DETECTIVES 2

DETECTIVES 2

THE TRIUMPHS OF EUGÈNE VALMONT

ROBERT BARR

MR. KEEN, THE TRACER OF LOST PERSONS

ROBERT W. CHAMBERS

COACHWHIP PUBLICATIONS
Landisville, Pennsylvania

2 Detectives: Eugène Valmont / Mr. Keen
The Triumphs of Eugène Valmont, by Robert Barr (1849-1912),
    published 1906.
The Tracer of Lost Persons, by Robert W. Chambers (1865-1933),
    published 1906.
Copyright © 2012 Coachwhip Publications
No claims made on public domain material.

ISBN 1-61646-116-0
ISBN-13 978-1-61646-116-4

CoachwhipBooks.com

CONTENTS

THE TRIUMPHS OF EUGÈNE VALMONT

MR. KEEN, THE TRACER OF LOST PERSONS

THE TRIUMPHS OF
EUGÈNE VALMONT

THE MYSTERY OF THE
FIVE HUNDRED DIAMONDS

I

When I say I am called Valmont, the name will convey no impression to the reader, one way or another. My occupation is that of private detective in London, but if you ask any policeman in Paris who Valmont was he will likely be able to tell you, unless he is a recent recruit. If you ask him where Valmont is now, he may not know, yet I have a good deal to do with the Parisian police.

For a period of seven years I was chief detective to the Government of France, and if I am unable to prove myself a great crime hunter, it is because the record of my career is in the secret archives of Paris.

I may admit at the outset that I have no grievances to air. The French Government considered itself justified in dismissing me, and it did so. In this action it was quite within its right, and I should be the last to dispute that right; but, on the other hand, I consider myself justified in publishing the following account of what actually occurred, especially as so many false rumours have been put abroad concerning the case. However, as I said at the beginning, I hold no grievance, because my worldly affairs are now much more prosperous than they were in Paris, my intimate knowledge of that city and the country of which it is the capital bringing to me many cases with which I have dealt more or less successfully since I established myself in London.

Without further preliminary I shall at once plunge into an account of the case which riveted the attention of the whole world a little more than a decade ago.

The year 1893 was a prosperous twelve months for France. The weather was good, the harvest excellent, and the wine of that vintage is celebrated to this day. Everyone was well off and reasonably happy, a marked contrast to the state of things a few years later, when dissension over the Dreyfus case rent the country in twain.

Newspaper readers may remember that in 1893 the Government of France fell heir to an unexpected treasure which set the civilised world agog, especially those inhabitants of it who are interested in historical relics. This was the finding of the diamond necklace in the Château de Chaumont, where it had rested undiscovered for a century in a rubbish heap of an attic. I believe it has not been questioned that this was the veritable necklace which the court jeweller, Boehmer, hoped to sell to Marie Antoinette, although how it came to be in the Château de Chaumont no one has been able to form even a conjecture. For a hundred years it was supposed that the necklace had been broken up in London, and its half a thousand stones, great and small, sold separately. It has always seemed strange to me that the Countess de Lamotte-Valois, who was thought to have profited by the sale of these jewels, should not have abandoned France if she possessed money to leave that country, for exposure was inevitable if she remained. Indeed, the unfortunate woman was branded and imprisoned, and afterwards was dashed to death from the third storey of a London house, when, in the direst poverty, she sought escape from the consequences of the debts she had incurred.

I am not superstitious in the least, yet this celebrated piece of treasure-trove seems actually to have exerted a malign influence over everyone who had the misfortune to be connected with it. Indeed, in a small way, I who write these words suffered dismissal and disgrace, though I caught but one glimpse of this dazzling scintillation of jewels. The jeweller who made the necklace met financial ruin; the Queen for whom it was constructed was beheaded; that high-born Prince Louis Réné Edouard, Cardinal de Rohan, who purchased it, was flung into prison; the unfortunate Countess, who said she acted as go-between until the transfer was concluded, clung for five awful minutes to a London window-sill before dropping to her death to the flags below; and now, a hundred and eight years later, up comes this devil's display of fireworks to the light again!

Droulliard, the working man who found the ancient box, seems to have pried it open, and ignorant though he was—he had probably never seen a diamond in his life before—realised that a fortune was in his grasp. The baleful glitter from the combination must have sent madness into his brain, working havoc therein as though the shafts of brightness were those mysterious rays which scientists have recently discovered. He might quite easily have walked through the main gate of the Château unsuspected and unquestioned with the diamonds concealed about his person, but instead of this he crept from the attic window on to the steep roof, slipped to the eaves, fell to the ground, and lay dead with a broken neck, while the necklace, intact, shimmered in the sunlight beside his body. No matter where these jewels had been found the Government would have insisted that they belonged to the Treasury of the Republic; but as the Château de Chaumont was a historical monument, and the property of France, there could be no question regarding the ownership of the necklace. The Government at once claimed it, and ordered it to be sent by a trustworthy military man to Paris. It was carried safely and delivered promptly to the authorities by Alfred Dreyfus, a young captain of artillery, to whom its custody had been entrusted.

In spite of its fall from the tall tower neither case nor jewels were perceptibly damaged. The lock of the box had apparently been forced by Droulliard's hatchet, or perhaps by the clasp knife found on his body. On reaching the ground the lid had flown open, and the necklace was thrown out.

I believe there was some discussion in the Cabinet regarding the fate of this ill-omened trophy, one section wishing it to be placed in a museum on account of its historical interest, another advocating the breaking up of the necklace and the selling of the diamonds for what they would fetch. But a third party maintained that the method to get the most money into the coffers of the country was to sell the necklace as it stood, for as the world now contains so many rich amateurs who collect undoubted rarities, regardless of expense, the historic associations of the jewelled collar would enhance the intrinsic value of the stones; and, this view prevailing, it was announced that the necklace would be sold by auction a month later in the rooms of Meyer, Renault and Co., in the Boulevard des Italians, near the Bank of the Crédit-Lyonnais.

This announcement elicited much comment from the newspapers of all countries, and it seemed that, from a financial point of view at least, the decision of the Government had been wise, for it speedily became evident that a notable coterie of wealthy buyers would be congregated in Paris on the thirteenth (unlucky day for me!) when the sale was to take place. But we of the inner circle were made aware of another result somewhat more disquieting, which was that the most expert criminals in the world were also gathering like vultures upon the fair city. The honour of France was at stake. Whoever bought that necklace must be assured of a safe conduct out of the country. We might view with equanimity whatever happened afterwards, but while he was a resident of France his life and property must not be endangered. Thus it came about that I was given full authority to ensure that neither murder nor theft nor both combined should be committed while the purchaser of the necklace remained within our boundaries, and for this purpose the police resources of France were placed unreservedly at my disposal. If I failed there should be no one to blame but myself; consequently, as I have remarked before, I do not complain of my dismissal by the Government.

The broken lock of the jewel-case had been very deftly repaired by an expert locksmith, who in executing his task was so unfortunate as to scratch a finger on the broken metal, whereupon blood poisoning set in, and although his life was saved, he was dismissed from the hospital with his right arm gone and his usefulness destroyed.

When the jeweller Boehmer made the necklace he asked a hundred and sixty thousand pounds for it, but after years of disappointment he was content to sell it to Cardinal de Rohan for sixty-four thousand pounds, to be liquidated in three instalments, not one of which was ever paid. This latter amount was probably somewhere near the value of the five hundred and sixteen separate stones, one of which was of tremendous size, a very monarch of diamonds, holding its court among seventeen brilliants each as large as a filbert. This iridescent concentration of wealth was, as one might say, placed in my care, and I had to see to it that no harm came to the necklace or to its prospective owner until they were safely across the boundaries of France.

The four weeks previous to the thirteenth proved a busy and anxious time for me. Thousands, most of whom were actuated by mere curiosity, wished to view the diamonds. We were compelled to discriminate, and sometimes discriminated against the wrong person, which caused unpleasantness. Three distinct attempts were made to rob the safe, but luckily these criminal efforts were frustrated, and so we came unscathed to the eventful thirteenth of the month.

The sale was to begin at two o'clock, and on the morning of that day I took the somewhat tyrannical precaution of having the more dangerous of our own malefactors, and as many of the foreign thieves as I could trump up charges against, laid by the heels, yet I knew very well it was not these rascals I had most to fear, but the suave, well-groomed gentlemen, amply supplied with unimpeachable credentials, stopping at our fine hotels and living like princes. Many of these were foreigners against whom we could prove nothing, and whose arrest might land us into temporary international difficulties. Nevertheless, I had each of them shadowed, and on the morning of the thirteenth if one of them had even disputed a cab fare I should have had him in prison half an hour later, and taken the consequences, but these gentlemen are very shrewd and do not commit mistakes.

I made up a list of all the men in the world who were able or likely to purchase the necklace. Many of them would not be present in person at the auction rooms; their bidding would be done by agents. This simplified matters a good deal, for the agents kept me duly informed of their purposes, and, besides, an agent who

handles treasure every week is an adept at the business, and does
not need the protection which must surround an amateur, who in
nine cases out of ten has but scant idea of the dangers that threaten
him, beyond knowing that if he goes down a dark street in a dangerous quarter he is likely to be maltreated and robbed.

There were no less than sixteen clients all told, whom we
learned were to attend personally on the day of the sale, any one
of whom might well have made the purchase. The Marquis of
Warlingham and Lord Oxtead from England were well-known jewel
fanciers, while at least half a dozen millionaires were expected from
the United States, with a smattering from Germany, Austria, and
Russia, and one each from Italy, Belgium, and Holland.

Admission to the auction rooms was allowed by ticket only, to
be applied for at least a week in advance, applications to be accompanied by satisfactory testimonials. It would possibly have
surprised many of the rich men collected there to know that they
sat cheek by jowl with some of the most noted thieves of England
and America, but I allowed this for two reasons: first, I wished to
keep these sharpers under my own eye until I knew who had bought
the necklace; and, secondly, I was desirous that they should not
know they were suspected.

I stationed trusty men outside on the Boulevard des Italiens,
each of whom knew by sight most of the probable purchasers of
the necklace. It was arranged that when the sale was over I should
walk out to the boulevard alongside the man who was the new
owner of the diamonds, and from that moment until he quitted
France my men were not to lose sight of him if he took personal
custody of the stones, instead of doing the sensible and proper
thing of having them insured and forwarded to his residence by
some responsible transit company, or depositing them in the bank.
In fact, I took every precaution that occurred to me. All police Paris
was on the *qui vive*, and felt itself pitted against the scoundrelism
of the world.

For one reason or another it was nearly half-past two before
the sale began. There had been considerable delay because of

forged tickets, and, indeed, each order for admittance was so closely scrutinised that this in itself took a good deal more time than we anticipated. Every chair was occupied, and still a number of the visitors were compelled to stand. I stationed myself by the swinging doors at the entrance end of the hall, where I could command a view of the entire assemblage. Some of my men were placed with backs against the wall, whilst others were distributed amongst the chairs, all in plain clothes. During the sale the diamonds themselves were not displayed, but the box containing them rested in front of the auctioneer and three policemen in uniform stood guard on either side.

II

Very quietly the auctioneer began by saying that there was no need for him to expatiate on the notable character of the treasure he was privileged to offer for sale, and with this preliminary, he requested those present to bid. Someone offered twenty thousand francs, which was received with much laughter; then the bidding went steadily on until it reached nine hundred thousand francs, which I knew to be less than half the reserve the Government had placed upon the necklace. The contest advanced more slowly until the million and a half was touched, and there it hung fire for a time, while the auctioneer remarked that this sum did not equal that which the maker of the necklace had been finally forced to accept for it. After another pause he added that, as the reserve was not exceeded, the necklace would be withdrawn, and probably never again offered for sale. He therefore urged those who were holding back to make their bids now. At this the contest livened until the sum of two million three hundred thousand francs had been offered, and now I knew the necklace would be sold. Nearing the three million mark the competition thinned down to a few dealers from Hamburg and the Marquis of Warlingham, from England, when a voice that had not yet been heard in the auction room was lifted in a tone of some impatience:

"One million dollars!"

There was an instant hush, followed by the scribbling of pen-
cils, as each person present reduced the sum to its equivalent in
his own currency—pounds for the English, francs for the French,
marks for the German, and so on. The aggressive tone and the clear-
cut face of the bidder proclaimed him an American, not less than
the financial denomination he had used. In a moment it was
realised that his bid was a clear leap of more than two million
francs, and a sigh went up from the audience as if this settled it,
and the great sale was done. Nevertheless the auctioneer's hammer hovered over the lid of his desk, and he looked up and down
the long line of faces turned towards him. He seemed reluctant to
tap the board, but no one ventured to compete against this tremendous sum, and with a sharp click the mallet fell.

"What name?" he asked, bending over towards the customer.

"Cash," replied the American; "here's a cheque for the amount.
I'll take the diamonds with me."

"Your request is somewhat unusual," protested the auctioneer
mildly.

"I know what you mean," interrupted the American; "you think
the cheque may not be cashed. You will notice it is drawn on the
Crédit-Lyonnais, which is practically next door. I must have the
jewels with me. Send round your messenger with the cheque; it
will take only a few minutes to find out whether or not the money
is there to meet it. The necklace is mine, and I insist on having it."

The auctioneer with some demur handed the cheque to the representative of the French Government who was present, and this
official himself went to the bank. There were some other things to
be sold and the auctioneer endeavoured to go on through the list,
but no one paid the slightest attention to him.

Meanwhile I was studying the countenance of the man who had
made the astounding bid, when I should instead have adjusted my
preparations to meet the new conditions now confronting me. Here
was a man about whom we knew nothing whatever. I had come to
the instant conclusion that he was a prince of criminals, and that a
sinister design, not at that moment fathomed by me, was on foot
to get possession of the jewels. The handing up of the cheque was

clearly a trick of some sort, and I fully expected the official to return and say the draft was good. I determined to prevent this man from getting the jewel box until I knew more of his game. Quickly I removed from my place near the door to the auctioneer's desk, having two objects in view; first, to warn the auctioneer not to part with the treasure too easily; and, second, to study the suspected man at closer range. Of all evil-doers the American is most to be feared; he uses more ingenuity in the planning of his projects, and will take greater risks in carrying them out than any other malefactor on earth.

From my new station I saw there were two men to deal with. The bidder's face was keen and intellectual; his hands refined, ladylike, clean and white, showing they were long divorced from manual labour, if indeed they had ever done any useful work. Coolness and imperturbability were his beyond a doubt. The companion who sat at his right was of an entirely different stamp. His hands were hairy and sun-tanned; his face bore the stamp of grim determination and unflinching bravery. I knew that these two types usually hunted in couples—the one to scheme, the other to execute, and they always formed a combination dangerous to encounter and difficult to circumvent.

There was a buzz of conversation up and down the hall as these two men talked together in low tones. I knew now that I was face to face with the most hazardous problem of my life.

I whispered to the auctioneer, who bent his head to listen. He knew very well who I was, of course.

"You must not give up the necklace," I began.

He shrugged his shoulders.

"I am under the orders of the official from the Ministry of the Interior. You must speak to him."

"I shall not fail to do so," I replied. "Nevertheless, do not give up the box too readily."

"I am helpless," he protested with another shrug. "I obey the orders of the Government."

Seeing it was useless to parley further with the auctioneer, I set my wits to work to meet the new emergency. I felt convinced that the cheque would prove to be genuine, and that the fraud,

wherever it lay, might not be disclosed in time to aid the authorities. My duty, therefore, was to make sure we lost sight neither of
the buyer nor the thing bought. Of course I could not arrest the
purchaser merely on suspicion; besides, it would make the Government the laughing-stock of the world if they sold a case of jewels and immediately placed the buyer in custody when they themselves had handed over his goods to him. Ridicule kills in France.
A breath of laughter may blow a Government out of existence in
Paris much more effectually than will a whiff of cannon smoke.
My duty then was to give the Government full warning, and never
lose sight of my man until he was clear of France; then my responsibility ended.

I took aside one of my own men in plain clothes and said to
him:

"You have seen the American who has bought the necklace?"

"Yes, sir."

"Very well. Go outside quietly, and station yourself there. He
is likely to emerge presently with the jewels in his possession. You
are not to lose sight of either the man or the casket. I shall follow
him and be close behind him as he emerges, and you are to shadow
us. If he parts with the case you must be ready at a sign from me to
follow either the man or the jewels. Do you understand?"

"Yes, sir," he answered, and left the room.

It is ever the unforeseen that baffles us; it is easy to be wise
after the event. I should have sent two men, and I have often
thought since how admirable is the regulation of the Italian Government which sends out its policemen in pairs. Or I should have
given my man power to call for help, but even as it was he did only
half as well as I had a right to expect of him, and the blunder he
committed by a moment's dull-witted hesitation—ah, well! there
is no use of scolding. After all the result might have been the same.

Just as my man disappeared between the two folding doors the
official from the Ministry of the Interior entered. I intercepted him
about half-way on his journey from the door to the auctioneer.

"Possibly the cheque appears to be genuine," I whispered to
him.

"But certainly," he replied pompously. He was an individual greatly impressed with his own importance; a kind of character with which it is always difficult to deal. Afterwards the Government asserted that this official had warned me, and the utterances of an empty-headed ass dressed in a little brief authority, as the English poet says, were looked upon as the epitome of wisdom.

"I advise you strongly not to hand over the necklace as has been requested," I went on.

"Why?" he asked.

"Because I am convinced the bidder is a criminal."

"If you have proof of that, arrest him."

"I have no proof at the present moment, but I request you to delay the delivery of the goods."

"That is absurd," he cried impatiently. "The necklace is his, not ours. The money has already been transferred to the account of the Government; we cannot retain the five million francs, and refuse to hand over to him what he has bought with them," and so the man left me standing there, nonplussed and anxious. The eyes of everyone in the room had been turned on us during our brief conversation, and now the official proceeded ostentatiously up the room with a grand air of importance; then, with a bow and a flourish of the hand, he said, dramatically:

"The jewels belong to Monsieur."

The two Americans rose simultaneously, the taller holding out his hand while the auctioneer passed to him the case he had apparently paid so highly for. The American nonchalantly opened the box and for the first time the electric radiance of the jewels burst upon that audience, each member of which craned his neck to behold it. It seemed to me a most reckless thing to do. He examined the jewels minutely for a few moments, then snapped the lid shut again, and calmly put the box in his outside pocket, and I could not help noticing that the light overcoat he wore possessed pockets made extraordinarily large, as if on purpose for this very case. And now this amazing man walked serenely down the room past miscreants who joyfully would have cut his throat for even the smallest diamond in that conglomeration; yet he did not take the trouble to put his hand on the pocket which contained the case, or in any way attempt to protect it. The assemblage seemed stricken dumb by his audacity. His friend followed closely at his heels, and the tall man disappeared through the folding doors. Not so the other. He turned quickly, and whipped two revolvers out of his pockets, which he presented at the astonished crowd. There had been a movement on the part of every one to leave the room, but the sight of these deadly weapons confronting them made each one shrink into his place again.

The man with his back to the door spoke in a loud and domineering voice, asking the auctioneer to translate what he had to say into French and German; he spoke in English.

"These here shiners are valuable; they belong to my friend who has just gone out. Casting no reflections on the generality of people in this room, there are, nevertheless, half a dozen 'crooks' among us whom my friend wishes to avoid. Now, no honest man here will object to giving the buyer of that there trinket five clear minutes in which to get away. It's only the 'crooks' that can kick. I ask these five minutes as a favour, but if they are not granted I am going to take them as a right. Any man who moves will get shot."

"I am an honest man," I cried, "and I object. I am chief detective of the French Government. Stand aside; the police will protect your friend."

"Hold on, my son," warned the American, turning one weapon directly upon me, while the other held a sort of roving commission, pointing all over the room. "My friend is from New York and he distrusts the police as much as he does the grafters. You may be twenty detectives, but if you move before that clock strikes three, I'll bring you down, and don't you forget it."

It is one thing to face death in a fierce struggle, but quite another to advance coldly upon it toward the muzzle of a pistol held so steadily that there could be no chance of escape. The gleam of determination in the man's eyes convinced me he meant what he said. I did not consider then, nor have I considered since, that the next five minutes, precious as they were, would be worth paying my life for. Apparently everyone else was of my opinion, for none moved hand or foot until the clock slowly struck three.

"Thank you, gentlemen," said the American, as he vanished between the spring-doors. When I say vanished, I mean that word and no other, because my men outside saw nothing of this individual then or later. He vanished as if he had never existed, and it was some hours before we found how this had been accomplished.

I rushed out almost on his heels, as one might say, and hurriedly questioned my waiting men. They had all seen the tall American come out with the greatest leisure and stroll towards the west. As he was not the man any of them were looking for they paid no further attention to him, as, indeed, is the custom with our Parisian force. They have eyes for nothing but what they are sent to look for, and this trait has its drawbacks for their superiors.

I ran up the boulevard, my whole thought intent on the diamonds and their owner. I knew my subordinate in command of the men inside the hall would look after the scoundrel with the pistols. A short distance up I found the stupid fellow I had sent out, standing in a dazed manner at the corner of the Rue Michodière, gazing alternately down that short street and towards the Place de l'Opéra. The very fact that he was there furnished proof that he had failed.

"Where is the American?" I demanded.

"He went down this street, sir."

"Then why are you standing here like a fool?"

"I followed him this far, when a man came up the Rue Michodière, and without a word the American handed him the jewel-box, turning instantly down the street up which the other had come. The other jumped into a cab, and drove towards the Place de l'Opéra."

"And what did you do? Stood here like a post, I suppose?"

"I didn't know what to do, sir. It all happened in a moment."

"Why didn't you follow the cab?"

"I didn't know which to follow, sir, and the cab was gone instantly while I watched the American."

"What was its number?"

"I don't know, sir."

"You clod! Why didn't you call one of our men, whoever was nearest, and leave him to shadow the American while you followed the cab?"

"I did shout to the nearest man, sir, but he said you told him to stay there and watch the English lord, and even before he had spoken both American and cabman were out of sight."

"Was the man to whom he gave the box an American also?"

"No, sir, he was French."

"How do you know?"

"By his appearance and the words he spoke."

"I thought you said he didn't speak."

"He did not speak to the American, sir, but he said to the cabman, 'Drive to the Madeleine as quickly as you can.'"

"Describe the man."

"He was a head shorter than the American, wore a black beard and moustache rather neatly trimmed, and seemed to be a superior sort of artisan."

"You did not take the number of the cab. Should you know the cabman if you saw him again?"

"Yes, sir, I think so."

Taking this fellow with me I returned to the now nearly empty auction room and there gathered all my men about me. Each in his notebook took down particulars of the cabman and his passenger from the lips of my incompetent spy; next I dictated a full description of the two Americans, then scattered my men to the various railway stations of the lines leading out of Paris, with orders to make inquiries of the police on duty there, and to arrest one or more of the four persons described should they be so fortunate as to find any of them.

I now learned how the rogue with the pistols vanished so completely as he did. My subordinate in the auction room had speedily solved the mystery. To the left of the main entrance of the auction room was a door that gave private access to the rear of the premises. As the attendant in charge confessed when questioned, he had been bribed by the American earlier in the day to leave this side door open and to allow the man to escape by the goods entrance. Thus the ruffian did not appear on the boulevard at all, and so had not been observed by any of my men.

Taking my futile spy with me I returned to my own office, and sent an order throughout the city that every cabman who had been in the Boulevard des Italiens between half-past two and half-past three that afternoon, should report immediately to me. The examination of these men proved a very tedious business indeed, but whatever other countries may say of us, we French are patient, and if the haystack is searched long enough, the needle will be found. I did not discover the needle I was looking for, but I came upon one quite as important, if not more so.

It was nearly ten o'clock at night when a cabman answered my oft-repeated questions in the affirmative.

"Did you take up a passenger a few minutes past three o'clock on the Boulevard des Italiens, near the Crédit-Lyonnais? Had he a short black beard? Did he carry a small box in his hand and order you to drive to the Madeleine?"

The cabman seemed puzzled.

"He wore a short black beard when he got out of the cab," he replied.

"What do you mean by that?"

"I drive a closed cab, sir. When he got in he was a smooth-faced gentleman; when he got out he wore a short black beard."

"Was he a Frenchman?"

"No, sir; he was a foreigner, either English or American."

"Was he carrying a box?"

"No, sir; he held in his hand a small leather bag."

"Where did he tell you to drive?"

"He told me to follow the cab in front, which had just driven off very rapidly towards the Madeleine. In fact, I heard the man, such as you describe, order the other cabman to drive to the Madeleine. I had come alongside the curb when this man held up his hand for a cab, but the open cab cut in ahead of me. Just then my passenger stepped up and said in French, but with a foreign accent: 'Follow that cab wherever it goes.'"

I turned with some indignation to my inefficient spy.

"You told me," I said, "that the American had gone down a side street. Yet he evidently met a second man, obtained from him the handbag, turned back, and got into the closed cab directly behind you."

"Well, sir," stammered the spy, "I could not look in two directions at the same time. The American certainly went down the side street, but of course I watched the cab which contained the jewels."

"And you saw nothing of the closed cab right at your elbow?"

"The boulevard was full of cabs, sir, and the pavement crowded with passers-by, as it always is at that hour of the day, and I have only two eyes in my head."

"I am glad to know you had that many, for I was beginning to think you were blind."

Although I said this, I knew in my heart it was useless to censure the poor wretch, for the fault was entirely my own in not sending two men, and in failing to guess the possibility of the jewels and their owner being separated. Besides, here was a clue to my hand at last, and no time must be lost in following it up. So I continued my interrogation of the cabman.

"The other cab was an open vehicle, you say?"

"Yes, sir."

"You succeeded in following it?"

"Oh, yes, sir. At the Madeleine the man in front redirected the coachman, who turned to the left and drove to the Place de la Concorde, then up the Champs-Elysées to the Arch and so down the Avenue de la Grande Armée, and the Avenue de Neuilly, to the Pont de Neuilly, where it came to a standstill. My fare got out, and I saw he now wore a short black beard, which he had evidently put on inside the cab. He gave me a ten-franc piece, which was very satisfactory."

"And the fare you were following? What did he do?"

"He also stepped out, paid the cabman, went down the bank of the river and got on board a steam launch that seemed to be waiting for him."

"Did he look behind, or appear to know that he was being followed?"

"No, sir."

"And your fare?"

"He ran after the first man, and also went aboard the steam launch, which instantly started down the river."

"And that was the last you saw of them?"

"Yes, sir."

"At what time did you reach the Pont de Neuilly?"

"I do not know, sir; I was compelled to drive rather fast, but the distance is seven to eight kilometres."

"You would do it under the hour?"

"But certainly, under the hour."

"Then you must have reached Neuilly bridge about four o'clock?"

"It is very likely, sir."

The plan of the tall American was now perfectly clear to me, and it comprised nothing that was contrary to law. He had evidently placed his luggage on board the steam launch in the morning. The handbag had contained various materials which would enable him to disguise himself, and this bag he had probably left in some shop down the side street, or else someone was waiting with it for him. The giving of the treasure to another man was not so risky as it had at first appeared, because he instantly followed that man, who was probably his confidential servant. Despite the windings of the river there was ample time for the launch to reach Havre before the American steamer sailed on Saturday morning. I surmised it was his intention to come alongside the steamer before she left her berth in Havre harbour, and thus transfer himself and his belongings unperceived by anyone on watch at the land side of the liner.

All this, of course, was perfectly justifiable, and seemed, in truth, merely a well-laid scheme for escaping observation. His only danger of being tracked was when he got into the cab. Once away from the neighbourhood of the Boulevard des Italiens he was reasonably sure to evade pursuit, and the five minutes which his friend with the pistols had won for him afforded just the time he needed to get so far as the Place Madeleine, and after that everything was easy. Yet, if it had not been for those five minutes secured by coercion, I should not have found the slightest excuse for arresting him. But he was accessory after the act in that piece of illegality—in fact, it was absolutely certain that he had been accessory before the act, and guilty of conspiracy with the man who had presented firearms to the auctioneer's audience, and who had interfered with an officer in the discharge of his duty by threatening me and my men. So I was now legally in the right if I arrested every person on board that steam launch.

III

With a map of the river before me I proceeded to make some calculations. It was now nearly ten o'clock at night. The launch had had six hours in which to travel at its utmost speed. It was doubtful if so small a vessel could make ten miles an hour, even with the current in its favour, which is rather sluggish because of the locks and the level country. Sixty miles would place her beyond Meulan, which is fifty-eight miles from the Pont Royal, and, of course, a lesser distance from the Pont de Neuilly. But the navigation of the river is difficult at all times, and almost impossible after dark. There were chances of the boat running aground, and then there was the inevitable delay at the locks. So I estimated that the launch could not yet have reached Meulan, which was less than twenty-five miles from Paris by rail. Looking up the timetable I saw there were still two trains to Meulan, the next at 10.25, which reached Meulan at 11.40. I therefore had time to reach St. Lazare station, and accomplish some telegraphing before the train left.

With three of my assistants I got into a cab and drove to the station. On arrival I sent one of my men to hold the train while I went into the telegraph office, cleared the wires, and got into communication with the lock master at Meulan. He replied that no steam launch had passed down since an hour before sunset. I then instructed him to allow the yacht to enter the lock, close the upper gate, let half of the water out, and hold the vessel there until I came. I also ordered the local Meulan police to send enough men to the lock to enforce this command. Lastly, I sent messages all along the river asking the police to report to me on the train the passage of the steam launch.

The 10.25 is a slow train, stopping at every station. However, every drawback has its compensation, and these stoppages enabled me to receive and to send telegraphic messages. I was quite well aware that I might be on a fool's errand in going to Meulan. The yacht could have put about before it had steamed a mile, and so returned back to Paris. There had been no time to learn whether this was so or not if I was to catch the 10.25. Also, it might have landed its passengers anywhere along the river. I may say at once that neither of these two things happened, and my calculations regarding her movements were accurate to the letter. But a trap most carefully set may be prematurely sprung by inadvertence, or more often by the over-zeal of some stupid ass who fails to understand his instructions, or oversteps them if they are understood. I received a most annoying telegram from Denouval, a lock about thirteen miles above that of Meulan. The local policeman, arriving at the lock, found that the yacht had just cleared. The fool shouted to the captain to return, threatening him with all the pains and penalties of the law if he refused. The captain did refuse, rung on full speed ahead, and disappeared in the darkness. Through this well-meant blunder of an understrapper those on board the launch had received warning that we were on their track. I telegraphed to the lock-keeper at Denouval to allow no craft to pass toward Paris until further orders. We thus held the launch in a thirteen-mile stretch of water, but the night was pitch dark, and passengers might be landed on either bank with all France before them, over which to effect their escape in any direction.

It was midnight when I reached the lock at Meulan, and, as was to be expected, nothing had been seen or heard of the launch.

It gave me some satisfaction to telegraph to that dunderhead at
Denouval to walk along the river bank to Meulan, and report if he
learnt the launch's whereabouts. We took up our quarters in the
lodgekeeper's house and waited. There was little sense in sending
men to scour the country at this time of night, for the pursued were
on the alert, and very unlikely to allow themselves to be caught if
they had gone ashore. On the other hand, there was every chance
that the captain would refuse to let them land, because he must
know his vessel was in a trap from which it could not escape, and
although the demand of the policeman at Denouval was quite
unauthorised, nevertheless the captain could not know that, while
he must be well aware of his danger in refusing to obey a command from the authorities. Even if he got away for the moment he
must know that arrest was certain, and that his punishment would
be severe. His only plea could be that he had not heard and understood the order to return. But this plea would be invalidated if he
aided in the escape of two men, whom he must know were wanted
by the police. I was therefore very confident that if his passengers
asked to be set ashore, the captain would refuse when he had had
time to think about his own danger. My estimate proved accurate,
for towards one o'clock the lockkeeper came in and said the green
and red lights of an approaching craft were visible, and as he spoke
the yacht whistled for the opening of the lock. I stood by the
lockkeeper while he opened the gates; my men and the local police
were concealed on each side of the lock. The launch came slowly
in, and as soon as it had done so I asked the captain to step ashore,
which he did.

"I wish a word with you," I said. "Follow me."

I took him into the lockkeeper's house and closed the door.

"Where are you going?"

"To Havre."

"Where did you come from?"

"Paris."

"From what quay?"

"From the Pont de Neuilly."

"When did you leave there?"

"At five minutes to four o'clock this afternoon."

"Yesterday afternoon, you mean?"

"Yesterday afternoon."

"Who engaged you to make this voyage?"

"An American; I do not know his name."

"He paid you well, I suppose?"

"He paid me what I asked."

"Have you received the money?"

"Yes, sir."

"I may inform you, captain, that I am Eugène Valmont, chief detective of the French Government, and that all the police of France at this moment are under my control. I ask you, therefore, to be careful of your answers. You were ordered by a policeman at Denouval to return. Why did you not do so?"

"The lockkeeper ordered me to return, but as he had no right to order me, I went on."

"You knew very well it was the police who ordered you, and you ignored the command. Again I ask you why you did so."

"I did not know it was the police."

"I thought you would say that. You knew very well, but were paid to take the risk, and it is likely to cost you dear. You had two passengers aboard?"

"Yes, sir."

"Did you put them ashore between here and Denouval?"

"No, sir; but one of them went overboard, and we couldn't find him again."

"Which one?"

"The short man."

"Then the American is still aboard?"

"What American, sir?"

"Captain, you must not trifle with me. The man who engaged you is still aboard?"

"Oh, no, sir; he has never been aboard."

"Do you mean to tell me that the second man who came on your launch at the Pont de Neuilly is not the American who engaged you?"

"No, sir; the American was a smooth-faced man; this man wore a black beard."

"Yes, a false beard."

"I did not know that, sir. I understood from the American that I was to take but one passenger. One came aboard with a small box in his hand; the other with a small bag. Each declared himself to be the passenger in question. I did not know what to do, so I left Paris with both of them on board."

"Then the tall man with the black beard is still with you?"

"Yes, sir."

"Well, captain, is there anything else you have to tell me? I think you will find it better in the end to make a clean breast of it."

The captain hesitated, turning his cap about in his hands for a few moments, then he said:

"I am not sure that the first passenger went overboard of his own accord. When the police hailed us at Denouval—"

"Ah, you knew it was the police, then?"

"I was afraid after I left it might have been. You see, when the bargain was made with me the American said that if I reached Havre at a certain time a thousand francs extra would be paid to me, so I was anxious to get along as quickly as I could. I told him it was dangerous to navigate the Seine at night, but he paid me well for attempting it. After the policeman called to us at Denouval the man with the small box became very much excited, and asked me to put him ashore, which I refused to do. The tall man appeared to be watching him, never letting him get far away. When I heard the splash in the water I ran aft, and I saw the tall man putting the box which the other had held into his handbag, although I said nothing of it at the time. We cruised back and forward about the spot where the other man had gone overboard, but saw nothing more of him. Then I came on to Meulan, intending to give information about what I had seen. That is all I know of the matter, sir."

"Was the man who had the jewels a Frenchman?"

"What jewels, sir?"

"The man with the small box."

"Oh, yes, sir; he was French."

"You have hinted that the foreigner threw him overboard. What grounds have you for such a belief if you did not see the struggle?"

"The night is very dark, sir, and I did not see what happened. I was at the wheel in the forward part of the launch, with my back turned to these two. I heard a scream, then a splash. If the man had jumped overboard as the other said he did, he would not have screamed. Besides, as I told you, when I ran aft I saw the foreigner put the little box in his handbag, which he shut up quickly as if he did not wish me to notice."

"Very good, captain. If you have told the truth it will go easier with you in the investigation that is to follow."

I now turned the captain over to one of my men, and ordered in the foreigner with his bag and bogus black whiskers. Before questioning him I ordered him to open the handbag, which he did with evident reluctance. It was filled with false whiskers, false moustaches, and various bottles, but on top of them all lay the jewel case. I raised the lid and displayed that accursed necklace. I looked up at the man, who stood there calmly enough, saying nothing in spite of the overwhelming evidence against him.

"Will you oblige me by removing your false beard?"

He did so at once, throwing it into the open bag. I knew the moment I saw him that he was not the American, and thus my theory had broken down, in one very important part at least. Informing him who I was, and cautioning him to speak the truth, I asked how he came in possession of the jewels.

"Am I under arrest?" he asked.

"But certainly," I replied.

"Of what am I accused?"

"You are accused, in the first place, of being in possession of property which does not belong to you."

"I plead guilty to that. What in the second place?"

"In the second place, you may find yourself accused of murder."

"I am innocent of the second charge. The man jumped overboard."

"If that is true, why did he scream as he went over?"

"Because, too late to recover his balance, I seized this box and held it."

"He was in rightful possession of the box; the owner gave it to him."

"I admit that; I saw the owner give it to him."

"Then why should he jump overboard?"

"I do not know. He seemed to become panic-stricken when the police at the last lock ordered us to return. He implored the captain to put him ashore, and from that moment I watched him keenly, expecting that if we drew near to the land he would attempt to escape, as the captain had refused to beach the launch. He remained quiet for about half an hour, seated on a camp chair by the rail, with his eyes turned toward the shore, trying, as I imagined, to penetrate the darkness and estimate the distance. Then suddenly he sprung up and made his dash. I was prepared for this, and instantly caught the box from his hand. He gave a half turn, trying either to save himself or to retain the box; then with a scream went down shoulders first into the water. It all happened within a second after he leaped from his chair."

"You admit yourself, then, indirectly responsible for his drowning, at least?"

"I see no reason to suppose that the man was drowned. If able to swim he could easily have reached the river bank. If unable to swim, why should he attempt it encumbered by the box?"

"You believe he escaped, then?"

"I think so."

"It will be lucky for you should that prove to be the case."

"Certainly."

"How did you come to be in the yacht at all?"

"I shall give you a full account of the affair, concealing nothing. I am a private detective, with an office in London. I was certain that some attempt would be made, probably by the most expert criminals at large, to rob the possessor of this necklace. I came over to Paris, anticipating trouble, determined to keep an eye upon the jewel case if this proved possible. If the jewels were stolen the crime was bound to be one of the most celebrated in legal annals. I was present during the sale, and saw the buyer of the necklace. I followed the official who went to the bank, and thus learned that the money was behind the cheque. I then stopped outside and waited for the buyer to appear. He held the case in his hand."

"In his pocket, you mean?" I interrupted.

"He had it in his hand when I saw him. Then the man who afterwards jumped overboard approached him, took the case without a word, held up his hand for a cab, and when an open vehicle approached the curb he stepped in, saying, 'The Madeleine.' I hailed a closed cab, instructed the cabman to follow the first, disguising myself with whiskers as near like those the man in front wore as I had in my collection."

"Why did you do that?"

"As a detective you should know why I did it. I wished as nearly as possible to resemble the man in front, so that if necessity arose I could pretend that I was the person commissioned to carry the jewel case. As a matter of fact, the crisis arose when we came to the end of our cab journey. The captain did not know which was his true passenger, and so let us both remain aboard the launch. And now you have the whole story."

"An extremely improbable one, sir. Even by your own account you had no right to interfere in this business at all."

"I quite agree with you there," he replied, with great nonchalance, taking a card from his pocketbook, which he handed to me.

"That is my London address; you may make inquiries, and you will find I am exactly what I represent myself to be."

The first train for Paris left Meulan at eleven minutes past four in the morning. It was now a quarter after two. I left the captain, crew, and launch in charge of two of my men, with orders to proceed to Paris as soon as it was daylight. I, supported by the third man, waited at the station with our English prisoner, and reached Paris at half-past five in the morning.

The English prisoner, though severely interrogated by the judge, stood by his story. Inquiry by the police in London proved that what he said of himself was true. His case, however, began to look very serious when two of the men from the launch asserted that they had seen him push the Frenchman overboard, and their statement could not be shaken. All our energies were bent for the next two weeks on trying to find something of the identity of the missing man, or to get any trace of the two Americans. If the tall American were alive, it seemed incredible that he should not have made application for the valuable property he had lost. All attempts to trace him by means of the cheque on the Crédit-Lyonnais proved futile. The bank pretended to give me every assistance, but I sometimes doubt if it actually did so. It had evidently been well paid for its services, and evinced no impetuous desire to betray so good a customer.

We made inquiries about every missing man in Paris, but also without result.

The case had excited much attention throughout the world, and doubtless was published in full in the American papers. The Englishman had been in custody three weeks when the chief of police in Paris received the following letter:

> "Dear Sir: On my arrival in New York by the English steamer *Lucania*, I was much amused to read in the papers accounts of the exploits of detectives, French and English. I am sorry that only one of them seems to be in prison; I think his French *confrère* ought to be there also. I regret exceedingly, however, that there is the rumour of the death by drowning of my friend Martin Dubois, of 375 Rue aux Juifs, Rouen. If this is indeed the case he has met his death through the blunders of the police. Nevertheless, I wish you would communicate with his family at the address I have given, and assure them that I will make arrangements for their future support.
>
> "I beg to inform you that I am a manufacturer of imitation diamonds, and through extensive advertising succeeded in accumulating a fortune of many millions. I was in Europe when the necklace was

found, and had in my possession over a thousand imitation diamonds of my own manufacture. It occurred to me that here was the opportunity of the most magnificent advertisement in the world. I saw the necklace, received its measurements, and also obtained photographs of it taken by the French Government. Then I set my expert friend Martin Dubois at work, and, with the artificial stones I gave him, he made an imitation necklace so closely resembling the original that you apparently do not know it is the unreal you have in your possession. I did not fear the villainy of the crooks as much as the blundering of the police, who would have protected me with brass-band vehemence if I could not elude them. I knew that the detectives would overlook the obvious, but would at once follow a clue if I provided one for them. Consequently, I laid my plans, just as you have discovered, and got Martin Dubois up from Rouen to carry the case I gave him down to Havre. I had had another box prepared and wrapped in brown paper, with my address in New York written thereon. The moment I emerged from the auction room, while my friend the cowboy was holding up the audience, I turned my face to the door, took out the genuine diamonds from the case and slipped it into the box I had prepared for mailing. Into the genuine case I put the bogus diamonds. After handing the box to Dubois, I turned down a side street, and then into another whose name I do not know, and there in a shop with sealing wax and string did up the real diamonds for posting. I labelled the package "Books," went to the nearest post office, paid letter postage, and handed it over unregistered as if it were of no particular value. After this I went to my rooms in the Grand Hotel where I had been staying under my own name for more than a month. Next morning I took train for London, and the day after sailed from Liverpool on the *Lucania*. I arrived before the *Gascogne*, which sailed from Havre on Saturday, met my box at the Customshouse, paid duty, and it now reposes in my safe. I intend to construct an imitation necklace which will be so like the genuine one that nobody can tell the two apart; then I shall come to Europe and exhibit the pair, for the publication of the truth of this matter will give me the greatest advertisement that ever was.

"Yours truly,

"John P. Hazard."

I at once communicated with Rouen and found Martin Dubois alive and well. His first words were:

"I swear I did not steal the jewels."

He had swum ashore, tramped to Rouen, and kept quiet in great fear while I was fruitlessly searching Paris for him. It took Mr. Hazard longer to make his imitation necklace than he supposed, and several years later he booked his passage with the two necklaces on the ill-fated steamer *Bourgogne*, and now rests beside them at the bottom of the Atlantic.

As the English poet says:

> *Full many a gem of purest ray serene,*
> *The dark unfathomed caves of ocean bear.*

THE SIAMESE TWIN OF A BOMB-THROWER

I

The events I have just related led to my dismissal by the French Government. It was not because I had arrested an innocent man; I had done that dozens of times before, with nothing said about it. It was not because I had followed a wrong clue, or because I had failed to solve the mystery of the five hundred diamonds. Every detective follows a wrong clue now and then, and every detective fails more often than he cares to admit. No. All these things would not have shaken my position, but the newspapers were so fortunate as to find something humorous in the case, and for weeks Paris rang with laughter over my exploits and my defeat. The fact that the chief French detective had placed the most celebrated English detective into prison, and that each of them were busily sleuth-hounding a bogus clue, deliberately flung across their path by an amateur, roused all France to great hilarity. The Government was furious. The Englishman was released and I was dismissed. Since the year 1893 I have been a resident of London.

When a man is, as one might say, the guest of a country, it does not become him to criticise that country. I have studied this strange people with interest, and often with astonishment, and if I now set down some of the differences between the English and the French, I trust that no note of criticism of the former will appear, even when my sympathies are entirely with the latter. These differences have sunk deeply into my mind, because, during the first years of my stay in London my lack of understanding them was often a cause of my own failure when I thought I had success in hand. Many a time did I come to the verge of starvation in Soho, through not appreciating the peculiar trend of mind which causes an Englishman to do inexplicable things—that is, of course, from my Gallic standpoint. For instance, an arrested man is presumed to be innocent until he is proved guilty. In England, if a murderer is caught red-handed over his victim, he is held guiltless until the judge sentences him. In France we make no such foolish assumption, and although I admit that innocent men have sometimes been punished, my experience enables me to state very emphatically that this happens not nearly so often as the public imagines. In ninety-nine cases out of a hundred an innocent man can at once prove his innocence without the least difficulty. I hold it is his duty towards the State to run the very slight risk of unjust imprisonment in order that obstacles may not be thrown in the way of the conviction of real criminals. But it is impossible to persuade an Englishman of this. *Mon Dieu!* I have tried it often enough.

Never shall I forget the bitterness of my disappointment when I captured Felini, the Italian anarchist, in connection with the Greenwich Park murder. At this time—it gives me no shame to confess it—I was myself living in Soho, in a state of extreme poverty. Having been employed so long by the French Government, I had formed the absurd idea that the future depended on my getting, not exactly a similar connection with Scotland Yard, but at least a subordinate position on the police force which would enable me to prove my capabilities, and lead to promotion. I had no knowledge, at that time, of the immense income which awaited me entirely outside the Government circle. Whether it is contempt for the foreigner, as has often been stated, or that native stolidity which spells complacency, the British official of any class rarely thinks it worth his while to discover the real cause of things in France, or Germany, or Russia, but plods heavily on from one mistake to another. Take, for example, those periodical outbursts of hatred against England which appear in the Continental Press. They create a dangerous international situation, and more than once have brought

Britain to the verge of a serious war. Britain sternly spends millions in defence and preparation, whereas, if she would place in my hand half a million pounds I would guarantee to cause Britannia to be proclaimed an angel with white wings in every European country.

When I attempted to arrive at some connection with Scotland Yard, I was invariably asked for my credentials. When I proclaimed that I had been chief detective to the Republic of France, I could see that this announcement made a serious impression, but when I added that the Government of France had dismissed me without credentials, recommendation, or pension, official sympathy with officialism at once turned the tables against me. And here I may be pardoned for pointing out another portentous dissimilarity between the two lands which I think is not at all to the credit of my countrymen.

I was summarily dismissed. You may say it was because I failed, and it is true that in the case of the Queen's necklace I had undoubtedly failed, but, on the other hand, I had followed unerringly the clue which lay in my path, and although the conclusion was not in accordance with the facts, it was in accordance with logic. No, I was not dismissed because I failed. I had failed on various occasions before, as might happen to any man in any profession. I was dismissed because I made France for the moment the laughing-stock of Europe and America. France dismissed me because France had been laughed at. No Frenchman can endure the turning of a joke against him, but the Englishman does not appear to care in the least. So far as failure is concerned, never had any man failed so egregiously as I did with Felini, a slippery criminal who possessed all the bravery of a Frenchman and all the subtlety of an Italian. Three times he was in my hands—twice in Paris, once in Marseilles—and each time he escaped me; yet I was not dismissed.

When I say that Signor Felini was as brave as a Frenchman, perhaps I do him a little more than justice. He was desperately afraid of one man, and that man was myself. Our last interview in France he is not likely to forget, and although he eluded me, he took good care to get into England as fast as train and boat could carry him, and never again, while I was at the head of the French detective force, did he set foot on French soil. He was an educated villain, a graduate of the University of Turin, who spoke Spanish, French, and English as well as his own language, and this education made him all the more dangerous when he turned his talents to crime.

Now, I knew Felini's handiwork, either in murder or in housebreaking, as well as I know my own signature on a piece of white paper, and as soon as I saw the body of the murdered man in Greenwich Park I was certain Felini was the murderer. The English authorities at that time looked upon me with a tolerant, good-natured contempt.

Inspector Standish assumed the manner of a man placing at my disposal plenty of rope with which I might entangle myself. He appeared to think me excitable, and used soothing expressions as if I were a fractious child to be calmed, rather than a sane equal to be reasoned with. On many occasions I had the facts at my finger ends, while he remained in a state of most complacent ignorance, and though this attitude of lowering himself to deal gently with one whom he evidently looked upon as an irresponsible lunatic was most exasperating, I nevertheless claim great credit for having kept my temper with him. However, it turned out to be impossible for me to overcome his insular prejudice. He always supposed me to be a frivolous, volatile person, and so I was unable to prove myself of any value to him in his arduous duties.

The Felini instance was my last endeavour to win his favour. Inspector Standish appeared in his most amiable mood when I was admitted to his presence, and this in spite of the fact that all London was ringing with the Greenwich Park tragedy, while the police possessed not the faintest idea regarding the crime or its perpetrator. I judged from Inspector Standish's benevolent smile that I was somewhat excited when I spoke to him, and perhaps used many gestures which seemed superfluous to a large man whom I should describe as immovable, and who spoke slowly, with no motion of the hand, as if his utterances were the condensed wisdom of the ages.

"Inspector Standish," I cried, "is it within your power to arrest a man on suspicion?"

"Of course it is," he replied; "but we must harbour the suspicion before we make the arrest."

"Have confidence in me," I exclaimed. "The man who committed the Greenwich Park murder is an Italian named Felini."

I gave the address of the exact room in which he was to be found, with cautions regarding the elusive nature of this individual. I said that he had been three times in my custody, and those three times he had slipped through my fingers. I have since thought that Inspector Standish did not credit a word I had spoken.

"What is your proof against this Italian?" asked the Inspector slowly.

"The proof is on the body of the murdered man, but, nevertheless, if you suddenly confront Felini with me without giving him any hint of whom he is going to meet, you shall have the evidence from his own lips before he recovers from his surprise and fright."

Something of my confidence must have impressed the official, for the order of arrest was made. Now, during the absence of the constable sent to bring in Felini, I explained to the inspector fully the details of my plan. Practically he did not listen to me, for his head was bent over a writing-pad on which I thought he was taking down my remarks, but when I had finished he went on writing as before, so I saw I had flattered myself unnecessarily. More than two hours passed before the constable returned, bringing with him the trembling Italian. I swung round in front of him, and cried, in a menacing voice:

"Felini! Regard me! You know Valmont too well to trifle with him! What have you to say of the murder in Greenwich Park?"

I give you my word that the Italian collapsed, and would have fallen to the floor in a heap had not the constables upheld him with hands under each arm. His face became of a pasty whiteness, and he began to stammer his confession, when this incredible thing happened, which could not be believed in France. Inspector Standish held up his finger.

"One moment," he cautioned solemnly, "remember that whatever you say will be used against you!"

The quick, beady black eyes of the Italian shot from Standish to me, and from me to Standish. In an instant his alert mind grasped the situation. Metaphorically I had been waved aside. I was not there in any official capacity, and he saw in a moment with what an opaque intellect he had to deal. The Italian closed his mouth like a steel trap, and refused to utter a word. Shortly after he was liberated, as there was no evidence against him. When at last complete proof was in the tardy hands of the British authorities, the agile Felini was safe in the Apennine mountains, and to-day is serving a life sentence in Italy for the assassination of a senator whose name I have forgotten.

Is it any wonder that I threw up my hands in despair at finding myself amongst such a people. But this was in the early days, and now that I have greater experience of the English, many of my first opinions have been modified.

I mention all this to explain why, in a private capacity, I often did what no English official would dare to do. A people who will send a policeman, without even a pistol to protect him, to arrest a desperate criminal in the most dangerous quarter of London, cannot be comprehended by any native of France, Italy, Spain, or Germany. When I began to succeed as a private detective in London, and had accumulated money enough for my project, I determined not to be hampered by this unexplainable softness of the English toward an accused person. I therefore reconstructed my flat, and placed in the centre of it a dark room strong as any Bastille cell. It was twelve feet square, and contained no furniture except a number of shelves, a lavatory in one corner, and a pallet on the floor. It was ventilated by two flues from the centre of the ceiling, in one of which operated an electric fan, which, when the room was occupied, sent the foul air up that flue, and drew down fresh air through the other. The entrance to this cell opened out from my bedroom, and the most minute inspection would have failed to reveal the door, which was of massive steel, and was opened and shut by electric buttons that were partially concealed by the head of my bed. Even if they had been discovered, they would have revealed nothing, because the first turn of the button lit the electric light at the head of my bed; the second turn put it out; and this would happen as often as the button was turned to the right. But turn it three times slowly to the left, and the steel door opened. Its juncture was completely concealed by panelling. I have brought many a scoundrel to reason within the impregnable walls of that small room.

Those who know the building regulations of London will wonder how it was possible for me to delude the Government inspector during the erection of this section of the Bastille in the midst of the modern metropolis. It was the simplest thing in the world. Liberty of the subject is the first great rule with the English people, and thus many a criminal is allowed to escape. Here was I laying plans for the contravening of this first great rule, and to do so I took advantage of the second great rule of the English people, which is, that property is sacred. I told the building authorities I was a rich man with a great distrust of banks, and I wished to build in my flat a safe or strong-room in which to deposit my valuables. I built then such a room as may be found in every bank, and many private premises of the City, and a tenant might have lived in my flat for a year and never suspected the existence of this prison. A railway engine might have screeched its whistle within it, and not a sound would have penetrated the apartments that surrounded it unless the door were open.

But besides M. Eugène Valmont, dressed in elegant attire as if he were still a boulevardier of Paris, occupier of the top floor in the Imperial Flats, there was another Frenchman in London to whom I must introduce you, namely, Professor Paul Ducharme, who occupied a squalid back room in the cheapest and most undesirable quarter of Soho. Valmont flatters himself he is not yet middle-aged, but poor Ducharme does not need his sparse gray beard to proclaim his advancing years. Valmont vaunts an air of prosperity; Ducharme wears the shabby habiliments and the shoulder-stoop of hopeless poverty. He shuffles cringingly along the street, a compatriot not to be proud of. There are so many Frenchmen anxious to give lessons in their language, that merely a small living is to be picked up by any one of them. You will never see the spruce Valmont walking alongside the dejected Ducharme.

"Ah!" you exclaim, "Valmont in his prosperity has forgotten those less fortunate of his nationality."

Pardon, my friends, it is not so. Behold, I proclaim to you, the exquisite Valmont and the threadbare Ducharme are one and the same person. That is why they do not promenade together. And, indeed, it requires no great histrionic art on my part to act the rôle of the miserable Ducharme, for when I first came to London, I warded off starvation in this wretched room, and my hand it was that nailed to the door the painted sign "Professor Paul Ducharme, Teacher of the French Language." I never gave up the room, even when I became prosperous and moved to Imperial Flats, with its concealed chamber of horrors unknown to British authority. I did not give up the Soho chamber principally for this reason: Paul Ducharme, if the truth were known about him, would have been regarded as a dangerous character; yet this was a character some-times necessary for me to assume. He was a member of the very inner circle of the International, an anarchist of the anarchists. This malign organisation has its real headquarters in London, and we who were officials connected with the Secret Service of the Con-tinent have more than once cursed the complacency of the British Government which allows such a nest of vipers to exist practically unmolested. I confess that before I came to know the English people as well as I do now, I thought that this complacency was due to utter selfishness, because the anarchists never commit an outrage in England. England is the one spot on the map of Europe where an anarchist cannot be laid by the heels unless there is evi-dence against him that will stand the test of open court. Anarchists take advantage of this fact, and plots are hatched in London which are executed in Paris, Berlin, Petersburg, or Madrid. I know now that this leniency on the part of the British Government does not arise from craft, but from their unexplainable devotion to their shibboleth—"The liberty of the subject." Time and again France has demanded the extradition of an anarchist, always to be met with the question:

"Where is your proof?"

I know many instances where our certainty was absolute, and also cases where we possessed legal proof as well, but legal proof which, for one reason or another, we dared not use in public; yet all this had no effect on the British authorities. They would never give up even the vilest criminal except on publicly attested legal evidence, and not even then, if the crime were political.

During my term of office under the French Government, no part of my duties caused me more anxiety than that which pertained to the political secret societies. Of course, with a large portion of the Secret Service fund at my disposal, I was able to buy expert assistance, and even to get information from anarchists themselves. This latter device, however, was always more or less unreliable. I have never yet met an anarchist I could believe on oath, and when one of them offered to sell exclusive information to the police, we rarely knew whether he was merely trying to get a few francs to keep himself from starving, or whether he was giving us false particulars which would lead us into a trap. I have always regarded our dealings with nihilists, anarchists, or other secret associations for the perpetrating of murder as the most dangerous service a detective is called upon to perform. Yet it is absolutely necessary that the authorities should know what is going on in these secret conclaves. There are three methods of getting this intelligence. First, periodical raids upon the suspected, accompanied by confiscation and search of all papers found. This method is much in favour with the Russian police. I have always regarded it as largely futile; first, because the anarchists are not such fools, speaking generally, as to commit their purposes to writing; and, second, because it leads to reprisal. Each raid is usually followed by a fresh outbreak of activity on the part of those left free. The second method is to bribe an anarchist to betray his comrades. I have never found any difficulty in getting these gentry to accept money. They are eternally in need, but I usually find the information they give in return to be either unimportant or inaccurate. There remains, then, the third method, which is to place a spy among them. The spy battalion is the forlorn hope of the detective service. In one year I lost three men on anarchist duty, among the victims being my most valuable helper, Henri Brisson. Poor Brisson's fate was an example of how a man may follow a perilous occupation for months with safety, and then by a slight mistake bring disaster on himself.

At the last gathering Brisson attended he received news of such immediate and fateful import that on emerging from the cellar where the gathering was held, he made directly for my residence instead of going to his own squalid room in the Rue Falgarie. My concierge said that he arrived shortly after one o'clock in the morning, and it would seem that at this hour he could easily have made himself acquainted with the fact that he was followed. Still, as there was on his track that human panther, Felini, it is not strange poor Brisson failed to elude him.

Arriving at the tall building in which my flat was then situated, Brisson rang the bell, and the concierge, as usual, in that strange state of semi-somnolence which envelops concierges during the night, pulled the looped wire at the head of his bed, and unbolted the door. Brisson assuredly closed the huge door behind him, and yet the moment before he did so, Felini must have slipped in unnoticed to the stone-paved courtyard. If Brisson had not spoken and announced himself, the concierge would have been wide awake in an instant. If he had given a name unknown to the concierge, the same result would have ensued. As it was he cried aloud "Brisson," whereupon the concierge of the famous chief of the French detective staff, Valmont, muttered "*Bon!*" and was instantly asleep again.

Now Felini had known Brisson well, but it was under the name of Revensky, and as an exiled Russian. Brisson had spent all his early years in Russia, and spoke the language like a native. The moment Brisson had uttered his true name he had pronounced his own death warrant. Felini followed him up to the first landing— my rooms were on the second floor—and there placed his sign manual on the unfortunate man, which was the swift downward stroke of a long, narrow, sharp poniard, entering the body below the shoulders, and piercing the heart. The advantage presented by this terrible blow is that the victim sinks instantly in a heap at the feet of his slayer, without uttering a moan. The wound left is a scarcely perceptible blue mark which rarely even bleeds. It was this mark I saw on the body of the Maire of Marseilles, and afterwards on one other in Paris besides poor Brisson. It was the mark found on the man in Greenwich Park; always just below the left shoulder-blade, struck from behind. Felini's comrades claim that there was this nobility in his action, namely, he allowed the traitor to prove himself before he struck the blow. I should be sorry to take away this poor shred of credit from Felini's character, but the reason he followed Brisson into the courtyard was to give himself time to escape. He knew perfectly the ways of the concierge. He knew that the body would lie there until the morning, as it actually did, and that this would give him hours in which to effect his retreat. And this was the man whom British law warned not to incriminate himself! What a people! What a people!

After Brisson's tragic death, I resolved to set no more valuable men on the track of the anarchists, but to place upon myself the task in my moments of relaxation. I became very much interested in the underground workings of the International. I joined the organisation under the name of Paul Ducharme, a professor of advanced opinions, who because of them had been dismissed his situation in Nantes. As a matter of fact there had been such a Paul Ducharme, who had been so dismissed, but he had drowned himself in the Loire, at Orleans, as the records show. I adopted the precaution of getting a photograph of this foolish old man from the police at Nantes, and made myself up to resemble him. It says much for my disguise that I was recognised as the professor by a delegate from Nantes, at the annual Convention held in Paris, which I attended, and although we conversed for some time together he never suspected that I was not the professor, whose fate was known to no one but the police of Orleans. I gained much credit among my comrades because of this encounter, which, during its first few moments, filled me with dismay, for the delegate from Nantes held me up as an example of a man well off, who had deliberately sacrificed his worldly position for the sake of principle.

Shortly after this I was chosen delegate to carry a message to our comrades in London, and this delicate undertaking passed off without mishap.

It was perhaps natural then, that when I came to London after my dismissal by the French Government, I should assume the name and appearance of Paul Ducharme, and adopt the profession of French teacher. This profession gave me great advantages. I could be absent from my rooms for hours at a time without attracting the least attention, because a teacher goes wherever there are pupils. If any of my anarchist comrades saw me emerging shabbily from the grand Imperial Flats where Valmont lived, he greeted me affably, thinking I was coming from a pupil.

The sumptuous flat was therefore the office in which I received my rich clients, while the squalid room in Soho was often the workshop in which the tasks entrusted to me were brought to completion.

II

I now come to very modern days indeed, when I spent much time with the emissaries of the International.

It will be remembered that the King of England made a round of visits to European capitals, the far-reaching results of which in the interest of peace we perhaps do not yet fully understand and appreciate. His visit to Paris was the beginning of the present *entente cordiale*, and I betray no confidence when I say that this brief official call at the French capital was the occasion of great anxiety to the Government of my own country and also of that in which I was domiciled. Anarchists are against all government, and would like to see each one destroyed, not even excepting that of Great Britain.

My task in connection with the visit of King Edward to Paris was entirely unofficial. A nobleman, for whom on a previous occasion I had been so happy as to solve a little mystery which troubled him, complimented me by calling at my flat about two weeks before the King's entry into the French capital. I know I shall be pardoned if I fail to mention this nobleman's name. I gathered that the intended visit of the King met with his disapproval. He asked if I knew anything, or could discover anything, of the purposes animating the anarchist clubs of Paris, and their attitude towards the royal function, which was now the chief topic in the newspapers. I replied that within four days I would be able to submit to him a complete report on the subject. He bowed coldly and withdrew. On the evening of the fourth day I permitted myself the happiness of waiting upon his lordship at his West End London mansion.

"I have the honour to report to your lordship," I began, "that the anarchists of Paris are somewhat divided in their opinions regarding His Majesty's forthcoming progress through that city. A minority, contemptible in point of number, but important so far as the extremity of their opinions are concerned, has been trying—"

"Excuse me," interrupted the nobleman, with some severity of tone, "are they going to attempt to injure the King or not?"

"They are not, your lordship," I replied, with what, I trust, is my usual urbanity of manner, despite his curt interpolation. "His most gracious Majesty will suffer no molestation, and their reason for quiescence—"

"Their reasons do not interest me," put in his lordship gruffly. "You are sure of what you say?"

"Perfectly sure, your lordship."

"No precautions need be taken?"

"None in the least, your lordship."

"Very well," concluded the nobleman shortly, "if you tell my secretary in the next room as you go out how much I owe you, he will hand you a cheque," and with that I was dismissed.

I may say that, mixing as I do with the highest in two lands, and meeting invariably such courtesy as I myself am always eager to bestow, a feeling almost of resentment arose at this cavalier treatment. However, I merely bowed somewhat ceremoniously in silence, and availed myself of the opportunity in the next room to double my bill, which was paid without demur.

Now, if this nobleman had but listened, he would have heard much that might interest an ordinary man, although I must say that during my three conversations with him his mind seemed closed to all outward impressions save and except the grandeur of his line, which he traced back unblemished into the northern part of my own country.

The King's visit had come as a surprise to the anarchists, and they did not quite know what to do about it. The Paris Reds were rather in favour of a demonstration, while London bade them, in God's name, to hold their hands, for, as they pointed out, England is the only refuge in which an anarchist is safe until some particular crime can be imputed to him, and what is more, proven up to the hilt.

It will be remembered that the visit of the King to Paris passed off without incident, as did the return visit of the President to London. On the surface all was peace and goodwill, but under the surface seethed plot and counterplot, and behind the scenes two great governments were extremely anxious, and high officials in the Secret Service spent sleepless nights. As no "untoward incident" had happened, the vigilance of the authorities on both sides of the Channel relaxed at the very moment when, if they had known their adversaries, it should have been redoubled. Always beware of the anarchist when he has been good: look out for the reaction. It annoys him to be compelled to remain quiet when there is a grand opportunity for strutting across the world's stage, and when he misses the psychological moment, he is apt to turn "nasty," as the English say.

When it first became known that there was to be a Royal procession through the streets of Paris, a few fanatical hot-heads, both in that city and in London, wished to take action, but they were overruled by the saner members of the organisation. It must not be supposed that anarchists are a band of lunatics. There are able brains among them, and these born leaders as naturally assume control in the underground world of anarchy as would have been the case if they had devoted their talents to affairs in ordinary life. They were men whose minds, at one period, had taken the wrong turning. These people, although they calmed the frenzy of the extremists, nevertheless regarded the possible *rapprochement* between England and France with grave apprehension. If France and England became as friendly as France and Russia, might not the refuge which England had given to anarchy become a thing of the past? I may say here that my own weight as an anarchist while attending these meetings in disguise under the name of Paul Du-charme was invariably thrown in to help the cause of moderation. My rôle, of course, was not to talk too much; not to make myself prominent, yet in such a gathering a man cannot remain wholly a spectator. Care for my own safety led me to be as inconspicuous as possible, for members of communities banded together against the laws of the land in which they live, are extremely suspicious of one another, and an inadvertent word may cause disaster to the person speaking it.

Perhaps it was this conservatism on my part that caused my advice to be sought after by the inner circle; what you might term the governing body of the anarchists; for, strange as it may appear, this organisation, sworn to put down all law and order, was itself most rigidly governed, with a Russian prince elected as its chairman, a man of striking ability, who, nevertheless, I believe, owed his election more to the fact that he was a nobleman than to the recognition of his intrinsic worth. And another point which interested me much was that this prince ruled his obstreperous subjects after the fashion of Russian despotism, rather than according to the liberal ideas of the country in which he was domiciled. I have known him more than once ruthlessly overturn the action of the majority, stamp his foot, smite his huge fist on the table, and declare so and so should not be done, no matter what the vote was. And the thing was not done, either.

At the more recent period of which I speak, the chairmanship of the London anarchists was held by a weak, vacillating man, and the mob had got somewhat out of hand. In the crisis that confronted us, I yearned for the firm fist and dominant boot of the uncompromising Russian. I spoke only once during this time, and assured my listeners that they had nothing to fear from the coming friendship of the two nations. I said the Englishman was so wedded to his grotesque ideas regarding the liberty of the subject he so worshipped absolute legal evidence, that we would never find our comrades disappear mysteriously from England as had been the case in continental countries.

Although restless during the exchange of visits between King and President, I believe I could have carried the English phalanx with me, if the international courtesies had ended there. But after it was announced that members of the British Parliament were to meet the members of the French Legislature, the Paris circle became alarmed, and when that conference did not end the *entente*, but merely paved the way for a meeting of business men belonging to the two countries in Paris, the French anarchists sent a delegate over to us, who made a wild speech one night, waving continually the red flag. This aroused all our own malcontents to a frenzy. The French speaker practically charged the English contingent with cowardice; said that as they were safe from molestation, they felt no sympathy for their comrades in Paris, at any time liable to summary arrest and the torture of the secret cross-examination. This Anglo-French love-feast must be wafted to the heavens in a halo of dynamite. The Paris anarchists were determined, and although they wished the co-operation of their London brethren, yet if the speaker did not bring back with him assurance of such co-operation, Paris would act on its own initiative.

The Russian despot would have made short work of this blood-blinded rhetoric, but alas, he was absent, and an overwhelming vote in favour of force was carried and accepted by the trembling chairman. My French *confrère* took back with him to Paris the unanimous consent of the English comrades to whom he had appealed. All that was asked of the English contingent was that it should arrange for the escape and safe keeping of the assassin who flung the bomb into the midst of the English visitors, and after the oratorical madman had departed, I, to my horror, was chosen to arrange for the safe transport and future custody of the bomb-thrower. It is not etiquette in anarchist circles for any member to decline whatever task is given him by the vote of his comrades. He knows the alternative, which is suicide. If he declines the task and still remains upon earth, the dilemma is solved for him, as the

Italian Felini solved it through the back of my unfortunate helper Brisson. I therefore accepted the unwelcome office in silence, and received from the treasurer the money necessary for carrying out the same.

I realised for the first time since joining the anarchist association years before that I was in genuine danger. A single false step, a single inadvertent word, might close the career of Eugène Valmont, and at the same moment terminate the existence of the quiet, inoffensive Paul Ducharme, teacher of the French language. I knew perfectly well I should be followed. The moment I received the money the French delegate asked when they were to expect me in Paris. He wished to know so that all the resources of their organisation might be placed at my disposal. I replied calmly enough that I could not state definitely on what day I should leave England. There was plenty of time, as the business men's representatives from London would not reach Paris for another two weeks. I was well known to the majority of the Paris organisation, and would present myself before them on the first night of my arrival. The Paris delegate exhibited all the energy of a new recruit, and he seemed dissatisfied with my vagueness, but I went on without heeding his displeasure. He was not personally known to me, nor I to him, but if I may say so, Paul Ducharme was well thought of by all the rest of those present.

I had learned a great lesson during the episode of the Queen's Necklace, which resulted in my dismissal by the French Government. I had learned that if you expect pursuit it is always well to leave a clue for the pursuer to follow. Therefore I continued in a low conversational tone:

"I shall want the whole of tomorrow for myself: I must notify my pupils of my absence. Even if my pupils leave me it will not so much matter. I can probably get others. But what does matter is my secretarial work with Monsieur Valmont of the Imperial Flats. I am just finishing for him the translation of a volume from French into English, and tomorrow I can complete the work, and get his permission to leave for a fortnight. This man, who is a compatriot of my own, has given me employment ever since I came to London.

From him I have received the bulk of my income, and if it had not been for his patronage, I do not know what I should have done. I not only have no desire to offend him, but I wish the secretarial work to continue when I return to London."

There was a murmur of approval at this. It was generally recognised that a man's living should not be interfered with, if possible. Anarchists are not poverty-stricken individuals, as most people think, for many of them hold excellent situations, some occupying positions of great trust, which is rarely betrayed.

It is recognised that a man's duty, not only to himself, but to the organisation, is to make all the money he can, and thus not be liable to fall back on the relief fund. This frank admission of my dependence on Valmont made it all the more impossible that any-one there listening should suspect that it was Valmont himself who was addressing the conclave.

"You will then take the night train tomorrow for Paris?" persisted the inquisitive French delegate.

"Yes, and no. I shall take the night train, and it shall be for Paris, but not from Charing Cross, Victoria, or Waterloo. I shall travel on the 8.30 Continental express from Liverpool Street to Harwich, cross to the Hook of Holland, and from there make my way to Paris through Holland and Belgium. I wish to investigate that route as a possible path for our comrade to escape. After the blow is struck, Calais, Boulogne, Dieppe, and Havre will be closely watched. I shall perhaps bring him to London by way of Antwerp and the Hook."

These amiable disclosures were so fully in keeping with Paul Ducharme's reputation for candour and caution that I saw they made an excellent impression on my audience, and here the chairman intervened, putting an end to further cross-examination by saying they all had the utmost confidence in the judgment of Monsieur Paul Ducharme, and the Paris delegate might advise his friends to be on the lookout for the London representative within the next three or four days.

I left the meeting and went directly to my room in Soho, without even taking the trouble to observe whether I was watched or not. There I stayed all night, and in the morning quitted Soho as Ducharme, with a gray beard and bowed shoulders, walked west to the Imperial Flats, took the lift to the top, and, seeing the corridor was clear, let myself in to my own flat. I departed from my flat promptly at six o'clock, again as Paul Ducharme, carrying this time a bundle done up in brown paper under my arm, and proceeded directly to my room in Soho. Later I took a bus, still carrying my brown paper parcel, and reached Liverpool Street in ample time for the Continental train. By a little private arrangement with the guard, I secured a compartment for myself, although up to the moment the train left the station, I could not be sure but that I might be compelled to take the trip to the Hook of Holland after all. If any one had insisted on coming into my compartment, I should have crossed the North Sea that night. I knew I should be followed from Soho to the station, and that probably the spy would go as far as Harwich, and see me on the boat. It was doubtful if he would cross. I had chosen this route for the reason that we have no organisation in Holland: the nearest circle is in Brussels, and if there had been time, the Brussels circle would have been warned to keep an eye on me. There was, however, no time for a letter, and anarchists never use the telegraph, especially so far as the Continent is concerned, unless in cases of the greatest emergency. If they telegraphed my description to Brussels the chances were it would not be an anarchist who watched my landing, but a member of the Belgian police force.

The 8.30 Continental express does not stop between Liverpool Street and Parkeston Quay, which it is timed to reach three minutes before ten. This gave me an hour and a half in which to change my apparel. The garments of the poor old professor I rolled up into a ball one by one and flung out through the open window, far into the marsh past which we were flying in a pitch dark night. Coat, trousers, and waistcoat rested in separate swamps at least ten miles apart. Gray whiskers and gray wig I tore into little pieces, and dropped the bits out of the open window.

I had taken the precaution to secure a compartment in the front of the train, and when it came to rest at Parkeston Quay Station, the crowd, eager for the steamer, rushed past me, and I stepped out into the midst of it, a dapper, well-dressed young man, with black beard and moustaches, my own closely cropped black hair covered by a new bowler hat. Anyone looking for Paul Ducharme would have paid small attention to me, and to any friend of Valmont's I was equally unrecognisable.

I strolled in leisurely manner to the Great Eastern Hotel on the Quay, and asked the clerk if a portmanteau addressed to Mr. John Wilkins had arrived that day from London. He said "Yes," whereupon I secured a room for the night, as the last train had already left for the metropolis.

Next morning, Mr. John Wilkins, accompanied by a brand new and rather expensive portmanteau, took the 8.57 train for Liverpool Street, where he arrived at half-past ten, stepped into a cab, and drove to the Savoy Restaurant, lunching there with the portmanteau deposited in the cloak room. When John Wilkins had finished an excellent lunch in a leisurely manner at the Café Parisien of the Savoy, and had paid his bill, he did not go out into the Strand over the rubber-paved court by which he had entered, but went through the hotel and down the stairs, and so out into the thoroughfare facing the Embankment. Then turning to his right he reached the Embankment entrance of the Hotel Cecil. This leads into a long, dark corridor, at the end of which the lift may be rung for. It does not come lower than the floor above unless specially summoned. In this dark corridor, which was empty, John Wilkins took off the black beard and moustache, hid it in the inside pocket of his coat, and there went up into the lift a few moments later to the office floor, I, Eugène Valmont, myself for the first time in several days.

Even then I did not take a cab to my flat, but passed under the arched Strand front of the "Cecil" in a cab, bound for the residence of that nobleman who had formerly engaged me to see after the safety of the King.

You will say that this was all very elaborate precaution to take when a man was not even sure he was followed. To tell you the truth, I do not know to this day whether anyone watched me or not, nor do I care. I live in the present: when once the past is done with, it ceases to exist for me. It is quite possible, nay, entirely probable, that no one tracked me farther than Liverpool Street Station the night before, yet it was for lack of such precaution that my assistant Brisson received the Italian's dagger under his shoulder blade fifteen years before. The present moment is ever the critical time; the future is merely for intelligent forethought. It was to prepare for the future that I was now in a cab on the way to my lord's residence. It was not the French anarchists I feared during the contest in which I was about to become engaged, but the Paris police. I knew French officialdom too well not to understand the futility of going to the authorities there and proclaiming my object. If I ventured to approach the chief of police with the information that I, in London, had discovered what it was his business in Paris to know, my reception would be far from cordial, even though, or rather because, I announced myself as Eugène Valmont. The exploits of Eugène had become part of the legends of Paris, and these legends were extremely distasteful to those men in power. My doings have frequently been made the subject of *feuilletons* in the columns of the Paris Press, and were, of course, exaggerated by the imagination of the writers, yet, nevertheless, I admit I did some good strokes of detection during my service with the French Government. It is but natural, then, that the present authorities should listen with some impatience when the name of Eugène Valmont is mentioned. I recognise this as quite in the order of things to be expected, and am honest enough to confess that in my own time I often hearkened to narratives regarding the performances of Lecocq with a doubting shrug of the shoulders.

Now, if the French police knew anything of this anarchist plot, which was quite within the bounds of possibility, and if I were in surreptitious communication with the anarchists, more especially with the man who was to fling the bomb, there was every chance I might find myself in the grip of French justice. I must, then, provide myself with credentials to show that I was acting, not against the peace and quiet of my country, but on the side of law and order. I therefore wished to get from the nobleman a commission in writing, similar to that command which he had placed upon me during the King's visit. This commission I should lodge at my bank in Paris, to be a voucher for me at the last extremity. I had no doubt his lordship would empower me to act in this instance as I had acted on two former occasions.

III

Perhaps if I had not lunched so well I might have approached his lordship with greater deference than was the case; but when ordering lunch I permitted a bottle of Château du Tertre, 1878, a most delicious claret, to be decanted carefully for my delectation at the table, and this caused a genial glow to permeate throughout my system, inducing a mental optimism which left me ready to salute the greatest of earth on a plane of absolute equality. Besides, after all, I am the citizen of a Republic.

The nobleman received me with frigid correctness, implying disapproval of my unauthorised visit, rather than expressing it. Our interview was extremely brief.

"I had the felicity of serving your lordship upon two occasions," I began.

"They are well within my recollection," he interrupted, "but I do not remember sending for you a third time."

"I have taken the liberty of coming unrequested, my lord, because of the importance of the news I carry. I surmise that you are interested in the promotion of friendship between France and England."

"Your surmise, sir, is incorrect. I care not a button about it. My only anxiety was for the safety of the King."

Even the superb claret was not enough to fortify me against words so harsh, and tones so discourteous, as those his lordship permitted himself to use.

"Sir," said I, dropping the title in my rising anger, "it may interest you to know that a number of your countrymen run the risk of being blown to eternity by an anarchist bomb in less than two weeks from today. A party of business men, true representatives of a class to which the pre-eminence of your Empire is due, are about to proceed—"

"Pray spare me," interpolated his lordship wearily, "I have read that sort of thing so often in the newspapers. If all these estimable City men are blown up, the Empire would doubtless miss them, as you hint, but I should not, and their fate does not interest me in the least, although you did me the credit of believing that it would. Thompson, you will show this person out? Sir, if I desire your presence here in future I will send for you."

"You may send for the devil!" I cried, now thoroughly enraged, the wine getting the better of me.

"You express my meaning more tersely than I cared to do," he replied coldly, and that was the last I ever saw of him.

Entering the cab I now drove to my flat, indignant at the reception I had met with. However, I knew the English people too well to malign them for the action of one of their number, and resentment never dwells long with me. Arriving at my rooms I looked through the newspapers to learn all I could of the proposed business men's excursion to Paris, and in reading the names of those most prominent in carrying out the necessary arrangements, I came across that of W. Raymond White, which caused me to sit back in my chair and wrinkle my brow in an endeavour to stir my memory. Unless I was much mistaken, I had been so happy as to oblige this gentleman some dozen or thirteen years before. As I remembered him, he was a business man who engaged in large transactions with France, dealing especially in Lyons and that district. His address was given in the newspaper as Old 'Change, so at once I resolved to see him. Although I could not recall the details of our previous meeting, if, indeed, he should turn out to be the same person, yet the mere sight of the name had produced a mental pleasure, as a chance chord struck may bring a grateful harmony to the mind. I determined to get my credentials from Mr. White if possible, for his recommendation would in truth be much more valuable than that of the gruff old nobleman to whom I had first applied, because, if I got into trouble with the police of Paris, I was well enough acquainted with the natural politeness of the authorities to know that a letter from one of the city's guests would secure my instant release.

I took a hansom to the head of that narrow thoroughfare known as Old 'Change, and there dismissed my cab. I was so fortunate as to recognise Mr. White coming out of his office. A moment later, and I should have missed him.

"Mr. White," I accosted him, "I desire to enjoy both the pleasure and the honour of introducing myself to you."

"Monsieur," replied Mr. White with a smile, "the introduction is not necessary, and the pleasure and honour are mine. Unless I am very much mistaken, this is Monsieur Valmont of Paris?"

"Late of Paris," I corrected.

"Are you no longer in Government service then?"

"For a little more than ten years I have been a resident of London."

"What, and have never let me know? That is something the diplomatists call an unfriendly act, monsieur. Now, shall we return to my office, or go to a *café*?"

"To your office, if you please, Mr. White. I come on rather important business."

Entering his private office the merchant closed the door, offered me a chair, and sat down himself by his desk. From the first he had addressed me in French, which he spoke with an accent so pure that it did my lonesome heart good to hear it.

"I called upon you half a dozen years ago," he went on, "when I was over in Paris on a festive occasion, where I hoped to secure your company, but I could not learn definitely whether you were still with the Government or not."

"It is the way of the French officialism," I replied. "If they knew my whereabouts they would keep the knowledge to themselves."

"Well, if you have been ten years in London, Monsieur Valmont, we may now perhaps have the pleasure of claiming you as an Englishman; so I beg you will accompany us on another festive occasion to Paris next week. Perhaps you have seen that a number of us are going over there to make the welkin ring."

"Yes; I have read all about the business men's excursion to Paris, and it is with reference to this journey that I wish to consult you," and here I gave Mr. White in detail the plot of the anarchists against the growing cordiality of the two countries. The merchant listened quietly without interruption until I had finished; then he said: "I suppose it will be rather useless to inform the police of Paris?"

"Indeed, Mr. White, it is the police of Paris I fear more than the anarchists. They would resent information coming to them from the outside, especially from an ex-official, the inference being that they were not up to their own duties. Friction and delay would ensue until the deed was inevitable. It is quite on the cards that the police of Paris may have some inkling of the plot, and in that case, just before the event, they are reasonably certain to arrest the wrong men. I shall be moving about Paris, not as Eugène Valmont, but as Paul Ducharme, the anarchist; therefore, there is some danger that as a stranger and a suspect I may be laid by the heels at the critical moment. If you would be so good as to furnish me with credentials which I can deposit somewhere in Paris in case of need, I may thus be able to convince the authorities that they have taken the wrong man."

Mr. White, entirely unperturbed by the prospect of having a bomb thrown at him within two weeks, calmly wrote several documents, then turned his untroubled face to me, and said, in a very confidential, winning tone: "Monsieur Valmont, you have stated the case with that clear comprehensiveness pertaining to a nation which understands the meaning of words, and the correct adjustment of them; that felicity of language which has given France the first place in the literature of nations. Consequently, I think I see very clearly the delicacies of the situation. We may expect hindrances, rather than help, from officials on either side of the Channel. Secrecy is essential to success. Have you spoken of this to anyone but me?"

"Only to Lord Blank," I replied; "and now I deeply regret having made a confidant of him."

"That does not in the least matter," said Mr. White, with a smile; "Lord Blank's mind is entirely occupied by his own greatness. Chemists tell me that you cannot add a new ingredient to a saturated solution; therefore your revelation will have made no impression upon his lordship's intellect. He has already forgotten all about it. Am I right in supposing that everything hinges on the man who is to throw the bomb?"

"Quite right, sir. He may be venal, he may be traitorous, he may be a coward, he may be revengeful, he may be a drunkard. Before I am in conversation with him for ten minutes, I shall know what his weak spot is. It is upon that spot I must act, and my action must be delayed till the very last moment; for, if he disappears too long before the event, his first, second, or third substitute will instantly step into his place."

"Precisely. So you cannot complete your plans until you have met this man?"

"*Parfaitement.*"

"Then I propose," continued Mr. White, "that we take no one into our confidence. In a case like this there is little use in going before a committee. I can see that you do not need any advice, and my own part shall be to remain in the background, content to support the most competent man that could have been chosen to grapple with a very difficult crisis."

I bowed profoundly. There was a compliment in his glance as well as in his words. Never before had I met so charming a man.

"Here," he continued, handing me one of the papers he had written, "is a letter to whom it may concern, appointing you my agent for the next three weeks, and holding myself responsible for all you see fit to do. Here," he went on, passing to me a second sheet, "is a letter of introduction to Monsieur Largent, the manager of my bank in Paris, a man well known and highly respected in all circles, both official and commercial. I suggest that you introduce yourself to him, and he will hold himself in readiness to respond to any call you may make, night or day. I assure you that his mere presence before the authorities will at once remove any ordinary difficulty. And now," he added, taking in hand the third slip of paper, speaking with some hesitation, and choosing his words with care, "I come to a point which cannot be ignored. Money is a magician's wand, which, like faith, will remove mountains. It may also remove an anarchist hovering about the route of a business man's procession."

He now handed to me what I saw was a draft on Paris for a thousand pounds.

"I assure you, monsieur," I protested, covered with confusion, "that no thought of money was in my mind when I took the liberty of presenting myself to you. I have already received more than I could have expected in the generous confidence you were good enough to repose in me, as exhibited by these credentials, and especially the letter to your banker. Thanks to the generosity of your countrymen, Mr. White, of which you are a most notable example, I am in no need of money."

"Monsieur Valmont, I am delighted to hear that you have got on well amongst us. This money is for two purposes. First, you will use what you need. I know Paris very well, monsieur, and have never found gold an embarrassment there. The second purpose is this: I suggest that when you present the letter of introduction to Monsieur Largent, you will casually place this amount to your account in his bank. He will thus see that besides writing you a letter of introduction, I transfer a certain amount of my own balance to your credit. That will do you no harm with him, I assure you. And now, Monsieur Valmont, it only remains for me to thank you for the opportunity you have given me, and to assure you that I shall march from the Gare du Nord without a tremor, knowing the outcome is in such capable custody."

And then this estimable man shook hands with me in action the most cordial. I walked away from Old 'Change as if I trod upon air; a feeling vastly different from that with which I departed from the residence of the old nobleman in the West End but a few hours before.

IV

Next morning I was in Paris, and next night I attended the underground meeting of the anarchists, held within a quarter of a mile of the Luxembourg. I was known to many there assembled, but my acquaintance of course was not so large as with the London circle. They had half expected me the night before, knowing that even going by the Hook of Holland I might have reached Paris in time for the conclave. I was introduced generally to the assemblage as the emissary from England, who was to assist the bomb-throwing brother to escape either to that country, or to such other point of safety as I might choose. No questions were asked me regarding my doings of the day before, nor was I required to divulge the plans for my fellow-member's escape. I was responsible; that was enough. If I failed through no fault of my own, it was but part of the ill-luck we were all prepared to face. If I failed through treachery, then a dagger in the back at the earliest possible moment. We all knew the conditions of our sinister contract, and we all recognised that the least said the better.

The cellar was dimly lighted by one oil lamp depending from the ceiling. From this hung a cord attached to an extinguisher, and one jerk of the cord would put out the light. Then, while the main entry doors were being battered down by police, the occupants of the room escaped through one of three or four human rat-holes provided for that purpose.

If any Parisian anarchist does me the honour to read these jottings, I beg to inform him that while I remained in office under the Government of France there was never a time when I did not know the exit of each of these underground passages, and could during any night there was conference have bagged the whole lot of those there assembled. It was never my purpose, however, to shake the anarchists' confidence in their system, for that merely meant the removal of the gathering to another spot, thus giving us the additional trouble of mapping out their new exits and entrances. When I did make a raid on anarchist headquarters in Paris, it was always to secure some particular man. I had my emissaries in plain clothes stationed at each exit. In any case, the rats were allowed to escape unmolested, sneaking forth with great caution into the night, but we always spotted the man we wanted, and almost invariably arrested him elsewhere, having followed him from his kennel. In each case my uniformed officers found a dark and empty cellar, and retired apparently baffled. But the coincidence that on the night of every raid some member there present was secretly arrested in another quarter of Paris, and perhaps given a free passage to Russia, never seemed to awaken suspicion in the minds of the conspirators.

I think the London anarchists' method is much better, and I have ever considered the English nihilist the most dangerous of this fraternity, for he is cool-headed and not carried away by his own enthusiasm, and consequently rarely carried away by his own police. The authorities of London meet no opposition in making a raid. They find a well-lighted room containing a more or less shabby coterie playing cards at cheap pine tables. There is no money visible, and, indeed, very little coin would be brought to light if the whole party were searched; so the police are unable to convict the players under the Gambling Act. Besides, it is difficult in any case to obtain a conviction under the Gambling Act, because the accused has the sympathy of the whole country with him. It has always been to me one of the anomalies of the English nature that a magistrate can keep a straight face while he fines some poor wretch for gambling, knowing that next race day (if the court is not sitting) the magistrate himself, in correct sporting costume, with binoculars hanging at his hip, will be on the lawn by the course backing his favourite horse.

After my reception at the anarchists' club of Paris, I remained seated unobtrusively on a bench waiting until routine business was finished, after which I expected an introduction to the man selected to throw the bomb. I am a very sensitive person, and sitting there quietly I became aware that I was being scrutinised with more than ordinary intensity by someone, which gave me a feeling of uneasiness. At last, in the semi-obscurity opposite me I saw a pair of eyes as luminous as those of a tiger peering fixedly at me. I returned the stare with such composure as I could bring to my aid, and the man, as if fascinated by a look as steady as his own, leaned forward, and came more and more into the circle of light.

Then I received a shock which it required my utmost self-control to conceal. The face, haggard and drawn, was none other than that of Adolph Simard, who had been my second assistant in the Secret Service of France during my last year in office. He was a most capable and rising young man at that time, and, of course, he knew me well. Had he, then, penetrated my disguise? Such an event seemed impossible; he could not have recognised my voice, for I had said nothing aloud since entering the room, my few words to the president being spoken in a whisper. Simard's presence there bewildered me; by this time he should be high up in the Secret Service. If he were now a spy, he would, of course, wish to familiarise himself with every particular of my appearance, as in my hands lay the escape of the criminal. Yet, if such were his mission, why did he attract the attention of all members by this open-eyed scrutiny? That he recognised me as Valmont I had not the least fear; my disguise was too perfect; and, even if I were there in my own proper person, I had not seen Simard, nor he me, for ten years, and great changes occur in a man's appearance during so long a period. Yet I remembered with disquietude that Mr. White recognised me, and here tonight I had recognised Simard. I could not move my bench farther back because it stood already against the wall.

Simard, on the contrary, was seated on one of the few chairs in the room, and this he periodically hitched forward, the better to continue his examination, which now attracted the notice of others besides myself. As he came forward, I could not help admiring the completeness of his disguise so far as apparel was concerned. He was a perfect picture of the Paris wastrel, and what was more, he wore on his head a cap of the Apaches, the most dangerous band of cut-throats that have ever cursed a civilised city. I could understand that even among lawless anarchists this badge of membership of the Apache band might well strike tenor. I felt that before the meeting adjourned I must speak with him, and I determined to begin our conversation by asking him why he stared so fixedly at me. Yet even then I should have made little progress. I did not dare to hint that he belonged to the Secret Service; nevertheless, if the authorities had this plot in charge, it was absolutely necessary we should work together, or, at least, that I should know they were in the secret, and steer my course accordingly. The fact that Simard appeared with undisguised face was not so important as might appear to an outsider.

It is always safer for a spy to preserve his natural appearance if that is possible, because a false beard or false moustache or wig run the risk of being deranged or torn away. As I have said, an anarchist assemblage is simply a room filled with the atmosphere of suspicion. I have known instances where an innocent stranger was suddenly set upon in the midst of solemn proceedings by two or three impetuous fellow-members, who nearly jerked his own whiskers from his face under the impression that they were false. If Simard, therefore, appeared in his own scraggy beard and unkempt hair it meant that he communicated with headquarters by some circuitous route. I realised, therefore, that a very touchy bit of diplomacy awaited me if I was to learn from himself his actual status. While I pondered over this perplexity, it was suddenly dissolved by the action of the president, and another substituted for it.

"Will Brother Simard come forward?" asked the president.

My former subordinate removed his eyes from me, slowly rose from his chair, and shuffled up to the president's table.

"Brother Ducharme," said that official to me in a quiet tone, "I introduce you to Brother Simard, whom you are commissioned to see into a place of safety when he has dispersed the procession."

Simard turned his fishy goggle eyes upon me, and a grin disclosed wolf-like teeth. He held out his hand, which, rising to my feet, I took. He gave me a flabby grasp, and all the time his inquiring eyes travelled over me.

"You don't look up to much," he said. "What are you?"

"I am a teacher of the French language in London."

"Umph!" growled Simard, evidently in no wise prepossessed by my appearance. "I thought you weren't much of a fighter. The *gendarmes* will make short work of this fellow," he growled to the chairman.

"Brother Ducharme is vouched for by the whole English circle," replied the president firmly.

"Oh, the English! I think very little of them. Still, it doesn't matter," and with a shrug of the shoulders he shuffled to his seat again, leaving me standing there in a very embarrassed state of mind; my brain in a whirl. That the man was present with his own face was bewildering enough, but that he should be here under his own name was simply astounding. I scarcely heard what the president said. It seemed to the effect that Simard would take me to his own room, where we might talk over our plans. And now Simard rose again from his chair, and said to the president that if nothing more were wanted of him, we should go. Accordingly we left the place of meeting together. I watched my comrade narrowly. There was now a trembling eagerness in his action, and without a word he hurried me to the nearest *café*, where we sat down before a little iron table on the pavement.

"*Garçon*," he shouted harshly, "bring me four absinthes. What will you drink, Ducharme?"

"A *café-cognac*, if you please."

"Bah!" cried Simard; "better have absinthe."

Then he cursed the waiter for his slowness. When the absinthe came he grasped the half-full glass and swallowed the liquid raw, a thing I had never seen done before. Into the next measure of the wormwood he poured the water impetuously from the *carafe*, another thing I had never seen done before, and dropped two lumps of sugar into it. Over the third glass he placed a flat perforated plated spoon, piled the sugar on this bridge, and now quite expertly allowed the water to drip through, the proper way of concocting this seductive mixture. Finishing his second glass he placed the perforated spoon over the fourth, and began now more calmly sipping the third while the water dripped slowly into the last glass.

Here before my eyes was enacted a more wonderful change than the gradual transformation of transparent absinthe into an opaque opalescent liquid. Simard, under the influence of the drink, was slowly becoming the Simard I had known ten years before. Remarkable! Absinthe having in earlier years made a beast of the man was now forming a man out of the beast. His staring eyes took on an expression of human comradeship. The whole mystery became perfectly clear to me without a question asked or an answer uttered. This man was no spy, but a genuine anarchist. However it happened, he had become a victim of absinthe, one of many with whom I was acquainted, although I never met any so far sunk as he. He was into his fourth glass, and had ordered two more when he began to speak.

"Here's to us," he cried, with something like a civilised smile on his gaunt face. "You're not offended at what I said in the meeting, I hope?"

"Oh, no," I answered.

"That's right. You see, I once belonged to the Secret Service, and if my chief was there today, we would soon find ourselves in a cool dungeon. We couldn't trip up Eugène Valmont."

At these words, spoken with sincerity, I sat up in my chair, and I am sure such an expression of enjoyment came into my face that if I had not instantly suppressed it, I might have betrayed myself.

"Who was Eugène Valmont?" I asked, in a tone of assumed indifference.

Mixing his fifth glass he nodded sagely.

"You wouldn't ask that question if you'd been in Paris a dozen years ago. He was the Government's chief detective, and he knew more of anarchists, yes, and of Apaches, too, than either you or I do. He had more brains in his little finger than that whole lot babbling there tonight. But the Government being a fool, as all governments are, dismissed him, and because I was his assistant, they dismissed me as well. They got rid of all his staff. Valmont disappeared. If I could have found him, I wouldn't be sitting here with you tonight; but he was right to disappear. The Government did all they could against us who had been his friends, and I for one came through starvation, and was near throwing myself in the Seine, which sometimes I wish I had done. Here, *garçon*, another absinthe. But by-and-by I came to like the gutter, and here I am. I'd rather have the gutter and absinthe than the Luxembourg without it. I've had my revenge on the Government many times since, for I knew their ways, and often have I circumvented the police. That's why they respect me among the anarchists. Do you know how I joined? I knew all their passwords, and walked right into one of their meetings, alone and in rags.

"'Here am I,' I said; 'Adolph Simard, late second assistant to Eugène Valmont, chief detective to the French Government.'

"There were twenty weapons covering me at once, but I laughed.

"'I'm starving,' I cried, 'and I want something to eat, and more especially something to drink. In return for that I'll show you every rat-hole you've got. Lift the president's chair, and there's a trap-door that leads to the Rue Blanc. I'm one of you, and I'll tell you the tricks of the police.'

"Such was my initiation, and from that moment the police began to pick their spies out of the Seine, and now they leave us alone. Even Valmont himself could do nothing against the anarchists since I have joined them."

Oh, the incredible self-conceit of human nature! Here was this ruffian proclaiming the limitations of Valmont, who half an hour before had shaken his hand within the innermost circle of his order! Yet my heart warmed towards the wretch who had remembered me and my exploits.

It now became my anxious and difficult task to lure Simard away from this *café* and its absinthe. Glass after glass of the poison had brought him up almost to his former intellectual level, but now it was shoving him rapidly down the hill again. I must know where his room was situated, yet if I waited much longer the man would be in a state of drunken imbecility which would not only render it impossible for him to guide me to his room, but likely cause both of us to be arrested by the police. I tried persuasion, and he laughed at me; I tried threats, whereat he scowled and cursed me as a renegade from England. At last the liquor overpowered him, and his head sunk on the metal table and the dark blue cap fell to the floor.

V

I was in despair, but now received a lesson which taught me that if a man leaves a city, even for a short time, he falls out of touch with its ways. I called the waiter, and said to him:

"Do you know my friend here?"

"I do not know his name," replied the *garçon*, "but I have seen him many times at this *café*. He is usually in this state when he has money."

"Do you know where he lives? He promised to take me with him, and I am a stranger in Paris."

"Have no discontent, monsieur. Rest tranquil; I will intervene."

With this he stepped across the pavement in front of the *café*, into the street, and gave utterance to a low, peculiar whistle. The *café* was now nearly deserted, for the hour was very late, or, rather, very early. When the waiter returned I whispered to him in some anxiety:

"Not the police, surely?"

"But no!" he cried in scorn; "certainly not the police."

He went on unconcernedly taking in the empty chairs and tables. A few minutes later there swaggered up to the *café* two of the most disreputable, low-browed scoundrels I had ever seen, each wearing a dark-blue cap, with a glazed peak over the eyes; caps exactly similar to the one which lay in front of Simard. The band of Apaches which now permeates all Paris has risen since my time, and Simard had been mistaken an hour before in asserting that Valmont was familiar with their haunts. The present Chief of Police in Paris and some of his predecessors confess there is a difficulty in dealing with these picked assassins, but I should very much like to take a hand in the game on the side of law and order. However, that is not to be; therefore, the Apaches increase and prosper.

The two vagabonds roughly smote Simard's cap on his prone head, and as roughly raised him to his feet.

"He is a friend of mine," I interposed, "and promised to take me home with him."

"Good! Follow us," said one of them; and now I passed through the morning streets of Paris behind three cut-throats, yet knew that I was safer than if broad daylight was in the thoroughfare, with a meridian sun shining down upon us. I was doubly safe, being in no fear of harm from midnight prowlers, and equally free from danger of arrest by the police. Every officer we met avoided us, and casually stepped to the other side of the street. We turned down a narrow lane, then through a still narrower one, which terminated at a courtyard. Entering a tall building, we climbed up five flights of stairs to a landing, where one of the scouts kicked open a door, into a room so miserable that there was not even a lock to protect its poverty. Here they allowed the insensible Simard to drop with a crash on the floor, thus they left us alone without even an adieu. The Apaches take care of their own—after a fashion.

I struck a match, and found part of a *bougie* stuck in the mouth of an absinthe bottle, resting on a rough deal table. Lighting the *bougie*, I surveyed the horrible apartment. A heap of rags lay in a corner, and this was evidently Simard's bed. I hauled him to it, and there he lay unconscious, himself a bundle of rags. I found one chair, or, rather, stool, for it had no back. I drew the table against the lockless door, blew out the light, sat on the stool, resting my arms on the table, and my head on my arms, and slept peacefully till long after daybreak.

Simard awoke in the worst possible humour. He poured forth a great variety of abusive epithets at me. To make himself still more agreeable, he turned back the rags on which he had slept, and brought to the light a round, black object, like a small cannon-ball, which he informed me was the picric bomb that was to scatter destruction among my English friends, for whom he expressed the greatest possible loathing and contempt. Then sitting up, he began playing with this infernal machine, knowing, as well as I, that if he allowed it to drop that was the end of us two.

I shrugged my shoulders at this display, and affected a nonchalance I was far from feeling, but finally put an end to his dangerous amusement by telling him that if he came out with me I would pay for his breakfast, and give him a drink of absinthe.

The next few days were the most anxious of my life. Never before had I lived on terms of intimacy with a picric bomb, that most deadly and uncertain of all explosive agencies. I speedily found that Simard was so absinthe-soaked I could do nothing with him. He could not be bribed or cajoled or persuaded or threatened. Once, indeed, when he talked with drunken affection of Eugène Valmont, I conceived a wild notion of declaring myself to him; but a moment's reflection showed the absolute uselessness of this course. It was not one Simard with whom I had to deal, but half a dozen or more. There was Simard, sober, half sober, quarter sober, drunk, half drunk, quarter drunk, or wholly drunk. Any bargain I might make with the one Simard would not be kept by any of the other six. The only safe Simard was Simard insensible through over-indulgence. I had resolved to get Simard insensibly drunk on the morning of the procession, but my plans were upset at a meeting of the anarchists, which luckily took place on an evening shortly after my arrival, and this gave me time to mature the plan which was actually carried out. Each member of the anarchists' club knew of Simard's slavery to absinthe, and fears were expressed that he might prove incapable on the day of the procession, too late for a substitute to take his place. It was, therefore, proposed that one or two others should be stationed along the route of the procession with bombs ready if Simard failed. This I strenuously opposed, and guaranteed that Simard would be ready to launch his missile. I met with little difficulty in persuading the company to agree, because, after all, every man among them feared he might be one of those selected, which choice was practically a sentence of death. I guaranteed that the bomb would be thrown, and this apparently was taken to mean that if Simard did not do the deed, I would.

This danger over, I next took the measurements, and estimated the weight, of the picric bomb. I then sought out a most amiable and expert pyrotechnist, a capable workman of genius, who with his own hand makes those dramatic firework arrangements which you sometimes see in Paris. As Eugène Valmont, I had rendered a great service to this man, and he was not likely to have forgotten it. During one of the anarchist scares a stupid policeman had arrested him, and when I intervened the man was just on the verge of being committed for life. France trembled in one of her panics, or, rather, Paris did, and demanded victims. This blameless little workman had indeed contributed with both material and advice, but any fool might have seen that he had done this innocently. His assistance had been invoked and secured under the pretence that his clients were promoting an amateur firework display, which was true enough, but the display cost the lives of three men, and intentionally so. I cheered up the citizen in the moment of his utmost despair, and brought such proof of his innocence to the knowledge of those above me that he was most reluctantly acquitted. To this

man I now went with my measurement of the bomb and the estimate of its weight.

"Sir," said I, "do you remember Eugène Valmont?"

"Am I ever likely to forget him?" he replied, with a fervour that
pleased me.

"He has sent me to you, and implores you to aid me, and that
aid will wipe out the debt you owe him."

"Willingly, willingly," cried the artisan, "so long as it has nothing to do with the anarchists or the making of bombs."

"It has to do exactly with those two things. I wish you to make
an innocent bomb which will prevent an anarchist outrage."

At this the little man drew back, and his face became pale.

"It is impossible," he protested; "I have had enough of innocent bombs. No, no, and in any case how can I be sure you come
from Eugène Valmont? No, monsieur, I am not to be trapped the
second time."

At this I related rapidly all that Valmont had done for him, and
even repeated Valmont's most intimate conversation with him. The
man was nonplussed, but remained firm.

"I dare not do it," he said.

We were alone in his back shop. I walked to the door and thrust
in the bolt; then, after a moment's pause, turned round, stretched
forth my right hand dramatically, and cried: "Behold, Eugène
Valmont!"

My friend staggered against the wall in his amazement, and I
continued in solemn tones: "Eugène Valmont, who by this removal
of his disguise places his life in your hands as your life was in his.
Now, monsieur, what will you do?"

He replied: "Monsieur Valmont, I shall do whatever you ask. If
I refused a moment ago, it was because I thought there was now in
France no Eugène Valmont to rectify my mistake if I made one."

I resumed my disguise, and told him I wished an innocent substitute for this picric bomb, and he at once suggested an earthenware globe, which would weigh the same as the bomb, and which
could be coloured to resemble it exactly.

"And now, Monsieur Valmont, do you wish smoke to issue from this imitation bomb?"

"Yes," I said, "in such quantity as you can compress within it."

"It is easily done," he cried, with the enthusiasm of a true French artist. "And may I place within some little design of my own which will astonish your friends the English, and delight my friends the French?"

"Monsieur," said I, "I am in your hands. I trust the project entirely to your skill," and thus it came about that four days later I substituted the bogus globe for the real one, and, unseen, dropped the picric bomb from one of the bridges into the Seine.

On the morning of the procession I was compelled to allow Simard several drinks of absinthe to bring him up to a point where he could be depended on, otherwise his anxiety and determination to fling the bomb, his frenzy against all government, made it certain that he would betray both of us before the fateful moment came. My only fear was that I could not stop him drinking when once he began, but somehow our days of close companionship, loathsome as they were to me, seemed to have had the effect of building up again the influence I held over him in former days, and his yielding more or less to my wishes appeared to be quite unconscious on his part.

The procession was composed entirely of carriages, each containing four persons—two Englishmen sat on the back seats, with two Frenchmen in front of them. A thick crowd lined each side of the thoroughfare, cheering vociferously. Right into the middle of the procession Simard launched his bomb. There was no crash of explosion. The missile simply went to pieces as if it were an earthenware jar, and there arose a dense column of very white smoke. In the immediate vicinity the cheering stopped at once, and the sinister word "bomb" passed from lip to lip in awed whispers. As the throwing had been unnoticed in the midst of the commotion, I held Simard firmly by the wrist, determined he should not draw attention to himself by his panic-stricken desire for immediate flight.

"Stand still, you fool!" I hissed into his ear and he obeyed trembling.

The pair of horses in front of which the bomb fell rose for a moment on their hind legs, and showed signs of bolting, but the coachman held them firmly, and uplifted his hand so that the procession behind him came to a momentary pause. No one in the carriages moved a muscle, then suddenly the tension was broken by a great and simultaneous cheer. Wondering at this I turned my eyes from the frightened horses to the column of pale smoke in front of us, and saw that in some manner it had resolved itself into a gigantic calla lily, pure white, while from the base of this sprung the lilies of France, delicately tinted. Of course, this could not have happened if there had been the least wind, but the air was so still that the vibration of the cheering caused the huge lily to tremble gently as it stood there marvellously poised; the lily of peace, surrounded by the lilies of France! That was the design, and if you ask me how it was done, I can only refer you to my pyrotechnist, and say that whatever a Frenchman attempts to do he will accomplish artistically.

And now these imperturbable English, who had been seated immobile when they thought a bomb was thrown, stood up in their carriages to get a better view of this aerial phenomenon, cheering and waving their hats. The lily gradually thinned and dissolved in little patches of cloud that floated away above our heads.

"I cannot stay here longer," groaned Simard, quaking, his nerves, like himself, in rags. "I see the ghosts of those I have killed floating around me."

"Come on, then, but do not hurry."

There was no difficulty in getting him to London, but it was absinthe, absinthe, all the way, and when we reached Charing Cross, I was compelled to help him, partly insensible, into a cab. I took him direct to Imperial Flats, and up into my own set of chambers, where I opened my strong room, and flung him inside to sleep off his intoxication, and subsist on bread and water when he became sober.

I attended that night a meeting of the anarchists, and detailed accurately the story of our escape from France. I knew we had been watched, and so skipped no detail. I reported that I had taken Simard directly to my compatriot's flat; to Eugène Valmont, the man who had given me employment, and who had promised to do what he could for Simard, beginning by trying to break him of the absinthe habit, as he was now a physical wreck through over-indulgence in that stimulant.

It was curious to note the discussion which took place a few nights afterwards regarding the failure of the picric bomb. Scientists among us said that the bomb had been made too long; that a chemical reaction had taken place which destroyed its power. A few superstitious ones saw a miracle in what had happened, and they forthwith left our organisation. Then again, things were made easier by the fact that the man who constructed the bomb, evidently terror-stricken at what he had done, disappeared the day before the procession, and has never since been heard of. The majority of the anarchists believed he had made a bogus bomb, and had fled to escape their vengeance rather than to evade the justice of the law.

Simard will need no purgatory in the next world. I kept him on bread and water for a month in my strong room, and at first he demanded absinthe with threats, then grovelled, begging and praying for it. After that a period of depression and despair ensued, but finally his naturally strong constitution conquered, and began to build itself up again. I took him from his prison one midnight, and gave him a bed in my Soho room, taking care in bringing him away that he would never recognise the place where he had been incarcerated. In my dealings with him I had always been that old man, Paul Ducharme. Next morning I said to him: "You spoke of Eugène Valmont. I have learned that he lives in London, and I advise you to call upon him. Perhaps he can get you something to do."

Simard was overjoyed, and two hours later, as Eugène Valmont, I received him in my flat, and made him my assistant on the spot. From that time forward, Paul Ducharme, language teacher, disappeared from the earth, and Simard abandoned his two A's—anarchy and absinthe.

THE CLUE OF THE SILVER SPOONS

I

When the card was brought in to me, I looked upon it with some misgiving, for I scented a commercial transaction, and, although such cases are lucrative enough, nevertheless I, Eugène Valmont, formerly high in the service of the French Government, do not care to be connected with them. They usually pertain to sordid business affairs, presenting little that is of interest to a man who, in his time, has dealt with subtle questions of diplomacy upon which the welfare of nations sometimes turned.

The name of Bentham Gibbes is familiar to everyone, connected as it is with the much-advertised pickles, whose glaring announcements in crude crimson and green strike the eye throughout Great Britain, and shock the artistic sense wherever seen. Me! I have never tasted them, and shall not so long as a French restaurant remains open in London. But I doubt not they are as pronounced to the palate as their advertisement is distressing to the eye. If then, this gross pickle manufacturer expected me to track down those who were infringing upon the recipes for making his so-called sauces, chutneys, and the like, he would find himself mistaken, for I was now in a position to pick and choose my cases, and a case of pickles did not allure me. "Beware of imitations," said the advertisement; "none genuine without a facsimile of the signature of Bentham Gibbes." Ah, well, not for me were either the pickles or the tracking of imitators. A forged cheque! yes, if you like, but the forged signature of Mr. Gibbes on a pickle bottle was out of my line. Nevertheless, I said to Armand:

"Show the gentleman in," and he did so.

To my astonishment there entered a young man, quite correctly dressed in the dark frock-coat, faultless waistcoat and trousers that proclaimed a Bond Street tailor. When he spoke his voice and language were those of a gentleman.

"Monsieur Valmont?" he inquired.

"At your service," I replied, bowing and waving my hand as Armand placed a chair for him, and withdrew.

"I am a barrister with chambers in the Temple," began Mr. Gibbes, "and for some days a matter has been troubling me about which I have now come to seek your advice, your name having been suggested by a friend in whom I confided."

"Am I acquainted with him?" I asked.

"I think not," replied Mr. Gibbes; "he also is a barrister with chambers in the same building as my own. Lionel Dacre is his name."

"I never heard of him."

"Very likely not. Nevertheless, he recommended you as a man who could keep his own counsel, and if you take up this case I desire the utmost secrecy preserved, whatever may be the outcome."

I bowed, but made no protestation. Secrecy is a matter of course with me.

The Englishman paused for a few moments as if he expected fervent assurances; then went on with no trace of disappointment on his countenance at not receiving them.

"On the night of the twenty-third, I gave a little dinner to six friends of mine in my own rooms. I may say that so far as I am aware they are all gentlemen of unimpeachable character. On the night of the dinner I was detained later than I expected at a reception, and in driving to the Temple was still further delayed by a block of traffic in Piccadilly, so that when I arrived at my chambers there was barely time for me to dress and receive my guests. My man Johnson had everything laid out ready for me in my dressing-room, and as I passed through to it I hurriedly flung off the coat I was wearing and carelessly left it hanging over the back of a chair in the dining-room, where neither Johnson nor myself noticed it until my attention was called to it after the dinner was over, and everyone rather jolly with wine.

"This coat contains an inside pocket. Usually any frock-coat I wear at an afternoon reception has not an inside pocket, but I had been rather on the rush all day.

"My father is a manufacturer whose name may be familiar to you, and I am on the directors' board of his company. On this occasion I took a cab from the city to the reception I spoke of, and had not time to go and change at my rooms. The reception was a somewhat bohemian affair, extremely interesting, of course, but not too particular as to costume, so I went as I was. In this inside pocket rested a thin package, composed of two pieces of cardboard, and between them rested five twenty-pound Bank of England notes, folded lengthwise, held in place by an elastic rubber band. I had thrown the coat across the chair-back in such a way that the inside pocket was exposed, leaving the ends of the notes plainly recognisable.

"Over the coffee and cigars one of my guests laughingly called attention to what he termed my vulgar display of wealth, and Johnson, in some confusion at having neglected to put away the coat, now picked it up, and took it to the reception-room where the wraps of my guests lay about promiscuously. He should, of course, have hung it up in my wardrobe, but he said afterwards he thought it belonged to the guest who had spoken. You see, Johnson was in my dressing-room when I threw my coat on the chair in the corner while making my way thither, and I suppose he had not noticed the coat in the hurry of arriving guests, otherwise he would have put it where it belonged. After everybody had gone Johnson came to me and said the coat was there, but the package was missing, nor has any trace of it been found since that night."

"The dinner was fetched in from outside, I suppose?"

"Yes."

"How many waiters served it?"

"Two. They are men who have often been in my employ on similar occasions, but, apart from that, they had left my chambers before the incident of the coat happened."

"Neither of them went into the reception-room, I take it?"

"No. I am certain that not even suspicion can attach to either of the waiters."

"Your man Johnson—?"

"Has been with me for years. He could easily have stolen much more than the hundred pounds if he had wished to do so, but I have never known him to take a penny that did not belong to him."

"Will you favour me with the names of your guests, Mr. Gibbes?"

"Viscount Stern sat at my right hand, and at my left Lord Templemere; Sir John Sanclere next to him, and Angus McKeller next to Sanclere. After Viscount Stern was Lionel Dacre, and at his right, Vincent Innis."

On a sheet of paper I had written the names of the guests, and noted their places at the table.

"Which guest drew your attention to the money?"

"Lionel Dacre."

"Is there a window looking out from the reception-room?"

"Two of them."

"Were they fastened on the night of the dinner party?"

"I could not be sure; very likely Johnson would know. You are hinting at the possibility of a thief coming in through a reception-room window while we were somewhat noisy over our wine. I think such a solution highly improbable. My rooms are on the third floor, and a thief would scarcely venture to make an entrance when he could not but know there was a company being entertained. Besides this, the coat was there less than an hour, and it appears to me that whoever stole those notes knew where they were."

"That seems reasonable," I had to admit. "Have you spoken to any one of your loss?"

"To no one but Dacre, who recommended me to see you. Oh, yes, and to Johnson, of course."

I could not help noting that this was the fourth or fifth time Dacre's name had come up during our conversation.

"What of Dacre?" I asked.

"Oh, well, you see, he occupies chambers in the same building on the ground floor. He is a very good fellow, and we are by way of being firm friends. Then it was he who had called attention to the money, so I thought he should know the sequel."

"How did he take your news?"

"Now that you call attention to the fact, he seemed slightly troubled. I should like to say, however, that you must not be mis-led by that. Lionel Dacre could no more steal than he could lie."

"Did he show any surprise when you mentioned the theft?"

Bentham Gibbes paused a moment before replying, knitting his brows in thought.

"No," he said at last; "and, come to think of it, it appeared as if he had been expecting my announcement."

"Doesn't that strike you as rather strange, Mr. Gibbes?"

"Really my mind is in such a whirl, I don't know what to think. But it's perfectly absurd to suspect Dacre. If you knew the man you would understand what I mean. He comes of an excellent fam-ily, and he is—oh! he is Lionel Dacre, and when you have said that you have made any suspicion absurd."

"I suppose you caused the rooms to be thoroughly searched. The packet didn't drop out and remain unnoticed in some corner?"

"No; Johnson and myself examined every inch of the premises."

"Have you the numbers of the notes?"

"Yes; I got them from the Bank next morning. Payment was stopped, and so far not one of the five has been presented. Of course, one or more may have been cashed at some shop, but none have been offered to any of the banks."

"A twenty-pound note is not accepted without scrutiny, so the chances are the thief may find some difficulty in disposing of them."

"As I told you, I don't mind the loss of the money at all. It is the uncertainty, the uneasiness caused by the incident which troubles me. You will comprehend how little I care about the notes when I say that if you are good enough to interest yourself in this case, I shall be dis-appointed if your fee does not exceed the amount I have lost."

Mr. Gibbes rose as he said this, and I accompanied him to the door assuring him that I should do my best to solve the mystery.

Whether he sprang from pickles or not, I realised he was a polished and generous gentleman, who estimated the services of a professional expert like myself at their true value.

I shall not set down the details of my researches during the following few days, because the trend of them must be gone over in the account of that remarkable interview in which I took part somewhat later. Suffice it to say that an examination of the rooms and a close cross-questioning of Johnson satisfied me he and the two waiters were innocent. I became certain no thief had made his way through the window, and finally I arrived at the conclusion that the notes were stolen by one of the guests. Further investigation convinced me that the thief was no other than Lionel Dacre, the only one of the six in pressing need of money at this time. I caused Dacre to be shadowed, and during one of his absences made the acquaintance of his man Hopper, a surly, impolite brute, who accepted my golden sovereign quickly enough, but gave me little in exchange for it. While I conversed with him, there arrived in the passage where we were talking together a huge case of champagne, bearing one of the best-known names in the trade, and branded as being of the vintage of '78. Now I knew that the product of Camelot Frères is not bought as cheaply as British beer, and I also had learned that two short weeks before Mr. Lionel Dacre was at his wits' end for money. Yet he was still the same briefless barrister he had ever been.

On the morning after my unsatisfactory conversation with his man Hopper, I was astonished to receive the following note, written on a dainty correspondence card:

"3 and 4 Vellum Buildings,
"Inner Temple, E.C.
"Mr. Lionel Dacre presents his compliments to Monsieur Eugène Valmont, and would be obliged if Monsieur Valmont could make it convenient to call upon him in his chambers tomorrow morning at eleven."

II

Had the young man become aware that he was being shadowed, or had the surly servant informed him of the inquiries made? I was soon to know. I called punctually at eleven next morning, and was received with charming urbanity by Mr. Dacre himself. The taciturn Hopper had evidently been sent away for the occasion.

"My dear Monsieur Valmont, I am delighted to meet you," began the young man with more of effusiveness than I had ever noticed in an Englishman before, although his very next words supplied an explanation that did not occur to me until afterwards as somewhat far-fetched. "I believe we are by way of being countrymen, and, therefore, although the hour is early, I hope you will allow me to offer you some of this bottled sunshine of the year '78 from *la belle France*, to whose prosperity and honour we shall drink together. For such a toast any hour is propitious," and to my amazement he brought forth from the case I had seen arrive two days before, a bottle of that superb Camelot Frères '78.

"Now," said I to myself, "it is going to be difficult to keep a clear head if the aroma of this nectar rises to the brain. But tempting as is the cup, I shall drink sparingly, and hope he may not be so judicious."

Sensitive, I already experienced the charm of his personality, and well understood the friendship Mr. Bentham Gibbes felt for him. But I saw the trap spread before me. He expected, under the influence of champagne and courtesy, to extract a promise from me which I must find myself unable to give.

"Sir, you interest me by claiming kinship with France. I had understood that you belonged to one of the oldest families of England."

"Ah, England!" he cried, with an expressive gesture of outspreading hands truly Parisian in its significance. "The trunk belongs to England, of course, but the root—ah! the root—Monsieur Valmont, penetrated the soil from which this wine of the gods has been drawn."

Then filling my glass and his own he cried:

"To France, which my family left in the year 1066!"

I could not help laughing at his fervent ejaculation.

"1066! With William the Conqueror! That is a long time ago, Mr. Dacre."

"In years perhaps; in feelings but a day. My forefathers came over to steal, and, lord! how well they accomplished it. They stole the whole country—something like a theft, say I—under that prince of robbers whom you have well named the Conqueror. In our secret hearts we all admire a great thief, and if not a great one, then an expert one, who covers his tracks so perfectly that the hounds of justice are baffled in attempting to follow them. Now even you, Monsieur Valmont (I can see you are the most generous of men, with a lively sympathy found to perfection only in France), even you must suffer a pang of regret when you lay a thief by the heels who has done his task deftly."

"I fear, Mr. Dacre, you credit me with a magnanimity to which I dare not lay claim. The criminal is a danger to society."

"True, true, you are in the right, Monsieur Valmont Still, admit there are cases that would touch you tenderly. For example, a man, ordinarily honest; a great need; a sudden opportunity. He takes that of which another has abundance, and he, nothing. What then, Monsieur Valmont? Is the man to be sent to perdition for a momentary weakness?"

His words astonished me. Was I on the verge of hearing a confession? It almost amounted to that already.

"Mr. Dacre," I said, "I cannot enter into the subtleties you pursue. My duty is to find the criminal."

"Again I say you are in the right, Monsieur Valmont, and I am enchanted to find so sensible a head on French shoulders. Although you are a more recent arrival, if I may say so, than myself, you nevertheless already give utterance to sentiments which do honour to England. It is your duty to hunt down the criminal. Very well. In that I think I can aid you, and thus have taken the liberty of requesting your attendance here this morning. Let me fill your glass again, Monsieur Valmont."

"No more, I beg of you, Mr. Dacre."

"What, do you think the receiver is as bad as the thief?"

I was so taken aback by this remark that I suppose my face showed the amazement within me. But the young man merely laughed with apparently free-hearted enjoyment, poured some wine into his own glass, and tossed it off. Not knowing what to say, I changed the current of conversation.

"Mr. Gibbes said you had been kind enough to recommend me to his attention. May I ask how you came to hear of me?"

"Ah! who has not heard of the renowned Monsieur Valmont," and as he said this, for the first time, there began to grow a suspicion in my mind that he was chaffing me, as it is called in England— a procedure which I cannot endure. Indeed, if this gentleman practiced such a barbarism in my own country he would find himself with a duel on his hands before he had gone far. However, the next instant his voice resumed its original fascination, and I listened to it as to some delicious melody.

"I need only mention my cousin, Lady Gladys Dacre, and you will at once understand why I recommended you to my friend. The case of Lady Gladys, you will remember, required a delicate touch which is not always to be had in this land of England, except when those who possess the gift do us the honour to sojourn with us."

I noticed that my glass was again filled, and bowing an acknowledgment of his compliment, I indulged in another sip of the delicious wine. I sighed, for I began to realise it was going to be very difficult for me, in spite of my disclaimer, to tell this man's friend he had stolen the money. All this time he had been sitting on the edge of the table, while I occupied a chair at its end. He sat there in careless fashion, swinging a foot to and fro. Now he sprang to the floor, and drew up a chair, placing on the table a blank sheet of paper. Then he took from the mantelshelf a packet of letters, and I was astonished to see they were held together by two bits of cardboard and a rubber band similar to the combination that had contained the folded bank notes. With great nonchalance he slipped off the rubber band, threw it and the pieces of cardboard on the table before me, leaving the documents loose to his hand.

"Now, Monsieur Valmont," he cried jauntily, "you have been occupied for several days on this case, the case of my dear friend Bentham Gibbes, who is one of the best fellows in the world."

"He said the same of you, Mr. Dacre."

"I am gratified to hear it. Would you mind letting me know to what point your researches have led you?"

"They have led me in a direction rather than to a point."

"Ah! In the direction of a man, of course?"

"Certainly."

"Who is he?"

"Will you pardon me if I decline to answer this question at the present moment?"

"That means you are not sure."

"It may mean, Mr. Dacre, that I am employed by Mr. Gibbes, and do not feel at liberty to disclose the results of my quest without his permission."

"But Mr. Bentham Gibbes and I are entirely at one in this matter. Perhaps you are aware that I am the only person with whom he has discussed the case beside yourself."

"That is undoubtedly true, Mr. Dacre; still, you see the difficulty of my position."

"Yes, I do, and so shall press you no further. But I also have been studying the problem in a purely amateurish way, of course. You will perhaps express no disinclination to learn whether or not my deductions agree with yours."

"None in the least. I should be very glad to know the conclusion at which you have arrived. May I ask if you suspect any one in particular?"

"Yes, I do."

"Will you name him?"

"No; I shall copy the admirable reticence you yourself have shown. And now let us attack this mystery in a sane and business-like manner. You have already examined the room. Well, here is a rough sketch of it. There is the table; in this corner stood the chair on which the coat was flung. Here sat Gibbes at the head of the table. Those on the left-hand side had their backs to the chair. I, being on the centre to the right, saw the chair, the coat, and the notes, and called attention to them. Now our first duty is to find a motive. If it were a murder, our motive might be hatred, revenge, robbery—what you like. As it is simply the stealing of money, the man must have been either a born thief or else some hitherto innocent person pressed to the crime by great necessity. Do you agree with me, Monsieur Valmont?"

"Perfectly. You follow exactly the line of my own reasoning."

"Very well. It is unlikely that a born thief was one of Mr. Gibbes's guests. Therefore we are reduced to look for a man under the spur of necessity; a man who has no money of his own but who must raise a certain amount, let us say, by a certain date. If we can find such a man in that company, do you not agree with me that he is likely to be the thief?"

"Yes, I do."

"Then let us start our process of elimination. Out goes Viscount Stern, a lucky individual with twenty thousand acres of land, and God only knows what income. I mark off the name of Lord Templemere, one of His Majesty's judges, entirely above suspicion. Next, Sir John Sanclere; he also is rich, but Vincent Innis is still richer, so the pencil obliterates both names. Now we arrive at Angus McKeller, an author of some note, as you are well aware, deriving a good income from his books and a better one from his plays; a canny Scot, so we may rub his name from our paper and our memory. How do my erasures correspond with yours, Monsieur Valmont?"

"They correspond exactly, Mr. Dacre."

"I am flattered to hear it. There remains one name untouched, Mr. Lionel Dacre, the descendant, as I have said, of robbers."

"I have not said so, Mr. Dacre."

"Ah! my dear Valmont, the politeness of your country asserts itself. Let us not be deluded, but follow our inquiry wherever it leads. I suspect Lionel Dacre. What do you know of his circumstances before the dinner of the twenty-third?"

As I made no reply he looked up at me with his frank, boyish face illumined by a winning smile.

"You know nothing of his circumstances?" he asked.

"It grieves me to state that I do. Mr. Lionel Dacre was penniless on the night of the dinner."

"Oh, don't exaggerate, Monsieur Valmont," cried Dacre with a gesture of pathetic protest; "his pocket held one sixpence, two pennies, and a halfpenny. How came you to suspect he was penniless?"

"I knew he ordered a case of champagne from the London representative of Camelot Frères, and was refused unless he paid the money down."

"Quite right, and then when you were talking to Hopper you saw that case of champagne delivered. Excellent! excellent! Monsieur Valmont. But will a man steal, think you, even to supply himself with so delicious a wine as this we have been tasting? And, by the way, forgive my neglect, allow me to fill your glass, Monsieur Valmont."

"Not another drop, if you will excuse me, Mr. Dacre."

"Ah, yes, champagne should not be mixed with evidence. When we have finished, perhaps. What further proof have you discovered, monsieur?"

"I hold proof that Mr. Dacre was threatened with bankruptcy, if, on the twenty-fourth, he did not pay a bill of seventy-eight pounds that had been long outstanding. I hold proof that this was paid, not on the twenty-fourth, but on the twenty-sixth. Mr. Dacre had gone to the solicitor and assured him he would pay the money on that date, whereupon he was given two days' grace."

"Ah, well, he was entitled to three, you know, in law. Yes, there, Monsieur Valmont, you touch the fatal point. The threat of bankruptcy will drive a man in Dacre's position to almost any crime. Bankruptcy to a barrister means ruin. It means a career blighted; it means a life buried, with little chance of resurrection. I see, you grasp the supreme importance of that bit of evidence. The case of champagne is as nothing compared with it, and this reminds me that in the crisis now upon us I shall take another sip, with your permission. Sure you won't join me?"

"Not at this juncture, Mr. Dacre."

"I envy your moderation. Here's to the success of our search, Monsieur Valmont."

I felt sorry for the gay young fellow as with smiling face he drank the champagne.

"Now, Monsieur," he went on, "I am amazed to learn how much you have discovered. Really, I think tradespeople, solicitors, and all such should keep better guard on their tongues than they do. Nevertheless, these documents at my elbow, which I expected would surprise you, are merely the letters and receipts. Here is the communication from the solicitor threatening me with bankruptcy; here is his receipt dated the twenty-sixth; here is the refusal of the wine merchant, and here is his receipt for the money. Here are smaller bills liquidated. With my pencil we will add them up. Seventy-eight pounds—the principal debt—bulks large. We add the smaller items and it reaches a total of ninety-three pounds seven shillings and fourpence. Let us now examine my purse. Here is a five-pound note; there is a golden sovereign. I now count out and place on the table twelve and sixpence in silver and two pence in coppers. The purse thus becomes empty. Let us add the silver and copper to the amount on the paper. Do my eyes deceive me, or is the sum exactly a hundred pounds? There is your money fully accounted for."

"Pardon me, Mr. Dacre," I said, "but I observe a sovereign resting on the mantelpiece."

Dacre threw back his head and laughed with greater heartiness than I had yet known him to indulge in during our short acquaintance.

"By Jove," he cried, "you've got me there. I'd forgotten entirely about that pound on the mantelpiece, which belongs to you."

"To me? Impossible!"

"It does, and cannot interfere in the least with our century calculation. That is the sovereign you gave to my man Hopper, who, knowing me to be hard-pressed, took it and shamefacedly presented it to me, that I might enjoy the spending of it. Hopper belongs to our family, or the family belongs to him. I am never sure which. You must have missed in him the deferential bearing of a man-servant in Paris, yet he is true gold, like the sovereign you bestowed upon him, and he bestowed upon me. Now here, Monsieur, is the evidence of the theft, together with the rubber

band and two pieces of cardboard. Ask my friend Gibbes to examine them minutely. They are all at your disposition, Monsieur, and
thus you learn how much easier it is to deal with the master than
with the servant. All the gold you possess would not have wrung
these incriminating documents from old Hopper. I was compelled
to send him away to the West End an hour ago, fearing that in his
brutal British way he might assault you if he got an inkling of your
mission."

"Mr. Dacre," said I slowly, "you have thoroughly convinced me—"

"I thought I would," he interrupted with a laugh.

"—that you did *not* take the money."

"Oho, this is a change of wind, surely. Many a man has been
hanged on a chain of circumstantial evidence much weaker than
this which I have exhibited to you. Don't you see the subtlety of
my action? Ninety-nine persons in a hundred would say: 'No man
could be such a fool as to put Valmont on his own track, and then
place in Valmont's hands such striking evidence.' But there comes
in my craftiness. Of course, the rock you run up against will be
Gibbes's incredulity. The first question he will ask you may be this:
'Why did not Dacre come and borrow the money from me?' Now
there you find a certain weakness in your chain of evidence. I knew
perfectly well that Gibbes would lend me the money, and he knew
perfectly well that if I were pressed to the wall I should ask him."

"Mr. Dacre," said I, "you have been playing with me. I should
resent that with most men, but whether it is your own genial manner or the effect of this excellent champagne, or both together, I
forgive you. But I am convinced of another thing. You know who
took the money."

"I don't know, but I suspect."

"Will you tell me whom you suspect?"

"That would not be fair, but I shall now take the liberty of filling your glass with champagne."

"I am your guest, Mr. Dacre."

"Admirably answered, monsieur," he replied, pouring out the
wine, "and now I offer you a clue. Find out all about the story of
the silver spoons."

"The story of the silver spoons! What silver spoons?"

"Ah! That is the point. Step out of the Temple into Fleet Street, seize the first man you meet by the shoulder, and ask him to tell you about the silver spoons. There are but two men and two spoons concerned. When you learn who those two men are, you will know that one of them did not take the money, and I give you my assurance that the other did."

"You speak in mystery, Mr. Dacre."

"But certainly, for I am speaking to Monsieur Eugène Valmont."

"I echo your words, sir. Admirably answered. You put me on my mettle, and I flatter myself that I see your kindly drift. You wish me to solve the mystery of this stolen money. Sir, you do me honour, and I drink to your health."

"To yours, monsieur," said Lionel Dacre, and thus we drank and parted.

On leaving Mr. Dacre I took a hansom to a café in Regent Street, which is a passable imitation of similar places of refreshment in Paris. There, calling for a cup of black coffee, I sat down to think. The clue of the silver spoons! He had laughingly suggested that I should take by the shoulders the first man I met, and ask him what the story of the silver spoons was. This course naturally struck me as absurd, and he doubtless intended it to seem absurd. Nevertheless, it contained a hint. I must ask somebody, and that the right person, to tell me the tale of the silver spoons.

Under the influence of the black coffee I reasoned it out in this way. On the night of the twenty-third one of the six guests there present stole a hundred pounds, but Dacre had said that an actor in the silver spoon episode was the actual thief. That person, then, must have been one of Mr. Gibbes's guests at the dinner of the twenty-third. Probably two of the guests were the participators in the silver spoon comedy, but, be that as it may, it followed that one at least of the men around Mr. Gibbes's table knew the episode of the silver spoons. Perhaps Bentham Gibbes himself was cognisant of it. It followed, therefore, that the easiest plan was to question each of the men who partook of that dinner. Yet if only one knew about the spoons, that one must also have some idea that these spoons formed the clue which attached him to the crime of the twenty-third, in which case he was little likely to divulge what he knew to an entire stranger.

Of course, I might go to Dacre himself and demand the story of the silver spoons, but this would be a confession of failure on my part, and I rather dreaded Lionel Dacre's hearty laughter when I admitted that the mystery was too much for me. Besides this I was very well aware of the young man's kindly intentions towards me. He wished me to unravel the coil myself, and so I determined not to go to him except as a last resource.

I resolved to begin with Mr. Gibbes, and, finishing my coffee, I got again into a hansom, and drove back to the Temple. I found Bentham Gibbes in his room, and after greeting me, his first inquiry was about the case.

"How are you getting on?" he asked.

"I think I'm getting on fairly well," I replied, "and expect to finish in a day or two, if you will kindly tell me the story of the silver spoons."

"The silver spoons?" he echoed, quite evidently not understanding me.

"There happened an incident in which two men were engaged, and this incident related to a pair of silver spoons. I want to get the particulars of that."

"I haven't the slightest idea what you are talking about," replied Gibbes, thoroughly bewildered. "You will need to be more definite, I fear, if you are to get any help from me."

"I cannot be more definite, because I have already told you all I know."

"What bearing has all this on our own case?"

"I was informed that if I got hold of the clue of the silver spoons I should be in a fair way of settling our case."

"Who told you that?"

"Mr. Lionel Dacre."

"Oh, does Dacre refer to his own conjuring?"

"I don't know, I'm sure. What was his conjuring?"

"A very clever trick he did one night at dinner here about two months ago."

"Had it anything to do with silver spoons?"

"Well, it was silver spoons or silver forks, or something of that kind. I had entirely forgotten the incident. So far as I recollect at the moment there was a sleight-of-hand man of great expertness in one of the music halls, and the talk turned upon him. Then Dacre said the tricks he did were easy, and holding up a spoon or a fork, I don't remember which, he professed his ability to make it disappear before our eyes, to be found afterwards in the clothing of some one there present. Several offered to bet that he could do nothing of the kind, but he said he would bet with no one but Innis, who sat opposite him. Innis, with some reluctance, accepted the bet, and then Dacre, with a great show of the usual conjurer's gesticulations, spread forth his empty hands, and said we should find the spoon in Innis's pocket, and there, sure enough, it was. It seemed a proper sleight-of-hand trick, but we were never able to get him to repeat it."

"Thank you very much, Mr. Gibbes; I think I see daylight now."

"If you do you are cleverer than I by a long chalk," cried Bentham Gibbes as I took my departure.

I went directly downstairs, and knocked at Mr. Dacre's door once more. He opened the door himself, his man not yet having returned.

"Ah, monsieur," he cried, "back already? You don't mean to tell me you have so soon got to the bottom of the silver spoon entanglement?"

"I think I have, Mr. Dacre. You were sitting at dinner opposite Mr. Vincent Innis. You saw him conceal a silver spoon in his pocket. You probably waited for some time to understand what he meant by this, and as he did not return the spoon to its place, you proposed a conjuring trick, made the bet with him, and thus the spoon was returned to the table."

"Excellent! excellent, monsieur! that is very nearly what occurred, except that I acted at once. I had had experiences with Mr.

Vincent Innis before. Never did he enter these rooms of mine without my missing some little trinket after he was gone. Although Mr. Innis is a very rich person, I am not a man of many possessions, so if anything is taken, I meet little difficulty in coming to a knowledge of my loss. Of course, I never mentioned these abstractions to him. They were all trivial, as I have said, and so far as the silver spoon was concerned, it was of no great value either. But I thought the bet and the recovery of the spoon would teach him a lesson; it apparently has not done so. On the night of the twenty-third he sat at my right hand, as you will see by consulting your diagram of the table and the guests. I asked him a question twice, to which he did not reply, and looking at him I was startled by the expression in his eyes. They were fixed on a distant corner of the room, and following his gaze I saw what he was staring at with such hypnotising concentration. So absorbed was he in contemplation of the packet there so plainly exposed, now my attention was turned to it, that he seemed to be entirely oblivious of what was going on around him. I roused him from his trance by jocularly calling Gibbes's attention to the display of money. I expected in this way to save Innis from committing the act which he seemingly did commit. Imagine then the dilemma in which I was placed when Gibbes confided to me the morning after what had occurred the night before. I was positive Innis had taken the money, yet I possessed no proof of it. I could not tell Gibbes, and I dare not speak to Innis. Of course, monsieur, you do not need to be told that Innis is not a thief in the ordinary sense of the word. He has no need to steal, and yet apparently cannot help doing so. I am sure that no attempt has been made to pass those notes. They are doubtless resting securely in his house at Kensington. He is, in fact, a kleptomaniac, or a maniac of some sort. And now, monsieur, was my hint regarding the silver spoons of any value to you?"

"Of the most infinite value, Mr. Dacre."

"Then let me make another suggestion. I leave it entirely to your bravery; a bravery which, I confess, I do not myself possess. Will you take a hansom, drive to Mr. Innis's house on the Cromwell Road, confront him quietly, and ask for the return of the packet? I am anxious to know what will happen. If he hands it to you, as I expect he will, then you must tell Mr. Gibbes the whole story."

"Mr. Dacre, your suggestion shall be immediately acted upon, and I thank you for your compliment to my courage."

I found that Mr. Innis inhabited a very grand house. After a time he entered the study on the ground floor, to which I had been conducted. He held my card in his hand, and was looking at it with some surprise.

"I think I have not the pleasure of knowing you, Monsieur Valmont," he said, courteously enough.

"No. I ventured to call on a matter of business. I was once investigator for the French Government, and now am doing private detective work here in London."

"Ah! And how is that supposed to interest me? There is nothing that I wish investigated. I did not send for you, did I?"

"No, Mr. Innis, I merely took the liberty of calling to ask you to let me have the package you took from Mr. Bentham Gibbes's frock-coat pocket on the night of the twenty-third."

"He wishes it returned, does he?"

"Yes."

Mr. Innis calmly walked to a desk, which he unlocked and opened, displaying a veritable museum of trinkets of one sort and another. Pulling out a small drawer he took from it the packet containing the five twenty-pound notes. Apparently it had never been opened. With a smile he handed it to me.

"You will make my apologies to Mr. Gibbes for not returning it before. Tell him I have been unusually busy of late."

"I shall not fail to do so," said I, with a bow.

"Thanks so much. Good-morning, Monsieur Valmont."

"Good-morning, Mr. Innis,"

And so I returned the packet to Mr. Bentham Gibbes, who pulled the notes from between their pasteboard protection, and begged me to accept them.

LORD CHIZELRIGG'S MISSING FORTUNE

The name of the late Lord Chizelrigg never comes to my mind without instantly suggesting that of Mr. T. A. Edison. I never saw the late Lord Chizelrigg, and I have met Mr. Edison only twice in my life, yet the two men are linked in my memory, and it was a remark the latter once made that in great measure enabled me to solve the mystery which the former had wrapped round his actions.

There is no memorandum at hand to tell me the year in which those two meetings with Edison took place. I received a note from the Italian Ambassador in Paris requesting me to wait upon him at the Embassy. I learned that on the next day a deputation was to set out from the Embassy to one of the chief hotels, there to make a call in state upon the great American inventor, and formally present to him various insignia accompanying certain honours which the King of Italy had conferred upon him. As many Italian nobles of high rank had been invited, and as these dignitaries would not only be robed in the costumes pertaining to their orders, but in many cases would wear jewels of almost inestimable value, my presence was desired in the belief that I might perhaps be able to ward off any attempt on the part of the deft-handed gentry who might possibly make an effort to gain these treasures, and I may add, with perhaps some little self-gratification, no *contretemps* occurred.

Mr. Edison, of course, had long before received notification of the hour at which the deputation would wait upon him, but when we entered the large parlour assigned to the inventor, it was evident to me at a glance that the celebrated man had forgotten all about the function. He stood by a bare table, from which the cloth had been jerked and flung into a corner, and upon that table were placed several bits of black and greasy machinery—cog wheels, pulleys, bolts, etc. These seemingly belonged to a French workman who stood on the other side of the table, with one of the parts in his grimy hand. Edison's own hands were not too clean, for he had palpably been examining the material, and conversing with the workman, who wore the ordinary long blouse of an iron craftsman in a small way. I judged him to be a man with a little shop of his own in some back street, who did odd jobs of engineering, assisted perhaps by a skilled helper or two, and a few apprentices. Edison looked sternly towards the door as the solemn procession filed in, and there was a trace of annoyance on his face at the interruption, mixed with a shade of perplexity as to what this gorgeous display all meant. The Italian is as ceremonious as the Spaniard where a function is concerned, and the official who held the ornate box which contained the jewellery resting on a velvet cushion, stepped slowly forward, and came to a stand in front of the bewildered American. Then the Ambassador, in sonorous voice, spoke some gracious words regarding the friendship existing between the United States and Italy, expressed a wish that their rivalry should ever take the form of benefits conferred upon the human race, and instanced the honoured recipient as the most notable example the world had yet produced of a man bestowing blessings upon all nations in the arts of peace. The eloquent Ambassador concluded by saying that, at the command of his Royal master, it was both his duty and his pleasure to present, and so forth and so forth.

Mr. Edison, visibly ill at ease, nevertheless made a suitable reply in the fewest possible words, and the *étalage* being thus at an end, the noblemen, headed by their Ambassador, slowly retired, myself forming the tail of the procession. Inwardly I deeply sympathised with the French workman who thus unexpectedly found himself confronted by so much magnificence. He cast one wild look about him, but saw that his retreat was cut off unless he displaced some of these gorgeous grandees. He tried then to shrink into himself, and finally stood helpless like one paralysed. In spite of Republican institutions, there is deep down in every Frenchman's heart a respect and awe for official pageants, sumptuously staged and costumed as this one was. But he likes to view it from afar, and supported by his fellows, not thrust incongruously into the midst of things, as was the case with this panic-stricken engineer. As I passed out, I cast a glance over my shoulder at the humble artisan content with a profit of a few francs a day, and at the millionaire inventor opposite him, Edison's face, which during the address had been cold and impassive, reminding me vividly of a bust of Napoleon, was now all aglow with enthusiasm as he turned to his humble visitor. He cried joyfully to the workman:

"A minute's demonstration is worth an hour's explanation. I'll call round tomorrow at your shop, about ten o'clock, and show you how to make the thing work."

I lingered in the hall until the Frenchman came out, then, introducing myself to him, asked the privilege of visiting his shop next day at ten. This was accorded with that courtesy which you will always find among the industrial classes of France, and next day I had the pleasure of meeting Mr. Edison. During our conversation I complimented him on his invention of the incandescent electric light, and this was the reply that has ever remained in my memory:

"It was not an invention, but a discovery. We knew what we wanted; a carbonised tissue, which would withstand the electric current in a vacuum for, say, a thousand hours. If no such tissue existed, then the incandescent light, as we know it, was not possible. My assistants started out to find this tissue, and we simply carbonised everything we could lay our hands on, and ran the current through it in a vacuum. At last we struck the right thing, as we were bound to do if we kept on long enough, and if the thing existed. Patience and hard work will overcome any obstacle."

This belief has been of great assistance to me in my profession. I know the idea is prevalent that a detective arrives at his solutions in a dramatic way through following clues invisible to the ordinary man. This doubtless frequently happens, but, as a general thing, the patience and hard work which Mr. Edison commends is a much safer guide. Very often the following of excellent clues had led me to disaster, as was the case with my unfortunate attempt to solve the mystery of the five hundred diamonds.

As I was saying, I never think of the late Lord Chizelrigg without remembering Mr. Edison at the same time, and yet the two were very dissimilar. I suppose Lord Chizelrigg was the most useless man that ever lived, while Edison is the opposite.

One day my servant brought in to me a card on which was engraved "Lord Chizelrigg."

"Show his lordship in," I said, and there appeared a young man of perhaps twenty-four or twenty-five, well dressed, and of most charming manners, who, nevertheless, began his interview by asking a question such as had never before been addressed to me, and which, if put to a solicitor, or other professional man, would have been answered with some indignation. Indeed, I believe it is a written or unwritten law of the legal profession that the acceptance of such a proposal as Lord Chizelrigg made to me, would, if proved, result in the disgrace and ruin of the lawyer.

"Monsieur Valmont," began Lord Chizelrigg, "do you ever take up cases on speculation?"

"On speculation, sir? I do not think I understand you."

His lordship blushed like a girl, and stammered slightly as he attempted an explanation.

"What I mean is, do you accept a case on a contingent fee? That is to say, monsieur—er—well, not to put too fine a point upon it, no results, no pay."

I replied somewhat severely:

"Such an offer has never been made to me, and I may say at once that I should be compelled to decline it were I favoured with the opportunity. In the cases submitted to me, I devote my time and attention to their solution. I try to deserve success, but I cannot command it, and as in the interim I must live, I am reluctantly compelled to make a charge for my time, at least. I believe the doctor sends in his bill, though the patient dies."

The young man laughed uneasily, and seemed almost too embarrassed to proceed, but finally he said:

"Your illustration strikes home with greater accuracy than probably you imagined when you uttered it. I have just paid my last penny to the physician who attended my late uncle, Lord Chizelrigg, who died six months ago. I am fully aware that the suggestion I made may seem like a reflection upon your skill, or rather, as implying a doubt regarding it. But I should be grieved, monsieur, if you fell into such an error. I could have come here and commissioned you to undertake some elucidation of the strange situation in which I find myself, and I make no doubt you would have accepted the task if your numerous engagements had permitted. Then, if you failed, I should have been unable to pay you, for I am practically bankrupt. My whole desire, therefore, was to make an honest beginning, and to let you know exactly how I stand. If you succeed, I shall be a rich man; if you do not succeed, I shall be what I am now, penniless. Have I made it plain now why I began with a question which you had every right to resent?"

"Perfectly plain, my lord, and your candour does you credit."

I was very much taken with the unassuming manners of the young man, and his evident desire to accept no service under false pretences. When I had finished my sentence the pauper nobleman rose to his feet, and bowed.

"I am very much your debtor, monsieur, for your courtesy in receiving me, and can only beg pardon for occupying your time on a futile quest. I wish you good-morning, monsieur."

"One moment, my lord," I rejoined, waving him to his chair again. "Although I am unprepared to accept a commission on the terms you suggest, I may, nevertheless, be able to offer a hint or two that will prove of service to you. I think I remember the announcement of Lord Chizelrigg's death. He was somewhat eccentric, was he not?"

"Eccentric?" said the young man, with a slight laugh, seating himself again—"well, *rather!*"

"I vaguely remember that he was accredited with the possession of something like twenty thousand acres of land?"

"Twenty-seven thousand, as a matter of fact," replied my visitor.

"Have you fallen heir to the lands as well as to the title?"

"Oh, yes; the estate was entailed. The old gentleman could not divert it from me if he would, and I rather suspect that fact must have been the cause of some worry to him."

"But surely, my lord, a man who owns, as one might say, a principality in this wealthy realm of England, cannot be penniless?"

Again the young man laughed.

"Well, no," he replied, thrusting his hand in his pocket and bringing to light a few brown coppers, and a white silver piece. "I possess enough money to buy some food tonight, but not enough to dine at the Hotel Cecil. You see, it is like this. I belong to a somewhat ancient family, various members of whom went the pace, and mortgaged their acres up to the hilt. I could not raise a further penny on my estates were I to try my hardest, because at the time the money was lent, land was much more valuable than it is today. Agricultural depression, and all that sort of thing, have, if I may put it so, left me a good many thousands worse off than if I had no land at all. Besides this, during my late uncle's life, Parliament, on his behalf, intervened once or twice, allowing him in the first place to cut valuable timber, and in the second place to sell the pictures of Chizelrigg Chase at Christie's for figures which make one's mouth water."

"And what became of the money?" I asked, whereupon once more this genial nobleman laughed. "That is exactly what I came up in the lift to learn if Monsieur Valmont could discover."

"My lord, you interest me," I said, quite truly, with an uneasy apprehension that I should take up his case after all, for I liked the young man already. His lack of pretence appealed to me, and that sympathy which is so universal among my countrymen enveloped him, as I may say, quite independent of my own will.

"My uncle," went on Lord Chizelrigg, "was somewhat of an anomaly in our family. He must have been a reversal to a very, very ancient type; a type of which we have no record. He was as miserly as his forefathers were prodigal. When he came into the title and estate some twenty years ago, he dismissed the whole retinue of servants, and, indeed, was defendant in several cases at law where retainers of our family brought suit against him for wrongful dismissal, or dismissal without a penny compensation in lieu of notice. I am pleased to say he lost all his cases, and when he pleaded poverty, got permission to sell a certain number of heirlooms, enabling him to make compensation, and giving him something on which to live. These heirlooms at auction sold so unexpectedly well, that my uncle acquired a taste, as it were, of what might be done. He could always prove that the rents went to the mortgagees, and that he had nothing on which to exist, so on several occasions he obtained permission from the courts to cut timber and sell pictures, until he denuded the estate and made an empty barn of the old manor house. He lived like any labourer, occupying himself sometimes as a carpenter, sometimes as a blacksmith; indeed, he made a blacksmith's shop of the library, one of the most noble rooms in Britain, containing thousands of valuable books which again and again he applied for permission to sell, but this privilege was never granted to him. I find on coming into the property that my uncle quite persistently evaded the law, and depleted this superb collection, book by book, surreptitiously through dealers in London. This, of course, would have got him into deep trouble if it had been discovered before his death, but now the valuable volumes are gone, and there is no redress. Many of them are doubtless in America, or in museums and collections of Europe."

"You wish me to trace them, perhaps?" I interpolated.

"Oh, no; they are past praying for. The old man made tens of thousands by the sale of the timber, and other thousands by disposing of the pictures. The house is denuded of its fine old furniture, which was immensely valuable, and then the books, as I have said, must have brought in the revenue of a prince, if he got anything like their value, and you may be sure he was shrewd enough to know their worth. Since the last refusal of the courts to allow him further relief, as he termed it, which was some seven years ago, he had quite evidently been disposing of books and furniture by a private sale, in defiance of the law. At that time I was under age, but my guardians opposed his application to the courts, and demanded an account of the moneys already in his hands. The judges upheld the opposition of my guardians, and refused to allow a further spoliation of the estate, but they did not grant the accounting my guardians asked, because the proceeds of the former sales were entirely at the disposal of my uncle, and were sanctioned by the law to permit him to live as befitted his station. If he lived meagrely instead of lavishly, as my guardians contended, that, the judges said, was his affair, and there the matter ended.

"My uncle took a violent dislike to me on account of this opposition to his last application, although, of course, I had nothing whatever to do with the matter. He lived like a hermit, mostly in the library, and was waited upon by an old man and his wife, and these three were the only inhabitants of a mansion that could comfortably house a hundred. He visited nobody, and would allow no one to approach Chizelrigg Chase. In order that all who had the misfortune to have dealing with him should continue to endure trouble after his death, he left what might be called a will, but which rather may be termed a letter to me. Here is a copy of it.

> "'My Dear Tom: You will find your fortune between a couple of sheets of paper in the library.
> "'Your affectionate uncle,
> "'Reginald Moran, *Earl of Chizelrigg*.'"

"I should doubt if that were a legal will," said I.

"It doesn't need to be," replied the young man with a smile. "I am next-of-kin, and heir to everything he possessed, although, of course, he might have given his money elsewhere if he had chosen to do so. Why he did not bequeath it to some institution, I do not know. He knew no man personally except his own servants, whom he misused and starved, but, as he told them, he misused and starved himself, so they had no cause to grumble. He said he was treating them like one of the family. I suppose he thought it would cause me more worry and anxiety if he concealed the money, and put me on the wrong scent, which I am convinced he has done, than to leave it openly to any person or charity."

"I need not ask if you have searched the library?"

"Searched it? Why, there never was such a search since the world began!"

"Possibly you put the task into incompetent hands?"

"You are hinting, Monsieur Valmont, that I engaged others until my money was gone, then came to you with a speculative proposal. Let me assure you such is not the case. Incompetent hands, I grant you, but the hands were my own. For the past six months I have lived practically as my uncle lived. I have rummaged that library from floor to ceiling. It was left in a frightful state, littered with old newspapers, accounts, and what-not. Then, of course, there were the books remaining in the library, still a formidable collection."

"Was your uncle a religious man?"

"I could not say. I surmise not. You see, I was unacquainted with him, and never saw him until after his death. I fancy he was not religious, otherwise he could not have acted as he did. Still, he proved himself a man of such twisted mentality that anything is possible."

"I knew a case once where an heir who expected a large sum of money was bequeathed a family Bible, which he threw into the fire, learning afterwards, to his dismay, that it contained many thousands of pounds in Bank of England notes, the object of the devisor being to induce the legatee to read the good Book or suffer through the neglect of it."

"I have searched the Scriptures," said the youthful Earl with a laugh, "but the benefit has been moral rather than material."

"Is there any chance that your uncle has deposited his wealth in a bank, and has written a cheque for the amount, leaving it between two leaves of a book?"

"Anything is possible, monsieur, but I think that highly improbable. I have gone through every tome, page by page, and I suspect very few of the volumes have been opened for the last twenty years."

"How much money do you estimate he accumulated?"

"He must have cleared more than a hundred thousand pounds, but speaking of banking it, I would like to say that my uncle evinced a deep distrust of banks, and never drew a cheque in his life so far as I am aware. All accounts were paid in gold by this old steward, who first brought the receipted bill in to my uncle, and then received the exact amount, after having left the room, and waited until he was rung for, so that he might not learn the repository from which my uncle drew his store. I believe if the money is ever found it will be in gold, and I am very sure that this will was written, if we may call it a will, to put us on the wrong scent."

"Have you had the library cleared out?"

"Oh, no, it is practically as my uncle left it. I realised that if I were to call in help, it would be well that the newcomer found it undisturbed."

"You were quite right, my lord. You say you examined all the papers?"

"Yes; so far as that is concerned, the room has been very fairly gone over, but nothing that was in it the day my uncle died has been removed, not even his anvil."

"His anvil?"

"Yes; I told you he made a blacksmith's shop, as well as bed-room, of the library. It is a huge room, with a great fireplace at one end which formed an excellent forge. He and the steward built the forge in the eastern fireplace of brick and clay, with their own hands, and erected there a second-hand blacksmith's bellows."

"What work did he do at his forge?"

"Oh, anything that was required about the place. He seems to have been a very expert ironworker. He would never buy a new implement for the garden or the house so long as he could get one second-hand, and he never bought anything second-hand while at his forge he might repair what was already in use. He kept an old cob, on which he used to ride through the park, and he always put the shoes on this cob himself, the steward informs me, so he must have understood the use of blacksmith's tools. He made a carpenter's shop of the chief drawing-room and erected a bench there. I think a very useful mechanic was spoiled when my uncle became an earl."

"You have been living at the Chase since your uncle died?"

"If you call it living, yes. The old steward and his wife have been looking after me, as they looked after my uncle, and, seeing me day after day, coatless, and covered with dust, I imagine they think me a second edition of the old man."

"Does the steward know the money is missing?"

"No; no one knows it but myself. This will was left on the anvil, in an envelope addressed to me."

"Your statement is exceedingly clear, Lord Chizelrigg, but I confess I don't see much daylight through it. Is there a pleasant country around Chizelrigg Chase?"

"Very; especially at this season of the year. In autumn and winter the house is a little draughty. It needs several thousand pounds to put it in repair."

"Draughts do not matter in the summer. I have been long enough in England not to share the fear of my countrymen for a *courant d'air*. Is there a spare bed in the manor house, or shall I take down a cot with me, or let us say a hammock?"

"Really," stammered the earl, blushing again, "you must not think I detailed all these circumstances in order to influence you to take up what may be a hopeless case. I, of course, am deeply interested, and, therefore, somewhat prone to be carried away when I begin a recital of my uncle's eccentricities. If I receive your permission, I will call on you again in a month or two. To tell you the truth, I borrowed a little money from the old steward, and visited London to see my legal advisers, hoping that in the circumstances I may get permission to sell something that will keep me from starvation. When I spoke of the house being denuded, I meant relatively, of course. There are still a good many antiquities which would doubtless bring me in a comfortable sum of money. I have been borne up by the belief that I should find my uncle's gold. Lately, I have been beset by a suspicion that the old gentleman thought the library the only valuable asset left, and for this reason wrote his note, thinking I would be afraid to sell anything from that room. The old rascal must have made a pot of money out of those shelves. The catalogue shows that there was a copy of the first book printed in England by Caxton, and several priceless

Shakespeares, as well as many other volumes that a collector would
give a small fortune for. All these are gone. I think when I show
this to be the case, the authorities cannot refuse me the right to
sell something, and, if I get this permission, I shall at once call
upon you."

"Nonsense, Lord Chizelrigg. Put your application in motion, if
you like. Meanwhile I beg of you to look upon me as a more
substantial banker than your old steward. Let us enjoy a good
dinner together at the Cecil tonight, if you will do me the honour
to be my guest. Tomorrow we can leave for Chizelrigg Chase. How
far is it?"

"About three hours," replied the young man, becoming as red
as a new Queen Anne villa. "Really, Monsieur Valmont, you over-
whelm me with your kindness, but nevertheless I accept your
generous offer."

"Then that's settled. What's the name of the old steward?"

"Higgins."

"You are certain he has no knowledge of the hiding-place of
this treasure?"

"Oh, quite sure. My uncle was not a man to make a confidant
of anyone, least of all an old babbler like Higgins."

"Well, I should like to be introduced to Higgins as a benighted
foreigner. That will make him despise me and treat me like a child."

"Oh, I say," protested the earl, "I should have thought you'd
lived long enough in England to have got out of the notion that we
do not appreciate the foreigner. Indeed, we are the only nation in
the world that extends a cordial welcome to him, rich or poor."

"*Certainement*, my lord, I should be deeply disappointed did
you not take me at my proper valuation, but I cherish no delusions
regarding the contempt with which Higgins will regard me. He will
look upon me as a sort of simpleton to whom the Lord had been
unkind by not making England my native land. Now, Higgins must
be led to believe that I am in his own class; that is, a servant of
yours. Higgins and I will gossip over the fire together, should these
spring evenings prove chilly, and before two or three weeks are
past I shall have learned a great deal about your uncle that you
never dreamed of. Higgins will talk more freely with a fellow-

servant than with his master, however much he may respect that master, and then, as I am a foreigner, he will babble down to my comprehension, and I shall get details that he never would think of giving to a fellow-countryman."

II

The young earl's modesty in such description of his home as he had given me, left me totally unprepared for the grandeur of the mansion, one corner of which he inhabited. It is such a place as you read of in romances of the Middle Ages; not a pinnacled or turreted French *château* of that period, but a beautiful and substantial stone manor house of a ruddy colour, whose warm hue seemed to add a softness to the severity of its architecture. It is built round an outer and an inner courtyard and could house a thousand, rather than the hundred with which its owner had accredited it. There are many stone-mullioned windows, and one at the end of the library might well have graced a cathedral. This superb residence occupies the centre of a heavily timbered park, and from the lodge at the gates we drove at least a mile and a half under the grandest avenue of old oaks I have ever seen. It seemed incredible that the owner of all this should actually lack the ready money to pay his fare to town!

Old Higgins met us at the station with a somewhat rickety cart, to which was attached the ancient cob that the late earl used to shoe. We entered a noble hall, which probably looked the larger because of the entire absence of any kind of furniture, unless two complete suits of venerable armour which stood on either hand might be considered as furnishing. I laughed aloud when the door was shut, and the sound echoed like the merriment of ghosts from the dim timbered roof above me.

"What are you laughing at?" asked the earl.

"I am laughing to see you put your modern tall hat on that mediaeval helmet."

"Oh, that's it! Well, put yours on the other. I mean no disrespect to the ancestor who wore this suit, but we are short of the harmless, necessary hat-rack, so I put my topper on the antique helmet, and thrust the umbrella (if I have one) in behind here, and down one of his legs. Since I came in possession, a very crafty-looking dealer from London visited me, and attempted to sound me regarding the sale of these suits of armour. I gathered he would give enough money to keep me in new suits, London made, for the rest of my life, but when I endeavoured to find out if he had had commercial dealings with my prophetic uncle, he became frightened and bolted. I imagine that if I had possessed presence of mind enough to have lured him into one of our most uncomfortable dungeons, I might have learned where some of the family treasures went to. Come up these stairs, Monsieur Valmont, and I will show you your room."

We had lunched on the train coming down, so after a wash in my own room I proceeded at once to inspect the library. It proved, indeed, a most noble apartment, and it had been scandalously used by the old reprobate, its late tenant. There were two huge fireplaces, one in the middle of the north wall and the other at the eastern end. In the latter had been erected a rude brick forge, and beside the forge hung a great black bellows, smoky with usage. On a wooden block lay the anvil, and around it rested and rusted several hammers, large and small. At the western end was a glorious window filled with ancient stained glass, which, as I have said, might have adorned a cathedral. Extensive as the collection of books was, the great size of this chamber made it necessary that only the outside wall should be covered with book cases, and even these were divided by tall windows. The opposite wall was blank, with the exception of a picture here and there, and these pictures offered a further insult to the room, for they were cheap prints, mostly coloured lithographs that had appeared in Christmas numbers of London weekly journals, encased in poverty-stricken frames, hanging from nails ruthlessly driven in above them. The floor was covered with a litter of papers, in some places knee-deep, and in the corner farthest from the forge still stood the bed on which the ancient miser had died.

"Looks like a stable, doesn't it?" commented the earl, when I had finished my inspection. "I am sure the old boy simply filled it up with this rubbish to give me the trouble of examining it. Higgins tells me that up to within a month before he died the room was reasonably clear of all this muck. Of course it had to be, or the place would have caught fire from the sparks of the forge. The old man made Higgins gather all the papers he could find anywhere about the place, ancient accounts, newspapers, and what not, even to the brown wrapping paper you see, in which parcels came, and commanded him to strew the floor with this litter, because, as he complained, Higgins's boots on the boards made too much noise, and Higgins, who is not in the least of an inquiring mind, accepted this explanation as entirely meeting the case."

Higgins proved to be a garrulous old fellow, who needed no urging to talk about the late earl; indeed, it was almost impossible to deflect his conversation into any other channel. Twenty years' intimacy with the eccentric nobleman had largely obliterated that sense of deference with which an English servant usually approaches his master. An English underling's idea of nobility is the man who never by any possibility works with his hands. The fact that Lord Chizelrigg had toiled at the carpenter's bench; had mixed cement in the drawing-room; had caused the anvil to ring out till midnight, aroused no admiration in Higgins's mind. In addition to this, the ancient nobleman had been penuriously strict in his examination of accounts, exacting the uttermost farthing, so the humble servitor regarded his memory with supreme contempt. I realised before the drive was finished from the station to Chizelrigg Chase that there was little use of introducing me to Higgins as a foreigner and a fellow-servant. I found myself completely unable to understand what the old fellow said. His dialect, was as unknown to me as the Choctaw language would have been, and the young earl was compelled to act as interpreter on the occasions when we set this garrulous talking-machine going.

The new Earl of Chizelrigg, with the enthusiasm of a boy, proclaimed himself my pupil and assistant, and said he would do whatever he was told. His thorough and fruitless search of the library had convinced him that the old man was merely chaffing him, as he put it, by leaving such a letter as he had written. His lordship was certain that the money had been hidden somewhere else; probably buried under one of the trees in the park. Of course this was possible, and represented the usual method by which a stupid person conceals treasure, yet I did not think it probable. All conversations with Higgins showed the earl to have been an extremely suspicious man; suspicious of banks, suspicious even of Bank of England notes, suspicious of every person on earth, not omitting Higgins himself. Therefore, as I told his nephew, the miser would never allow the fortune out of his sight and immediate reach.

From the first the oddity of the forge and anvil being placed in his bedroom struck me as peculiar, and I said to the young man:

"I'll stake my reputation that forge or anvil, or both, contain the secret. You see, the old gentleman worked sometimes till midnight, for Higgins could hear his hammering. If he used hard coal on the forge the fire would last through the night, and being in continual terror of thieves, as Higgins says, barricading the castle every evening before dark as if it were a fortress, he was bound to place the treasure in the most unlikely spot for a thief to get at it. Now, the coal fire smouldered all night long, and if the gold was in the forge underneath the embers, it would be extremely difficult to get at. A robber rummaging in the dark would burn his fingers in more senses than one. Then, as his lordship kept no less than four loaded revolvers under his pillow, all he had to do, if a thief entered his room was to allow the search to go on until the thief started at the forge, then doubtless, as he had the range with reasonable accuracy night or day, he might sit up in bed and blaze away with revolver after revolver. There were twenty-eight shots that could be fired in about double as many seconds, so you see the robber stood little chance in the face of such a fusillade. I propose that we dismantle the forge."

Lord Chizelrigg was much taken by my reasoning, and one morning early we cut down the big bellows, tore it open, found it empty, then took brick after brick from the forge with a crowbar, for the old man had builded better than he knew with Portland cement. In fact, when we cleared away the rubbish between the bricks and the core of the furnace we came upon one cube of cement which was as hard as granite. With the aid of Higgins, and a set of rollers and levers, we managed to get this block out into the park, and attempted to crush it with the sledge-hammers belonging to the forge, in which we were entirely unsuccessful. The more it resisted our efforts, the more certain we became that the coins would be found within it. As this would not be treasure-trove in the sense that the Government might make a claim upon it, there was no particular necessity for secrecy, so we had up a man from the mines near by with drills and dynamite, who speedily shattered the block into a million pieces, more or less. Alas! there was no trace in its debris of "pay dirt," as the western miner puts it. While the dynamite expert was on the spot, we induced him to shatter the anvil as well as the block of cement, and then the workman, doubtless thinking the new earl was as insane as the old one had been, shouldered his tools, and went back to his mine.

The earl reverted to his former opinion that the gold was concealed in the park, while I held even more firmly to my own belief that the fortune rested in the library.

"It is obvious," I said to him, "that if the treasure is buried outside, someone must have dug the hole. A man so timorous and so reticent as your uncle would allow no one to do this but himself. Higgins maintained the other evening that all picks and spades were safely locked up by himself each night in the tool-house. The mansion itself was barricaded with such exceeding care that it would have been difficult for your uncle to get outside even if he wished to do so. Then such a man as your uncle is described to have been would continually desire ocular demonstration that his savings were intact, which would be practically impossible if the gold had found a grave in the park. I propose now that we abandon violence and dynamite, and proceed to an intellectual search of the library."

"Very well," replied the young earl, "but as I have already searched the library very thoroughly, your use of the word 'intellectual,' Monsieur Valmont, is not in accord with your customary politeness. However, I am with you. 'Tis for you to command, and me to obey."

"Pardon me, my lord," I said, "I used the word 'intellectual' in contradistinction to the word 'dynamite.' It had no reference to your former search. I merely propose that we now abandon the use of chemical reaction, and employ the much greater force of mental activity. Did you notice any writing on the margins of the newspapers you examined?"

"No, I did not."

"Is it possible that there may have been some communication on the white border of a newspaper?"

"It is, of course, possible."

"Then will you set yourself to the task of glancing over the margin of every newspaper, piling them away in another room when your scrutiny of each is complete? Do not destroy anything, but we must clear out the library completely. I am interested in the accounts, and will examine them."

It was exasperatingly tedious work, but after several days my assistant reported every margin scanned without result, while I had collected each bill and memorandum, classifying them according to date. I could not get rid of a suspicion that the contrary old beast had written instructions for the finding of the treasure on the back of some account, or on the fly-leaf of a book, and as I looked at the thousands of volumes still left in the library, the prospect of such a patient and minute search appalled me. But I remembered Edison's words to the effect that if a thing exist, search, exhaustive enough, will find it. From the mass of accounts I selected several; the rest I placed in another room, alongside the heap of the earl's newspapers.

"Now," said I to my helper, "if it please you, we will have Higgins in, as I wish some explanation of these accounts."

"Perhaps I can assist you," suggested his lordship drawing up a chair opposite the table on which I had spread the statements. "I have lived here for six months, and know as much about things as Higgins does. He is so difficult to stop when once he begins to talk. What is the first account you wish further light upon?"

"To go back thirteen years I find that your uncle bought a second-hand safe in Sheffield. Here is the bill. I consider it necessary to find that safe."

"Pray forgive me, Monsieur Valmont," cried the young man, springing to his feet and laughing; "so heavy an article as a safe should not slip readily from a man's memory, but it did from mine. The safe is empty, and I gave no more thought to it."

Saying this the earl went to one of the bookcases that stood against the wall, pulled it round as if it were a door, books and all, and displayed the front of an iron safe, the door of which he also drew open, exhibiting the usual empty interior of such a receptacle.

"I came on this," he said, "when I took down all these volumes. It appears that there was once a secret door leading from the library into an outside room, which has long since disappeared; the walls are very thick. My uncle doubtless caused this door to be taken off its hinges, and the safe placed in the aperture, the rest of which he then bricked up."

"Quite so," said I, endeavouring to conceal my disappointment. "As this strong box was bought second-hand and not made to order, I suppose there can be no secret crannies in it?"

"It looks like a common or garden safe," reported my assistant, "but we'll have it out if you say so."

"Not just now," I replied; "we've had enough of dynamiting to make us feel like housebreakers already."

"I agree with you. What's the next item on the programme?"

"Your uncle's mania for buying things at second-hand was broken in three instances so far as I have been able to learn from a scrutiny of these accounts. About four years ago he purchased a new book from Denny and Co., the well-known booksellers of the Strand. Denny and Co. deal only in new books. Is there any comparatively new volume in the library?"

"Not one."

"Are you sure of that?"

"Oh, quite; I searched all the literature in the house. What is the name of the volume he bought?"

"That I cannot decipher. The initial letter looks like 'M,' but the rest is a mere wavy line. I see, however, that it cost twelve-and-sixpence, while the cost of carriage by parcel post was sixpence, which shows it weighed something under four pounds. This, with the price of the book, induces me to think that it was a scientific work, printed on heavy paper and illustrated."

"I know nothing of it," said the earl.

"The third account is for wallpaper; twenty-seven rolls of an expensive wallpaper, and twenty-seven rolls of a cheap paper, the latter being just half the price of the former. This wallpaper seems to have been supplied by a tradesman in the station road in the village of Chizelrigg."

"There's your wallpaper," cried the youth, waving his hand; "he was going to paper the whole house, Higgins told me, but got tired after he had finished the library, which took him nearly a year to accomplish, for he worked at it very intermittently, mixing the paste in the boudoir, a pailful at a time as he needed it. It was a scandalous thing to do, for underneath the paper is the most exquisite oak panelling, very plain, but very rich in colour."

I rose and examined the paper on the wall. It was dark brown, and answered the description of the expensive paper on the bill.

"What became of the cheap paper?" I asked.

"I don't know."

"I think," said I, "we are on the track of the mystery. I believe that paper covers a sliding panel or concealed door."

"It is very likely," replied the earl. "I intended to have the paper off, but I had no money to pay a workman, and I am not so industrious as was my uncle. What is your remaining account?"

"The last also pertains to paper, but comes from a firm in Budge Row, London, E.C. He has had, it seems, a thousand sheets of it, and it appears to have been frightfully expensive. This bill is also illegible, but I take it a thousand sheets were supplied, although of course it may have been a thousand quires, which would be a little more reasonable for the price charged, or a thousand reams, which would be exceedingly cheap."

"I don't know anything about that. Let's turn on Higgins."

Higgins knew nothing of this last order of paper either. The wallpaper mystery he at once cleared up. Apparently the old earl had discovered by experiment that the heavy, expensive wallpaper would not stick to the glossy panelling, so he had purchased a cheaper paper, and had pasted that on first. Higgins said he had gone all over the panelling with a yellowish-white paper, and after that was dry, he pasted over it the more expensive rolls.

"But," I objected, "the two papers were bought and delivered at the same time; therefore, he could not have found by experiment that the heavy paper would not stick."

"I don't think there is much in that," commented the earl; "the heavy paper may have been bought first, and found to be unsuitable, and then the coarse, cheap paper bought afterwards. The bill merely shows that the account was sent in on that date. Indeed, as the village of Chizelrigg is but a few miles away, it would have been quite possible for my uncle to have bought the heavy paper in the morning, tried it, and in the afternoon sent for the commoner lot; but in any case, the bill would not have been presented until months after the order, and the two purchases were thus lumped together."

I was forced to confess that this seemed reasonable.

Now, about the book ordered from Denny's. Did Higgins remember anything regarding it? It came four years ago.

Ah, yes, Higgins did; he remembered it very well indeed. He had come in one morning with the earl's tea, and the old man was sitting up in bed reading his volume with such interest that he was unaware of Higgins's knock, and Higgins himself, being a little hard of hearing, took for granted the command to enter. The earl hastily thrust the book under the pillow, alongside the revolvers, and rated Higgins in a most cruel way for entering the room before getting permission to do so. He had never seen the earl so angry before, and he laid it all to this book. It was after the book had come that the forge had been erected and the anvil bought. Higgins never saw the book again, but one morning, six months before the earl died, Higgins, in raking out the cinders of the forge, found what he supposed was a portion of the book's cover. He believed his master had burnt the volume.

Having dismissed Higgins, I said to the earl:

"The first thing to be done is to enclose this bill to Denny and Co., booksellers, Strand. Tell them you have lost the volume, and ask them to send another. There is likely someone in the shop who can decipher the illegible writing. I am certain the book will give us a clue. Now, I shall write to Braun and Sons, Budge Row. This is evidently a French company; in fact, the name as connected with paper-making runs in my mind, although I cannot at this moment place it. I shall ask them the use of this paper that they furnished to the late earl."

This was done accordingly, and now, as we thought, until the answers came, we were two men out of work. Yet the next morning, I am pleased to say, and I have always rather plumed myself on the fact, I solved the mystery before replies were received from London. Of course, both the book and the answer of the paper agents, by putting two and two together, would have given us the key.

After breakfast, I strolled somewhat aimlessly into the library, whose floor was now strewn merely with brown wrapping paper, bits of string, and all that. As I shuffled among this with my feet, as if tossing aside dead autumn leaves in a forest path, my attention was suddenly drawn to several squares of paper, unwrinkled, and never used for wrapping. These sheets seemed to me strangely familiar. I picked one of them up, and at once the significance of the name Braun and Sons occurred to me. They are paper makers in France, who produce a smooth, very tough sheet, which, dear as it is, proves infinitely cheap compared with the fine vellum it deposed in a certain branch of industry. In Paris, years before, these sheets had given me the knowledge of how a gang of thieves disposed of their gold without melting it. The paper was used instead of vellum in the rougher processes of manufacturing gold-leaf. It stood the constant beating of the hammer nearly as well as the vellum, and here at once there flashed on me the secret of the old man's midnight anvil work. He was transforming his sovereigns into gold-leaf, which must have been of a rude, thick kind, because to produce the gold-leaf of commerce he still needed the vellum as well as a "clutch" and other machinery, of which we had found no trace.

"My lord," I called to my assistant; he was at the other end of the room; "I wish to test a theory on the anvil of your own fresh common sense."

"Hammer away," replied the earl, approaching me with his usual good-natured, jocular expression.

"I eliminate the safe from our investigations because it was purchased thirteen years ago, but the buying of the book, of wall covering, of this tough paper from France, all group themselves into a set of incidents occurring within the same month as the purchase of the anvil and the building of the forge; therefore, I think they are related to one another. Here are some sheets of paper he got from Budge Row. Have you ever seen anything like it? Try to tear this sample."

"It's reasonably tough," admitted his lordship, fruitlessly endeavouring to rip it apart.

"Yes. It was made in France, and is used in gold beating. Your uncle beat his sovereigns into gold-leaf. You will find that the book from Denny's is a volume on gold beating, and now as I remember that scribbled word which I could not make out, I think the title of the volume is 'Metallurgy.' It contains, no doubt, a chapter on the manufacture of gold-leaf."

"I believe you," said the earl; "but I don't see that the discovery sets us any further forward. We're now looking for gold-leaf instead of sovereigns."

"Let's examine this wallpaper," said I.

I placed my knife under a corner of it at the floor, and quite easily ripped off a large section. As Higgins had said, the brown paper was on top, and the coarse, light-coloured paper underneath. But even that came away from the oak panelling as easily as though it hung there from habit, and not because of paste.

"Feel the weight of that," I cried, handing him the sheet I had torn from the wall.

"By Jove!" said the earl, in a voice almost of awe.

I took it from him, and laid it, face downwards, on the wooden table, threw a little water on the back, and with a knife scraped away the porous white paper. Instantly there gleamed up at us the baleful yellow of the gold. I shrugged my shoulders and spread out my hands. The Earl of Chizelrigg laughed aloud and very heartily.

"You see how it is," I cried. "The old man first covered the entire wall with this whitish paper. He heated his sovereigns at the forge and beat them out on the anvil, then completed the process rudely between the sheets of this paper from France. Probably he pasted the gold to the wall as soon as he shut himself in for the night, and covered it over with the more expensive paper before Higgins entered in the morning."

We found afterwards, however, that he had actually fastened the thick sheets of gold to the wall with carpet tacks.

His lordship netted a trifle over a hundred and twenty-three thousand pounds through my discovery, and I am pleased to pay tribute to the young man's generosity by saying that his voluntary settlement made my bank account swell stout as a City alderman.

THE ABSENT-MINDED COTERIE

I

Some years ago I enjoyed the unique experience of pursuing a man for one crime, and getting evidence against him of another. He was innocent of the misdemeanour, the proof of which I sought, but was guilty of another most serious offence, yet he and his confederates escaped scot-free in circumstances which I now purpose to relate.

You may remember that in Rudyard Kipling's story, "Bedalia Herodsfoot," the unfortunate woman's husband ran the risk of being arrested as a simple drunkard, at a moment when the blood of murder was upon his boots. The case of Ralph Summertrees was rather the reverse of this. The English authorities were trying to fasten upon him a crime almost as important as murder, while I was collecting evidence which proved him guilty of an action much more momentous than that of drunkenness.

The English authorities have always been good enough, when they recognise my existence at all, to look down upon me with amused condescension. If today you ask Spenser Hale, of Scotland Yard, what he thinks of Eugène Valmont, that complacent man will put on the superior smile which so well becomes him, and if you are a very intimate friend of his, he may draw down the lid of his right eye, as he replies:

"Oh, yes, a very decent fellow, Valmont, but he's a Frenchman," as if, that said, there was no need of further inquiry.

Myself, I like the English detective very much, and if I were to be in a *mêlée* tomorrow, there is no man I would rather find beside me than Spenser Hale. In any situation where a fist that can fell an ox is desirable, my friend Hale is a useful companion, but for intellectuality, mental acumen, finesse—ah, well! I am the most modest of men, and will say nothing.

It would amuse you to see this giant come into my room during an evening, on the bluff pretence that he wishes to smoke a pipe with me. There is the same difference between this good-natured giant and myself as exists between that strong black pipe of his and my delicate cigarette, which I smoke feverishly when he is present, to protect myself from the fumes of his terrible tobacco. I look with delight upon the huge man, who, with an air of the utmost good humour, and a twinkle in his eye as he thinks he is twisting me about his finger, vainly endeavours to obtain a hint regarding whatever case is perplexing him at that moment. I baffle him with the ease that an active greyhound eludes the pursuit of a heavy mastiff, then at last I say to him with a laugh:

"Come *mon ami* Hale, tell me all about it, and I will help you if I can."

Once or twice at the beginning he shook his massive head, and replied the secret was not his. The last time he did this I assured him that what he said was quite correct, and then I related full particulars of the situation in which he found himself, excepting the names, for these he had not mentioned. I had pieced together his perplexity from scraps of conversation in his half-hour's fishing for my advice, which, of course, he could have had for the plain asking. Since that time he has not come to me except with cases he feels at liberty to reveal, and one or two complications I have happily been enabled to unravel for him.

But, staunch as Spenser Hale holds the belief that no detective service on earth can excel that centering in Scotland Yard, there is one department of activity in which even he confesses that Frenchmen are his masters, although he somewhat grudgingly qualifies his admission by adding that we in France are constantly allowed to do what is prohibited in England. I refer to the minute search of a house during the owner's absence. If you read that excellent story, entitled "The Purloined Letter," by Edgar Allan Poe, you will find a record of the kind of thing I mean, which is better than any description I, who have so often taken part in such a search, can set down.

Now, these people among whom I live are proud of their phrase, "The Englishman's house is his castle," and into that castle even a policeman cannot penetrate without a legal warrant. This may be all very well in theory, but if you are compelled to march up to a man's house, blowing a trumpet, and rattling a snare drum, you need not be disappointed if you fail to find what you are in search of when all the legal restrictions are complied with. Of course, the English are a very excellent people, a fact to which I am always proud to bear testimony, but it must be admitted that for cold common sense the French are very much their superiors. In Paris, if I wish to obtain an incriminating document, I do not send the possessor a *carte postale* to inform him of my desire, and in this procedure the French people sanely acquiesce. I have known men who, when they go out to spend an evening on the boulevards, toss their bunch of keys to the concierge, saying:

"If you hear the police rummaging about while I'm away, pray assist them, with an expression of my distinguished consideration."

I remember while I was chief detective in the service of the French Government being requested to call at a certain hour at the private hotel of the Minister for Foreign Affairs. It was during the time that Bismarck meditated a second attack upon my country, and I am happy to say that I was then instrumental in supplying the Secret Bureau with documents which mollified that iron man's purpose, a fact which I think entitled me to my country's gratitude, not that I ever even hinted such a claim when a succeeding ministry forgot my services. The memory of a republic, as has been said by a greater man than I, is short. However, all that has nothing to do with the incident I am about to relate. I merely mention the crisis to excuse a momentary forgetfulness on my part which in any other country might have been followed by serious results to myself. But in France—ah, we understand those things, and nothing happened.

I am the last person in the world to give myself away, as they say in the great West. I am usually the calm, collected Eugène Valmont whom nothing can perturb, but this was a time of great tension, and I had become absorbed. I was alone with the minister in his private house, and one of the papers he desired was in his bureau at the Ministry for Foreign Affairs; at least, he thought so, and said:

"Ah, it is in my desk at the bureau. How annoying! I must send for it!"

"No, Excellency," I cried, springing up in a self-oblivion the most complete, "it is here." Touching the spring of a secret drawer, I opened it, and taking out the document he wished, handed it to him.

It was not until I met his searching look, and saw the faint smile on his lips that I realised what I had done.

"Valmont," he said quietly, "on whose behalf did you search my house?"

"Excellency," I replied in tones no less agreeable than his own, "tonight at your orders I pay a domiciliary visit to the mansion of Baron Dumoulaine, who stands high in the estimation of the President of the French Republic. If either of those distinguished gentlemen should learn of my informal call and should ask me in whose interests I made the domiciliary visit, what is it you wish that I should reply?"

"You should reply, Valmont, that you did it in the interests of the Secret Service."

"I shall not fail to do so, Excellency, and in answer to your question just now, I had the honour of searching this mansion in the interests of the Secret Service of France."

The Minister for Foreign Affairs laughed; a hearty laugh that expressed no resentment.

"I merely wished to compliment you, Valmont, on the efficiency of your search, and the excellence of your memory. This is indeed the document which I thought was left in my office."

I wonder what Lord Lansdowne would say if Spenser Hale showed an equal familiarity with his private papers! But now that we have returned to our good friend Hale, we must not keep him waiting any longer.

II

I well remember the November day when I first heard of the Summertrees case, because there hung over London a fog so thick that two or three times I lost my way, and no cab was to be had at any price. The few cabmen then in the streets were leading their animals slowly along, making for their stables. It was one of those depressing London days which filled me with *ennui* and a yearning for my own clear city of Paris, where, if we are ever visited by a slight mist, it is at least clean, white vapour, and not this horrible London mixture saturated with suffocating carbon. The fog was too thick for any passer to read the contents bills of the newspapers plastered on the pavement, and as there were probably no races that day the newsboys were shouting what they considered the next most important event—the election of an American President. I bought a paper and thrust it into my pocket. It was late when I reached my flat, and, after dining there, which was an unusual thing for me to do, I put on my slippers, took an easy-chair before the fire, and began to read my evening journal. I was distressed to learn that the eloquent Mr. Bryan had been defeated. I knew little about the silver question, but the man's oratorical powers had appealed to me, and my sympathy was aroused because he owned many silver mines, and yet the price of the metal was so low that apparently he could not make a living through the operation of them. But, of course, the cry that he was a plutocrat, and a reputed millionaire over and over again, was bound to defeat him in a democracy where the average voter is exceedingly poor and not comfortably well-to-do as is the case with our peasants in France. I always took great interest in the affairs of the huge republic to the west, having been at some pains to inform myself accurately regarding its politics, and although, as my readers know, I seldom quote anything complimentary that is said of me, nevertheless, an American client of mine once admitted that he never knew the true inwardness—I think that was the phrase he used—of American politics until he heard me discourse upon them. But then, he added, he had been a very busy man all his life.

I had allowed my paper to slip to the floor, for in very truth the fog was penetrating even into my flat, and it was becoming difficult to read, notwithstanding the electric light. My man came in, and announced that Mr. Spenser Hale wished to see me, and, indeed, any night, but especially when there is rain or fog outside, I am more pleased to talk with a friend than to read a newspaper.

"*Mon Dieu*, my dear Monsieur Hale, it is a brave man you are to venture out in such a fog as is abroad tonight."

"Ah, Monsieur Valmont," said Hale with pride, "you cannot raise a fog like this in Paris!"

"No. There you are supreme," I admitted, rising and saluting my visitor, then offering him a chair.

"I see you are reading the latest news," he said, indicating my newspaper, "I am very glad that man Bryan is defeated. Now we shall have better times."

I waved my hand as I took my chair again. I will discuss many things with Spenser Hale, but not American politics; he does not understand them. It is a common defect of the English to suffer complete ignorance regarding the internal affairs of other countries.

"It is surely an important thing that brought you out on such a night as this. The fog must be very thick in Scotland Yard."

This delicate shaft of fancy completely missed him, and he answered stolidly:

"It's thick all over London, and, indeed, throughout most of England."

"Yes, it is," I agreed, but he did not see that either.

Still a moment later he made a remark which, if it had come from some people I know, might have indicated a glimmer of comprehension.

"You are a very, very clever man, Monsieur Valmont, so all I need say is that the question which brought me here is the same as that on which the American election was fought. Now, to a countryman, I should be compelled to give further explanation, but to you, monsieur, that will not be necessary."

There are times when I dislike the crafty smile and partial closing of the eyes which always distinguishes Spenser Hale when he places on the table a problem which he expects will baffle me. If I said he never did baffle me, I would be wrong, of course, for sometimes the utter simplicity of the puzzles which trouble him leads me into an intricate involution entirely unnecessary in the circumstances.

I pressed my fingertips together, and gazed for a few moments at the ceiling. Hale had lit his black pipe, and my silent servant placed at his elbow the whisky and soda, then tiptoed out of the room. As the door closed my eyes came from the ceiling to the level of Hale's expansive countenance.

"Have they eluded you?" I asked quietly.

"Who?"

"The coiners."

Hale's pipe dropped from his jaw, but he managed to catch it before it reached the floor. Then he took a gulp from the tumbler.

"That was just a lucky shot," he said.

"*Parfaitement*," I replied carelessly.

"Now, own up, Valmont, wasn't it?"

I shrugged my shoulders. A man cannot contradict a guest in his own house.

"Oh, stow that!" cried Hale impolitely. He is a trifle prone to strong and even slangy expressions when puzzled. "Tell me how you guessed it."

"It is very simple, *mon ami*. The question on which the American election was fought is the price of silver, which is so low that it has ruined Mr. Bryan, and threatens to ruin all the farmers of the west who possess silver mines on their farms. Silver troubled America, ergo silver troubles Scotland Yard.

"Very well, the natural inference is that someone has stolen bars of silver. But such a theft happened three months ago, when the metal was being unloaded from a German steamer at Southampton, and my dear friend Spenser Hale ran down the thieves very cleverly as they were trying to dissolve the marks off the bars with acid. Now crimes do not run in series, like the numbers in roulette at Monte Carlo. The thieves are men of brains. They say to themselves, 'What chance is there successfully to steal bars of silver while Mr. Hale is at Scotland Yard?' Eh, my good friend?"

"Really, Valmont," said Hale, taking another sip, "sometimes you almost persuade me that you have reasoning powers."

"Thanks, comrade. Then it is not a *theft* of silver we have now to deal with. But the American election was fought on the *price* of silver. If silver had been high in cost, there would have been no silver question. So the crime that is bothering you arises through the low price of silver, and this suggests that it must be a case of illicit coinage, for there the low price of the metal comes in. You have, perhaps, found a more subtle illegitimate act going forward than heretofore. Someone is making your shillings and your half-crowns from real silver, instead of from baser metal, and yet there is a large profit which has not hitherto been possible through the high price of silver. With the old conditions you were familiar, but this new element sets at nought all your previous formulae. That is how I reasoned the matter out."

"Well, Valmont, you have hit it. I'll say that for you; you have hit it. There is a gang of expert coiners who are putting out real silver money, and making a clear shilling on the half-crown. We can find no trace of the coiners, but we know the man who is shoving the stuff."

"That ought to be sufficient," I suggested.

"Yes, it should, but it hasn't proved so up to date. Now I came tonight to see if you would do one of your French tricks for us, right on the quiet."

"What French trick, Monsieur Spenser Hale?" I inquired with some asperity, forgetting for the moment that the man invariably became impolite when he grew excited.

"No offence intended," said this blundering officer, who really is a good-natured fellow, but always puts his foot in it, and then apologises. "I want someone to go through a man's house without a search warrant, spot the evidence, let me know, and then we'll rush the place before he has time to hide his tracks."

"Who is this man, and where does he live?"

"His name is Ralph Summertrees, and he lives in a very natty little *bijou* residence, as the advertisements call it, situated in no less a fashionable street than Park Lane."

"I see. What has aroused your suspicions against him?"

"Well, you know, that's an expensive district to live in; it takes a bit of money to do the trick. This Summertrees has no ostensible business, yet every Friday he goes to the United Capital Bank in Piccadilly, and deposits a bag of swag, usually all silver coin."

"Yes, and this money?"

"This money, so far as we can learn, contains a good many of these new pieces which never saw the British Mint."

"It's not all the new coinage, then?"

"Oh, no, he's a bit too artful for that. You see, a man can go round London, his pockets filled with new coinage five-shilling pieces, buy this, that, and the other, and come home with his change in legitimate coins of the realm—half-crowns, florins, shillings, sixpences, and all that."

"I see. Then why don't you nab him one day when his pockets are stuffed with illegitimate five-shilling pieces?"

"That could be done, of course, and I've thought of it, but you see, we want to land the whole gang. Once we arrested him, without knowing where the money came from, the real coiners would take flight."

"How do you know he is not the real coiner himself?"

Now poor Hale is as easy to read as a book. He hesitated before answering this question, and looked confused as a culprit caught in some dishonest act.

"You need not be afraid to tell me," I said soothingly after a pause. "You have had one of your men in Mr. Summertrees' house, and so learned that he is not the coiner. But your man has not succeeded in getting you evidence to incriminate other people."

"You've about hit it again, Monsieur Valmont. One of my men has been Summertrees' butler for two weeks, but, as you say, he has found no evidence."

"Is he still butler?"

"Yes."

"Now tell me how far you have got. You know that Summertrees deposits a bag of coin every Friday in the Piccadilly bank, and I suppose the bank has allowed you to examine one or two of the bags."

"Yes, sir, they have, but, you see, banks are very difficult to treat with. They don't like detectives bothering round, and whilst they do not stand out against the law, still they never answer any more questions than they're asked, and Mr. Summertrees has been a good customer at the United Capital for many years."

"Haven't you found out where the money comes from?"

"Yes, we have; it is brought there night after night by a man who looks like a respectable city clerk, and he puts it into a large safe, of which he holds the key, this safe being on the ground floor, in the dining-room."

"Haven't you followed the clerk?"

"Yes. He sleeps in the Park Lane house every night, and goes up in the morning to an old curiosity shop in Tottenham Court Road, where he stays all day, returning with his bag of money in the evening."

"Why don't you arrest and question him?"

"Well, Monsieur Valmont, there is just the same objection to his arrest as to that of Summertrees himself. We could easily arrest both, but we have not the slightest evidence against either of them, and then, although we put the go-betweens in clink, the worst criminals of the lot would escape."

"Nothing suspicious about the old curiosity shop?"

"No. It appears to be perfectly regular."

"This game has been going on under your noses for how long?"

"For about six weeks."

"Is Summertrees a married man?"

"No."

"Are there any women servants in the house?"

"No, except that three charwomen come in every morning to do up the rooms."

"Of what is his household comprised?"

"There is the butler, then the valet, and last, the French cook."

"Ah," cried I, "the French cook! This case interests me. So Summertrees has succeeded in completely disconcerting your man? Has he prevented him going from top to bottom of the house?"

"Oh no, he has rather assisted him than otherwise. On one occasion he went to the safe, took out the money, had Podgers—

that's my chap's name—help him to count it, and then actually sent Podgers to the bank with the bag of coin."

"And Podgers has been all over the place?"

"Yes."

"Saw no signs of a coining establishment?"

"No. It is absolutely impossible that any coining can be done there. Besides, as I tell you, that respectable clerk brings him the money."

"I suppose you want me to take Podgers' position?"

"Well, Monsieur Valmont, to tell you the truth, I would rather you didn't. Podgers has done everything a man can do, but I thought if you got into the house, Podgers assisting, you might go through it night after night at your leisure."

"I see. That's just a little dangerous in England. I think I should prefer to assure myself the legitimate standing of being the amiable Podgers' successor. You say that Summertrees has no business?"

"Well, sir, not what you might call a business. He is by the way of being an author, but I don't count that any business."

"Oh, an author, is he? When does he do his writing?"

"He locks himself up most of the day in his study."

"Does he come out for lunch?"

"No; he lights a little spirit lamp inside, Podgers tells me, and makes himself a cup of coffee, which he takes with a sandwich or two."

"That's rather frugal fare for Park Lane."

"Yes, Monsieur Valmont, it is, but he makes it up in the evening, when he has a long dinner with all them foreign kickshaws you people like, done by his French cook."

"Sensible man! Well, Hale, I see I shall look forward with pleasure to making the acquaintance of Mr. Summertrees. Is there any restriction on the going and coming of your man Podgers?"

"None in the least. He can get away either night or day."

"Very good, friend Hale, bring him here tomorrow, as soon as our author locks himself up in his study, or rather, I should say, as soon as the respectable clerk leaves for Tottenham Court Road, which I should guess, as you put it, is about half an hour after his master turns the key of the room in which he writes."

"You are quite right in that guess, Valmont. How did you hit it?"

"Merely a surmise, Hale. There is a good deal of oddity about that Park Lane house, so it doesn't surprise me in the least that the master gets to work earlier in the morning than the man. I have also a suspicion that Ralph Summertrees knows perfectly well what the estimable Podgers is there for."

"What makes you think that?"

"I can give no reason except that my opinion of the acuteness of Summertrees has been gradually rising all the while you were speaking, and at the same time my estimate of Podgers' craft has been as steadily declining. However, bring the man here tomorrow, that I may ask him a few questions."

III

Next day, about eleven o'clock, the ponderous Podgers, hat in hand, followed his chief into my room. His broad, impassive, immobile smooth face gave him rather more the air of a genuine butler than I had expected, and this appearance, of course, was enhanced by his livery. His replies to my questions were those of a well-trained servant who will not say too much unless it is made worth his while. All in all, Podgers exceeded my expectations, and really my friend Hale had some justification for regarding him, as he evidently did, a triumph in his line.

"Sit down, Mr. Hale, and you, Podgers."

The man disregarded my invitation, standing like a statue until his chief made a motion; then he dropped into a chair. The English are great on discipline.

"Now, Mr. Hale, I must first congratulate you on the make-up of Podgers. It is excellent. You depend less on artificial assistance than we do in France, and in that I think you are right."

"Oh, we know a bit over here, Monsieur Valmont," said Hale, with pardonable pride.

"Now then, Podgers, I want to ask you about this clerk. What time does he arrive in the evening?"

"At prompt six, sir."

"Does he ring, or let himself in with a latchkey?"

"With a latchkey, sir."

"How does he carry the money?"

"In a little locked leather satchel, sir, flung over his shoulder."

"Does he go direct to the dining-room?"

"Yes, sir."

"Have you seen him unlock the safe and put in the money?"

"Yes, sir."

"Does the safe unlock with a word or a key?"

"With a key, sir. It's one of the old-fashioned kind."

"Then the clerk unlocks his leather money bag?"

"Yes, sir."

"That's three keys used within as many minutes. Are they separate or in a bunch?"

"In a bunch, sir."

"Did you ever see your master with this bunch of keys?"

"No, sir."

"You saw him open the safe once, I am told?"

"Yes, sir."

"Did he use a separate key, or one of a bunch?"

Podgers slowly scratched his head, then said:

"I don't just remember, sir."

"Ah, Podgers, you are neglecting the big things in that house. Sure you can't remember?"

"No, sir."

"Once the money is in and the safe locked up, what does the clerk do?"

"Goes to his room, sir."

"Where is this room?"

"On the third floor, sir."

"Where do you sleep?"

"On the fourth floor with the rest of the servants, sir."

"Where does the master sleep?"

"On the second floor, adjoining his study."

"The house consists of four stories and a basement, does it?"

"Yes, sir."

"I have somehow arrived at the suspicion that it is a very narrow house. Is that true?"

"Yes, sir."

"Does the clerk ever dine with your master?"

"No, sir. The clerk don't eat in the house at all, sir."

"Does he go away before breakfast?"

"No, sir."

"No one takes breakfast to his room?"

"No, sir."

"What time does he leave the house?"

"At ten o'clock, sir."

"When is breakfast served?"

"At nine o'clock, sir."

"At what hour does your master retire to his study?"

"At half-past nine, sir."

"Locks the door on the inside?"

"Yes, sir."

"Never rings for anything during the day?"

"Not that I know of, sir."

"What sort of a man is he?"

Here Podgers was on familiar ground, and he rattled off a description minute in every particular.

"What I meant was, Podgers, is he silent, or talkative, or does he get angry? Does he seem furtive, suspicious, anxious, terrorised, calm, excitable, or what?"

"Well, sir, he is by way of being very quiet, never has much to say for himself; never saw him angry, or excited."

"Now, Podgers, you've been at Park Lane for a fortnight or more. You are a sharp, alert, observant man. What happens there that strikes you as unusual?"

"Well, I can't exactly say, sir," replied Podgers, looking rather helplessly from his chief to myself, and back again.

"Your professional duties have often compelled you to enact the part of butler before, otherwise you wouldn't do it so well. Isn't that the case?"

Podgers did not reply, but glanced at his chief. This was evidently a question pertaining to the service, which a subordinate was not allowed to answer. However, Hale said at once:

"Certainly. Podgers has been in dozens of places."

"Well, Podgers, just call to mind some of the other households where you have been employed, and tell me any particulars in which Mr. Summertrees' establishment differs from them."

Podgers pondered a long time.

"Well, sir, he do stick to writing pretty close."

"Ah, that's his profession, you see, Podgers. Hard at it from half-past nine till towards seven, I imagine?"

"Yes, sir."

"Anything else, Podgers? No matter how trivial."

"Well, sir, he's fond of reading too; leastways, he's fond of newspapers."

"When does he read?"

"I've never seen him read 'em, sir; indeed, so far as I can tell, I never knew the papers to be opened, but he takes them all in, sir."

"What, all the morning papers?"

"Yes, sir, and all the evening papers too."

"Where are the morning papers placed?"

"On the table in his study, sir."

"And the evening papers?"

"Well, sir, when the evening papers come, the study is locked. They are put on a side table in the dining-room, and he takes them upstairs with him to his study."

"This has happened every day since you've been there?"

"Yes, sir."

"You reported that very striking fact to your chief, of course?"

"No, sir, I don't think I did," said Podgers, confused.

"You should have done so. Mr. Hale would have known how to make the most of a point so vital."

"Oh, come now, Valmont," interrupted Hale, "you're chaffing us. Plenty of people take in all the papers!"

"I think not. Even clubs and hotels subscribe to the leading journals only. You said *all*, I think, Podgers?"

"Well, *nearly* all, sir."

"But which is it? There's a vast difference."

"He takes a good many, sir."

"How many?"

"I don't just know, sir."

"That's easily found out, Valmont," cried Hale, with some impatience, "if you think it really important."

"I think it so important that I'm going back with Podgers myself. You can take me into the house, I suppose, when you return?"

"Oh, yes, sir."

"Coming back to these newspapers for a moment, Podgers. What is done with them?"

"They are sold to the ragman, sir, once a week."

"Who takes them from the study?"

"I do, sir."

"Do they appear to have been read very carefully?"

"Well, no, sir; leastways, some of them seem never to have been opened, or else folded up very carefully again."

"Did you notice that extracts have been clipped from any of them?"

"No, sir."

"Does Mr. Summertrees keep a scrapbook?"

"Not that I know of, sir."

"Oh, the case is perfectly plain," said I, leaning back in my chair, and regarding the puzzled Hale with that cherubic expression of self-satisfaction which I know is so annoying to him.

"*What's* perfectly plain?" he demanded, more gruffly perhaps than etiquette would have sanctioned.

"Summertrees is no coiner, nor is he linked with any band of coiners."

"What is he, then?"

"Ah, that opens another avenue of enquiry. For all I know to the contrary, he may be the most honest of men. On the surface it would appear that he is a reasonably industrious tradesman in Tottenham Court Road, who is anxious that there should be no visible connection between a plebian employment and so aristocratic a residence as that in Park Lane."

At this point Spenser Hale gave expression to one of those rare flashes of reason which are always an astonishment to his friends.

"That is nonsense, Monsieur Valmont," he said, "the man who is ashamed of the connection between his business and his house is one who is trying to get into Society, or else the women of his family are trying it, as is usually the case. Now Summertrees has no family. He himself goes nowhere, gives no entertainments, and accepts no invitations. He belongs to no club, therefore to say that he is ashamed of his connection with the Tottenham Court Road shop is absurd. He is concealing the connection for some other reason that will bear looking into."

"My dear Hale, the goddess of Wisdom herself could not have made a more sensible series of remarks. Now, *mon ami*, do you want my assistance, or have you enough to go on with?"

"Enough to go on with? We have nothing more than we had when I called on you last night."

"Last night, my dear Hale, you supposed this man was in league with coiners. Today you know he is not."

"I know you *say* he is not."

I shrugged my shoulders, and raised my eyebrows, smiling at him.

"It is the same thing, Monsieur Hale."

"Well, of all the conceited—" and the good Hale could get no further.

"If you wish my assistance, it is yours."

"Very good. Not to put too fine a point upon it, I do."

"In that case, my dear Podgers, you will return to the residence of our friend Summertrees, and get together for me in a bundle all of yesterday's morning and evening papers, that were delivered to the house. Can you do that, or are they mixed up in a heap in the coal cellar?"

"I can do it, sir. I have instructions to place each day's papers in a pile by itself in case they should be wanted again. There is always one week's supply in the cellar, and we sell the papers of the week before to the rag men."

"Excellent. Well, take the risk of abstracting one day's journals, and have them ready for me. I will call upon you at half-past three o'clock exactly, and then I want you to take me upstairs to the clerk's bedroom in the third story, which I suppose is not locked during the daytime?"

"No, sir, it is not."

With this the patient Podgers took his departure. Spenser Hale rose when his assistant left.

"Anything further I can do?" he asked.

"Yes; give me the address of the shop in Tottenham Court Road. Do you happen to have about you one of those new five-shilling pieces which you believe to be illegally coined?"

He opened his pocket-book, took out the bit of white metal, and handed it to me.

"I'm going to pass this off before evening," I said, putting it in my pocket, "and I hope none of your men will arrest me."

"That's all right," laughed Hale as he took his leave.

At half-past three Podgers was waiting for me, and opened the front door as I came up the steps, thus saving me the necessity of ringing. The house seemed strangely quiet. The French cook was evidently down in the basement, and we had probably all the upper part to ourselves, unless Summertrees was in his study, which I doubted. Podgers led me directly upstairs to the clerk's room on the third floor, walking on tiptoe, with an elephantine air of silence and secrecy combined, which struck me as unnecessary.

"I will make an examination of this room," I said. "Kindly wait for me down by the door of the study."

The bedroom proved to be of respectable size when one considers the smallness of the house. The bed was all nicely made up, and there were two chairs in the room, but the usual washstand and swing-mirror were not visible. However, seeing a curtain at the farther end of the room, I drew it aside, and found, as I expected, a fixed lavatory in an alcove of perhaps four feet deep by five in width. As the room was about fifteen feet wide, this left two-thirds of the space unaccounted for. A moment later, I opened a door which exhibited a closet filled with clothes hanging on hooks. This left a space of five feet between the clothes closet and the lavatory. I thought at first that the entrance to the secret stairway must have issued from the lavatory, but examining the boards closely, although they sounded hollow to the knuckles, they were quite evidently plain matchboarding, and not a concealed door. The entrance to the stairway, therefore, must issue from the clothes closet. The right hand wall proved similar to the matchboarding of the lavatory as far as the casual eye or touch was concerned, but I saw at once it was a door. The latch turned out to be somewhat ingeniously operated by one of the hooks which held a pair of old trousers. I found that the hook, if pressed upward, allowed the door to swing outward, over the stairhead. Descending to the second floor, a similar latch let me in to a similar clothes closet in the room beneath. The two rooms were identical in size, one directly above the other, the only difference being that the lower room door gave into the study, instead of into the hall, as was the case with the upper chamber.

The study was extremely neat, either not much used, or the abode of a very methodical man. There was nothing on the table except a pile of that morning's papers. I walked to the farther end, turned the key in the lock, and came out upon the astonished Podgers.

"Well, I'm blowed!" exclaimed he.

"Quite so," I rejoined, "you've been tiptoeing past an empty room for the last two weeks. Now, if you'll come with me, Podgers, I'll show you how the trick is done."

When he entered the study, I locked the door once more, and led the assumed butler, still tiptoeing through force of habit, up the stair into the top bedroom, and so out again, leaving every-thing exactly as we found it. We went down the main stair to the front hall, and there Podgers had my parcel of papers all neatly wrapped up. This bundle I carried to my flat, gave one of my assis-tants some instructions, and left him at work on the papers.

IV

I took a cab to the foot of Tottenham Court Road, and walked up that street till I came to J. Simpson's old curiosity shop. After gazing at the well-filled windows for some time, I stepped aside, having selected a little iron crucifix displayed behind the pane; the work of some ancient craftsman.

I knew at once from Podgers's description that I was waited upon by the veritable respectable clerk who brought the bag of money each night to Park Lane, and who I was certain was no other than Ralph Summertrees himself.

There was nothing in his manner differing from that of any other quiet salesman. The price of the crucifix proved to be seven-and-six, and I threw down a sovereign to pay for it.

"Do you mind the change being all in silver, sir?" he asked, and I answered without any eagerness, although the question aroused a suspicion that had begun to be allayed:

"Not in the least."

He gave me half-a-crown, three two-shilling pieces, and four separate shillings, all the coins being well-worn silver of the realm, the undoubted inartistic product of the reputable British Mint. This seemed to dispose of the theory that he was palming off illegiti-mate money. He asked me if I were interested in any particular branch of antiquity, and I replied that my curiosity was merely general, and exceedingly amateurish, whereupon he invited me to look around. This I proceeded to do, while he resumed the address-ing and stamping of some wrapped-up pamphlets which I surmised to be copies of his catalogue.

He made no attempt either to watch me or to press his wares upon me. I selected at random a little ink-stand, and asked its price. It was two shillings, he said, whereupon I produced my fraudulent five-shilling piece. He took it, gave me the change without com-ment, and the last doubt about his connection with coiners flick-ered from my mind.

At this moment a young man came in, who, I saw at once, was not a customer. He walked briskly to the farther end of the shop, and disappeared behind a partition which had one pane of glass in it that gave an outlook towards the front door.

"Excuse me a moment," said the shopkeeper, and he followed the young man into the private office.

As I examined the curious heterogeneous collection of things for sale, I heard the clink of coins being poured out on the lid of a desk or an uncovered table, and the murmur of voices floated out to me. I was now near the entrance of the shop, and by a sleight-of-hand trick, keeping the corner of my eye on the glass pane of the private office, I removed the key of the front door without a sound, and took an impression of it in wax, returning the key to its place unobserved. At this moment another young man came in, and walked straight past me into the private office. I heard him say:

"Oh, I beg pardon, Mr. Simpson. How are you, Rogers?"

"Hallo, Macpherson," saluted Rogers, who then came out, bidding good-night to Mr. Simpson, and departed whistling down the street, but not before he had repeated his phrase to another young man entering, to whom he gave the name of Tyrrel.

I noted these three names in my mind. Two others came in together, but I was compelled to content myself with memorising their features, for I did not learn their names. These men were evidently collectors, for I heard the rattle of money in every case; yet here was a small shop, doing apparently very little business, for I had been within it for more than half an hour, and yet remained the only customer. If credit were given, one collector would certainly have been sufficient, yet five had come in, and had poured their contributions into the pile Summertrees was to take home with him that night.

I determined to secure one of the pamphlets which the man had been addressing. They were piled on a shelf behind the counter, but I had no difficulty in reaching across and taking the one on top, which I slipped into my pocket. When the fifth young man went down the street Summertrees himself emerged, and this time he carried in his hand the well-filled locked leather satchel, with the straps dangling. It was now approaching half-past five, and I saw he was eager to close up and get away.

"Anything else you fancy, sir?" he asked me.

"No, or rather yes and no. You have a very interesting collection here, but it's getting so dark I can hardly see."

"I close at half-past five, sir."

"Ah, in that case," I said, consulting my watch, "I shall be pleased to call some other time."

"Thank you, sir," replied Summertrees quietly, and with that I took my leave.

From the corner of an alley on the other side of the street I saw him put up the shutters with his own hands, then he emerged with overcoat on, and the money satchel slung across his shoulder. He locked the door, tested it with his knuckles, and walked down the street, carrying under one arm the pamphlets he had been address-ing. I followed him some distance, saw him drop the pamphlets into the box at the first post office he passed, and walk rapidly towards his house in Park Lane.

When I returned to my flat and called in my assistant, he said:

"After putting to one side the regular advertisements of pills, soap, and what not, here is the only one common to all the news-papers, morning and evening alike. The advertisements are not identical, sir, but they have two points of similarity, or perhaps I should say three. They all profess to furnish a cure for absent-mindedness; they all ask that the applicant's chief hobby shall be stated, and they all bear the same address: Dr. Willoughby, in Tottenham Court Road."

"Thank you," said I, as he placed the scissored advertisements before me.

I read several of the announcements. They were all small, and perhaps that is why I had never noticed one of them in the news-papers, for certainly they were odd enough. Some asked for lists of absent-minded men, with the hobbies of each, and for these lists, prizes of from one shilling to six were offered. In other clippings Dr. Willoughby professed to be able to cure absent-mindedness. There were no fees, and no treatment, but a pamphlet would be sent, which, if it did not benefit the receiver, could do no harm. The doctor was unable to meet patients personally, nor could he enter into correspondence with them. The address was the same as that of the old curiosity shop in Tottenham Court Road. At this juncture I pulled the pamphlet from my pocket, and saw it was entitled Christian Science and Absent-Mindedness, by Dr.

Stamford Willoughby, and at the end of the article was the statement contained in the advertisements, that Dr Willoughby would
neither see patients nor hold any correspondence with them.

I drew a sheet of paper towards me, wrote to Dr. Willoughby
alleging that I was a very absent-minded man, and would be glad
of his pamphlet, adding that my special hobby was the collecting
of first editions. I then signed myself, "Alport Webster, Imperial
Flats, London, W."

I may here explain that it is often necessary for me to see people
under some other name than the well-known appellation of Eugène
Valmont. There are two doors to my flat, and on one of these is
painted, "Eugène Valmont"; on the other there is a receptacle, into
which can be slipped a sliding panel bearing any *nom de guerre* I
choose. The same device is arranged on the ground floor, where
the names of all the occupants of the building appear on the right-
hand wall.

I sealed, addressed, and stamped my letter, then told my man
to put out the name of Alport Webster, and if I did not happen to
be in when anyone called upon that mythical person, he was to
make an appointment for me.

It was nearly six o'clock next afternoon when the card of Angus Macpherson was brought in to Mr. Alport Webster. I recognised
the young man at once as the second who had entered the little
shop carrying his tribute to Mr. Simpson the day before. He held
three volumes under his arm, and spoke in such a pleasant, in-
sinuating sort of way, that I knew at once he was an adept in his
profession of canvasser.

"Will you be seated, Mr. Macpherson? In what can I serve you?"

He placed the three volumes, backs upward, on my table.

"Are you interested at all in first editions, Mr. Webster?"

"It is the one thing I am interested in," I replied; "but unfortunately they often run into a lot of money."

"That is true," said Macpherson sympathetically, "and I have
here three books, one of which is an exemplification of what you
say. This one costs a hundred pounds. The last copy that was sold
by auction in London brought a hundred and twenty-three pounds.

This next one is forty pounds, and the third ten pounds. At these prices I am certain you could not duplicate three such treasures in any book shop in Britain."

I examined them critically, and saw at once that what he said was true. He was still standing on the opposite side of the table.

"Please take a chair, Mr. Macpherson. Do you mean to say you go round London with a hundred and fifty pounds worth of goods under your arm in this careless way?"

The young man laughed.

"I run very little risk, Mr. Webster. I don't suppose anyone I meet imagines for a moment there is more under my arm than perhaps a trio of volumes I have picked up in the fourpenny box to take home with me."

I lingered over the volume for which he asked a hundred pounds, then said, looking across at him:

"How came you to be possessed of this book, for instance?"

He turned upon me a fine, open countenance, and answered without hesitation in the frankest possible manner:

"I am not in actual possession of it, Mr. Webster. I am by way of being a connoisseur in rare and valuable books myself, although, of course, I have little money with which to indulge in the collection of them. I am acquainted, however, with the lovers of desirable books in different quarters of London. These three volumes, for instance, are from the library of a private gentleman in the West End. I have sold many books to him, and he knows I am trustworthy. He wishes to dispose of them at something under their real value, and has kindly allowed me to conduct the negotiation. I make it my business to find out those who are interested in rare books, and by such trading I add considerably to my income."

"How, for instance, did you learn that I was a bibliophile?"

Mr. Macpherson laughed genially.

"Well, Mr. Webster, I must confess that I chanced it. I do that very often. I take a flat like this, and send in my card to the name on the door. If I am invited in, I ask the occupant the question I asked you just now: 'Are you interested in rare editions?' If he says no, I simply beg pardon and retire. If he says yes, then I show my wares."

"I see," said I, nodding. What a glib young liar he was, with that innocent face of his, and yet my next question brought forth the truth.

"As this is the first time you have called upon me, Mr. Macpherson, you have no objection to my making some further inquiry, I suppose. Would you mind telling me the name of the owner of these books in the West End?"

"His name is Mr. Ralph Summertrees, of Park Lane."

"Of Park Lane? Ah, indeed."

"I shall be glad to leave the books with you, Mr. Webster, and if you care to make an appointment with Mr. Summertrees, I am sure he will not object to say a word in my favour."

"Oh, I do not in the least doubt it, and should not think of troubling the gentleman."

"I was going to tell you," went on the young man, "that I have a friend, a capitalist, who, in a way, is my supporter; for, as I said, I have little money of my own. I find it is often inconvenient for people to pay down any considerable sum. When, however, I strike a bargain, my capitalist buys the book, and I make an arrangement with my customer to pay a certain amount each week, and so even a large purchase is not felt, as I make the instalments small enough to suit my client."

"You are employed during the day, I take it?"

"Yes, I am a clerk in the City."

Again we were in the blissful realms of fiction!

"Suppose I take this book at ten pounds, what instalment should I have to pay each week?"

"Oh, what you like, sir. Would five shillings be too much?"

"I think not."

"Very well, sir, if you pay me five shillings now, I will leave the book with you, and shall have pleasure in calling this day week for the next instalment."

I put my hand into my pocket, and drew out two half-crowns, which I passed over to him.

"Do I need to sign any form or undertaking to pay the rest?"

The young man laughed cordially.

"Oh, no, sir, there is no formality necessary. You see, sir, this is largely a labour of love with me, although I don't deny I have my eye on the future. I am getting together what I hope will be a very valuable connection with gentlemen like yourself who are fond of books, and I trust some day that I may be able to resign my place with the insurance company and set up a choice little business of my own, where my knowledge of values in literature will prove useful."

And then, after making a note in a little book he took from his pocket, he bade me a most graceful good-bye and departed, leaving me cogitating over what it all meant.

Next morning two articles were handed to me. The first came by post and was a pamphlet on Christian Science and Absent-Mindedness, exactly similar to the one I had taken away from the old curiosity shop; the second was a small key made from my wax impression that would fit the front door of the same shop—a key fashioned by an excellent anarchist friend of mine in an obscure street near Holborn.

That night at ten o'clock I was inside the old curiosity shop, with a small storage battery in my pocket, and a little electric glow-lamp at my buttonhole, a most useful instrument for either burglar or detective.

I had expected to find the books of the establishment in a safe, which, if it was similar to the one in Park Lane, I was prepared to open with the false keys in my possession or to take an impression of the keyhole and trust to my anarchist friend for the rest. But to my amazement I discovered all the papers pertaining to the concern in a desk which was not even locked. The books, three in number, were the ordinary day book, journal, and ledger referring to the shop; book-keeping of the older fashion; but in a portfolio lay half a dozen foolscap sheets, headed "Mr. Rogers's List", "Mr. Macpherson's", "Mr Tyrrel's", the names I had already learned, and three others. These lists contained in the first column, names; in the second column, addresses; in the third, sums of money; and then in the small, square places following were amounts ranging from two-and-sixpence to a pound. At the bottom of Mr. Mac-pherson's list was the name Alport Webster, Imperial Flats, £10; then in the small, square place, five shillings. These six sheets, each headed by a canvasser's name, were evidently the record of current collections, and the innocence of the whole thing was so apparent that if it were not for my fixed rule never to believe that I am at the bottom of any case until I have come on something suspicious, I would have gone out empty-handed as I came in.

The six sheets were loose in a thin portfolio, but standing on a shelf above the desk were a number of fat volumes, one of which I took down, and saw that it contained similar lists running back several years. I noticed on Mr. Macpherson's current list the name of Lord Semptam, an eccentric old nobleman whom I knew slightly. Then turning to the list immediately before the current one the name was still there; I traced it back through list after list until I found the first entry, which was no less than three years previous, and there Lord Semptam was down for a piece of furniture costing fifty pounds, and on that account he had paid a pound a week for more than three years, totalling a hundred and seventy pounds at the least, and instantly the glorious simplicity of the scheme dawned upon me, and I became so interested in the swindle that I lit the gas, fearing my little lamp would be exhausted before my investigation ended, for it promised to be a long one.

In several instances the intended victim proved shrewder than old Simpson had counted upon, and the word "Settled" had been written on the line carrying the name when the exact number of instalments was paid. But as these shrewd persons dropped out, others took their places, and Simpson's dependence on their ab-sent-mindedness seemed to be justified in nine cases out of ten. His collectors were collecting long after the debt had been paid. In Lord Semptam's case, the payment had evidently become chronic, and the old man was giving away his pound a week to the suave Macpherson two years after his debt had been liquidated.

From the big volume I detached the loose leaf, dated 1893, which recorded Lord Semptam's purchase of a carved table for fifty pounds, and on which he had been paying a pound a week from that time to the date of which I am writing, which was November, 1896. This single document taken from the file of three years previous, was not likely to be missed, as would have been the case if I had selected a current sheet. I nevertheless made a copy of the names and addresses of Macpherson's present clients; then, carefully placing everything exactly as I had found it, I extinguished the gas, and went out of the shop, locking the door behind me. With the 1893 sheet in my pocket I resolved to prepare a pleasant little surprise for my suave friend Macpherson when he called to get his next instalment of five shillings.

Late as was the hour when I reached Trafalgar Square, I could not deprive myself of the felicity of calling on Mr. Spenser Hale, who I knew was then on duty. He never appeared at his best during office hours, because officialism stiffened his stalwart frame. Mentally he was impressed with the importance of his position, and added to this he was not then allowed to smoke his big, black pipe and terrible tobacco. He received me with the curtness I had been taught to expect when I inflicted myself upon him at his office. He greeted me abruptly with:

"I say, Valmont, how long do you expect to be on this job?"

"What job?" I asked mildly.

"Oh, you know what I mean: the Summertrees affair."

"Oh, that!" I exclaimed, with surprise. "The Summertrees case is already completed, of course. If I had known you were in a hurry, I should have finished up everything yesterday, but as you and Podgers, and I don't know how many more, have been at it sixteen or seventeen days, if not longer, I thought I might venture to take as many hours, as I am working entirely alone. You said nothing about haste, you know."

"Oh, come now, Valmont, that's a bit thick. Do you mean to say you have already got evidence against the man?"

"Evidence absolute and complete."

"Then who are the coiners?"

"My most estimable friend, how often have I told you not to jump at conclusions? I informed you when you first spoke to me about the matter that Summertrees was neither a coiner nor a confederate of coiners. I secured evidence sufficient to convict him of quite another offence, which is probably unique in the annals of crime. I have penetrated the mystery of the shop, and discovered the reason for all those suspicious actions which quite properly set you on his trail. Now I wish you to come to my flat next Wednesday night at a quarter to six, prepared to make an arrest."

"I must know who I am to arrest, and on what counts."

"Quite so, *mon ami* Hale; I did not say you were to make an arrest, but merely warned you to be prepared. If you have time now to listen to the disclosures, I am quite at your service. I promise you there are some original features in the case. If, however, the present moment is inopportune, drop in on me at your convenience, previously telephoning so that you may know whether I am there or not, and thus your valuable time will not be expended purposelessly."

With this I presented to him my most courteous bow, and although his mystified expression hinted a suspicion that he thought I was chaffing him, as he would call it, official dignity dissolved somewhat, and he intimated his desire to hear all about it then and there. I had succeeded in arousing my friend Hale's curiosity. He listened to the evidence with perplexed brow, and at last ejaculated he would be blessed.

"This young man," I said, in conclusion, "will call upon me at six on Wednesday afternoon, to receive his second five shillings. I propose that you, in your uniform, shall be seated there with me to receive him, and I am anxious to study Mr. Macpherson's countenance when he realises he has walked in to confront a policeman. If you will then allow me to cross-examine him for a few moments, not after the manner of Scotland Yard, with a warning lest he incriminate himself, but in the free and easy fashion we adopt in Paris, I shall afterwards turn the case over to you to be dealt with at your discretion."

"You have a wonderful flow of language, Monsieur Valmont," was the officer's tribute to me. "I shall be on hand at a quarter to six on Wednesday."

"Meanwhile," said I, "kindly say nothing of this to anyone. We must arrange a complete surprise for Macpherson. That is essential. Please make no move in the matter at all until Wednesday night."

Spenser Hale, much impressed, nodded acquiescence, and I took a polite leave of him.

V

The question of lighting is an important one in a room such as mine, and electricity offers a good deal of scope to the ingenious. Of this fact I have taken full advantage. I can manipulate the lighting of my room so that any particular spot is bathed in brilliancy, while the rest of the space remains in comparative gloom, and I arranged the lamps so that the full force of their rays impinged against the door that Wednesday evening, while I sat on one side of the table in semi-darkness and Hale sat on the other, with a light beating down on him from above which gave him the odd, sculptured look of a living statue of Justice, stern and triumphant. Anyone entering the room would first be dazzled by the light, and next would see the gigantic form of Hale in the full uniform of his order.

When Angus Macpherson was shown into this room he was quite visibly taken aback, and paused abruptly on the threshold, his gaze riveted on the huge policeman. I think his first purpose was to turn and run, but the door closed behind him, and he doubtless heard, as we all did, the sound of the bolt being thrust in its place, thus locking him in.

"I—I beg your pardon," he stammered, "I expected to meet Mr. Webster."

As he said this, I pressed the button under my table, and was instantly enshrouded with light. A sickly smile overspread the countenance of Macpherson as he caught sight of me, and he made a very creditable attempt to carry off the situation with nonchalance.

"Oh, there you are, Mr. Webster; I did not notice you at first."

It was a tense moment. I spoke slowly and impressively.

"Sir, perhaps you are not unacquainted with the name of Eugène Valmont."

He replied brazenly:

"I am sorry to say, sir, I never heard of the gentleman before."

At this came a most inopportune "Haw-haw" from that blockhead Spenser Hale, completely spoiling the dramatic situation I had elaborated with such thought and care. It is little wonder the English possess no drama, for they show scant appreciation of the sensational moments in life.

"Haw-haw," brayed Spenser Hale, and at once reduced the emotional atmosphere to a fog of commonplace. However, what is a man to do? He must handle the tools with which it pleases Providence to provide him. I ignored Hale's untimely laughter.

"Sit down, sir," I said to Macpherson, and he obeyed.

"You have called on Lord Semptam this week," I continued sternly.

"Yes, sir."

"And collected a pound from him?"

"Yes, sir."

"In October, 1893, you sold Lord Semptam a carved antique table for fifty pounds?"

"Quite right, sir."

"When you were here last week you gave me Ralph Summertrees as the name of a gentleman living in Park Lane. You knew at the time that this man was your employer?"

Macpherson was now looking fixedly at me, and on this occasion made no reply. I went on calmly:

"You also knew that Summertrees, of Park Lane, was identical with Simpson, of Tottenham Court Road?"

"Well, sir," said Macpherson, "I don't exactly see what you're driving at, but it's quite usual for a man to carry on a business under an assumed name. There is nothing illegal about that."

"We will come to the illegality in a moment, Mr. Macpherson. You, and Rogers, and Tyrrel, and three others, are confederates of this man Simpson."

"We are in his employ; yes, sir, but no more confederates than clerks usually are."

"I think, Mr. Macpherson, I have said enough to show you that the game is, what you call, up. You are now in the presence of Mr. Spenser Hale, from Scotland Yard, who is waiting to hear your confession."

Here the stupid Hale broke in with his—

"And remember, sir, that anything you say will be—"

"Excuse me, Mr. Hale," I interrupted hastily, "I shall turn over the case to you in a very few moments, but I ask you to remember our compact, and to leave it for the present entirely in my hands. Now, Mr. Macpherson, I want your confession, and I want it at once."

"Confession? Confederates?" protested Macpherson with admirably simulated surprise. "I must say you use extraordinary terms, Mr—Mr—What did you say the name was?"

"Haw-haw," roared Hale. "His name is Monsieur Valmont."

"I implore you, Mr. Hale, to leave this man to me for a very few moments. Now, Macpherson, what have you to say in your defence?"

"Where nothing criminal has been alleged, Monsieur Valmont, I see no necessity for defence. If you wish me to admit that somehow you have acquired a number of details regarding our business, I am perfectly willing to do so, and to subscribe to their accuracy. If you will be good enough to let me know of what you complain, I shall endeavour to make the point clear to you if I can. There has evidently been some misapprehension, but for the life of me, without further explanation, I am as much in a fog as I was on my way coming here, for it is getting a little thick outside."

Macpherson certainly was conducting himself with great discretion, and presented, quite unconsciously, a much more diplomatic figure than my friend, Spenser Hale, sitting stiffly opposite me. His tone was one of mild expostulation, mitigated by the intimation that all misunderstanding speedily would be cleared away. To outward view he offered a perfect picture of innocence, neither protesting too much nor too little. I had, however, another surprise in store for him, a trump card, as it were, and I played it down on the table.

"There!" I cried with vim, "have you ever seen that sheet before?"

He glanced at it without offering to take it in his hand.

"Oh, yes," he said, "that has been abstracted from our file. It is what I call my visiting list."

"Come, come, sir," I cried sternly, "you refuse to confess, but I warn you we know all about it. You never heard of Dr. Willoughby, I suppose?"

"Yes, he is the author of the silly pamphlet on Christian Science."

"You are in the right, Mr. Macpherson; on Christian Science and Absent-Mindedness."

"Possibly. I haven't read it for a long while."

"Have you ever met this learned doctor, Mr. Macpherson?"

"Oh, yes. Dr. Willoughby is the pen-name of Mr. Summertrees. He believes in Christian Science and that sort of thing, and writes about it."

"Ah, really. We are getting your confession bit by bit, Mr. Macpherson. I think it would be better to be quite frank with us."

"I was just going to make the same suggestion to you, Monsieur Valmont. If you will tell me in a few words exactly what is your charge against either Mr. Summertrees or myself, I will know then what to say."

"We charge you, sir, with obtaining money under false pretences, which is a crime that has landed more than one distinguished financier in prison."

Spenser Hale shook his fat forefinger at me, and said:

"Tut, tut, Valmont; we mustn't threaten, we mustn't threaten, you know;" but I went on without heeding him.

"Take for instance, Lord Semptam. You sold him a table for fifty pounds, on the instalment plan. He was to pay a pound a week, and in less than a year the debt was liquidated. But he is an absent-minded man, as all your clients are. That is why you came to me. I had answered the bogus Willoughby's advertisement. And so you kept on collecting and collecting for something more than three years. Now do you understand the charge?"

Mr. Macpherson's head during this accusation was held slightly inclined to one side. At first his face was clouded by the most clever imitation of anxious concentration of mind I had ever seen, and this was gradually cleared away by the dawn of awakening perception. When I had finished, an ingratiating smile hovered about his lips.

"Really, you know," he said, "that is rather a capital scheme. The absent-minded league, as one might call them. Most ingenious. Summertrees, if he had any sense of humour, which he hasn't, would be rather taken by the idea that his innocent fad for Christian Science had led him to be suspected of obtaining money under false pretences. But, really, there are no pretensions about the matter at all. As I understand it, I simply call and receive the money through the forgetfulness of the persons on my list, but where I think you would have both Summertrees and myself, if there was anything in your audacious theory, would be an indictment for conspiracy. Still, I quite see how the mistake arises. You have jumped to the conclusion that we sold nothing to Lord Semptam except that carved table three years ago. I have pleasure in pointing out to you that his lordship is a frequent customer of ours, and has had many things from us at one time or another. Sometimes he is in our debt; sometimes we are in his. We keep a sort of running contract with him by which he pays us a pound a week. He and several other customers deal on the same plan, and in return for an income that we can count upon, they get the first offer of anything in which they are supposed to be interested. As I have told you, we call these sheets in the office our visiting lists, but to make the visiting lists complete you need what we term our encyclopaedia. We call it that because it is in so many volumes; a volume for each year, running back I don't know how long. You will notice little figures here from time to time above the amount stated on this visiting list. These figures refer to the page of the encyclopaedia for the current year, and on that page is noted the new sale, and the amount of it, as it might be set down, say, in a ledger."

"That is a very entertaining explanation, Mr. Macpherson. I suppose this encyclopaedia, as you call it, is in the shop at Tottenham Court Road?"

"Oh, no, sir. Each volume of the encyclopaedia is self-locking. These books contain the real secret of our business, and they are kept in the safe at Mr. Summertrees' house in Park Lane. Take Lord Semptam's account, for instance. You will find in faint figures under a certain date, 102. If you turn to page 102 of the encyclopaedia for that year, you will then see a list of what Lord Semptam has bought, and the prices he was charged for them. It is really a very simple matter. If you will allow me to use your telephone for a moment, I will ask Mr. Summertrees, who has not yet begun dinner, to bring with him here the volume for 1893, and, within a quarter of an hour, you will be perfectly satisfied that everything is quite legitimate."

I confess that the young man's naturalness and confidence staggered me, the more so as I saw by the sarcastic smile on Hale's lips that he did not believe a single word spoken. A portable telephone stood on the table, and as Macpherson finished his explanation, he reached over and drew it towards him. Then Spenser Hale interfered.

"Excuse *me*," he said, "I'll do the telephoning. What is the call number of Mr. Summertrees?"

"140 Hyde Park."

Hale at once called up Central, and presently was answered from Park Lane. We heard him say:

"Is this the residence of Mr. Summertrees? Oh, is that you, Podgers? Is Mr. Summertrees in? Very well. This is Hale. I am in Valmont's flat—Imperial Flats—you know. Yes, where you went with me the other day. Very well, go to Mr. Summertrees, and say to him that Mr. Macpherson wants the encyclopaedia for 1893. Do you get that? Yes, encyclopaedia. Oh, he'll understand what it is. Mr. Macpherson. No, don't mention my name at all. Just say Mr. Macpherson wants the encyclopaedia for the year 1893, and that you are to bring it. Yes, you may tell him that Mr. Macpherson is at Imperial Flats, but don't mention my name at all. Exactly. As soon as he gives you the book, get into a cab, and come here as quickly as possible with it. If Summertrees doesn't want to let the book go, then tell him to come with you. If he won't do that, place him under arrest, and bring both him and the book here. All right. Be as quick as you can; we're waiting."

Macpherson made no protest against Hale's use of the telephone; he merely sat back in his chair with a resigned expression on his face which, if painted on canvas, might have been entitled "The Falsely Accused." When Hale rang off, Macpherson said:

"Of course you know your own business best, but if your man arrests Summertrees, he will make you the laughing-stock of London. There is such a thing as unjustifiable arrest, as well as getting money under false pretences, and Mr. Summertrees is not the man to forgive an insult. And then, if you will allow me to say so, the more I think over your absent-minded theory, the more absolutely grotesque it seems, and if the case ever gets into the newspapers, I am sure, Mr. Hale, you'll experience an uncomfortable half-hour with your chiefs at Scotland Yard."

"I'll take the risk of that, thank you," said Hale stubbornly.

"Am I to consider myself under arrest?" inquired the young man.

"No, sir."

"Then, if you will pardon me, I shall withdraw. Mr. Summertrees will show you everything you wish to see in his books, and can explain his business much more capably than I, because he knows more about it; therefore, gentlemen, I bid you goodnight."

"No you don't. Not just yet awhile," exclaimed Hale, rising to his feet simultaneously with the young man.

"Then I *am* under arrest," protested Macpherson.

"You're not going to leave this room until Podgers brings that book."

"Oh, very well," and he sat down again.

And now, as talking is dry work, I set out something to drink, a box of cigars, and a box of cigarettes. Hale mixed his favourite brew, but Macpherson, shunning the wine of his country, contented himself with a glass of plain mineral water, and lit a cigarette. Then he awoke my high regard by saying pleasantly as if nothing had happened:

"While we are waiting, Monsieur Valmont, may I remind you that you owe me five shillings?"

I laughed, took the coin from my pocket, and paid him, whereupon he thanked me.

"Are you connected with Scotland Yard, Monsieur Valmont?" asked Macpherson, with the air of a man trying to make conversation to bridge over a tedious interval; but before I could reply, Hale blurted out:

"Not likely!"

"You have no official standing as a detective, then, Monsieur Valmont?"

"None whatever," I replied quickly, thus getting in my oar ahead of Hale.

"This is a loss to our country," pursued this admirable young man, with evident sincerity.

I began to see I could make a good deal of so clever a fellow if he came under my tuition.

"The blunders of our police," he went on, "are something deplorable. If they would but take lessons in strategy, say, from France, their unpleasant duties would be so much more acceptably performed, with much less discomfort to their victims."

"France," snorted Hale in derision, "why, they call a man guilty there until he's proven innocent."

"Yes, Mr. Hale, and the same seems to be the case in Imperial Flats. You have quite made up your mind that Mr. Summertrees is guilty, and will not be content until he proves his innocence. I venture to predict that you will hear from him before long in a manner that may astonish you."

Hale grunted and looked at his watch. The minutes passed very slowly as we sat there smoking, and at last even I began to get uneasy. Macpherson, seeing our anxiety, said that when he came in the fog was almost as thick as it had been the week before, and that there might be some difficulty in getting a cab. Just as he was speaking the door was unlocked from the outside, and Podgers entered, bearing a thick volume in his hand. This he gave to his superior, who turned over its pages in amazement, and then looked at the back, crying:

"'Encyclopaedia of Sport, 1893'! What sort of a joke is this, Mr. Macpherson?"

There was a pained look on Mr. Macpherson's face as he reached forward and took the book. He said with a sigh:

"If you had allowed me to telephone, Mr. Hale, I should have made it perfectly plain to Summertrees what was wanted. I might have known this mistake was liable to occur. There is an increasing demand for out-of-date books of sport, and no doubt Mr. Summertrees thought this was what I meant. There is nothing for it but to send your man back to Park Lane and tell Mr. Summertrees that what we want is the locked volume of accounts for 1893, which we call the encyclopaedia. Allow me to write an order that will bring it. Oh, I'll show you what I have written before your man takes it," he said, as Hale stood ready to look over his shoulder.

On my notepaper he dashed off a request such as he had outlined, and handed it to Hale, who read it and gave it to Podgers.

"Take that to Summertrees, and get back as quickly as possible. Have you a cab at the door?"

"Yes, sir."

"Is it foggy outside?"

"Not so much, sir, as it was an hour ago. No difficulty about the traffic now, sir."

"Very well, get back as soon as you can."

Podgers saluted, and left with the book under his arm. Again the door was locked, and again we sat smoking in silence until the stillness was broken by the tinkle of the telephone. Hale put the receiver to his ear.

"Yes, this is the Imperial Flats. Yes. Valmont. Oh, yes; Macpherson is here. What? Out of what? Can't hear you. Out of print. What, the encyclopaedia's out of print? Who is that speaking? Dr. Willoughby; thanks."

Macpherson rose as if he would go to the telephone, but instead (and he acted so quietly that I did not notice what he was doing until the thing was done), he picked up the sheet which he called his visiting list, and walking quite without haste, held it in the glowing coals of the fireplace until it disappeared in a flash of flame up the chimney. I sprang to my feet indignant, but too late to make even a motion outwards saving the sheet. Macpherson regarded us both with that self-deprecatory smile which had several times lighted up his face.

"How dared you burn that sheet?" I demanded.

"Because, Monsieur Valmont, it did not belong to you; because you do not belong to Scotland Yard; because you stole it; because you had no right to it; and because you have no official standing in this country. If it had been in Mr. Hale's possession I should not have dared, as you put it, to destroy the sheet, but as this sheet was abstracted from my master's premises by you, an entirely unauthorised person, whom he would have been justified in shooting dead if he had found you housebreaking and you had resisted him on his discovery, I took the liberty of destroying the document. I have always held that these sheets should not have been kept, for, as has been the case, if they fell under the scrutiny of so intelligent a person as Eugène Valmont, improper inferences might have been drawn. Mr. Summertrees, however, persisted in keeping them, but made this concession, that if I ever telegraphed him or telephoned him the word 'Encyclopaedia,' he would at once burn these records, and he, on his part, was to telegraph or telephone to me 'The Encyclopaedia is out of print,' whereupon I would know that he had succeeded.

"Now, gentlemen, open this door, which will save me the trouble of forcing it. Either put me formally under arrest, or cease to restrict my liberty. I am very much obliged to Mr. Hale for telephoning, and I have made no protest to so gallant a host as Monsieur Valmont is, because of the locked door. However, the farce is now terminated. The proceedings I have sat through were entirely illegal, and if you will pardon me, Mr. Hale, they have been a little too

French to go down here in old England, or to make a report in the newspapers that would be quite satisfactory to your chiefs. I demand either my formal arrest, or the unlocking of that door."

In silence I pressed a button, and my man threw open the door. Macpherson walked to the threshold, paused, and looked back at Spenser Hale, who sat there silent as a sphinx.

"Good-evening, Mr. Hale."

There being no reply, he turned to me with the same ingratiating smile:

"Good-evening, Monsieur Eugène Valmont," he said, "I shall give myself the pleasure of calling next Wednesday at six for my five shillings."

THE GHOST WITH THE CLUB-FOOT

I

Celebrated critics have written with scorn of what they call "the long arm of coincidence" in fiction. Coincidence is supposed to be the device of a novelist who does not possess ingenuity enough to construct a book without it. In France our incomparable writers pay no attention to this, because they are gifted with a keener insight into real life than is the case with the British. The superb Charles Dickens, possibly as well known in France as he is wherever the English language is read, and who loved French soil and the French people, probably probed deeper into the intricacies of human character than any other novelist of modern times, and if you read his works, you will see that he continually makes use of coincidence. The experience that has come to me throughout my own strange and varied career convinces me that coincidence happens in real life with exceeding frequency, and this fact is especially borne in upon me when I set out to relate my conflict with the Rantremly ghost, which wrought startling changes upon the lives of two people, one an objectionable, domineering man, and the other a humble and crushed woman. Of course, there was a third person, and the consequences that came to him were the most striking of all, as you will learn if you do me the honour to read this account of the episode.

So far as coincidence is concerned, there was first the arrival of the newspaper clipping, then the coming of Sophia Brooks, and when that much-injured woman left my flat I wrote down this sentence on a sheet of paper:

"Before the week is out, I predict that Lord Rantremly himself will call to see me."

Next day my servant brought in the card of Lord Rantremly.

I must begin with the visit of Sophia Brooks, for though that comes second, yet I had paid no attention in particular to the newspaper clipping until the lady told her story. My man brought me a typewritten sheet of paper on which were inscribed the words:

"Sophia Brooks, Typewriting and Translating Office, First Floor, No. 51 Beaumont Street, Strand, London, W.C."

I said to my servant:

"Tell the lady as kindly as possible that I have no typewriting work to give out, and that, in fact, I keep a stenographer and typewriting machine on the premises."

A few moments later my man returned, and said the lady wished to see me, not about typewriting, but regarding a case in which she hoped to interest me. I was still in some hesitation about admitting her, for my transactions had now risen to a higher plane than when I was new to London. My expenses were naturally very heavy, and it was not possible for me, in justice to myself, to waste time in commissions from the poor, which even if they resulted successfully meant little money added to my banking account, and often nothing at all, because the client was unable to pay. As I remarked before, I possess a heart the most tender, and therefore must greatly to my grief, steel myself against the enlisting of my sympathy, which, alas! has frequently led to my financial loss. Still, sometimes the apparently poor are involved in matters of extreme importance, and England is so eccentric a country that one may find himself at fault if he closes his door too harshly. Indeed, ever since my servant, in the utmost good faith, threw downstairs the persistent and tattered beggar-man, who he learned later to his sorrow was actually his Grace the Duke of Ventnor, I have always cautioned my subordinates not to judge too hastily from appearances.

"Show the lady in," I said, and there came to me, hesitating, backward, abashed, a middle-aged woman, dressed with distressing plainness, when one thinks of the charming costumes to be seen on a Parisian boulevard. Her subdued manner was that of one to whom the world had been cruel. I rose, bowed profoundly, and placed a chair at her disposal, with the air I should have used if my caller had been a Royal Princess. I claim no credit for this; it is of my nature. There you behold Eugène Valmont. My visitor was a woman. *Voilà!*

"Madam," I said politely, "in what may I have the pleasure of serving you?"

The poor woman seemed for the moment confused, and was, I feared, on the verge of tears, but at last she spoke, and said:

"Perhaps you have read in the newspapers of the tragedy at Rantremly Castle?"

"The name, madam, remains in my memory, associated elusively with some hint of seriousness. Will you pardon me a moment?" and a vague thought that I had seen the castle mentioned either in a newspaper, or a clipping from one, caused me to pick up the latest bunch which had come from my agent. I am imbued with no vanity at all; still it is amusing to note what the newspapers say of one, and therefore I have subscribed to a clipping agency. In fact, I indulge in two subscriptions—one personal; the other calling for any pronouncement pertaining to the differences between England and France; for it is my determination yet to write a book on the comparative characteristics of the two people. I hold a theory that the English people are utterly incomprehensible to the rest of humanity, and this will be duly set out in my forthcoming volume.

I speedily found the clipping I was in search of. It proved to be a letter to the *Times*, and was headed: "Proposed Destruction of Rantremly Castle." The letter went on to say that this edifice was one of the most noted examples of Norman architecture in the north of England; that Charles II had hidden there for some days after his disastrous defeat at Worcester. Part of the castle had been battered down by Cromwell, and later it again proved the refuge of a Stuart when the Pretender made it a temporary place of conceal-ment. The new Lord Rantremly, it seemed, had determined to de-molish this ancient stronghold, so interesting architecturally and historically, and to build with its stones a modern residence. Against this act of vandalism the writer strongly protested, and suggested that England should acquire the power which France constantly exerts, in making an historical monument of an edifice so interwoven with the fortunes of the country.

"Well, madam," I said, "all this extract alludes to is the coming demolition of Rantremly Castle. Is that the tragedy of which you speak?"

"Oh no," she exclaimed; "I mean the death of the eleventh Lord Rantremly about six weeks ago. For ten years Lord Rantremly lived practically alone in the castle. Servants would not remain there because the place was haunted, and well it may be, for a terrible family the Rantremlys have been, and a cruel, as I shall be able to tell you. Up to a month and a half ago Lord Rantremly was waited on by a butler older than himself, and if possible, more wicked. One morning this old butler came up the stairs from the kitchen, with Lord Rantremly's breakfast on a silver tray, as was his cus-tom. His lordship always partook of breakfast in his own room. It is not known how the accident happened, as the old servant was going up the stairs instead of coming down, but the steps are very smooth and slippery, and without a carpet; at any rate, he seems to have fallen from the top to the bottom, and lay there with a bro-ken neck. Lord Rantremly, who was very deaf, seemingly did not hear the crash, and it is supposed that after ringing and ringing in vain, and doubtless working himself into a violent fit of temper— alas! too frequent an occurrence—the old nobleman got out of bed, and walked barefooted down the stair, coming at last upon the body of his ancient servant. There the man who arrived every morning to light the fires found them, the servant dead, and Lord Rantremly helpless from an attack of paralysis. The physicians say that only his eyes seemed alive, and they were filled with a great fear, and indeed that is not to be wondered at, after his wicked, wicked life.

His right hand was but partially disabled, and with that he tried to scribble something which proved indecipherable. And so he died, and those who attended him at his last moments say that if ever a soul had a taste of future punishment before it left this earth, it was the soul of Lord Rantremly as it shone through those terror-stricken eyes."

Here the woman stopped, with a catch in her breath, as if the fear of that grim death-bed had communicated itself to her. I interjected calmness into an emotional situation by remarking in a commonplace tone: "And it is the present Lord Rantremly who proposes to destroy the Castle, I suppose?"

"Yes."

"Is he the son of the late lord?"

"No; he is a distant relative. The branch of the family to which he belongs has been engaged in commerce, and, I believe, its members are very wealthy."

"Well, madam, no doubt this is all extremely interesting, and rather gruesome. In what way are you concerned in these occurrences?"

"Ten years ago I replied to an advertisement, there being required one who knew shorthand, who possessed a typewriting machine and a knowledge of French, to act as secretary to a nobleman. I was at that time twenty-three years old, and for two years had been trying to earn my living in London through the typing of manuscript. But I was making a hard struggle of it, so I applied for this position and got it. There are in the library of Rantremly Castle many documents relating to the Stuart exile in France. His lordship wished these documents sorted and catalogued, as well as copies taken of each. Many of the letters were in the French language, and these I was required to translate and type. It was a sombre place of residence, but the salary was good, and I saw before me work enough to keep me busy for years. Besides this, the task was extremely congenial, and I became absorbed in it, being young and romantically inclined. Here I seemed to live in the midst of these wonderful intrigues of long ago. Documents passed through my hands whose very possession at one period meant capital danger, bringing up even now visions of block, axe, and masked headsman. It seemed strange to me that so sinister a man as Lord Rantremly, who, I had heard, cared for nothing but drink and gambling, should have desired to promote this historical research, and, indeed, I soon found he felt nothing but contempt for it. However, he had undertaken it at the instance of his only son, then a young man of my own age, at Oxford University.

"Lord Rantremly at that time was sixty-five years old. His countenance was dark, harsh, and imperious, and his language brutal. He indulged in frightful outbursts of temper, but he paid so well for service that there was no lack of it, as there has been since the ghost appeared some years ago. He was very tall, and of commanding appearance, but had a deformity in the shape of a club-foot, and walked with the halting step of those so afflicted. There were at that time servants in plenty at the castle, for although a tradition existed that the ghost of the founder of the house trod certain rooms, this ghost, it was said, never demonstrated its presence when the living representative of the family was a man with a club-foot. Tradition further affirmed that if this club-footed ghost allowed its halting footsteps to be heard while the reigning lord possessed a similar deformity, the conjunction foreshadowed the passing of title and estates to a stranger. The ghost haunted the castle only when it was occupied by a descendant whose two feet were normal. It seems that the founder of the house was a club-footed man, and this disagreeable peculiarity often missed one generation, and sometimes two, while at other times both father and son had club-feet, as was the case with the late Lord Rantremly and the young man at Oxford. I am not a believer in the supernatural, of course, but nevertheless it is strange that within the past few years everyone residing in the castle has heard the club-footed ghost, and now title and estates descend to a family that were utter strangers to the Rantremlys."

"Well, madam, this also sounds most alluring, and were my time not taken up with affairs more material than those to which you allude, I should be content to listen all day, but as it is—" I spread my hands and shrugged my shoulders.

The woman with a deep sigh said:

"I am sorry to have taken so long, but I wished you to understand the situation, and now I will come direct to the heart of the case. I worked alone in the library, as I told you, much interested in what I was doing. The chaplain, a great friend of Lord Rantremly's son, and, indeed, a former tutor of his, assisted me with the documents that were in Latin, and a friendship sprang up between us. He was an elderly man, and extremely unworldly. Lord Rantremly never concealed his scorn of this clergyman, but did not interfere with him because of the son.

"My work went on very pleasantly up to the time that Reginald, the heir of his lordship, came down from Oxford. Then began the happiest days of a life that has been otherwise full of hardships and distress. Reginald was as different as possible from his father. In one respect only did he bear any resemblance to that terrible old man, and this resemblance was the deformity of a club-foot, a blemish which one soon forgot when one came to know the gentle and high-minded nature of the young man. As I have said, it was at his instance that Lord Rantremly had engaged me to set in order those historical papers. Reginald became enthusiastic at the progress I had made, and thus the young nobleman, the chaplain, and myself continued our work together with ever-increasing enthusiasm.

"To cut short a recital which must be trying to your patience, but which is necessary if you are to understand the situation, I may say that our companionship resulted in a proposal of marriage to me, which I, foolishly, perhaps, and selfishly, it may be, accepted. Reginald knew that his father would never consent, but we enlisted the sympathy of the chaplain, and he, mild, unworldly man, married us one day in the consecrated chapel of the castle.

"As I have told you, the house at that time contained many servants, and I think, without being sure, that the butler, whom I feared even more than Lord Rantremly himself, got some inkling of what was going forward. But, be that as it may, he and his lordship entered the chapel just as the ceremony was finished, and there followed an agonising scene. His lordship flung the ancient

chaplain from his place, and when Reginald attempted to interfere, the maddened nobleman struck his son full in the face with
his clenched fist, and my husband lay as one dead on the stone
floor of the chapel. By this time the butler had locked the doors,
and had rudely torn the vestments from the aged, half-insensible
clergyman, and with these tied him hand and foot. All this took
place in a very few moments, and I stood there as one paralysed,
unable either to speak or scream, not that screaming would have
done me any good in that horrible place of thick walls. The butler
produced a key, and unlocked a small, private door at the side of
the chapel which led from the apartments of his lordship to the
family pew. Then taking my husband by feet and shoulders, Lord
Rantremly and the butler carried him out, locking the door, and
leaving the clergyman and me prisoners in the chapel. The rever-
end old gentleman took no notice of me. He seemed to be dazed,
and when at last I found my voice and addressed him, he merely
murmured over and over texts of Scripture pertaining to the marriage service.

"In a short time I heard the key turn again in the lock of the
private door, and the butler entered alone. He unloosened the
bands around the clergyman's knees, escorted him out, and once
more locked the door behind him. A third time that terrible servant came back, grasped me roughly by the wrist, and without a
word dragged me with him, along a narrow passage, up a stair,
and finally to the main hall, and so to my lord's private study, which
adjoined his bedroom, and there on a table I found my typewriting
machine brought up from the library.

"I have but the most confused recollection of what took place.
I am not a courageous woman, and was in mortal terror both of
Lord Rantremly and his attendant. His lordship was pacing up and
down the room, and, when I came in, used the most unseemly language to me; then ordered me to write at his dictation, swearing
that if I did not do exactly as he told me, he would finish his son,
as he put it. I sat down at the machine, and he dictated a letter to
himself, demanding two thousand pounds to be paid to me, otherwise I should claim that I was the wife of his son, secretly married.

This, placing pen and ink before me, he compelled me to sign, and when I had done so, pleading to be allowed to see my husband, if only for a moment, I thought he was going to strike me, for he shook his fist in my face, and used words which were appalling to hear. That was the last I ever saw of Lord Rantremly, my husband, the clergyman, or the butler. I was at once sent off to London with my belongings, the butler himself buying my ticket, and flinging a handful of sovereigns into my lap as the train moved out."

Here the woman stopped, buried her face in her hands, and began to weep.

"Have you done nothing about this for the past ten years?"

She shook her head.

"What could I do?" she gasped. "I had little money, and no friends. Who would believe my story? Besides this, Lord Rantremly retained possession of a letter, signed by myself, that would convict me of attempted blackmail, while the butler would swear to anything against me."

"You have no marriage certificate, of course?"

"No."

"What has become of the clergyman?"

"I do not know."

"And what of Lord Rantremly's son?"

"It was announced that he had gone on a voyage to Australia for his health in a sailing ship, which was wrecked on the African coast, and everyone on board lost."

"What is your own theory?"

"Oh, my husband was killed by the blow given him in the chapel."

"Madam, that does not seem credible. A blow from the fist seldom kills."

"But he fell backwards, and his head struck the sharp stone steps at the foot of the altar. I know my husband was dead when the butler and his father carried him out."

"You think the clergyman was also murdered?"

"I am sure of it. Both master and servant were capable of any crime or cruelty."

"You received no letters from the young man?"

"No. You see, during our short friendship we were constantly together, and there was no need of correspondence."

"Well, madam, what do you expect of me?"

"I hoped you would investigate, and find perhaps where Reginald and the clergyman are buried. I realise that I have no proof, but in that way my strange story will be corroborated."

I leaned back in my chair and looked at her. Truth to tell, I only partially credited her story myself, and yet I was positive she believed every word of it. Ten years brooding on a fancied injustice by a woman living alone, and doubtless often in dire poverty, had mixed together the actual and the imaginary until now, what had possibly been an aimless flirtation on the part of the young man, unexpectedly discovered by the father, had formed itself into the tragedy which she had told me.

"Would it not be well," I suggested, "to lay the facts before the present Lord Rantremly?"

"I have done so," she answered simply.

"With what result?"

"His lordship said my story was preposterous. In examining the late lord's private papers, he discovered the letter which I typed and signed. He said very coldly that the fact that I had waited until everyone who could corroborate or deny my story was dead, united with the improbability of the narrative itself, would very likely consign me to prison if I made public a statement so incredible."

"Well, you know, madam, I think his lordship is right."

"He offered me an annuity of fifty pounds, which I refused."

"In that refusal, madam, I think you are wrong. If you take my advice, you will accept the annuity."

The woman rose slowly to her feet.

"It is not money I am after," she said, "although, God knows, I have often been in sore need of it. But I am the Countess of Rantremly, and I wish my right to that name acknowledged. My character has been under an impalpable shadow for ten years. On several occasions mysterious hints have reached me that in some manner I left the castle under a cloud. If Lord Rantremly will destroy the letter which I was compelled to write under duress, and if he will give me written acknowledgment that there was nothing to be alleged against me during my stay in the castle, he may enjoy his money in peace for all of me. I want none of it."

"Have you asked him to do this?"

"Yes. He refuses to give up or destroy the letter, although I told him in what circumstances it had been written. But, desiring to be fair, he said he would allow me a pound a week for life, entirely through his own generosity."

"And this you refused?"

"Yes, I refused."

"Madam, I regret to say that I cannot see my way to do anything with regard to what I admit is very unjust usage. We have absolutely nothing to go upon except your unsupported word. Lord Rantremly was perfectly right when he said no one would credit your story. I could not go down to Rantremly Castle and make investigations there. I should have no right upon the premises at all, and would get into instant trouble as an interfering trespasser. I beg you to heed my advice, and accept the annuity."

Sophia Brooks, with that mild obstinacy of which I had received indications during her recital, slowly shook her head.

"You have been very kind to listen for so long," she said, and then, with a curt "Good-day!" turned and left the room. On the sheet of paper underneath her address, I wrote this prophecy: "Before the week is out, I predict that Lord Rantremly himself will call to see me."

II

Next morning, at almost the same hour that Miss Brooks had arrived the day before, the Earl of Rantremly's card was brought in to me.

His lordship proved to be an abrupt, ill-mannered, dapper business man; purse-proud, I should call him, as there was every reason he should be, for he had earned his own fortune. He was doubtless equally proud of his new title, which he was trying to live up to, assuming now and then a haughty, domineering attitude, and again relapsing into the keen, incisive manner of the man of affairs; shrewd financial sense waging a constant struggle with the glamour of an ancient name. I am sure he would have shone to better advantage either as a financier or as a nobleman, but the combination was too much for him. I formed an instinctive dislike to the man, which probably would not have happened had he been wearing the title for twenty years, or had I met him as a business man, with no thought of the aristocratic honour awaiting him. There seemed nothing in common between him and the former holder of the title. He had keen, ferrety eyes, a sharp financial nose, a thin-lipped line of mouth which indicated little of human kindness. He was short of stature, but he did not possess the club-foot, which was one advantage. He seated himself before I had time to offer him a chair, and kept on his hat in my presence, which he would not have done if he had either been a genuine nobleman or a courteous business man.

"I am Lord Rantremly," he announced pompously, which announcement was quite unnecessary, because I held his card in my hand.

"Quite so, my lord. And you have come to learn whether or no I can lay the ghost in that old castle to the north which bears your name?"

"Well, I'm blessed!" cried his lordship, agape. "How could you guess that?"

"Oh, it is not a guess, but rather a choice of two objects, either of which might bring you to my rooms. I chose the first motive because I thought you might prefer to arrange the second problem with your solicitor, and he doubtless told you that Miss Sophia Brooks's claim was absurd; that you were quite right in refusing to give up or destroy the typewritten letter she had signed ten years ago, and that it was weakness on your part, without consulting him, to offer her an annuity of fifty-two pounds a year."

Long before this harangue was finished, which I uttered in an easy and nonchalant tone of voice, as if reciting something that everybody knew, his lordship stood on his feet again, staring at me like a man thunderstruck. This gave me the opportunity of exercising that politeness which his abrupt entrance and demeanour had forestalled. I rose, and bowing, said:

"I pray you to be seated, my lord."

He dropped into the chair, rather than sat down in it.

"And now," I continued, with the utmost suavity, stretching forth my hand, "may I place your hat on this shelf out of the way, where it will not incommode you during our discourse?"

Like a man in a dream, he took his hat from his head, and passively handed it to me, and after placing it in safety I resumed my chair with the comfortable feeling that his lordship and I were much nearer a plane of equality than when he entered the room.

"How about the ghost with a club-foot, my lord?" said I genially. "May I take it that in the City, that sensible, commercial portion of London, no spirits are believed in except those sold over the bars?"

"If you mean," began his lordship, struggling to reach his dignity once more, "if you mean to ask if there is any man fool enough to place credit in the story of a ghost, I answer no. I am a practical man, sir. I now possess in the north property representing, in farming lands, in shooting rights, and what not, a locked-up capital of many a thousand pounds. As you seem to know everything, sir, perhaps you are aware that I propose to build a modern mansion on the estate."

"Yes; I saw the letter in the *Times*."

"Very well, sir. It has come to a fine pass if, in this country of law and the rights of property, a man may not do what he pleases with his own."

"I think, my lord, cases may be cited where the decisions of your courts have shown a man may not do what he likes with his own. Nevertheless, I am quite certain that if you level Rantremly Castle with the ground, and build a modern mansion in its place, the law will not hinder you."

"I should hope not, sir, I should hope not," said his lordship gruffly. "Nevertheless, I am not one who wishes to ride roughshod over public opinion.

"I am chairman of several companies which depend more or less on popular favour for success. I deplore unnecessary antagonism. Technically, I might assert my right to destroy this ancient stronghold tomorrow if I wished to do so, and if that right were seriously disputed, I should, of course, stand firm. But it is not seriously disputed. The British nation, sir, is too sensible a people to object to the removal of an antiquated structure that has long outlived its usefulness, and the erection of a mansion replete with all modern improvements would be a distinct addition to the country, sir. A few impertinent busybodies protest against the demolition of Rantremly Castle, but that is all."

"Ah, then you do intend to destroy it?" I rejoined, and it is possible that a touch of regret was manifest in my tones.

"Not just at present; not until this vulgar clamour has had time to subside. Nevertheless, as a business man, I am forced to recognise that a large amount of unproductive capital is locked up in that property."

"And why is it locked up?"

"Because of an absurd belief that the place is haunted. I could let it tomorrow at a good figure, if it were not for that rumour."

"But surely sensible men do not pay any attention to such a rumour."

"Sensible men may not, but sensible men are often married to silly women, and the women object. It is only the other day that I was in negotiation with Bates, of Bates, Sturgeon and Bates, a very wealthy man, quite able and willing to pay the price I demanded. He cared nothing about the alleged ghost, but his family absolutely refused to have anything to do with the place, and so the arrangement fell through."

"What is your theory regarding this ghost, my lord?"

He answered me with some impatience.

"How can a sane man hold a theory about a ghost? I can, however, advance a theory regarding the noises heard in the castle. For years that place has been the resort of questionable characters."

"I understand the Rantremly family is a very old one," I commented innocently, but his lordship did not notice the innuendo.

"Yes, we are an old family," he went on with great complacency. "The castle, as perhaps you are aware, is a huge, ramshackle place, honeycombed underneath with cellars. I dare say in the old days some of these cellars and caves were the resort of smugglers, and the receptacle of their contraband wares, doubtless with the full knowledge of my ancestors, who, I regret to admit, as a business man, were not too particular in their respect for law. I make no doubt that the castle is now the refuge of a number of dangerous characters, who, knowing the legends of the place, frighten away fools by impersonating ghosts."

"You wish me to uncover their retreat, then?"

"Precisely."

"Could I get accommodation in the castle itself?"

"Lord bless you, no! Nor within two miles of it. You might secure bed and board at the porter's lodge, perhaps, or in the village, which is three miles distant."

"I should prefer to live in the castle night and day, until the mystery is solved."

"Ah, you are a practical man. That is a very sensible resolution. But you can persuade no one in that neighbourhood to bear you company. You would need to take some person down with you from London, and the chances are, that person will not stay long."

"Perhaps, my lord, if you used your influence, the chief of police in the village might allow a constable to bear me company. I do not mind roughing it in the least, but I should like someone to prepare my meals, and to be on hand in case of a struggle, should your surmise concerning the ghost prove correct."

"I regret to inform you," said his lordship, "that the police in that barbarous district are as superstitious as the peasantry. I, myself, told the chief constable my theory, and for six weeks he has been trying to run down the miscreants, who, I am sure, are making a rendezvous of the castle. Would you believe it, sir, that the constabulary, after a few nights' experience in the castle, threatened to resign in a body if they were placed on duty at Rantremly? They said they heard groans and shrieks, and the measured beat of a club-foot on the oaken floors. Perfectly absurd, of course, but there you are! Why, I cannot even get a charwoman or labourer to clear up the evidences of the tragedy which took place there six weeks ago. The beds are untouched, the broken china and the silver tray lie today at the foot of the stairway, and everything remains just as it was when the inquest took place."

"Very well, my lord, the case presents many difficulties, and so, speaking as one business man to another, you will understand that my compensation must be correspondingly great."

All the assumed dignity which straightened up this man whenever I addressed him as "my lord," instantly fell from him when I enunciated the word "compensation." His eyes narrowed, and all the native shrewdness of an adept skinflint appeared in his face. I shall do him the justice to say that he drove the very best bargain he could with me, and I, on my part, very deftly concealed from him the fact that I was so much interested in the affair that I should have gone down to Rantremly for nothing rather than forgo the privilege of ransacking Rantremly Castle.

When the new earl had taken his departure, walking to the door with the haughty air of a nobleman, then bowing to me with the affability of a business man, I left my flat, took a cab, and speedily found myself climbing the stair to the first floor of 51 Beaumont Street, Strand. As I paused at the door on which were painted the words, "S. Brooks, Stenography, Typewriting, Translation," I heard the rapid click-click of a machine inside. Knocking at the door the writing ceased, and I was bidden to enter. The room was but meagrely furnished, and showed scant signs of prosperity. On a small side-table, clean, but uncovered, the breakfast dishes, washed, but not yet put away, stood, and the kettle on the hob by the dying fire led me to infer that the typewriting woman was her own cook. I suspected that the awkward-looking sofa which partly occupied one side of the room, concealed a bed. By the lone front window stood the typewriting machine on a small stand, and in front of it sat the woman who had visited me the morning before. She was now gazing at me, probably hoping I was a customer, for there was no recognition in her eyes.

"Good-morning, Lady Rantremly," was my greeting, which caused her to spring immediately to her feet, with a little exclamation of surprise.

"Oh," she said at last, "you are Monsieur Valmont. Excuse me that I am so stupid. Will you take a chair?"

"Thank you, madam. It is I who should ask to be excused for so unceremonious a morning call. I have come to ask you a question. Can you cook?"

The lady looked at me with some surprise, mingled perhaps with so much of indignation as such a mild person could assume. She did not reply, but, glancing at the kettle, and then turning towards the breakfast dishes on the table by the wall, a slow flush of colour suffused her wan cheeks.

"My lady," I said at last, as the silence became embarrassing, "you must pardon the impulse of a foreigner who finds himself constantly brought into conflict with prejudices which he fails to understand. You are perhaps offended at my question. The last person of whom I made that inquiry was the young and beautiful Madame la Comtesse de Valérie-Moberanne, who enthusiastically clapped her hands with delight at the compliment, and replied impulsively:

"'Oh, Monsieur Valmont, let me compose for you an omelette which will prove a dream,' and she did. One should not forget that Louis XVIII himself cooked the *truffes à la purée d'ortolans* that caused the Duc d'Escars, who partook of the royal dish, to die of an indigestion. Cooking is a noble, yes, a regal art. I am a Frenchman, my lady, and, like all my countrymen, regard the occupation of a *cuisinière* as infinitely superior to the manipulation of that machine, which is your profession, or the science of investigation, which is mine."

"Sir," she said, quite unmollified by my harangue, speaking with a lofty pride which somehow seemed much more natural than that so intermittently assumed by my recent visitor, "Sir, have you come to offer me a situation as cook?"

"Yes, madam, at Rantremly Castle."

"You are going there?" she demanded, almost breathlessly.

"Yes, madam, I leave on the ten o'clock train tomorrow morning. I am commissioned by Lord Rantremly to investigate the supposed presence of the ghost in that mouldering dwelling. I am allowed to bring with me whatever assistants I require, and am assured that no one in the neighbourhood can be retained who dare sleep in the castle. You know the place very well, having lived there, so I shall be glad of your assistance if you will come. If there is any person whom you can trust, and who is not afraid of ghosts, I shall be delighted to escort you both to Rantremly Castle tomorrow."

"There is an old woman," she said, "who comes here to clear up my room, and do whatever I wish done. She is so deaf that she will hear no ghosts, and besides, monsieur, she can cook."

I laughed in acknowledgment of this last sly hit at me, as the English say.

"That will do excellently," I replied, rising, and placing a ten-pound note before her. "I suggest, madam, that you purchase with this anything you may need. My man has instructions to send by passenger train a huge case of provisions, which should arrive there before us. If you could make it convenient to meet me at Euston Station about a quarter of an hour before the train leaves, we may be able to discover all you wish to know regarding the mystery of Rantremly Castle."

Sophia Brooks accepted the money without demur, and thanked me. I could see that her thin hands were trembling with excitement as she put the crackling banknote into her purse.

III

Darkness was coming on next evening before we were installed in the grim building, which at first sight seemed more like a fortress than a residence. I had telegraphed from London to order a wagonette for us, and in this vehicle we drove to the police station, where I presented the written order from Lord Rantremly for the keys of the castle. The chief constable himself, a stolid, taciturn person, exhibited, nevertheless, some interest in my mission, and he was good enough to take the fourth seat in the wagonette, and accompany us through the park to the castle, returning in that conveyance to the village as nightfall approached, and I could not but notice that this grave official betrayed some uneasiness to get off before dusk had completely set in. Silent as he was, I soon learned that he entirely disbelieved Lord Rantremly's theory that the castle harboured dangerous characters, yet so great was his inherent respect for the nobility that I could not induce him to dispute with any decisiveness his lordship's conjecture. It was plain to be seen, however, that the chief constable believed implicitly in the club-footed ghost. I asked him to return the next morning, as I should spend the night in investigation, and might possibly have some questions to ask him, questions which none but the chief constable could answer. The good man promised, and left us rather hurriedly, the driver of the wagonette galloping his horse down the long, sombre avenue towards the village outside the gates.

I found Sophia Brooks but a doleful companion, and of very little assistance that evening. She seemed overcome by her remembrances. She had visited the library where her former work was done, doubtless the scene of her brief love episode, and she returned with red eyes and trembling chin, telling me haltingly that the great tome from which she was working ten years ago, and which had been left open on the solid library table, was still there exactly as she had placed it before being forced to abandon her work. For a decade apparently no one had entered that library. I could not but sympathise with the poor lady, thus revisiting, almost herself like a ghost, the haunted arena of her short happiness. But though she proved so dismal a companion, the old woman who came with her was a treasure. Having lived all her life in some semi-slum near the Strand, and having rarely experienced more than a summer's-day glimpse of the country, the long journey had delighted her, and now this rambling old castle in the midst of the forest seemed to realise all the dreams which a perusal of halfpenny fiction had engendered in her imagination. She lit a fire, and cooked for us a very creditable supper, bustling about the place, singing to herself in a high key.

Shortly after supper Sophia Brooks, exhausted as much by her emotions and memories as by her long journey of that day, retired to rest. After being left to myself I smoked some cigarettes, and finished a bottle of superb claret which stood at my elbow. A few

hours before I had undoubtedly fallen in the estimation of the stolid
constable when, instead of asking him questions regarding the tragedy, I had inquired the position of the wine cellar, and obtained
possession of the key that opened its portal. The sight of bin after
bin of dust-laden, cobwebbed bottles, did more than anything else
to reconcile me to my lonely vigil. There were some notable vin-
tages represented in that dismal cavern.

It was perhaps half-past ten or eleven o'clock when I began my
investigations. I had taken the precaution to provide myself with
half a dozen so-called electric torches before I left London. These
give illumination for twenty or thirty hours steadily, and much
longer if the flash is used only now and then. The torch is a thick
tube, perhaps a foot and a half long, with a bull's-eye of glass at
one end. By pressing a spring the electric rays project like the illumination of an engine's headlight. A release of the spring causes
instant darkness. I have found this invention useful in that it con-
centrates the light on any particular spot desired, leaving all the
surroundings in gloom, so that the mind is not distracted, even
unconsciously, by the eye beholding more than is necessary at the
moment. One pours a white light over any particular substance as
water is poured from the nozzle of a hose.

The great house was almost painfully silent. I took one of these
torches, and went to the foot of the grand staircase where the
wicked butler had met his death. There, as his lordship had said,
lay the silver tray, and nearby a silver jug, a pair of spoons, a knife
and fork, and scattered all around the fragments of broken plates,
cups, and saucers. With an exclamation of surprise at the stupidity of the researchers who had preceded me, I ran up the stair two
steps at a time, turned to the right, and along the corridor until I
came to the room occupied by the late earl. The coverings of the
bed lay turned down just as they were when his lordship sprang to
the floor, doubtless, in spite of his deafness, having heard faintly
the fatal crash at the foot of the stairs. A great oaken chest stood
at the head of the bed, perhaps six inches from the wall. Leaning
against this chest at the edge of the bed inclined a small, round
table, and the cover of the table had slipped from its sloping

surface until it partly concealed the chest lid. I mounted on this carven box of old black oak and directed the rays of electric light into the chasm between it and the wall. Then I laughed aloud, and was somewhat startled to hear another laugh directly behind me. I jumped down on the floor again, and swung round my torch like a searchlight on a battleship at sea. There was no human presence in that chamber except myself. Of course, after my first moment of surprise, I realised that the laugh was but an echo of my own. The old walls of the old house were like sounding-boards. The place resembled an ancient fiddle, still tremulous with the music that had been played on it. It was easy to understand how a superstitious population came to believe in its being haunted; in fact, I found by experiment that if one trod quickly along the uncovered floor of the corridor, and stopped suddenly, one seemed to hear the sound of steps still going on.

I now returned to the stair head, and examined the bare polished boards with most gratifying results. Amazed at having learnt so much in such a short time, I took from my pocket the paper on which the dying nobleman had attempted to write with his half-paralysed hand. The chief constable had given the document to me, and I sat on the stair head, spread it out on the floor and scrutinised it. It was all but meaningless. Apparently two words and the initial letter of a third had been attempted. Now, however grotesque a piece of writing may be, you can sometimes decipher it by holding it at various angles, as those puzzles are solved which remain a mystery when gazed at direct. By partially closing the eyes you frequently catch the intent, as in those pictures where a human figure is concealed among the outlines of trees and leaves. I held the paper at arm's length, and with the electric light gleaming upon it, examined it at all angles, with eyes wide open, and eyes half closed. At last, inclining it away from me, I saw that the words were intended to mean, "The Secret." The secret, of course, was what he was trying to impart, but he had apparently got no further than the title of it. Deeply absorbed in my investigation, I was never more startled in my life than to hear in the stillness down the corridor the gasped words, "Oh, God!"

I swept round my light, and saw leaning against the wall, in an almost fainting condition, Sophia Brooks, her eyes staring like those of a demented person, and her face white as any ghost's could have been. Wrapped round her was a dressing-gown. I sprang to my feet.

"What are you doing there?" I cried.

"Oh, is that you, Monsieur Valmont? Thank God, thank God! I thought I was going insane. I saw a hand, a bodiless hand, holding a white sheet of paper."

"The hand was far from bodiless, madam, for it belonged to me. But why are you here? It must be near midnight."

"It *is* midnight," answered the woman; "I came here because I heard my husband call me three times distinctly, 'Sophia, Sophia, Sophia!' just like that."

"Nonsense, madam," I said, with an asperity I seldom use where the fair sex is concerned; but I began to see that this hysterical creature was going to be in the way during a research that called for coolness and calmness. I was sorry I had invited her to come. "Nonsense, madam, you have been dreaming."

"Indeed, Monsieur Valmont, I have not. I have not even been asleep, and I heard the words quite plainly. You must not think I am either mad or superstitious."

I thought she was both, and next moment she gave further evidence of it, running suddenly forward, and clutching me by the arm.

"Listen! listen!" she whispered. "You hear nothing?"

"Nonsense!" I cried again, almost roughly for my patience was at an end, and I wished to go on with my inquiry undisturbed.

"Hist, hist!" she whispered; "listen!" holding up her finger. We both stood like statues, and suddenly I felt that curious creeping of the scalp which shows that even the most civilised among us have not yet eliminated superstitious fear. In the tense silence I heard someone slowly coming up the stair; I heard the halting step of a lame man. In the tension of the moment I had allowed the light to go out; now recovering myself, I pressed the spring, and waved its rays backward and forward down the stairway. The space was entirely empty, yet the hesitating footsteps approached us, up and up. I could almost have sworn on which step they last struck. At this interesting moment Sophia Brooks uttered a piercing shriek and collapsed into my arms, sending the electric torch rattling down the steps, and leaving us in impenetrable darkness. Really, I profess myself to be a gallant man, but there are situations which have a tendency to cause annoyance. I carried the limp creature cautiously down the stairs, fearing the fate of the butler, and at last got her into the dining-room, where I lit a candle, which gave a light less brilliant, perhaps, but more steady than my torch. I dashed some water in her face, and brought her to her senses, then uncorking another bottle of wine, I bade her drink a glassful, which she did.

"What was it?" she whispered.

"Madam, I do not know. Very possibly the club-footed ghost of Rantremly."

"Do you believe in ghosts, Monsieur Valmont?"

"Last night I did not, but at this hour I believe in only one thing, which is that it is time everyone was asleep."

She rose to her feet at this, and with a tremulous little laugh apologised for her terror, but I assured her that for the moment there were two panic-stricken persons at the stair head. Taking the candle, and recovering my electric torch, which luckily was uninjured by its roll down the incline the butler had taken, I escorted the lady to the door of her room, and bade her good-night, or rather, good-morning.

The rising sun dissipated a slight veil of mist which hung over the park, and also dissolved, so far as I was concerned, the phantoms which my imagination had conjured up at midnight. It was about half-past ten when the chief constable arrived. I flatter myself I put some life into that unimaginative man before I was done with him.

"What made you think that the butler was mounting the stair when he fell?"

"He was going up with my lord's breakfast," replied the chief.

"Then did it not occur to you that if such were the case, the silver pitcher would not have been empty, and, besides the broken dishes, there would have been the rolls, butter, toast, or what not, strewn about the floor?"

The chief constable opened his eyes.

"There was no one else for him to bring breakfast to," he objected.

"That is where you are very much mistaken. Bring me the boots the butler wore."

"He did not wear boots, sir. He wore a pair of cloth slippers."

"Do you know where they are?"

"Yes; they are in the boot closet."

"Very well, bring them out, examine their soles, and sticking in one of them you will find a short sliver of pointed oak."

The constable, looking slightly more stupefied than ever, brought the slippers, and I heard him ejaculate: "Well, I'm blowed!" as he approached me. He handed me the slippers soles upward, and there, as I have stated, was the fragment of oak, which I pulled out.

"Now, if you take this piece of oak to the top of the stair, you will see that it fits exactly a slight interstice at the edge of one of the planks. It is as well to keep one's eyes open, constable, when investigating a case like this."

"Well, I'm blowed!" he said again, as we walked up the stair together.

I showed him that the sliver taken from the slipper fitted exactly the interstice I had indicated.

"Now," said I to him, "the butler was not going up the stairs, but was coming down. When he fell headlong he must have made a fearful clatter. Shuffling along with his burden, his slipper was impaled by this sliver, and the butler's hands being full, he could not save himself, but went head foremost down the stair. The startling point, however, is the fact that he was not carrying my lord's breakfast to him, or taking it away from him, but that there is someone else in the castle for whom he was caterer. Who is that person?"

"I'm blessed if I know," said the constable, "but I think you are wrong there. He may not have been carrying up the breakfast, but he certainly was taking away the tray, as is shown by the empty dishes, which you have just a moment ago pointed out."

"No, constable; when his lordship heard the crash, and sprang impulsively from his bed, he upset the little table on which had been placed his own tray; it shot over the oaken chest at the head of the bed, and if you look between it and the wall you will find tray, dishes, and the remnants of a breakfast."

"Well, I'm blessed!" exclaimed the chief constable once again.

"The main point of all this," I went on calmly, "is not the disaster to the butler, nor even the shock to his lordship, but the fact that the tray the serving man carried brought food to a prisoner, who probably for six weeks has been without anything to eat."

"Then," said the constable, "he is a dead man."

"I find it easier," said I, "to believe in a living man than in a dead man's ghost. I think I heard his footsteps at midnight, and they seemed to me the footsteps of a person very nearly exhausted. Therefore, constable, I have awaited your arrival with some impatience. The words his late lordship endeavoured to write on the paper were 'The Secret.' I am sure that the hieroglyphics with which he ended his effort stood for the letter 'R,' and if he finished his sentence, it would have stood: 'The secret room.' Now, constable, it is a matter of legend that a secret room exists in this castle. Do you know where it is?"

"No one knows where the secret room is, or the way to enter it, except the Lords of Rantremly."

"Well, I can assure you that the Lord of Rantremly who lives in London knows nothing about it. I have been up and about since daylight, taking some rough measurements by stepping off distances. I surmise that the secret room is to the left of this stairway. Probably a whole suite of rooms exists, for there is certainly a stair coinciding with this one, and up that stair at midnight I heard a club-footed man ascend. Either that, or the ghost that has frightened you all, and, as I have said, I believe in the man."

Here the official made the first sensible remark I had yet heard him utter:

"If the walls are so thick that a prisoner's cry has not been heard, how could you hear his footsteps, which make much less noise?"

"That is very well put, constable, and when the same thing occurred to me earlier this morning, I began to study the architecture of this castle. In the first place, the entrance hall is double as wide at the big doors as it is near the stairway. If you stand with your back to the front door you will at once wonder why the builders made this curious and unnecessary right angle, narrowing the farther part of the hall to half its width. Then, as you gaze at the stair, and see that marvellous carved oak newel post standing like a monumental column, you guess, if you have any imagination, that the stairway, like the hall, was once double as wide as it is now. We are seeing only half of it, and doubtless we shall find a similar newel post within the hidden room. You must remember, constable, that these secret apartments are no small added chambers. Twice they have sheltered a king."

The constable's head bent low at the mention of royalty. I saw that his insular prejudice against me and my methods was vanishing, and that he had come to look upon me with greater respect than was shown at first.

"The walls need not be thick to be impenetrable to sound. Two courses of brick, and a space between filled with deafening would do it. The secret apartment has been cut off from the rest of the house since the castle was built, and was not designed by the original architect. The partition was probably built in a hurry to fulfil a pressing need, and it was constructed straight up the middle of the stair, leaving the stout planks intact, each step passing thus, as it were, through the wall. Now, when a man walks up the secret stairway, his footsteps reverberate until one would swear that some unseen person was treading the visible boards on the outside."

"By Jove!" said the constable, in an awed tone of voice.

"Now, officer, I have here a pickaxe and a crowbar. I propose that we settle the question at once."

But to this proposal the constable demurred.

"You surely would not break the wall without permission from his lordship in London?"

"Constable, I suspect there is no Lord Rantremly in London, and that we will find a very emaciated but genuine Lord Rantremly within ten feet of us. I need not tell you that if you are instrumental in his immediate rescue without the exercise of too much red tape, your interests will not suffer because you the more speedily brought food and drink to the lord paramount of your district."

"Right you are," cried the constable, with an enthusiasm for which I was not prepared. "Where shall we begin?"

"Oh, anywhere; this wall is all false from the entrance hall to some point up here. Still, as the butler was carrying the meal upstairs I think we shall save time if we begin on the landing."

I found the constable's brawn much superior to his brain. He worked like a *sans-culotte* on a barricade. When we had torn down part of the old oak panelling, which it seemed such a pity to mutilate with axe and crowbar, we came upon a brick wall, that quickly gave way before the strength of the constable. Then we pulled out some substance like matting, and found a second brick wall, beyond which was a further shell of panelling. The hole we made revealed nothing but darkness inside, and although we shouted, there was no answer. At last, when we had hewn it large enough for a man to enter, I took with me an electric torch, and stepped inside, the constable following, with crowbar still in hand. I learned, as I had surmised, that we were in the upper hall of a staircase nearly as wide as the one on the outside. A flash of the light showed a door corresponding with the fireplace of the upper landing, and this door not being locked, we entered a large room, rather dimly lighted by strongly barred windows that gave into a blind courtyard, of which there had been no indication heretofore, either outside or inside the castle. Broken glass crunched under our feet, and I saw that the floor was strewn with wine bottles whose necks had been snapped off to save the pulling of the cork. On a mattress at the farther end of the room lay a man with gray hair, and shaggy, unkempt iron-gray beard. He seemed either asleep or dead, but when I turned my electric light full on his face he proved to be still alive, for he rubbed his eyes languidly, and groaned, rather than spoke:

"Is that you at last, you beast of a butler? Bring me something to eat, in Heaven's name!"

I shook him wider awake. He seemed to be drowsed with drink, and was fearfully emaciated. When I got him on his feet, I noticed then the deformity that characterised one of them. We assisted him through the aperture, and down into the dining-room, where he cried out continually for something to eat, but when we placed food before him, he could scarcely touch it. He became more like a human being when he had drunk two glasses of wine, and I saw at once he was not as old as his gray hair seemed to indicate. There was a haunted look in his eyes, and he watched the door as if apprehensive.

"Where is that butler?" he asked at last.

"Dead," I replied.

"Did I kill him?"

"No; he fell down the stairway and broke his neck."

The man laughed harshly.

"Where is my father?"

"Who is your father?"

"Lord Rantremly."

"He is dead also."

"How came he to die?"

"He died from a stroke of paralysis on the morning the butler was killed."

The rescued man made no comment on this, but turned and ate a little more of his food. Then he said to me:

"Do you know a girl named Sophia Brooks?"

"Yes. For ten years she thought you dead."

"Ten years! Good God, do you mean to say I've been in there only ten years? Why, I'm an old man. I must be sixty at least."

"No; you're not much over thirty."

"Is Sophia—" He stopped, and the haunted look came into his eyes again.

"No. She is all right, and she is here."

"Here?"

"Somewhere in the grounds. I sent her and the servant out for a walk, and told them not to return till luncheon time, as the constable and I had something to do, and did not wish to be interrupted."

The man ran his hand through his long tangled beard.

"I should like to be trimmed up a bit before I see Sophia," he said.

"I can do that for you, my lord," cried the constable.

"My lord?" echoed the man. "Oh, yes, I understand. You are a policeman, are you not?"

"Yes, my lord, chief constable."

"Then I shall give myself up to you. I killed the butler."

"Oh, impossible, my lord!"

"No, it isn't. The beast, as I called him, was getting old, and one morning he forgot to close the door behind him. I followed him stealthily out, and at the head of the stair planted my foot in the small of his back, which sent him headlong. There was an infernal crash. I did not mean to kill the brute, but merely to escape, and just as I was about to run down the stairway, I was appalled to see my father looking like—looking like—well, I won't attempt to say what he looked like; but all my old fear of him returned. As he strode towards me, along the corridor, I was in such terror that I jumped through the secret door and slammed it shut."

"Where is the secret door?" I asked.

"The secret door is that fireplace. The whole fireplace moves inward if you push aside the carved ornament at the left-hand corner."

"Is it a dummy fireplace, then?"

"No, you may build a fire in it, and the smoke will escape up the chimney. But I killed the butler, constable, though not intending it, I swear."

And now the constable shone forth like the real rough diamond he was.

"My lord, we'll say nothing about that. Legally you didn't do it. You see, there's been an inquest on the butler and the jury brought in the verdict, 'Death by accident, through stumbling from the top of the stair.' You can't go behind a coroner's inquest, my lord."

"Indeed," said his lordship, with the first laugh in which he had indulged for many a year. "I don't want to go behind anything, constable, I've been behind that accursed chimney too long to wish any further imprisonment."

THE LIBERATION OF WYOMING ED

I

A man should present the whole truth to his doctor, his lawyer, or his detective. If a doctor is to cure, he must be given the full confidence of the patient; if a lawyer is to win a case he needs to know what tells against his client as well as the points in his favour; if a secret agent is to solve a mystery all the cards should be put on the table. Those who half trust a professional man need not be disappointed when results prove unsatisfactory.

A partial confidence reposed in me led to the liberation of a dangerous criminal, caused me to associate with a robber much against my own inclination, and brought me within danger of the law. Of course, I never pretend to possess that absolute confidence in the law which seems to be the birthright of every Englishman. I have lived too intimately among the machinery of the law, and have seen too many of its ghastly mistakes, to hold it in that blind esteem which appears to be prevalent in the British Isles.

There is a doggerel couplet which typifies this spirit better than anything I can write, and it runs:

> *No rogue e'er felt the halter draw,*
> *With a good opinion of the law.*

Those lines exemplify the trend of British thought in this direction. If you question a verdict of their courts you are a rogue, and that ends the matter. And yet when an Englishman undertakes to circumvent the law, there is no other man on earth who will go to greater lengths. An amazing people! Never understandable by the sane of other countries.

It was entirely my own fault that I became involved in affairs which were almost indefensible and wholly illegal.

My client first tried to bribe me into compliance with his wishes, which bribe I sternly refused. Then he partially broke down and, quite unconsciously as I take it, made an appeal to the heart—a strange thing for an Englishman to do. My kind heart has ever been my most vulnerable point. We French are sentimentalists. France has before now staked its very existence for an ideal, while other countries fight for continents, cash, or commerce. You cannot pierce me with a lance of gold, but wave a wand of sympathy, and I am yours.

There waited upon me in my flat a man who gave his name as Douglas Sanderson, which may or may not have been his legitimate title. This was a question into which I never probed, and at the moment of writing am as ignorant of his true cognomen, if that was not it, as on the morning he first met me. He was an elderly man of natural dignity and sobriety, slow in speech, almost sombre in dress. His costume was not quite that of a professional man, and not quite that of a gentleman. I at once recognised the order to which he belonged, and a most difficult class it is to deal with. He was the confidential servant or steward of some ancient and probably noble family, embodying in himself all the faults and virtues, each a trifle accentuated, of the line he served, and to which, in order to produce him and his like, his father, grandfather, and great-grandfather had doubtless been attached. It is frequently the case that the honour of the house he serves is more dear to him than it is to the representative of that house. Such a man is almost always the repository of family secrets; a repository whose inviolability gold cannot affect, threats sway, or cajolery influence.

I knew, when I looked at him, that practically I was looking at his master, for I have known many cases where even the personal appearance of the two was almost identical, which may have given rise to the English phrase, "Like master, like man." The servant was a little more haughty, a little less kind, a little more exclusive, a little less confidential, a little more condescending, a little less human, a little more Tory, and altogether a little less pleasant and easy person to deal with.

"Sir," he began, when I had waved him to a seat, "I am a very rich man, and can afford to pay well for the commission I request you to undertake. To ask you to name your own terms may seem unbusinesslike, so I may say at the outset I am not a business man. The service I shall ask will involve the utmost secrecy, and for that I am willing to pay. It may expose you to risk of limb or liberty, and for that I am willing to pay. It will probably necessitate the expenditure of a large sum of money; that sum is at your disposal."

Here he paused; he had spoken slowly and impressively, with a touch of arrogance in his tone which aroused to his prejudice, the combativeness latent in my nature. However, at this juncture I merely bowed my head, and replied in accents almost as supercilious as his own:

"The task must either be unworthy or unwelcome. In mentioning first the compensation, you are inverting the natural order of things. You should state at the outset what you expect me to do, then, if I accept the commission, it is time to discuss the details of expenditure."

Either he had not looked for such a reply, or was loath to open his budget, for he remained a few moments with eyes bent upon the floor, and lips compressed in silence. At last he went on, without change of inflection, without any diminution of that air of condescension, which had so exasperated me in the beginning, and which was preparing a downfall for himself that would rudely shake the cold dignity which encompassed him like a cloak:

"It is difficult for a father to confide in a complete stranger the vagaries of a beloved son, and before doing so you must pledge your word that my communication will be regarded as strictly confidential."

"*Cela va sans dire.*"

"I do not understand French," said Mr. Sanderson severely, as if the use of the phrase were an insult to him.

I replied nonchalantly:

"It means, as a matter of course; that goes without saying. Whatever you care to tell me about your son will be mentioned to no one. Pray proceed, without further circumlocution, for my time is valuable."

"My son was always a little wild and impatient of control. Although everything he could wish was at his disposal here at home, he chose to visit America, where he fell into bad company. I assure you there is no real harm in the boy, but he became implicated with others, and has suffered severely for his recklessness. For five years he has been an inmate of a prison in the West. He was known and convicted under the name of Wyoming Ed."

"What was his crime?"

"His alleged crime was the stopping, and robbing, of a railway train."

"For how long was he sentenced?"

"He was sentenced for life."

"What do you wish me to do?"

"Every appeal has been made to the governor of the State in an endeavour to obtain a pardon. These appeals have failed. I am informed that if money enough is expended it may be possible to arrange my son's escape."

"In other words, you wish me to bribe the officials of the jail?"

"I assure you the lad is innocent."

For the first time a quiver of human emotion came into the old man's voice.

"Then, if you can prove that, why not apply for a new trial?"

"Unfortunately, the circumstances of the case, of his arrest on the train itself, the number of witnesses against him, give me no hope that a new trial would end in a different verdict, even if a new trial could be obtained, which I am informed is not possible. Every legal means tending to his liberation has already been tried."

"I see. And now you are determined to adopt illegal means? I refuse to have anything to do with the malpractice you propose. You objected to a phrase in French, Mr. Sanderson, perhaps one in Latin will please you better. It is '*Veritas praevalebit*,' which means, 'Truth will prevail.' I shall set your mind entirely at rest regarding your son. Your son at this moment occupies a humble, if honourable, position in the great house from which you came, and he hopes in time worthily to fill his father's shoes, as you have filled the shoes of your father. You are not a rich man, but a servant. Your son never was in America, and never will go there. It is your master's son, the heir to great English estates, who became the Wyoming Ed of the Western prison. Even from what you say, I do not in the least doubt he was justly convicted, and you may go back to your master and tell him so. You came here to conceal the shameful secret of a wealthy and noble house; you may return knowing that secret has been revealed, and that the circumstances in which you so solemnly bound me to secrecy never existed. Sir, that is the penalty of lying."

The old man's contempt for me had been something to be felt, so palpable was it. The armour of icy reserve had been so complete that actually I had expected to see him rise with undiminished hauteur, and leave the room, disdaining further parley with one who had insulted him. Doubtless that is the way in which his master would have acted, but even in the underling I was unprepared for the instantaneous crumbling of this monument of pomp and pride. A few moments after I began to speak in terms as severe as his own, his trembling hands grasped the arms of the chair in which he sat, and his ever-widening eyes, which came to regard me with something like superstitious dread as I went on, showed me I had launched my random arrow straight at the bull's-eye of fact. His face grew mottled and green rather than pale. When at last I accused him of lying, he arose slowly, shaking like a man with a palsy, but, unable to support himself erect, sank helplessly back into his chair again. His head fell forward to the table before him, and he sobbed aloud.

"God help me!" he cried, "it is not my own secret I am trying to guard."

I sprang to the door, and turned the key in the lock so that by no chance might we be interrupted; then, going to the sideboard, I poured him out a *liqueur* glass full of the finest Cognac ever imported from south of the Loire, and tapping him on the shoulder, said brusquely:

"Here, drink this. The case is no worse than it was half an hour ago. I shall not betray the secret."

He tossed off the brandy, and with some effort regained his self-control.

"I have done my errand badly," he wailed. "I don't know what I have said that has led you to so accurate a statement of the real situation, but I have been a blundering fool. God forgive me, when so much depended on my making no mistake."

"Don't let that trouble you," I replied; "nothing you said gave me the slightest clue."

"You called me a liar," he continued, "and that is a hard word from one man to another, but I would not lie for myself, and when I do it for one I revere and respect, my only regret is that I have done it without avail."

"My dear sir," I assured him, "the fault is not with yourself at all. You were simply attempting the impossible. Stripped and bare, your proposal amounts to this. I am to betake myself to the United States, and there commit a crime, or a series of crimes, in bribing sworn officials to turn traitor to their duty and permit a convict to escape."

"You put it very harshly, sir. You must admit that, especially in new countries, there is lawlessness within the law as well as outside of it. The real criminals in the robbery of the railway train escaped; my young master, poor fellow, was caught. His father, one of the proudest men in England, has grown prematurely old under the burden of this terrible dishonour. He is broken-hearted, and a dying man, yet he presents an impassive front to the world, with all the ancient courage of his race. My young master is an only son, and failing his appearance, should his father die, title and estate will pass to strangers. Our helplessness in this situation adds to its horror. We dare not make any public move. My old master is one with such influence among the governing class of this country, of which he has long been a member, that the average Englishman, if his name were mentioned, would think his power limitless. Yet that power he dare not exert to save his own son from a felon's life and death. However much he or another may suffer, publicity must be avoided, and this is a secret which cannot safely be shared with more than those who know it now."

"How many know it?"

"In this country, three persons. In an American prison, one."

"Have you kept up communication with the young man?"

"Oh, yes."

"Direct?"

"No; through a third person. My young master has implored his father not to write to him direct."

"This go-between, as we may call him, is the third person in the secret? Who is he?"

"That I dare not tell you!"

"Mr. Sanderson, it would be much better for your master and his son that you should be more open with me. These half-confidences are misleading. Has the son made any suggestion regarding his release?"

"Oh yes, but not the suggestion I have put before you. His latest letter was to the effect that within six months or so there is to be an election for governor. He proposes that a large sum of money shall be used to influence this election so that a man pledged to pardon him may sit in the governor's chair."

"I see. And this sum of money is to be paid to the third person you referred to?"

"Yes."

"May I take it that this third person is the one to whom various sums have been paid during the last five years in order to bribe the governor to pardon the young man?"

Sanderson hesitated a moment before answering; in fact, he appeared so torn between inclination and duty; anxious to give me whatever information I deemed necessary, yet hemmed in by the instructions with which his master had limited him, that at last I waved my hand and said:

"You need not reply, Mr. Sanderson. That third party is the crux of the situation. I strongly suspect him of blackmail. If you would but name him, and allow me to lure him to these rooms, I possess a little private prison of my own into which I could thrust him, and I venture to say that before he had passed a week in darkness, on bread and water, we should have the truth about this business."

Look you now the illogical nature of an Englishman! Poor old Sanderson, who had come to me with a proposal to break the law of America, seemed horror-stricken when I airily suggested the immuring of a man in a dungeon here in England. He gazed at me in amazement, then cast his eyes furtively about him, as if afraid a trap door would drop beneath him, and land him in my private *oubliette*.

"Do not be alarmed, Mr. Sanderson, you are perfectly safe. You are beginning at the wrong end of this business, and it seems to me five years of contributions to this third party without any result might have opened the eyes of even the most influential nobleman in England, not to mention those of his faithful servant."

"Indeed, sir," said Sanderson, "I must confess to you that I have long had a suspicion of this third person, but my master has clung to him as his only hope, and if this third person were interfered with, I may tell you that he has deposited in London at some place unknown to us, a full history of the case, and if it should happen that he disappears for more than a week at a time, this record will be brought to light."

"My dear Mr. Sanderson, that device is as old as Noah and his ark. I should chance that. Let me lay this fellow by the heels, and I will guarantee that no publicity follows."

Sanderson sadly shook his head.

"Everything might happen as you say, sir, but all that would put us no further forward. The only point is the liberation of my young master. It is possible that the person unmentioned, whom we may call Number Three, has been cheating us throughout, but that is a matter of no consequence."

"Pardon me, but I think it is. Suppose your young master here, and at liberty. This Number Three would continue to maintain the power over him which he seems to have held over his father for the last five years."

"I think we can prevent that, sir, if my plan is carried out."

"The scheme for bribing the American officials is yours, then?"

"Yes, sir, and I may say I am taking a great deal upon myself in coming to you. I am, in fact, disobeying the implied commands of my master, but I have seen him pay money, and very large sums of money, to this Number Three for the last five years and nothing has come of it. My master is an unsuspicious man, who has seen little of the real world, and thinks everyone as honest as himself."

"Well, that may be, Mr. Sanderson, but permit me to suggest that the one who proposes a scheme of bribery, and, to put it mildly, an evasion of the law, shows some knowledge of the lower levels of this world, and is not quite in a position to plume himself on his own honesty."

"I am coming to that, Mr. Valmont. My master knows nothing whatever of my plan. He has given me the huge sum of money demanded by Number Three, and he supposes that amount has been already paid over. As a matter of fact, it has not been paid over, and will not be until my suggestion has been carried out, and failed. In fact, I am about to use this money, all of it if necessary, if you will undertake the commission. I have paid Number Three his usual monthly allowance, and will continue to do so. I have told him my master has his proposal under consideration; that there are still six months to come and go upon, and that my master is not one who decides in a hurry."

"Number Three says there is an election in six months for governor. What is the name of the state?"

Sanderson informed me. I walked to my book-case, and took down a current American Year Book, consulted it, and returned to the table.

"There is no election in that State, Mr. Sanderson, for eighteen months. Number Three is simply a blackmailer, as I have suspected."

"Quite so, sir," replied Sanderson, taking a newspaper from his pocket. "I read in this paper an account of a man immured in a Spanish dungeon. His friends arranged it with the officials in this way: The prisoner was certified to have died, and his body was turned over to his relatives. Now, if that could be done in America, it would serve two purposes. It would be the easiest way to get my young master out of the jail. It would remain a matter of record that he had died, therefore there could be no search for him, as would be the case if he simply escaped. If you were so good as to undertake this task you might perhaps see my young master in his cell, and ask him to write to this Number Three with whom he is in constant communication, telling him he was very ill. Then you could arrange with the prison doctor that this person was informed of my young master's death."

"Very well, we can try that, but a blackmailer is not so easily thrown off the scent. Once he has tasted blood he is a human man-eating tiger. But still, there is always my private dungeon in the background, and if your plan for silencing him fails, I guarantee that my more drastic and equally illegal method will be a success."

II

It will be seen that my scruples concerning the acceptance of this commission, and my first dislike for the old man had both faded away during the conversation which I have set down in the preceding chapter. I saw him under the stress of deep emotion, and latterly began to realise the tremendous chances he was taking in contravening the will of his imperious master. If the large sum of money was long withheld from the blackmailer, Douglas Sanderson ran the risk of Number Three opening up communication direct with his master. Investigation would show that the old servant had come perilously near laying himself open to a charge of breach of trust, and even of defalcation with regard to the money, and all this danger he was heroically incurring for the unselfish purpose of serving the interests of his employer. During our long interview old Sanderson gradually became a hero in my eyes, and entirely in opposition to the resolution I had made at the beginning, I accepted his commission at the end of it.

Nevertheless, my American experiences are those of which I am least proud, and all I care to say upon the subject is that my expedition proved completely successful. The late convict was my companion on the *Arontic*, the first steamship sailing for England after we reached New York from the west. Of course I knew that two or three years roughing it in mining camps and on ranches, followed by five years in prison, must have produced a radical effect not only on the character, but also in the personal appearance of a man who had undergone these privations. Nevertheless, making due allowance for all this, I could not but fear that the ancient English family, of which this young man was the hope and pride, would be exceedingly disappointed with him. In spite of the change which grooming and the wearing of a civilised costume made, Wyoming Ed still looked much more the criminal than the gentleman. I considered myself in honour bound not to make any inquiries of the young man regarding his parentage. Of course, if I had wished to possess myself of the secret, I had but to touch a button under the table when Sanderson left my rooms in the Imperial Flats, which would have caused him to be shadowed and run to earth. I may also add that the ex-prisoner volunteered no particulars about himself or his family. Only once on board ship did he attempt to obtain some information from me as we walked up and down the deck together.

"You are acting for someone else, I suppose?" he said.

"Yes."

"For someone in England?"

"Yes."

"He put up the money, did he?"

"Yes."

There was a pause, during which we took two or three turns in silence.

"Of course, there's no secret about it," he said at last. "I expected help from the other side, but Colonel Jim has been so mighty long about it, I was afraid he'd forgotten me."

"Who is Colonel Jim?"

"Colonel Jim Baxter. Wasn't it him gave you the money?"

"I never heard of the man before."

"Then who put up the coin?"

"Douglas Sanderson," I replied, looking at him sidewise as I mentioned the name. It had apparently no effect upon him. He wrinkled his brow for a moment, then said:

"Well, if you never heard of Baxter, I never heard of Sanderson."

This led me to suspect that Douglas Sanderson did not give me his own name, and doubtless the address with which he had furnished me was merely temporary. I did not cable to him from America regarding the success of the expedition, because I could not be certain it was a success until I was safely on English ground, and not even then, to tell the truth. Anyhow, I wished to leave no trail behind me, but the moment the *Arontic* reached Liverpool, I telegraphed Sanderson to meet us that evening at my flat.

He was waiting for me when Wyoming Ed and I entered together. The old man was quite evidently in a state of nervous tension. He had been walking up and down the room with hands clenched behind his back, and now stood at the end farthest from the door as he heard us approach, with his hands still clasped behind his back, and an expression of deep anxiety upon his rugged face. All the electric lamps were turned on, and the room was bright as day.

"Have you not brought him with you?" he cried.

"Brought him with me?" I echoed. "Here is Wyoming Ed!"

The old man glared at him for a moment or two stupefied, then moaned:

"Oh, my God, my God, that is not the man!"

I turned to my short-haired fellow traveller.

"You told me you were Wyoming Ed!"

He laughed uneasily.

"Well, in a manner of speaking, so I have been for the last five years, but I wasn't Wyoming Ed before that. Say, old man, are you acting for Colonel Jim Baxter?"

Sanderson, on whom a dozen years seemed to have fallen since we entered the room, appeared unable to speak, and merely shook his head in a hopeless sort of way.

"I say, boys," ejaculated the ex-convict, with an uneasy laugh, half-comic, half-bewildered, "this is a sort of mix-up, isn't it? I wish

Colonel Jim was here to explain. I say, Boss," he cried suddenly, turning sharp on me, "this here misfit's not my fault. I didn't change the children in the cradle. You don't intend to send me back to that hell-hole, do you?"

"No," I said, "not if you tell the truth. Sit down."

The late prisoner seated himself in a chair as close to the door as possible, hitching a little nearer as he sat down. His face had taken on a sharp, crafty aspect like that of a trapped rat.

"You are perfectly safe," I assured him. "Sit over here by the table. Even if you bolted through that door, you couldn't get out of this flat. Mr. Sanderson, take a chair."

The old man sank despondently into the one nearest at hand. I pressed a button, and when my servant entered, I said to him:

"Bring some Cognac and Scotch whisky, glasses, and two syphons of soda."

"You haven't got any Kentucky or Canadian?" asked the prisoner, moistening his lips. The jail whiteness in his face was now accentuated by the pallor of fear, and the haunted look of the escaped convict glimmered from his eyes. In spite of the comfort I had attempted to bestow upon him, he knew that he had been rescued in mistake for another, and for the first time since he left prison realised he was among strangers, and not among friends. In his trouble he turned to the beverage of his native continent.

"Bring a bottle of Canadian whisky," I said to the servant, who disappeared, and shortly returned with what I had ordered. I locked the door after him, and put the key in my pocket.

"What am I to call you?" I asked the ex-convict.

With a forced laugh he said; "You can call me Jack for short."

"Very well, Jack, help yourself," and he poured out a very liberal glass of the Dominion liquor, refusing to dilute it with soda. Sanderson took Scotch, and I helped myself to a *petit verre* of brandy.

"Now, Jack," I began, "I may tell you plainly that if I wished to send you back to prison, I could not do so without incriminating myself. You are legally dead, and you have now a chance to begin life anew, an opportunity of which I hope you will take advantage.

If you were to apply three weeks from today at the prison doors, they would not dare admit you. You are dead. Does that console you?"

"Well, squire, you can bet your bottom dollar I never thought I'd be pleased to hear I was dead, but I'm glad if it's all fixed as you say, and you can bet your last pair of boots I'm going to keep out of the jug in future if I can."

"That's right. Now, I can promise that if you answer all my questions truthfully, you shall be given money enough to afford you a new beginning in life."

"Good enough," said Jack briefly.

"You were known in prison as Wyoming Ed?"

"Yes, sir."

"If that was not your name, why did you use it?"

"Because Colonel Jim, on the train, asked me to do that. He said it would give him a pull in England to get me free."

"Did you know Wyoming Ed?"

"Yes, sir, he was one of us three that held up the train."

"What became of him?"

"He was shot dead."

"By one of the passengers?"

There was silence, during which the old man groaned, and bowed his head. Jack was studying the floor. Then he looked up at me and said:

"You don't expect me to give a pal away, do you?"

"As that pal has given you away for the last five years, it seems to me you need not show very much consideration for him."

"I'm not so sure he did."

"I am; but never mind that point. Colonel Jim Baxter shot Wyoming Ed and killed him. Why?"

"See here, my friend, you're going a little too fast. I didn't say that."

He reached somewhat defiantly for the bottle from Canada.

"Pardon me," I said, rising quietly, and taking possession of the bottle myself, "it grieves me more than I can say to restrict my hospitality. I have never done such a thing in my life before, but this is not a drinking bout; it is a very serious conference. The whisky you have already taken has given you a bogus courage, and a false view of things. Are you going to tell me the truth, or are you not?"

Jack pondered on this for a while, then he said:

"Well, sir, I'm perfectly willing to tell you the truth as far as it concerns myself, but I don't want to rat on a friend."

"As I have said, he isn't your friend. He told you to take the name of Wyoming Ed, so that he might blackmail the father of Wyoming Ed. He has done so for the last five years, living in luxury here in London, and not moving a finger to help you. In fact, nothing would appall him more than to learn that you are now in this country. By this time he has probably received the news from the prison doctor that you are dead, and so thinks himself safe for ever."

"If you can prove that to me—" said Jack.

"I can and will," I interrupted; then, turning to Sanderson, I demanded:

"When are you to meet this man next?"

"Tonight, at nine o'clock," he answered. "His monthly payment is due, and he is clamouring for the large sum I told you of."

"Where do you meet him? In London?"

"Yes."

"At your master's town house?"

"Yes."

"Will you take us there, and place us where we can see him and he can't see us?"

"Yes. I trust to your honour, Mr. Valmont. A closed carriage will call for me at eight, and you can accompany me. Still, after all, Mr. Valmont, we have no assurance that he is the same person this young man refers to."

"I am certain he is. He does not go under the name of Colonel Jim Baxter, I suppose?"

"No."

The convict had been looking from one to the other of us during this colloquy. Suddenly he drew his chair up closer to the table.

"Look here," he said, "you fellows are square, I can see that, and after all's said and done, you're the man that got me out of clink. Now, I half suspicion you're right about Colonel Jim, but, anyhow, I'll tell you exactly what happened. Colonel Jim was a Britisher, and I suppose that's why he and Wyoming Ed chummed together a good deal. We called Jim Baxter Colonel, but he never said he was a colonel or anything else. I was told he belonged to the British army, and that something happened in India so that he had to light out. He never talked about himself, but he was a mighty taking fellow when he laid out to please anybody. We called him Colonel because he was so straight in the back, and walked as if he were on parade. When this young English tenderfoot came out, he and the Colonel got to be as thick as thieves, and the Colonel won a good deal of money from him at cards, but that didn't make any difference in their friendship. The Colonel most always won when he played cards, and perhaps that's what started the talk about why he left the British army. He was the luckiest beggar I ever knew in that line of business. We all met in the rush to the new gold-fields, which didn't pan out worth a cent, and one after another of the fellows quit and went somewhere else. But Wyoming Ed, he held on, even after Colonel Jim wanted to quit. As long as there were plenty of fellows there, Colonel Jim never lacked money, al-though he didn't dig it out of the ground, but when the population thinned down to only a few of us, then we all struck hard times. Now, I knew Colonel Jim was going to hold up a train. He asked me if I would join him, and I said I would if there wasn't too many in the gang. I'd been into that business afore, and I knew there was no greater danger than to have a whole mob of fellows. Three men can hold up a train better than three dozen. Everybody's scared except the express messenger, and it's generally easy to settle him, for he stands where the light is, and we shoot from the dark. Well, I thought at first Wyoming Ed was on to the scheme, because when we were waiting in the cut to signal the train he talked about us going on with her to San Francisco, but I thought he was only jok-ing. I guess that Colonel Jim imagined that when it came to the pinch, Ed wouldn't back out and leave us in the lurch: he knew Ed was as brave as a lion. In the cut, where the train would be on the up grade, the Colonel got his lantern ready, lit it, and wrapped a thin red silk handkerchief round it. The express was timed to pass up there about midnight, but it was near one o'clock when her head-light came in sight. We knew all the passengers would be in bed in the sleepers, and asleep in the smoking car and the day coach. We didn't intend to meddle with them. The Colonel had brought a stick or two of dynamite from the mines, and was going to blow open the safe in the express car, and climb out with whatever was in-side.

"The train stopped to the signal all right, and the Colonel fired a couple of shots just to let the engineer know we meant business. The engineer and fireman at once threw up their hands, then the Colonel turns to Ed, who was standing there like a man pole-axed, and says to him mighty sharp, just like if he was speaking to a regi-ment of soldiers:

"'You keep these two men covered. Come on, Jack!' he says to me, and then we steps up to the door of the express car, which the fellow inside had got locked and bolted. The Colonel fires his re-volver in through the lock, then flung his shoulder agin the door, and it went in with a crash, which was followed instantly by an-other crash, for the little expressman was game right through. He had put out the lights and was blazing away at the open door. The Colonel sprang for cover inside the car, and wasn't touched, but one of the shots took me just above the knee, and broke my leg, so I went down in a heap. The minute the Colonel counted seven shots he was on to that express messenger like a tiger, and had him tied up in a hard knot before you could shake a stick. Then, quick as a wink he struck a match, and lit the lamp. Plucky as the express messenger was, he looked scared to death, and now, when Colonel Jim held a pistol to his head, he gave up the keys and told him how to open the safe. I had fallen back against the corner of the car, inside, and was groaning with Pain. Colonel Jim was scooping out the money from the shelves of the safe, and stuffing it into a sack.

"'Are you hurt, Jack?' he cried.

"'Yes, my leg's broke.'

"'Don't let that trouble you; we'll get you clear all right. Do you think you can ride your horse?'

"'I don't believe it,' said I. 'I guess I'm done for,' and I thought I was.

"Colonel Jim never looked round, but he went through that safe in a way that'd make your hair curl, throwing aside the bulky packages after tearing them open, taking only cash, which he thrust into a bag he had with him, till he was loaded like a millionaire. Then suddenly he swore, for the train began to move.

"'What is that fool Ed doing?' he shouted, rising to his feet.

"At that minute Ed came in, pistol in each hand, and his face ablaze.

"'Here, you cursed thief!' he cried, 'I didn't come with you to rob a train!'

"'Get outside, you fool!' roared Colonel Jim, 'get outside and stop this train. Jack has got his leg broke. Don't come another step towards me, or I'll kill you!'

"But Ed, he walked right on, Colonel Jim backing, then there was a shot that rang like cannon fire in the closed car, and Ed fell forward on his face. Colonel Jim turned him over, and I saw he had been hit square in the middle of the forehead. The train was now going at good speed, and we were already miles away from where our horses were tied. I never heard a man swear like Colonel Jim. He went through the pockets of Ed, and took a bundle of papers that was inside his coat, and this he stuffed away in his own clothes. Then he turned to me, and his voice was like a lamb.

"'Jack, old man,' he said, 'I can't help you. They're going to nab you, but not for murder. The expressman there will be your witness. It isn't murder anyhow on my part, but self-defence. You saw he was coming at me when I warned him to keep away.'

"All this he said in a loud voice, for the expressman to hear, then he bent over to me and whispered:

"'I'll get the best lawyer I can for you, but I'm afraid they're bound to convict you, and if they do, I will spend every penny of this money to get you free. You call yourself Wyoming Ed at the trial. I've taken all this man's papers so that he can't be identified. And don't you worry if you're sentenced, for remember I'll be working night and day for you, and if money can get you out, you'll be got out, because these papers will help me to get the cash required. Ed's folks are rich in England, so they'll fork over to get you out if you pretend to be him.' With that he bade me good-bye and jumped off the train. There, gentlemen, that's the whole story just as it happened, and that's why I thought it was Colonel Jim had sent you to get me free."

There was not the slightest doubt in my mind that the convict had told the exact truth, and that night, at nine o'clock, he identified Major Renn as the former Colonel Jim Baxter. Sanderson placed us in a gallery where we could see, but could not hear. The old man seemed determined that we should not know where we were, and took every precaution to keep us in the dark. I suppose he put us out of earshot, so that if the Major mentioned the name of the nobleman we should not be any the wiser. We remained in the gallery for some time after the major had left before Sanderson came to us again, carrying with him a packet.

"The carriage is waiting at the door," he said, "and with your permission, Monsieur Valmont, I will accompany you to your flat."

I smiled at the old man's extreme caution, but he continued very gravely:

"It is not that, Monsieur Valmont. I wish to consult with you, and if you will accept it, I have another commission to offer."

"Well," said I, "I hope it is not so unsavoury as the last." But to this the old man made no response.

There was silence in the carriage as we drove back to my flat. Sanderson had taken the precaution of pulling down the blinds of the carriage, which he need not have troubled to do, for, as I have said, it would have been the simplest matter in the world for me to have discovered who his employer was, if I had desired to know. As a matter of fact, I do not know to this day whom he represented.

Once more in my room with the electric light turned on, I was shocked and astonished to see the expression on Sanderson's face. It was the face of a man who would grimly commit murder and hang for it. If ever the thirst for vengeance was portrayed on a human countenance, it was on his that night. He spoke very quietly, laying down the packet before him on the table.

"I think you will agree with me," he said, "that no punishment on earth is too severe for that creature calling himself Major Renn."

"I'm willing to shoot him dead in the streets of London tomorrow," said the convict, "if you give the word."

Sanderson went on implacably: "He not only murdered the son, but for five years has kept the father in an agony of sorrow and apprehension, bleeding him of money all the time, which was the least of his crimes. Tomorrow I shall tell my master that his son has been dead these five years, and heavy as that blow must prove, it will be mitigated by the fact that his son died an honest and honourable man. I thank you for offering to kill this vile criminal. I intend that he shall die, but not so quickly or so mercifully."

Here he untied the packet, and took from it a photograph, which he handed to the convict.

"Do you recognise that?"

"Oh yes; that's Wyoming Ed as he appeared at the mine; as, indeed, he appeared when he was shot."

The photograph Sanderson then handed to me.

"An article that I read about you in the paper, Monsieur Valmont, said you could impersonate anybody. Can you impersonate this young man?"

"There's no difficulty in that," I replied.

"Then will you do this? I wish you two to dress in that fashion. I shall give you particulars of the haunts of Major Renn. I want you to meet him together and separately, as often as you can, until you drive him mad or to suicide. He believes you to be dead," said Sanderson, addressing Jack. "I am certain he has the news, by his manner tonight. He is extremely anxious to get the lump sum of money which I have been holding back from him. You may address him, for he will recognise your voice as well as your person, but Monsieur Valmont had better not speak, as then he might know it was not the voice of my poor young master. I suggest that you meet him first together, always at night. The rest I leave in your hands, Monsieur Valmont."

With that the old man rose and left us.

Perhaps I should stop this narration here, for I have often wondered if practically I am guilty of manslaughter.

We did not meet Major Renn together, but arranged that he should encounter Jack under one lamp-post, and me under the next. It was just after midnight, and the streets were practically deserted. The theatre crowds had gone, and the traffic was represented by the last 'buses, and a belated cab now and then. Major Renn came down the steps of his club, and under the first lamp-post, with the light shining full upon him, Jack the convict stepped forth.

"Colonel Jim," he said, "Ed and I are waiting for you. There were three in that robbery, and one was a traitor. His dead comrades ask the traitor to join them."

The Major staggered back against the lamp-post, drew his hand across his brow, and muttered, Jack told me afterwards:

"I must stop drinking! I must stop drinking!"

Then he pulled himself together, and walked rapidly towards the next lamp-post. I stood out square in front of him, but made no sound. He looked at me with distended eyes, while Jack shouted out in his boisterous voice, that had no doubt often echoed over the plain:

"Come on, Wyoming Ed, and never mind him. He must follow."

Then he gave a war whoop. The Major did not turn round, but continued to stare at me, breathing stertorously like a person with apoplexy. I slowly pushed back my hat, and on my brow he saw the red mark of a bullet hole. He threw up his hands and fell with a crash to the pavement.

"Heart failure" was the verdict of the coroner's jury.

LADY ALICIA'S EMERALDS

I

Many Englishmen, if you speak to them of me, indulge themselves in a detraction that I hope they will not mind my saying is rarely graced by the delicacy of innuendo with which some of my own countrymen attempt to diminish whatever merit I may possess. Mr. Spenser Hale, of Scotland Yard, whose lack of imagination I have so often endeavoured to amend, alas! without perceptible success, was good enough to say, after I had begun these reminiscences, which he read with affected scorn, that I was wise in setting down my successes, because the life of Methuselah himself would not be long enough to chronicle my failures, and the man to whom this was said replied that it was only my artfulness, a word of which these people are very fond; that I intended to use my successes as bait, issue a small pamphlet filled with them, and then record my failures in a thousand volumes, after the plan of a Chinese encyclopaedia, selling these to the public on the instalment plan.

Ah, well; it is not for me to pass comment on such observations. Every profession is marred by its little jealousies, and why should the coterie of detection be exempt? I hope I may never follow an example so deleterious, and thus be tempted to express my contempt for the stupidity with which, as all persons know, the official detective system of England is imbued. I have had my failures, of course. Did I ever pretend to be otherwise than human? But what has been the cause of these failures? They have arisen through the conservatism of the English. When there is a mystery to be solved, the average Englishman almost invariably places it in the hands of the regular police. When these good people are utterly baffled; when their big boots have crushed out all evidences that the grounds may have had to offer to a discerning mind; when their clumsy hands have obliterated the clues which are everywhere around them, I am at last called in, and if I fail, they say:

"What could you expect; he is a Frenchman."

This was exactly what happened in the case of Lady Alicia's emeralds. For two months the regular police were not only befogged, but they blatantly sounded the alarm to every thief in Europe. All the pawnbrokers' shops of Great Britain were ransacked, as if a robber of so valuable a collection would be foolish enough to take it to a pawnbroker. Of course, the police say that they thought the thief would dismantle the cluster, and sell the gems separately. As to this necklace of emeralds, possessing as it does an historical value which is probably in excess of its intrinsic worth, what more natural than that the holder of it should open negotiations with its rightful owner, and thus make more money by quietly restoring it than by its dismemberment and sale piecemeal? But such a fuss was kicked up, such a *furore* created, that it is no wonder the receiver of the goods lay low, and said nothing. In vain were all ports giving access to the Continent watched; in vain were the police of France, Belgium, and Holland warned to look out for this treasure. Two valuable months were lost, and then the Marquis of Blair sent for me! I maintain that the case was hopeless from the moment I took it up.

It may be asked why the Marquis of Blair allowed the regular police to blunder along for two precious months, but anyone who is acquainted with that nobleman will not wonder that he clung so long to a forlorn hope. Very few members of the House of Peers are richer than Lord Blair, and still fewer more penurious. He maintained that, as he paid his taxes, he was entitled to protection from theft; that it was the duty of the Government to restore the gems, and if this proved impossible, to make compensation for them. This theory is not acceptable in the English Courts, and while

Scotland Yard did all it could during those two months, what but failure was to be expected from its limited mental equipment?

When I arrived at the Manor of Blair, as his lordship's very ugly and somewhat modern mansion house is termed, I was instantly admitted to his presence. I had been summoned from London by a letter in his lordship's own hand, on which the postage was not paid. It was late in the afternoon when I arrived, and our first conference was what might be termed futile. It was take up entirely with haggling about terms, the marquis endeavouring to beat down the price of my services to a sum so insignificant that it would barely have paid my expenses from London to Blair and back. Such bargaining is intensely distasteful to me. When the marquis found all his offers declined with a politeness which left no opening for anger on his part, he endeavoured to induce me to take up the case on a commission contingent upon my recovery of the gems, and as I had declined this for the twentieth time, darkness had come on, and the gong rang for dinner. I dined alone in the *salle à manger*, which appeared to be set apart for those calling at the mansion on business, and the meagreness of the fare, together with the indifferent nature of the claret, strengthened my determination to return to London as early as possible next morning.

When the repast was finished, the dignified servingman said gravely to me:

"The Lady Alicia asks if you will be good enough to give her a few moments in the drawing-room, sir."

I followed the man to the drawing-room, and found the young lady seated at the piano, on which she was strumming idly and absentmindedly, but with a touch, nevertheless, that indicated advanced excellence in the art of music. She was not dressed as one who had just risen from the dining table, but was somewhat grimly and commonly attired, looking more like a cottager's daughter than a member of the great country family. Her head was small, and crowned with a mass of jet black hair. My first impression on entering the large, rather dimly lighted room was unfavourable, but that vanished instantly under the charm of a manner so graceful and vivacious, that in a moment I seemed to be standing in a brilliant Parisian *salon* rather than in the sombre drawing-room of an English country house. Every poise of her dainty head; every gesture of those small, perfect hands; every modulated tone of the voice, whether sparkling with laughter or caressing in confidential speech, reminded me of the *grandes dames* of my own land. It was strange to find this perfect human flower amidst the gloomy ugliness of a huge square house built in the time of the Georges; but I remembered now that the Blairs are the English equivalent of the de Bellairs of France, from which family sprang the fascinating Marquise de Bellairs, who adorned the Court of Louis XIV. Here, advancing towards me, was the very reincarnation of the lovely marquise, who gave lustre to this dull world nearly three hundred years ago. Ah, after all, what are the English but a conquered race! I often forget this, and I trust I never remind them of it, but it enables one to forgive them much. A vivid twentieth-century marquise was Lady Alicia, in all except attire. What a dream some of our Parisian dress artists could have made of her, and here she was immured in this dull English house in the high-necked costume of a labourer's wife. "Welcome, Monsieur Valmont," she cried, in French of almost faultless intonation. "I am so glad you have arrived," and she greeted me as if I were an old friend of the family. There was nothing of condescension in her manner; no display of her own affability, while at the same time teaching me my place, and the difference in our stations of life. I can stand the rudeness of the nobility, but I detest their condescension. No; Lady Alicia was a true de Bellairs, and in my confusion, bending over her slender hand, I said:

"Madame la Marquise, it is a privilege to extend to you my most respectful salutations."

She laughed at this quietly, with the melting laugh of the nightingale.

"Monsieur, you mistake my title. Although my uncle is a marquis, I am but Lady Alicia."

"Your pardon, my lady. For the moment I was back in that scintillating Court which surrounded Louis le Grand."

"How flatteringly you introduce yourself, monsieur. In the gallery upstairs there is a painting of the Marquise de Bellairs, and when I show it to your tomorrow, you will then understand how charmingly you have pleased a vain woman by your reference to that beautiful lady. But I must not talk in this frivolous strain, monsieur. There is serious business to be considered, and I assure you I looked forward to your coming, monsieur, with the eagerness of Sister Anne in the tower of Bluebeard."

I fear my expression as I bowed to her must have betrayed my gratification at hearing these words, so confidentially uttered by lips so sweet, while the glance of her lovely eyes was even more eloquent than her words. Instantly I felt ashamed of my chaffering over terms with her uncle; instantly I forgot my resolution to depart on the morrow; instantly I resolved to be of what assistance I could to this dainty lady. Alas! the heart of Valmont is today as unprotected against the artillery of inspiring eyes as ever it was in his extreme youth.

"This house," she continued vivaciously, "has been practically in a state of siege for two months. I could take none of my usual walks in the gardens, on the lawns, or through the park, without some clumsy policeman in uniform crashing his way through the bushes, or some detective in plain clothes accosting me and questioning me under the pretence that he was a stranger who had lost his way. The lack of all subtlety in our police is something deplorable. I am sure the real criminal might have passed through their hands a dozen times unmolested, while our poor innocent servants, and the strangers within our gates, were made to feel that the stern eye of the law was upon them night and day."

The face of the young lady was an entrancing picture of animated indignation as she gave utterance to this truism which her countrymen are so slow to appreciate. I experienced a glow of satisfaction.

"Yes," she went on, "they sent down from London an army of stupid men, who have kept our household in a state of abject terror for eight long weeks, and where are the emeralds?"

As she suddenly asked this question, in the most Parisian of accents, with a little outward spreading of the hand, a flash of the eye, and a toss of the head, the united effect was something indescribable through the limitations of the language I am compelled to use.

"Well, monsieur, your arrival has put to flight this tiresome brigade, if, indeed, the word flight is not too airy a term to use towards a company so elephantine, and I assure you a sigh of relief has gone up from the whole household with the exception of my uncle. I said to him at dinner tonight: 'If Monsieur Valmont had been induced to take an interest in the case at first, the jewels would have been in my possession long before tonight.'"

"Ah, my lady," I protested, "I fear you overrate my poor ability. It is quite true that if I had been called in on the night of the robbery, my chances of success would have been infinitely greater than they are now."

"Monsieur," she cried, clasping her hands over her knees, and leaning towards me, hypnotising me with those starry eyes, "Monsieur, I am perfectly confident that before a week is past you will restore the necklace, if such restoration be possible. I have said so from the first. Now, am I right in my conjecture, monsieur, that you come here alone; that you bring with you no train of followers and assistants?"

"That is as you have stated it, my lady."

"I was sure of it. It is to be a contest of trained mentality in opposition to our two months' experience of brute force."

Never before had I felt such ambition to succeed, and a determination not to disappoint took full possession of me. Appreciation is a needed stimulant, and here it was offered to me in its most intoxicating form. Ah, Valmont, Valmont, will you never grow old! I am sure that at this moment, if I had been eighty, the same thrill of enthusiasm would have tingled to my fingers' ends. Leave the Manor of Blair in the morning? Not for the Bank of France!

"Has my uncle acquainted you with particulars of the robbery?"

"No, madame, we were talking of other things."

The lady leaned back in her low chair, partially closed her eyes, and breathed a deep sigh.

"I can well imagine the subject of your conversation," she said at last. "The Marquis of Blair was endeavouring to impose usurer's terms upon you, while you, nobly scorning such mercenary considerations, had perhaps resolved to leave us at the earliest opportunity."

"I assure you, my lady, that if any such conclusion had been arrived at on my part, it vanished the moment I was privileged to set foot in this drawing-room."

"It is kind of you to say that, monsieur, but you must not allow your conversation with my uncle to prejudice you against him. He is an old man now, and, of course, has his fancies. You would think him mercenary, perhaps, and so he is; but then so, too, am I. Oh, yes, I am, monsieur, frightfully mercenary. To be mercenary, I believe, means to be fond of money. No one is fonder of money than I, except, perhaps, my uncle; but you see, monsieur, we occupy the two extremes. He is fond of money to hoard it; I am fond of money to spend it. I am fond of money for the things it will buy. I should like to scatter largesse as did my fair ancestress in France. I should love a manor house in the country, and a mansion in Mayfair. I could wish to make everyone around me happy if the expenditure of money would do it."

"That is a form of money-love, Lady Alicia, which will find a multitude of admirers."

The girl shook her head and laughed merrily.

"I should so dislike to forfeit your esteem, Monsieur Valmont, and therefore I shall not reveal the depth of my cupidity. You will learn that probably from my uncle, and then you will understand my extreme anxiety for the recovery of these jewels."

"Are they very valuable?"

"Oh, yes; the necklace consists of twenty stones, no one of which weighs less than an ounce. Altogether, I believe, they amount to two thousand four hundred or two thousand five hundred carats, and their intrinsic value is twenty pounds a carat at least. So you see that means nearly fifty thousand pounds, yet even this sum is trivial compared with what it involves. There is something like a million at stake, together with my coveted manor house in the country, and my equally coveted mansion in Mayfair. All this is within my grasp if I can but recover the emeralds."

The girl blushed prettily as she noticed how intently I regarded her while she evolved this tantalising mystery. I thought there was a trace of embarrassment in her laugh when she cried:

"Oh, what will you think of me when you understand the situation? Pray, pray do not judge me harshly. I assure you the position I aim at will be used for the good of others as well as for my own pleasure. If my uncle does not make a confidant of you, I must take my courage in both hands, and give you all the particulars, but not tonight. Of course, if one is to unravel such a snarl as that in which we find ourselves, he must be made aware of every particular, must he not?"

"Certainly, my lady."

"Very well, Monsieur Valmont, I shall supply any deficiencies that occur in my uncle's conversation with you. There is one point on which I should like to warn you. Both my uncle and the police have made up their minds that a certain young man is the culprit. The police found several clues which apparently led in his direction, but they were unable to find enough to justify his arrest. At first I could have sworn he had nothing whatever to do with the matter, but lately I am not so sure. All I ask of you until we secure another opportunity of consulting together is to preserve an open mind. Please do not allow my uncle to prejudice you against him."

"What is the name of this young man?"

"He is the Honourable John Haddon."

"The Honourable! Is he a person who could do so dishonourable an action?"

The young lady shook her head.

"I am almost sure he would not, and yet one never can tell. I think at the present moment there are one or two noble lords in prison, but their crimes have not been mere vulgar housebreaking."

"Am I to infer, Lady Alicia, that you are in possession of certain facts unknown either to your uncle or the police?"

"Yes."

"Pardon me, but do these facts tend to incriminate the young man?" Again the young lady leaned back in her chair, and gazed past me, a wrinkle of perplexity on her fair brow. Then she said very slowly:

"You will understand, Monsieur Valmont, how loath I am to speak against one who was formerly a friend. If he had been content to remain a friend, I am sure this incident, which has caused us all such worry and trouble, would never have happened. I do not wish to dwell on what my uncle will tell you was a very unpleasant episode, but the Honourable John Haddon is a poor man, and it is quite out of the question for one brought up as I have been to marry into poverty. He was very headstrong and reckless about the matter, and involved my uncle in a bitter quarrel while discussing it, much to my chagrin and disappointment. It is as necessary for him to marry wealth as it is for me to make a good match, but he could not be brought to see that. Oh, he is not at all a sensible young man, and my former friendship for him has ceased. Yet I should dislike very much to take any action that might harm him, therefore I have spoken to no one but you about the evidence that is in my hands, and this you must treat as entirely confidential, giving no hint to my uncle, who is already bitter enough against Mr. Haddon."

"Does this evidence convince you that he stole the necklace?"

"No; I do not believe that he actually stole it, but I am persuaded he was an accessory after the fact—is that the legal term? Now, Monsieur Valmont, we will say no more tonight. If I talk any longer about this crisis, I shall not sleep, and I wish, assured of your help, to attack the situation with a very clear mind tomorrow."

When I retired to my room, I found that I, too, could not sleep, although I needed a clear mind to face the problem of tomorrow. It is difficult for me to describe accurately the effect this interview had upon my mind, but to use a bodily simile, I may say that it seemed as if I had indulged too freely in a subtle champagne which appeared exceedingly excellent at first, but from which the exhilaration had now departed. No man could have been more completely under a spell than I was when Lady Alicia's eyes first told me more than her lips revealed; but although I had challenged her right to the title "mercenary" when she applied it to herself, I could not but confess that her nonchalant recital regarding the friend who desired to be a lover jarred upon me. I found my sympathy extending itself to that unknown young man, on whom it appeared the shadow of suspicion already rested. I was confident that if he had actually taken the emeralds it was not at all from motives of cupidity. Indeed that was practically shown by the fact that Scotland Yard found itself unable to trace the jewels, which at least they might have done if the necklace had been sold either as a whole or dismembered. Of course, an emerald weighing an ounce is by no means unusual. The Hope emerald, for example, weighs six ounces, and the gem owned by the Duke of Devonshire measures two and a quarter inches through its greatest diameter. Nevertheless, such a constellation as the Blair emeralds was not to be disposed of very easily, and I surmised no attempt had been made either to sell them or to raise money upon them. Now that I had removed myself from the glamour of her presence, I began to suspect that the young lady, after all, although undoubtedly possessing the brilliancy of her jewels, retained also something of their hardness. There had been no expression of sympathy for the discarded friend; it was too evident, recalling what had latterly passed between us, that the young woman's sole desire, and a perfectly natural desire, was to recover her missing treasure. There was something behind all this which I could not comprehend, and I resolved in the morning to question the Marquis of Blair as shrewdly as he cared to allow. Failing him, I should cross-question the niece in a somewhat dryer light than that which had enshrouded me during this interesting evening. I care not who knows it, but I have been befooled more than once by a woman, but I determined that in clear daylight I should resist the hypnotising influence of those glorious eyes. *Mon Dieu! Mon Dieu!* how easy it is for me to make good resolutions when I am far from temptation!

II

It was ten o'clock next morning when I was admitted to the study of the aged bachelor Marquis of Blair. His keen eyes looked through and through me as I seated myself before him.

"Well!" he said shortly.

"My lord," I began deliberately, "I know nothing more of the case than was furnished by the accounts I have read in the newspapers. Two months have elapsed since the robbery. Every day that passed made the detection of the criminal more difficult. I do not wish to waste either my time or your money on a forlorn hope. If, therefore, you will be good enough to place me in possession of all the facts known to you, I shall tell you at once whether or not I can take up the case."

"Do you wish me to give you the name of the criminal?" asked his lordship.

"Is his name known to you?" I asked in return.

"Yes. John Haddon stole the necklace."

"Did you give that name to the police?"

"Yes."

"Why didn't they arrest him?"

"Because the evidence against him is so small, and the improbability of his having committed the crime is so great."

"What is the evidence against him?"

His lordship spoke with the dry deliberation of an aged solicitor.

"The robbery was committed on the night of October the fifth. All day there had been a heavy rain, and the grounds were wet. For reasons into which I do not care to enter, John Haddon was familiar with this house, and with our grounds. He was well known to my servants, and, unfortunately, popular with them, for he is an openhanded spendthrift. The estate of his elder brother, Lord Steffenham, adjoins my own to the west, and Lord Steffenham's house is three miles from where we sit. On the night of the fifth a ball was given in the mansion of Lord Steffenham, to which, of course, my niece and myself were invited, and which invitation we accepted. I had no quarrel with the elder brother. It was known to John Haddon that my niece intended to wear her necklace of emeralds. The robbery occurred at a time when most crimes of that nature are committed in country houses, namely, while we were at dinner, an hour during which the servants are almost invariably in the lower part of the house. In October the days are getting short. The night was exceptionally dark, for, although the rain had ceased, not a star was visible. The thief placed a ladder against the sill of one of the upper windows, opened it, and came in. He must have been perfectly familiar with the house, for there are evidences that he went direct to the boudoir where the jewel case had been carelessly left on my niece's dressing table when she came down to dinner. It had been taken from the strong room about an hour before. The box was locked, but, of course, that made no difference. The thief wrenched the lid off, breaking the lock, stole the necklace, and escaped by the way he came."

"Did he leave the window open, and the ladder in place?"

"Yes."

"Doesn't that strike you as very extraordinary?"

"No. I do not assert that he is a professional burglar, who would take all the precautions against the discovery that might have been expected from one of the craft. Indeed, the man's carelessness in going straight across the country to his brother's house, and leaving footsteps in the soft earth, easily traceable almost to the very boundary fence, shows he is incapable of any serious thought."

"Is John Haddon rich?"

"He hasn't a penny."

"Did you go to the ball that night?"

"Yes, I had promised to go."

"Was John Haddon there?"

"Yes; but he appeared late. He should have been present at the opening, and his brother was seriously annoyed by his absence. When he did come he acted in a wild and reckless manner, which gave the guests the impression that he had been drinking. Both my niece and myself were disgusted with his actions."

"Do you think your niece suspects him?"

"She certainly did not at first, and was indignant when I told her, coming home from the ball, that her jewels were undoubtedly in Steffenham House, even though they were not round her neck, but latterly I think her opinion has changed."

"To go back a moment. Did any of your servants see him prowling about the place?"

"They all say they didn't, but I myself saw him, just before dusk, coming across the fields towards this house, and next morning we found the same footprints both going and coming. It seems to me the circumstantial evidence is rather strong."

"It's a pity that no one but yourself saw him. What more evidence are the authorities waiting for?"

"They are waiting until he attempts to dispose of the jewels."

"You think, then, he has not done so up to date?"

"I think he will never do so."

"Then why did he steal them?"

"To prevent the marriage of my niece with Jonas Carter, of Sheffield, to whom she is betrothed. They were to be married early in the New Year."

"My lord, you amaze me. If Mr. Carter and Lady Alicia are engaged, why should the theft of the jewels interfere with the ceremony?"

"Mr. Jonas Carter is a most estimable man, who, however, does not move in our sphere of life. He is connected with the steel or cutlery industry, and is a person of great wealth, rising upwards of a million, with a large estate in Derbyshire, and a house fronting Hyde Park, in London. He is a very strict business man, and both my niece and myself agree that he is also an eligible man. I myself am rather strict in matters of business, and I must admit that Mr. Carter showed a very generous spirit in arranging the preliminaries of the engagement with me. When Alicia's father died he had run through all the money he himself possessed or could borrow from his friends. Although a man of noble birth, I never liked him. He was married to my only sister. The Blair emeralds, as perhaps you know, descend down the female line. They, therefore, came to my niece from her mother. My poor sister had long been disillusioned before death released her from the titled scamp she had married, and she very wisely placed the emeralds in my custody to be held in trust for her daughter. They constitute my niece's only fortune, and would produce, if offered in London today, probably seventy-five or a hundred thousand pounds, although actually they are not worth so much. Mr. Jonas Carter very amiably consented to receive my niece with a dowry of only fifty thousand pounds, and that money I offered to advance, if I was allowed to retain the jewels as security. This was arranged between Mr. Carter and myself."

"But surely Mr. Carter does not refuse to carry out his engagement because the jewels have been stolen?"

"He does. Why should he not?"

"Then surely you will advance the fifty thousand necessary?"

"I will not. Why should I?"

"Well, it seems to me," said I, with a slight laugh, "the young man has very definitely checkmated both of you."

"He has, until I have laid him by the heels, which I am determined to do if he were the brother of twenty Lord Steffenhams."

"Please answer one more question. Are you determined to put the young man in prison, or would you be content with the return of the emeralds intact?"

"Of course I should prefer to put him in prison and get the emeralds too, but if there's no choice in the matter, I must content myself with the necklace."

"Very well, my lord, I will undertake the case."

This conference had detained us in the study till after eleven, and then, as it was a clear, crisp December morning, I went out through the gardens into the park, that I might walk along the well-kept private road and meditate upon my course of action, or, rather, think over what had been said, because I could not map my route until I had heard the secret which the Lady Alicia promised to impart. As at present instructed, it seemed to me the best way to go direct to the young man, show him as effectively as I could the danger in which he stood, and, if possible, persuade him to deliver up the necklace to me. As I strolled along under the grand old leafless trees, I suddenly heard my name called impulsively two or three times, and turning round saw the Lady Alicia running toward me. Her cheeks were bright with Nature's rouge, and her eyes sparkled more dazzlingly than any emerald that ever tempted man to wickedness.

"Oh, Monsieur Valmont, I have been waiting for you, and you escaped me. Have you seen my uncle?"

"Yes, I have been with him since ten o'clock."

226 ROBERT BARR

"Well?"

"Your ladyship, that is exactly the word with which he accosted me."

"Ah, you see an additional likeness between my uncle and myself this morning, then? Has he told you about Mr. Carter?"

"Yes."

"So now you understand how important it is that I should regain possession of my property?"

"Yes," I said with a sigh; "the house near Hyde Park and the great estate in Derbyshire."

She clapped her hands with glee, eyes and feet dancing in unison, as she capered along gaily beside me; a sort of skippety-hop, skippety-hop, sideways, keeping pace with my more stately step, as if she were a little girl of six instead of a young woman of twenty.

"Not only that!" she cried, "but one million pounds to spend! Oh, Monsieur Valmont, you know Paris, and yet you do not seem to comprehend what that plethora of money means!"

"Well, madame, I have seen Paris, and I have seen a good deal of the world, but I am not so certain you will secure the million to spend."

"What!" she cried, stopping short, that little wrinkle which betokened temper appearing on her brow. "Do you think we won't get the emeralds then?"

"Oh, I am sure we will get the emeralds. I, Valmont, pledge you my word. But if Mr. Jonas Carter before marriage calls a halt upon the ceremony until your uncle places fifty thousand pounds upon the table, I confess I am very pessimistic about your obtaining control of the million afterwards."

All her vivacity instantaneously returned.

"Pooh!" she cried, dancing round in front of me, and standing there directly in my path, so that I came to a stand. "Pooh!" she repeated, snapping her fingers, with an inimitable gesture of that lovely hand. "Monsieur Valmont, I am disappointed in you. You are not nearly so nice as you were last evening. It is very uncomplimentary in you to intimate that when once I am married to Mr.

Jonas I shall not wheedle from him all the money I want. Do not rest your eyes on the ground; look at me and answer!"

I glanced up at her, and could not forbear laughing. The witchery of the wood was in that girl; yes, and a perceptible trace of the Gallic devil flickered in those enchanting eyes of hers. I could not help myself.

"Ah, Madame la Marquise de Bellairs, how jauntily you would scatter despair in that susceptible Court of Louis!"

"Ah, Monsieur Eugène de Valmont," she cried, mimicking my tones, and imitating my manner with an exactitude that amazed me, "you are once more my dear de Valmont of last night. I dreamed of you, I assure you I did, and now to find you in the morning, oh, so changed!" She clasped her little hands and inclined her head, while the sweet voice sank into a cadence of melancholy which seemed so genuine that the mocking ripple of a laugh immediately following was almost a shock to me. Where had this creature of the dull English countryside learnt all such *frou-frou* of gesture and tone?

"Have you ever seen Sarah Bernhardt?" I asked.

Now the average English woman would have inquired the genesis of so inconsequent a question, but Lady Alicia followed the trend of my thought, and answered at once as if my query had been quite expected:

"*Mais non*, monsieur. Sarah the Divine! Ah, she comes with my million a year and the house of Hyde Park. No, the only inhabitant of my real world whom I have yet seen is Monsieur Valmont, and he, alas! I find so changeable. But now, adieu frivolity, we must be serious," and she walked sedately by my side.

"Do you know where you are going, monsieur? You are going to church. Oh, do not look frightened, not to a service. I am decorating the church with holly, and you shall help me and get thorns in your poor fingers."

The private road, which up to this time had passed through a forest, now reached a secluded glade in which stood a very small, but exquisite, church, evidently centuries older than the mansion we had left. Beyond it were gray stone ruins, which Lady Alicia pointed out to me as remnants of the original mansion that had been built in the reign of the second Henry. The church, it was thought, formed the private chapel to the hall, and it had been kept in repair by the various lords of the manor.

"Now hearken to the power of the poor, and learn how they may flout the proud marquis," cried Lady Alicia gleefully; "the poorest man in England may walk along this private road on Sunday to the church, and the proud marquis is powerless to prevent him. Of course, if the poor man prolongs his walk then is he in danger from the law of trespass. On weekdays, however, this is the most secluded spot on the estate, and I regret to say that my lordly uncle does not trouble it even on Sundays. I fear we are a degenerate race, Monsieur Valmont, for doubtless a fighting and deeply religious ancestor of mine built this church, and to think that when the useful masons cemented those stones together, Madame la Marquise de Bellairs or Lady Alicia were alike unthought of, and though three hundred years divide them this ancient chapel makes them seem, as one might say, contemporaries. Oh, Monsieur Valmont, what is the use of worrying about emeralds or anything else? As I look at this beautiful old church, even the house of Hyde Park appears as naught," and to my amazement, the eyes that Lady Alicia turned upon me were wet.

The front door was unlocked, and we walked into the church in silence. Around the pillars holly and ivy were twined. Great armfuls of the shrubs had been flung here and there along the walls in heaps, and a step-ladder stood in one of the aisles, showing that the decoration of the edifice was not yet complete. A subdued melancholy had settled down on my erstwhile vivacious companion, the inevitable reaction so characteristic of the artistic temperament, augmented doubtless by the solemnity of the place, around whose walls in brass and marble were sculptured memorials of her ancient race.

"You promised," I said at last, "to tell me how you came to suspect—"

"Not here, not here," she whispered; then rising from the pew in which she had seated herself, she said:

"Let us go, I am in no mood for working this morning. I shall finish the decoration in the afternoon."

We came out into the cool and brilliant sunlight again, and as we turned homeward, her spirits immediately began to rise.

"I am anxious to know," I persisted, "why you came to suspect a man whom at first you believed innocent."

"I am not sure but I believe him innocent now, although I am forced to the conclusion that he knows where the treasure is."

"What forces you to that conclusion, my lady?"

"A letter I received from himself, in which he makes a proposal so extraordinary that I am almost disinclined to accede to it, even though it leads to the discovery of my necklace. However, I am determined to leave no means untried if I receive the support of my friend, Monsieur Valmont."

"My lady," said I, with a bow, "it is but yours to command, mine to obey. What were the contents of that letter?"

"Read it," she replied, taking the folded sheet from her pocket, and handing it to me.

She had been quite right in characterising the note as an extraordinary epistle. The Honourable John Haddon had the temerity to propose that she should go through a form of marriage with him in the old church we had just left. If she did that, he said, it would console him for the mad love he felt for her. The ceremony would have no binding force upon her whatever, and she might bring whom she pleased to perform it. If she knew no one that she could trust, he would invite an old college chum, and bring him to the church next morning at half-past seven o'clock. Even if an ordained clergyman performed the ceremony, it would not be legal unless it took place between the hours of eight in the morning, and three in the afternoon. If she consented to this, the emeralds were hers once more.

"This is the proposal of a madman," said I, as I handed back the letter.

"Well," she replied, with a nonchalant shrug of her shoulders, "he has always said he was madly in love with me, and I quite believe it. Poor young man, if this mummery were to console him for the rest of his life, why should I not indulge him in it?"

"Lady Alicia, surely you would not countenance the profaning of that lovely old edifice with a mock ceremonial? No man in his senses could suggest such a thing!"

Once more her eyes were twinkling with merriment.

"But the Honourable John Haddon, as I have told you, is not in his senses."

"Then why should you indulge him?"

"Why? How can you ask such a question? Because of the emeralds. It is only a mad lark, after all, and no one need know of it. Oh, Monsieur Valmont," she cried pleadingly, clasping her hands, and yet it seemed to me with an undercurrent of laughter in her beseeching tones, "will you not enact for us the part of clergyman? I am sure if your face were as serious as it is at this moment, the robes of a priest would become you."

"Lady Alicia, you are incorrigible. I am somewhat of a man of the world, yet I should not dare to counterfeit the sacred office, and I hope you but jest. In fact, I am sure you do, my lady."

She turned away from me with a very pretty pout.

"Monsieur Valmont, your knighthood is, after all, but surface deep. 'Tis not mine to command, and yours to obey. Certainly I did but jest. John shall bring his own imitation clergyman with him."

"Are you going to meet him tomorrow?"

"Certainly I am. I have promised. I must secure my necklace."

"You seem to place great confidence in the belief that he will produce it."

"If he fails to do so, then I play Monsieur Valmont as my trump card. But, monsieur, although you quite rightly refuse to comply with my first request, you will surely not reject my second. Please meet me tomorrow at the head of the avenue, promptly at a quarter-past seven, and escort me to the church."

For a moment the negative trembled on my tongue's end, but she turned those enchanting eyes upon me, and I was undone.

"Very well," I answered.

She seized both my hands, like a little girl overjoyed at a promised excursion.

"Oh, Monsieur Valmont, you are a darling! I feel as if I'd known you all my life. I am sure you will never regret having humoured me," then added a moment later, "if we get the emeralds."

"Ah," said I, "*if* we get the emeralds."

We were now within sight of the house, and she pointed out our rendezvous for the following day, and with that I bade her good-bye.

It was shortly after seven o'clock next morning when I reached the meeting-place. The Lady Alicia was somewhat long in coming, but when she arrived her face was aglow with girlish delight at the solemn prank she was about to play.

"You have not changed your mind?" I asked, after the morning's greetings.

"Oh, no, Monsieur Valmont," she replied, with a bright laugh. "I am determined to recover those emeralds."

"We must hurry, Lady Alicia, or we will be too late."

"There is plenty of time," she remarked calmly; and she proved to be right, because when we came in sight of the church, the clock pointed to the hour of half-past seven.

"Now," she said "I shall wait here until you steal up to the church and look in through one of the windows that do not contain stained glass. I should not for the world arrive before Mr. Haddon and his friend are there."

I did as requested, and saw two young men standing together in the centre aisle, one in the full robes of a clergyman, the other in his ordinary dress, whom I took to be the Honourable John Haddon. His profile was toward me, and I must admit there was very little of the madman in his calm countenance. His was a well-cut face, clean shaven, and strikingly manly. In one of the pews was seated a woman—I learned afterwards she was Lady Alicia's maid, who had been instructed to come and go from the house by a footpath, while we had taken the longer road. I returned and escorted Lady Alicia to the church, and there was introduced to Mr. Haddon and his friend, the made-up divine. The ceremony was at once performed, and, man of the world as I professed myself to be, this enacting of private theatricals in a church grated upon me. When the maid and I were asked to sign the book as witnesses, I said:

"Surely this is carrying realism a little too far?"

Mr. Haddon smiled, and replied:

"I am amazed to hear a Frenchman objecting to realism going to its full length, and speaking for myself, I should be delighted to see the autograph of the renowned Eugène Valmont," and with that he proffered me the pen, whereupon I scrawled my signature. The maid had already signed, and disappeared. The reputed clergyman bowed us out of the church, standing in the porch to see us walk up the avenue.

"Ed," cried John Haddon, "I'll be back within half an hour, and we'll attend to the clock. You won't mind waiting?"

"Not in the least, dear boy. God bless you both," and the tremor in his voice seemed to me carrying realism one step further still.

The Lady Alicia, with downcast head, hurried us on until we were within the gloom of the forest, and then, ignoring me, she turned suddenly to the young man, and placed her two hands on his shoulders.

"Oh, Jack, Jack!" she cried.

He kissed her twice on the lips.

"Jack, Monsieur Valmont insists on the emeralds."

The young man laughed. Her ladyship stood fronting him with her back towards me. Tenderly the young man unfastened something at the throat of that high-necked dress of hers, then there was a snap, and he drew out an amazing, dazzling, shimmering sheen of green, that seemed to turn the whole bleak December landscape verdant as with a touch of spring. The girl hid her rosy face against him, and over her shoulder, with a smile, he handed me the celebrated Blair emeralds.

"There is the treasure, Valmont," he cried, "on condition that you do not molest the culprit."

"Or the accessory after the fact," gurgled Lady Alicia in smothered tones, with a hand clasping together her high-necked dress at the throat.

"We trust to your invention, Valmont, to deliver that necklace to uncle with a detective story that will thrill him to his very heart."

We heard the clock strike eight; then a second later smaller bells chimed a quarter-past, and another second after they tinkled the half-hour. "Hallo!" cried Haddon, "Ed has attended to the clock himself. What a good fellow he is."

I looked at my watch; it was twenty-five minutes to nine.

"Was the ceremony genuine then?" I asked.

"Ah, Valmont," said the young man, patting his wife affectionately on the shoulder, "nothing on earth can be more genuine than that ceremony was."

And the volatile Lady Alicia snuggled closer to him.

Mr. Keen,
The Tracer of Lost Persons

ONE

He was thirty-three, agreeable to look at, equipped with as much culture and intelligence as is tolerated east of Fifth Avenue and west of Madison. He had a couple of elaborate rooms at the Lenox Club, a larger income than seemed to be good for him, and no profession. It follows that he was a pessimist before breakfast. Besides, it's a bad thing for a man at thirty-three to come to the conclusion that he has seen all the most attractive girls in the world and that they have been vastly overrated. So, when a club servant with gilt buttons on his coat tails knocked at the door, the invitation to enter was not very cordial. He of the buttons knocked again to take the edge off before he entered; then opened the door and unburdened himself as follows:

"Mr. Gatewood, sir, Mr. Kerns's compliments, and wishes to know if 'e may 'ave 'is coffee served at your tyble, sir."

Gatewood, before the mirror, gave a vicious twist to his tie, inserted a pearl scarf pin, and regarded the effect with gloomy approval.

"Say to Mr. Kerns that I am—flattered," he replied morosely; "and tell Henry I want him."

"'Enry, sir? Yes, sir."

The servant left; one of the sleek club valets came in, softly sidling.

"Henry!"

"Sir?"

"I'll wear a white waistcoat, if you don't object."

The valet laid out half a dozen.

"Which one do you usually wear when I'm away, Henry? Which is *your* favorite?"

"Sir?"

"Pick it out and don't look injured, and *don't* roll up your eyes. I merely desire to borrow it for one day."

"Very good, sir."

"And, Henry, hereafter always help yourself to my *best* cigars. Those I smoke may injure you. I've attempted to conceal the keys, but you will, of course, eventually discover them under that loose tile on the hearth."

"Yes, sir; thanky', sir," returned the valet gravely.

"And—Henry!"

"Sir?" with martyred dignity.

"When you are tired of searching for my olivine and opal pin, just find it, for a change. I'd like to wear that pin for a day or two if it would not inconvenience you."

"Very good, sir; I will 'unt it hup, sir."

Gatewood put on his coat, took hat and gloves from the unabashed valet, and sauntered down to the sunny breakfast room, where he found Kerns inspecting a morning paper and leisurely consuming grapefruit with a cocktail on the side.

"Hullo," observed Kerns briefly.

"I'm not on the telephone," snapped Gatewood.

"I beg your pardon; how are you, dear friend?"

"*I* don't know how I am," retorted Gatewood irritably; "how the devil should a man know how he is?"

"Everything going to the bowwows, *as* usual, dear friend?"

"*As* usual. Oh, read your paper, Tommy! You know well enough I'm not one of those tail-wagging imbeciles who wakes up in the morning singing like a half-witted lark. Why should I, with this taste in my mouth, and the laundress using vitriol, and Henry sneering at my cigars?" He yawned and cast his eyes toward the ceiling. "Besides, there's too much gilt all over this club! There's too much everywhere. Half the world is stucco, the rest rococo. Where's that Martini I bid for?"

Kerns, undisturbed, applied himself to cocoa and toasted muffins. Grapefruit and an amber-tinted accessory were brought for the other and sampled without mirth. However, a little later Gatewood said: "Well, are you going to read your paper all day?"

"What you need," said Kerns, laying the paper aside, "is a job—any old kind would do, dear friend."

"I don't want to make any more money."

"I don't want you to. I mean a job where you'd lose a lot and be scared into thanking Heaven for carfare. *You're* a nice object for the breakfast table!"

"Bridge. I will be amiable enough by noon time."

"Yes, you're endurable by noon time, as a rule. When you're forty you may be tolerated after five o'clock; when you're fifty your wife and children might even venture to emerge from the cellar after dinner—"

"Wife!"

"I said wife," replied Kerns, as he calmly watched his man.

He had managed it well, so far, and he was wise enough not to overdo it. An interval of silence was what the situation required.

"I wish I *had* a wife," muttered Gatewood after a long pause.

"Oh, haven't you said that every day for five years? Wife! Look at the willing assortment of dreams playing Sally Waters around town. Isn't this borough a bower of beauty—a flowery thicket where the prettiest kind in all the world grow under glass or outdoors? And what do you do? You used to pretend to prowl about inspecting the yearly crop of posies, growling, cynical, dissatisfied; but you've even given that up. Now you only point your nose skyward and squall for a mate, and yowl mournfully that you never have seen your ideal. *I* know *you*."

"I never have seen my ideal," retorted Gatewood sulkily, "but I know she exists—somewhere between heaven and Hoboken."

"You're sure, are you?"

"Oh, *I'm* sure. And, rich or poor, good or bad, she was fashioned for me alone. That's a theory of mine; *you* needn't accept it; in fact, it's none of your business, Tommy."

"All the same," insisted Kerns, "did you ever consider that if your ideal does exist somewhere, it is morally up to you to find her?"

"Haven't I inspected every débutante for ten years? You don't expect me to advertise for an ideal, do you—object, matrimony?"

Kerns regarded him intently. "Now, I'm going to make a vivid suggestion, Jack. In fact, that's why I subjected myself to the ordeal of breakfasting with you. It's none of my business, as you so kindly put it, but—*shall* I suggest something?"

"Go ahead," replied Gatewood, tranquilly lighting a cigarette. "I know what you'll say."

"No, you don't. Firstly, you are having such a good time in this world that you don't really enjoy yourself—isn't that so?"

"I—well I—well, let it go at that."

"Secondly, with all your crimes and felonies, you have one decent trait left: you really would like to fall in love. And I suspect you'd even marry."

"There are grounds," said Gatewood guardedly, "for your suspicions. *Et après?*"

"Good. Then there's a way! I know—"

"Oh, don't tell me you 'know a girl,' or anything like that!" began Gatewood sullenly. "I've heard that before, and I won't meet her."

"I don't want you to; I don't know anybody. All I desire to say is this: I do know a way. The other day I noticed a sign on Fifth Avenue:

KEEN & CO.
TRACERS OF LOST PERSONS

It was a most extraordinary sign; and having a little unemployed imagination I began to speculate on how Keen & Co. might operate, and I wondered a little, too, that, the conditions of life in this city could enable a firm to make a living by devoting itself exclusively to the business of hunting up missing people."

Kerns paused, partly to light a cigarette, partly for diplomatic reasons.

"What has all this to do with me?" inquired Gatewood curiously; and diplomacy scored one.

"Why not try Keen & Co.?"

"Try them? Why? I haven't lost anybody, have I?"

"You haven't, precisely *lost anybody*, but the fact remains that you can't *find somebody*," returned Kerns coolly. "Why not employ Keen & Co. to look for her?"

"Look for whom, in Heaven's name?"

"Your ideal."

"Look for—for my ideal! Kerns, you're crazy. How the mischief can anybody hunt for somebody who doesn't exist?"

"You *say* that she *does* exist."

"But I can't prove it, man."

"You don't have to; it's up to Keen & Co. to prove it. That's why you employ them."

"What wild nonsense you talk! Keen & Co. might, perhaps, be able to trace the concrete, but how are they going to trace and find the abstract?"

"She isn't abstract; she is a lovely, healthy, and youthful concrete object—if, as you say, she *does* exist."

"How can I *prove* she exists?"

"You don't have to; they do that."

"Look here," said Gatewood almost angrily, "do you suppose that if I were ass enough to go to these people and tell them that I wanted to find my ideal—"

"*Don't* tell them *that!*"

"But how—"

"There is no necessity for going into such trivial details. All you need say is: 'I am very anxious to find a young lady'—and then describe her as minutely as you please. Then, when they locate a girl of that description they'll notify you; you will go, judge for yourself whether she is the one woman on earth—and, if disappointed, you need only shake your head and murmur: 'Not *the same!*' And it's for them to find another."

"I won't do it!" said Gatewood hotly.

"Why not? At least, it would be amusing. You haven't many mental resources, and it might occupy you for a week or two."

Gatewood glared.

"You have a pleasant way of putting things this morning, haven't you?"

"I don't want to be pleasant: I want to jar you. Don't I care enough about you to breakfast with you? Then I've a right to be pleasantly unpleasant. I can't bear to watch your mental and spiritual dissolution—a man like you, with all your latent ability and capacity for being nobody in particular—which is the sort of man this nation needs. Do you want to turn into a club-window gazer like Van Bronk? Do you want to become another Courtlandt Allerton and go rocking down the avenue—a grimacing, tailor-made sepulcher?—the pompous obsequies of a dead intellect?—a funeral on two wavering legs, carrying the corpse of all that should be deathless in a man? Why, Jack, I'd rather see you in bankruptcy—I'd rather see you trying to lead a double life in a single flat on seven dollars and a half a week—I'd almost rather see you every day at breakfast than have it come to that!

"Wake up and get jocund with life! Why, you could have all good citizens stung to death if you chose. It isn't that I want you to make money; but I want you to worry over somebody besides yourself—not in Wall Street—a pool and its money are soon parted. But in your own home, where a beautiful wife and seven angel children have you dippy and close to the ropes; where the housekeeper gets a rake off, and the cook is red-headed and comes from Sligo, and the butler's cousin will bear watching, and the chauffeur is a Frenchman, and the coachman's uncle is a Harlem vet, and every scullion in the establishment lies, drinks, steals, and supports twenty satiated relatives at your expense. That would mean the making of you; for, after all, Jack, you are no genius—you're a plain, non-partisan, uninspired, clean-built, wholesome citizen, thank God!—the sort whose unimaginative mission is to pitch in with eighty-odd millions of us and, like the busy coral creatures, multiply with all your might, and make this little old Republic the greatest, biggest, finest article that an overworked world has ever yet put up! . . . Now you can call for help if you choose."

Gatewood's breath returned slowly. In an intimacy of many years he had never suspected that sort of thing from Kerns. That is why, no doubt, the opinions expressed by Kerns stirred him to an astonishment too innocent to harbor anger or chagrin.

And when Kerns stood up with an unembarrassed laugh, saying, "I'm going to the office; see you this evening?" Gatewood replied rather vacantly: "Oh, yes; I'm dining here. Good-by, Tommy."

Kerns glanced at his watch, lingering. "Was there anything you wished to ask me, Jack?" he inquired guilelessly.

"Ask you? No, I don't think so."

"Oh; I had an idea you might care to know where Keen & Co. were to be found."

"*That*," said Gatewood firmly, "is foolish."

"I'll write the address for you, anyway," rejoined Kerns, scribbling it and handing the card to his friend.

Then he went down the stairs, several at a time, eased in conscience, satisfied that he had done his duty by a friend he cared enough for to breakfast with.

"Of course," he ruminated as he crawled into a hansom and lay back buried in meditation— "of course there may be nothing in this Keen & Co. business. But it will stir him up and set him thinking; and the longer Keen & Co. take to hunt up an imaginary lady that doesn't exist, the more anxious and impatient poor old Jack Gatewood will become, until he'll catch the fever and go cantering about with that one fixed idea in his head. And," added Kerns softly, "no New Yorker in his right mind can go galloping through these five boroughs very long before he's roped, tied, and marked by the 'only girl in the world'—the *only* girl—if you don't care to turn around and look at another million girls precisely like her. O Lord!—precisely like her!"

Here was a nice exhorter to incite others to matrimony.

TWO

Meanwhile, Gatewood was walking along Fifth Avenue, more or less soothed by the May sunshine. First, he went to his hatters, looked at straw hats, didn't like them, protested, and bought one, wishing he had strength of mind enough to wear it home. But he hadn't. Then he entered the huge white marble palace of his jeweler, left his watch to be regulated, caught a glimpse of a girl whose hair and neck resembled the hair and neck of his ideal, sidled around until he discovered that she was chewing gum, and backed off, with a bitter smile, into the avenue once more.

Every day for years he had had glimpses of girls whose hair, hands, figures, eyes, hats, carriage, resembled the features required by his ideal; there always was something wrong somewhere. And, as he strolled moodily, a curious feeling of despair seized him—something that, even in his most sentimental moments, even amid the most unexpected disappointment, he had never before experienced.

"I do want to love *somebody*!" he found himself saying half aloud; "I want to marry; I—" He turned to look after three pretty children with their maids— "I want several like those—several!—seven—ten—I don't care how many! I want a house to worry me, just as Tommy described it; I want to see the same girl across the breakfast table—or she can sip her cocoa in bed if she desires—" A slow, modest blush stole over his features; it was one of the nicest things he ever did. Glancing up, he beheld across the way a white sign, ornamented with strenuous crimson lettering:

KEEN & CO.
TRACERS OF LOST PERSONS

The moment he discovered it, he realized he had been covertly hunting for it; he also realized that he was going to climb the stairs. He hadn't quite decided what he meant to do after that; nor was his mind clear on the matter when he found himself opening a door of opaque glass on which was printed in red:

KEEN & CO.

He was neither embarrassed nor nervous when he found himself in a big carpeted anteroom where a negro attendant bowed him to a seat and took his card; and he looked calmly around to see what was to be seen.

Several people occupied easy chairs in various parts of the room—an old woman very neatly dressed, clutching in her withered hand a photograph which she studied and studied with tear-dimmed eyes; a young man wearing last year's most fashionable styles in everything except his features: and soap could have aided him there; two policemen, helmets resting on their knees; and, last of all, a rather thin child of twelve, staring open-mouthed at everybody, a bundle of soiled clothing under one arm. Through an open door he saw a dozen young women garbed in black, with white cuffs and collars, all rattling away steadily at typewriters. Every now and then, from some hidden office, a bell rang decisively, and one of the girls would rise from her machine and pass noiselessly out of sight to obey the summons. From time to time, too, the darky servant with marvelous manners would usher somebody through the room where the typewriters were rattling, into the unseen office. First the old woman went—shakily, clutching her photograph; then the thin child with the bundle, staring at everything; then the two fat policemen, in portentous single file, helmets in their white-gloved hands, oiled hair glistening.

Gatewood's turn was approaching; he waited without any definite emotion, watching newcomers enter to take the places of those

ROBERT W. CHAMBERS

who had been summoned. He hadn't the slightest idea of what he was to say; nor did it worry him. A curious sense of impending good fortune left him pleasantly tranquil; he picked up, from the silver tray on the table at his elbow, one of the firm's business cards, and scanned it with interest:

KEEN & CO.
TRACERS OF LOST PERSONS
Keen & Co. are prepared to locate the where-abouts of anybody on earth. No charges will be made unless the person searched for is found.
Blanks on application.
WESTREL KEEN, *Manager.*

"Mistuh Keen will see you, suh," came a persuasive voice at his elbow; and he rose and followed the softly moving colored servant out of the room, through a labyrinth of demure young women at their typewriters, then sharply to the right and into a big, hand-somely furnished office, where a sleepy-looking elderly gentleman rose from an armchair and bowed. There could not be the slightest doubt that he *was* a gentleman; every movement, every sound he uttered, settled the fact.

"Mr. Keen?"

"Mr. Gatewood?"—with a quiet certainty which had its charm. "This is very good of you."

Gatewood sat down and looked at his host. Then he said: "I'm searching for somebody, Mr. Keen, whom you are not likely to find."

"I doubt it," said Keen pleasantly.

Gatewood smiled. "If," he said, "you will undertake to find the person *I* cannot find, I must ask you to accept a retainer."

"We don't require retainers," replied Keen. "Unless we find the person sought for, we make no charges, Mr. Gatewood."

"I must ask you to do so in my case. It is not fair that you should undertake it on other terms. I desire to make a special arrange-ment with you. Do you mind?"

"What arrangement had you contemplated?" inquired Keen, amused.

"Only this: charge me in advance exactly what you would charge if successful. And, on the other hand, do not ask me for detailed information—I mean, do not insist on any information that I decline to give. Do you mind taking up such an extraordinary and unbusinesslike proposition, Mr. Keen?"

The Tracer of Lost Persons looked up sharply:

"About how much information *do* you decline to give, Mr. Gatewood?"

"About enough to incriminate and degrade," replied the young man, laughing.

The elderly gentleman sat silent, apparently buried in meditation. Once or twice his pleasant steel-gray eyes wandered over Gatewood as an expert, a connoisseur, glances at a picture and assimilates its history, its value, its artistic merit, its every detail in one practiced glance.

"I think we may take up this matter for you, Mr. Gatewood," he said, smiling his singularly agreeable smile.

"But—but you would first desire to know something about me—would you not?"

Keen looked at him: "You will not mistake me—you will consider it entirely inoffensive—if I say that I know something about you, Mr. Gatewood?"

"About *me*? How can you? Of course, there is the social register and the club lists and all that—"

"And many, many sources of information which are necessary in such a business as this, Mr. Gatewood. It is a necessity for us to be almost as well informed as our clients' own lawyers. I could pay you no sincerer compliment than to undertake your case. I am half inclined to do so even *without* a retainer. Mind, I haven't yet said that I *will* take it."

"I prefer to regulate any possible indebtedness in advance," said Gatewood.

"As you wish," replied the older man, smiling. "In that case, suppose you draw your check" (he handed Gatewood a fountain pen as the young man fished a check-book from his pocket)— "your check for—well, say for $5,000, to the order of Keen & Co."

Gatewood met his eye without wincing; he was in for it now; and he was always perfectly game. He had brought it upon himself; it was his own proposition. Not that he would have for a moment considered the sum as high—or any sum exorbitant—if there had been a chance of success; one cannot compare and weigh such matters. But how could there be any chance for success?

As he slowly smoothed out the check and stub, pen poised, Keen was saying: "Of course, we should succeed sooner or later—if we took up your case. We might succeed to-morrow—to-day. That would mean a large profit for us. But we might not succeed to-day, or next month, or even next year. That would leave us little or no profit; and, as it is our custom to go on until we do succeed, no matter how long it may require, you see, Mr. Gatewood, I should be taking all sorts of chances. It might even cost us double your retainer before we found her—"

"Her? How did—*why* do you say '*her*'?"

"Am I wrong?" asked Keen, smiling.

"No—you are right."

The Tracer of Lost Persons sank into abstraction again. Gatewood waited, hoping that his case might be declined, yet ready to face any music started at his own request.

"She is young," mused Keen aloud, "very beautiful and accomplished. *Is* she wealthy?" He looked up mildly.

Gatewood said: "I don't know—the truth is I don't care—" And stopped.

"O-ho!" mused Keen slowly. "I—think—I understand. Am I wrong, Mr. Gatewood, in surmising that this young lady whom you seek is, in your eyes, very—I may say ideally gifted?"

"She is my ideal," replied the young man, coloring.

"*Ex*actly. And—her general allure?"

"Charming!"

"*Ex*actly; but to be a trifle more precise—if you could give me a sketch, an idea, a mere outline delicately tinted, now. *Is* she more blond than brunette?"

"Yes—but her eyes are brown. I—I insist on that."

"Why should you not? *You* know her; I don't," said Keen, laughing. "I merely wished to form a mental picture. . . . You say her hair is—is—"

"It's full of sunny color; that's all I can say."

"*Ex*actly—I see. A rare and lovely combination with brown eyes and creamy skin, Mr. Gatewood. I fancy she might be, perhaps, an inch or two under your height?"

"Just about that. Her hands should be—*are* beautiful—"

"*Ex*actly. The ensemble is most vividly portrayed, Mr. Gatewood; and—you have intimated that her lack of fortune—er—we might almost say her pecuniary distress—is more than compensated for by her accomplishments, character, and very unusual beauty. . . . *Did* I so understand you, Mr. Gatewood?"

"That's what I meant, anyhow," he said, flushing up.

"You *did* mean it?"

"I did: I do."

"Then we take your case, Mr. Gatewood. . . . No haste about the check, my dear sir—pray consider us at your service."

But Gatewood doggedly filled in the check and handed it to the Tracer of Lost Persons.

"I wish you happiness," said the older man in a low voice. "The lady you describe exists; it is for us to discover her."

"Thank you," stammered Gatewood, astounded.

Keen touched an electric button; a moment later a young girl entered the room.

"Miss Southerland, Mr. Gatewood. Will you be kind enough to take Mr. Gatewood's dictation in Room 19?"

For a second Gatewood stared—as though in the young girl before him the ghost of his ideal had risen to confront him—only for a second; then he bowed, matching her perfect acknowledgment of his presence by a bearing and courtesy which must have been inbred to be so faultless.

And he followed her to Room 19.

What had Keen meant by saying, "The lady you describe exists!" Did this remarkable elderly gentleman suspect that it was to be a hunt for an ideal? Had he deliberately entered into such a bargain? Impossible!

His disturbed thoughts reverted to the terms of the bargain, the entire enterprise, the figures on his check. His own amazing imbecility appalled him. What idiocy! What sudden madness had seized him to entangle himself in such unheard-of negotiations! True, he had played bridge until dawn the night before, but, on awaking, he had discovered no perceptible hold-over. It must have been sheer weakness of intellect that permitted him to be dominated by the suggestions of Kerns. And now the game was on: the jack declared, cards dealt, and his ante was up. Had he openers?

Room 19, duly labeled with its number on the opaque glass door, contained a desk, a table and typewriter, several comfortable chairs, and a window opening on Fifth Avenue, through which the eastern sun poured a stream of glory, washing curtain, walls, and ceiling with palest gold.

And all this time, preoccupied with new impressions and his own growing chagrin, he watched the girl who conducted him with all the unconscious assurance and grace of a young chatelaine passing through her own domain under escort of a distinguished guest.

When they had entered Room 19, she half turned, but he forestalled her and closed the door, and she passed before him with a perceptible inclination of her finely modeled head, seating herself at the desk by the open window. He took an armchair at her elbow and removed his gloves, looking at her expectantly.

THREE

"This is a list of particular and general questions for you to answer, Mr. Gatewood," she said, handing him a long slip of printed matter. "The replies to such questions as you are able or willing to answer you may dictate to me." The beauty of her modulated voice was scarcely a surprise—no woman who moved and carried herself as did this tall young girl in black and white could reasonably be expected to speak with less distinction—yet the charm of her voice, from the moment her lips unclosed, so engrossed him that the purport of her speech escaped him.

"Would you mind saying it once more?" he asked.

She did so; he attempted to concentrate his attention, and succeeded sufficiently to look as though some vestige of intellect remained in him. He saw her pick up a pad and pencil; the contour and grace of two deliciously fashioned hands arrested his mental process once more.

"I *beg* your pardon," he said hastily; "what were you saying, Miss Southerland?"

"Nothing, Mr. Gatewood. I did not speak." And he realized, hazily, that she had not spoken—that it was the subtle eloquence of her youth and loveliness that had appealed like a sudden voice— a sound faintly exquisite echoing his own thought of her.

Troubled, he looked at the slip of paper in his hand; it was headed:

SPECIAL DESCRIPTION BLANK
(*Form K*)

And he read it as carefully as he was able to—the curious little clamor of his pulses, the dazed sense of elation, almost of expectation, distracting his attention all the time.

"I wish you would read it to me," he said; "that would give me time to think up answers."

"If you wish," she assented pleasantly, swinging around toward him in her desk chair. Then she crossed one knee over the other to support the pad, and, bending above it, lifted her brown eyes. She could have done nothing in the world more distracting at that moment.

"What is the sex of the person you desire to find, Mr. Gatewood?"

"Her sex? I—well, I fancy it is feminine."

She wrote after "Sex" the words "She is probably feminine"; looked at him absently, glanced at what she had written, flushed a little, rubbed out the "she is probably," wondering why a moment's mental wandering should have committed her to absurdity.

"Married?" she asked with emphasis.

"No," he replied, startled; then, vexed, "I beg your pardon—you mean to ask if *she* is married!"

"Oh, I didn't mean *you*, Mr. Gatewood; it's the next question, you see"—she held out the blank toward him. "Is the person you are looking for married?"

"Oh, no; she isn't married, either—at least—trust—not—because if she *is* I don't want to find her!" he ended, entangled in an explanation which threatened to involve him deeper than he desired. And, looking up, he saw the beautiful brown eyes regarding him steadily. They reverted to the paper at once, and the white fingers sent the pencil flying.

"He trusts that she is unmarried, but if she *is* (underlined) married he doesn't want to find her," she wrote.

"That," she explained, "goes under the head of 'General Remarks' at the bottom of the page"—she held it out, pointing with her pencil. He nodded, staring at her slender hand.

"Age?" she continued, setting the pad firmly on her rounded, yielding knee and looking up at him.

"Age? Well, I—as a matter of fact, I could only venture a surmise. You know," he said earnestly, "how difficult it is to guess ages, don't you, Miss Southerland?"

"How old do you *think* she is? Could you not hazard a guess—judging, say, from her appearance?"

"I have no data—no experience to guide me." He was becoming involved again. "Would you, for practice, permit me first to guess your age, Miss Southerland?"

"Why—yes—if you think that might help you to guess hers."

So he leaned back in his armchair and considered her a very long time—having a respectable excuse to do so. Twenty times he forgot he was looking at her for any purpose except that of disinterested delight, and twenty times he remembered with a guilty wince that it was a matter of business.

"Perhaps I had better tell you," she suggested, her color rising a little under his scrutiny.

"Is it eighteen? Just *her* age!"

"Twenty-one, Mr. Gatewood—and you *said* you didn't know her age."

"I have just remembered that I *thought* it might be eighteen; but I dare say I was shy three years in her case, too. You may put it down at twenty-one."

For the slightest fraction of a second the brown eyes rested on his, the pencil hovered in hesitation. Then the eyes fell, and the moving fingers wrote.

"Did you write 'twenty-one'?" he inquired carelessly.

"I did not, Mr. Gatewood."

"What did you write?"

"I wrote: 'He doesn't appear to know much about her age.'"

"But I *do* know—"

"You said—" They looked at one another earnestly.

"The next question," she continued with composure, "is: 'Date and place of birth?' Can you answer any part of *that* question?"

"I trust I may be able to—some day. . . . What *are* you writing?"

"I'm writing: 'He trusts he may be able to, some day.' Wasn't that what you said?"

"Yes, I did say that. I—I'm not perfectly sure what I meant by it."

She passed to the next question:

"Height?"

"About five feet six," he said, fascinated gaze on her.

"Hair?"

"More gold than brown—full of—er—gleams—" She looked up quickly; his eyes reverted to the window rather suddenly. He had been looking at her hair.

"Complexion?" she continued after a shade of hesitation.

"It's a sort of delicious mixture—bisque, tinted with a pinkish bloom—ivory and rose—" He was explaining volubly, when she began to shake her head, timing each shake to his words.

"Really, Mr. Gatewood, I think you are hopelessly vague on that point—unless you desire to convey the impression that she is speckled."

"Speckled!" he repeated, horrified. "Why, I am describing a woman who is my ideal of beauty—"

But she had already gone to the next question:

"Teeth?"

"P-p-perfect p-p-pearls!" he stammered. The laughing red mouth closed like a flower at dusk, veiling the sparkle of her teeth.

Was he trying to be impertinent? Was he deliberately describing her? He did not look like that sort of man; yet *why* was he watching her so closely, so curiously at every question? Why did he look at her teeth when she laughed?

"Eyes?" Her own dared him to continue what, coincidence or not, was plainly a description of herself.

"B-b-b—" He grew suddenly timorous, hesitating, pretending to a perplexity which was really a healthy scare. For she was frowning.

"Curious I can't think of the color of her eyes," he said; "is—isn't it?"

She coldly inspected her pad and made a correction; but all she did was to rub out a comma and put another in its place. Meanwhile, Gatewood, chin in his hand, sat buried in profound thought.

"*Were* they blue?" he murmured to himself aloud, "or *were* they brown? Blue begins with a *b* and brown begins with a *b*. I'm convinced that her eyes began with a *b*. They were not, therefore, gray or green, because," he added in a burst of confidence, "it is utterly impossible to spell gray or green with a *b*!"

Miss Southerland looked slightly astonished.

"All you can recollect, then, is that the color of her eyes began with the letter *b*?"

"That is absolutely all I can remember; but I *think* they *were*—brown."

"If they *were* brown they must be brown now," she observed, looking out of the window.

"That's true! Isn't it curious I never thought of that? What are you writing?"

"Brown," she said, so briefly that it sounded something like a snub.

"Mouth?" inquired the girl, turning a new leaf on her pad.

"Perfect. Write it: there is no other term fit to describe its color, shape, its sensitive beauty, its—*What* did you write just then?"

"I wrote, 'Mouth, ordinary.'"

"I don't want you to! I want—"

"Really, Mr. Gatewood, a rhapsody on a girl's mouth is proper in poetry, but scarcely germane to the record of a purely business transaction. Please answer the next question tersely, if you don't mind: 'Figure?'"

"Oh, I *do* mind! I can't! Any poem is much too brief to describe her figure—"

"Shall we say 'Perfect'?" asked the girl, raising her brown eyes in a glimmering transition from vexation to amusement. For, after all, it could be *only* a coincidence that this young man should be describing features peculiar to herself.

"Couldn't you write, 'Venus-of-Milo-like'?" he inquired. "That is laconic."

"I could—if it's true. But if you mean it for praise—I—don't think any modern woman would be flattered."

"I always supposed that she of Milo had an ideal figure," he said, perplexed.

She wrote, "A good figure." Then, propping her rounded chin on one lovely white hand, she glanced at the next question:

"Hands?"

"White, beautiful, rose-tipped, slender yet softly and firmly rounded—"

"How *can* they be soft and firm, too, Mr. Gatewood?" she protested; then, surprising his guilty eyes fixed on her hands, hastily dropped them and sat up straight, level-browed, cold as marble. *Was* he deliberately being rude to her?

FOUR

As a matter of fact, he was not. Too poor in imagination to invent, on the spur of the moment, charms and qualities suited to his ideal, he had, at first unconsciously, taken as a model the girl before him; quite unconsciously and innocently at first—then furtively, and with a dawning perception of the almost flawless beauty he was secretly plagiarizing. Aware, now, that something had annoyed her; aware, too, at the same moment that there appeared to be nothing lacking in her to satisfy his imagination of the ideal, he began to turn redder than he had ever turned in all his life.

Several minutes of sixty seconds each ensued before he ventured to stir a finger. And it was only when she bent again very gravely over her pad that he cautiously eased a cramped muscle or two, and drew a breath—a long, noiseless, deep and timid respiration. He realized the enormity of what he had been doing—how close he had come to giving unpardonable offense by drawing a perfect portrait of her as the person he desired to find through the good offices of Keen & Co.

But there was no such person—unless she had a double: for what more could a man desire than the ideal traits he had been able to describe only by using her as his inspiration.

When he ventured to look at her, one glance was enough to convince him that she, too, had noticed the parallel—had been forced to recognize her own features in the portrait he had constructed of an ideal. And she had caught him in absent-minded contemplation of the hands he had been describing. He knew that his face was the face of a guilty man.

"What is the next question?" he stammered, eager to answer it in a manner calculated to allay her suspicions.

"The next question?" She glanced at the list, then with a voice of velvet which belied the eyes, clear as frosty brown pools in November: "The next question requires a description of her feet."

"Feet! Oh—they—they're rather large—why, her feet are enormous, I believe—"

She looked at him as though stunned; suddenly a flood of pink spread, wave on wave, from the white nape of her neck to her hair; she bent low over her pad and wrote something, remaining in that attitude until her face cooled.

"Somehow or other I've done it again!" he thought, horrified. "The best thing I can do is to end it and go home."

In his distress he began to hedge, saying: "Of course, she is rather tall and her feet are in some sort of proportion—in fact, they are perfectly symmetrical feet—"

Never in his life had he encountered a pair of such angrily beautiful eyes. Speech stopped with a dry gulp.

"We now come to 'General Remarks,'" she said in a voice made absolutely steady and emotionless. "Have you any remarks of that description to offer, Mr. Gatewood?"

"I'm willing to make remarks," he said, "if I only knew what you wished me to say."

She mused, eyes on the sunny window, then looked up. "Where did you last see her?"

"Near Fifth Avenue."

"And what street?"

He named the street.

"Near *here*?"

"Rather," he said timidly.

She ruffled the edges of her pad, wrote something and erased it, bit her scarlet upper lip, and frowned.

"Out of doors, of course?"

"No; indoors," he admitted furtively.

She looked up with a movement almost nervous.

"Do you dare—I mean, care—to be more concise?"

"I would rather not," he replied in a voice from which he hoped he had expelled the tremors of alarm.

"As you please, Mr. Gatewood. And would you care to answer any of these other questions: Who and what are or were her parents? Give all particulars concerning all her relatives. Is she employed or not? What are her social, financial, and general circumstances? Her character, personal traits, aims, interests, desires? Has she any vices? Any virtues? Talents? Ambitions? Caprices? Fads? Are you in love with her? Is—"

"Yes," he said, "I am."

"Is she in love with you?"

"No; she hates me—I'm afraid."

"Is she in love with anybody?"

"That is a very difficult—"

The girl wrote: "He doesn't know," with a satisfaction apparently causeless.

"Is she a relative of yours, Mr. Gatewood?" very sweetly.

"No, Miss Southerland," very positively.

"You—you desire to marry her—you say?"

"I do. But I didn't say it."

She was silent; then:

"What is her name?" in a low voice which started several agreeable thrills chasing one another over him.

"I—I decline to answer," he stammered.

"On what grounds, Mr. Gatewood?"

He looked her full in the eyes; suddenly he bent forward and gazed at the printed paper from which she had been apparently reading.

"Why, all those questions you are scaring me with are not there!" he exclaimed indignantly. "You are making them up?"

"I—I know, but"—she was flushing furiously— "but they are on the other forms—some of them. Can't you see you are answering 'Form K'? That is a special form—"

"But why do you ask me questions that are *not* on Form K?"

"Because it is my duty to do all I can to secure evidence which may lead to the discovery of the person you desire to find. I—I assure you, Mr. Gatewood, this duty is not—not always agreeable—and some people make it harder still."

Gatewood looked out of the window. Various emotions—among them shame, mortification, chagrin—pervaded him, and chased each other along his nervous system, coloring his neck and ears a fiery red for the enlightenment of any observer.

"I—I did not mean to offend you," said the girl in a low voice—such a gently regretful voice that Gatewood swung around in his chair.

"There is nothing I would not be glad to tell you about the woman I have fallen in love with," he said. "She is overwhelmingly lovely; and—when I dare—I will tell you her name and where I first saw her—and where I saw her last—if you desire. Shall I?"

"It would be advisable. When will you do this?"

"When I dare."

"You—you don't dare—now?"

"No . . . not now."

She absently wrote on her pad: "He doesn't dare tell me now." Then, with head still bent, she lifted her mischief-making, trouble-breeding brown eyes to his once more.

"I am to come here, of course, to consult you?" he asked dizzily.

"Mr. Keen will receive you—"

"He may be busy."

"He may be," she repeated dreamily.

"So—I'll ask for you."

"We *could* write you, Mr. Gatewood."

He said hastily: "It's no trouble for me to come; I walk every morning."

"But there would be no use, I think, in your coming very soon. All I—all Mr. Keen could do for a while would be to report progress—"

"That is all I dare look for: progress—for the present."

During the time that he remained—which was not very long—neither of them spoke until he arose to take his departure.

"Good-by, Miss Southerland. I hope you may find the person I have been searching for."

"Good-by, Mr. Gatewood. . . . I hope we shall; . . . but I—don't—know."

And, as a matter of fact, she did not know; she was rather excited over nothing, apparently; and also somewhat preoccupied with several rather disturbing emotions the species of which she was interested in determining. But to label and catalogue each of these emotions separately required privacy and leisure to think—and she also wished to look very earnestly at the reflection of her own face in the mirror of her own chamber. For it is a trifle exciting—though but an innocent coincidence—to be compared, feature by feature, to a young man's ideal. As far as that went, she excelled it, too; and, as she stood by the desk, alone, gathering up her notes, she suddenly bent over and lifted the hem of her gown a trifle—sufficient to reassure herself that the dainty pair of shoes she wore, would have baffled the efforts of any Venus ever sculptured. And she was perfectly right.

"Of course," she thought to herself, "his ideal runaway hasn't enormous feet. He, too, must have been struck with the similarity between me and his ideal, and when he realized that I also noticed it, he was frightened by my frown into saying that her feet were enormous. How silly! . . . For I didn't *mean* to frighten him. . . . He frightened me—once or twice—I mean he irritated me—no, interested me, is what I *do* mean. . . . Heigho! I wonder why she ran away? I wonder why he can't find her? . . . It's—it's silly to run away from a man like that. . . . Heigho! . . . She doesn't deserve to be found. There is nothing to be afraid of—nothing to alarm anybody in a man like that."

So she gathered up her notes and walked slowly out and across to the private office of the Tracer of Lost Persons.

"Come in," said the Tracer when she knocked. He was using the telephone; she seated herself rather listlessly beside the window, where spring sunshine lay in gilded patches on the rug and spring breezes stirred the curtains. She was a little tired, but there seemed to be no good reason why. Yet, with the soft wind blowing on her cheek, the languor grew; she rested her face on one closed hand, shutting her eyes.

When they opened again it was to meet the fixed gaze of Mr. Keen.

"Oh—I beg your pardon!"

"There is no need of it, child. Be seated. Never mind that report just now." He paced the length of the room once or twice, hands clasped behind him; then, halting to confront her:

"What sort of a man is this young Gatewood?"

"What *sort*, Mr. Keen? Why—I think he is the—the sort—that—"

"I see that you don't think much of him," said Keen, laughing.

"Oh, indeed I did not mean that at all; I mean that he appeared to be—to be—"

"Rather a cad?"

"Why, *no!*" she said, flushing up. "He is absolutely well-bred, Mr. Keen."

"You received no unpleasant impression of him?"

"On the contrary!" she said rather warmly—for it hurt her sense of justice that Keen should so misjudge even a stranger in whom she had no personal interest.

"You think he looks like an honest man?"

"Honest?" She was rosy with annoyance. "Have you any idea that he is dishonest?"

"Have you?"

"Not the slightest," she said with emphasis.

"Suppose a man should set us hunting for a person who does not exist—on our terms, which are no payment unless successful? Would that be honest?" asked Keen gravely.

"Did—did *he* do that?"

"No, child."

"I knew he *couldn't* do such a thing!"

"No, he—er—couldn't, because I wouldn't allow it—not that he tried to!" added Keen hastily as the indignant brown eyes sparkled ominously. "Really, Miss Southerland, he must be all you say he is, for he has a stanch champion to vouch for him."

"All I *say* he is? I haven't said anything about him!"

Mr. Keen nodded. "*Ex*actly. Let us drop him for a moment. . . . Are you perfectly well, Miss Southerland?"

"Why, yes."

"I'm glad of it. You are a trifle pale; you seem to be a little languid. . . . When do you take your vacation?"

"You suggested May, I believe," she said wistfully.

The Tracer leaned back in his chair, joining the tips of his fingers reflectively.

"Miss Southerland," he said, "you have been with us a year. I thought it might interest you to know that I am exceedingly pleased with you."

She colored charmingly.

"But," he added, "I'm terribly afraid we're going to lose you."

"Why?" she asked, startled.

"However," he continued, ignoring her half-frightened question with a smile, "I am going to promote you—for faithful and efficient service."

"O-h!"

"With an agreeable increase of salary, and new duties which will take you into the open air. . . . You ride?"

"I—I used to before—"

"*Ex*actly; before you were obliged to earn your living. Please have yourself measured for habit and boots this afternoon. I shall arrange for horse, saddle, and groom. You will spend most of your time riding in the Park—for the present."

"But—Mr. Keen—am I to be one of your agents—a sort of detective?"

Keen regarded her absently, then crossed one leg over the other.

"Read me your notes," he said with a smile.

She read them, folded them, and he took them from her, thoughtfully regarding her.

"Did you know that your mother and I were children together?" he asked.

"No!" She stared. "Is *that* why you sent for me that day at the school of stenography?"

"That is why . . . When I learned that my playmate—your mother—was dead, is it not reasonable to suppose that I should wish her daughter to have a chance?"

Miss Southerland looked at him steadily.

"She was like you—when she married . . . I never married . . . Do you wonder that I sent for you, child?"

Nothing but the clock ticking there in the sunny room, and an old man staring into two dimmed brown eyes, and the little breezes at the open window whispering of summers past.

"This young man, Gatewood," said the Tracer, clearing his voice of its hoarseness— "this young man ought to be all right, if I did not misjudge his father—years ago, child, years ago. And he *is* all right—" He half turned toward a big letter-file; "his record is clean, so far. The trouble with him is idleness. He ought to marry."

"Isn't he trying to?" she asked.

"It looks like it. Miss Southerland, we *must* find this woman!"

"Yes, but I don't see how you are going to—on such slight information—"

"Information! Child, I have all I want—all I could desire." He laughed, passing his hands over his gray hair. "We are going to find the girl he is in love with before the week ends!"

"Do you really think so?" she exclaimed.

"Yes. But you must do a great deal in this case."

"I?"

"*Exactly.*"

"And—and what am I to do?"

"Ride in the Park, child! And if you see Mr. Gatewood, don't you dare take your eyes off him for one moment. Watch him; observe everything he does. If he should recognize you and speak to you, be as amiable to him as though it were not by my orders."

"Then—then I *am* to be a detective!" she faltered.

The Tracer did not appear to hear her. He took up the notes, turned to the telephone, and began to send out a general alarm, reading the description of the person whom Gatewood had described. The vast, intricate and delicate machinery under his control was being set in motion all over the Union.

"Not that I expect to find her outside the borough of Manhattan," he said, smiling, as he hung up the receiver and turned to her; "but it's as well to know how many types of that species exist in this Republic, and who they are—in case any other young man comes here raving of brown eyes and 'gleams' in the hair."

Miss Southerland, to her own intense consternation, blushed.

"I think you had better order that habit at once," said the Tracer carelessly.

"Tell me, Mr. Keen," she asked tremulously, "am I to spy upon Mr. Gatewood? And report to you? . . . For I simply cannot bear to do it—"

"Child, you need report nothing unless you desire to. And when there is something to report, it will be about the woman I am searching for. *Don't* you understand? I have already located her. You will find her in the Park. And when you are *sure* she is the right one—and if you care to report it to me—I shall be ready to listen . . . I am always ready to listen to you."

"But—I warn you, Mr. Keen, that I have perfect faith in the honor of Mr. Gatewood. I *know* that I could have nothing unworthy to report."

"I am sure of it," said the Tracer of Lost Persons, studying her with eyes that were not quite clear. "Now, I think you had better order that habit . . . Your mother sat her saddle perfectly . . . We rode very often—my lost playmate and I."

He turned, hands clasped behind his back, absently pacing the room, backward, forward, there in the spring sunshine. Nor did he notice her lingering, nor mark her as she stole from the room, brown eyes saddened and thoughtful, wondering, too, that there should be in the world so much room for sorrow.

FIVE

Gatewood, burdened with restlessness and gnawed by curiosity, consumed a week in prowling about the edifice where Keen & Co. carried on an interesting profession.

His first visit resulted merely in a brief interview with Mr. Keen, who smilingly reported progress and suavely bowed him out. He looked about for Miss Southerland as he was leaving, but did not see her.

On his second visit he mustered the adequate courage to ask for her, and experienced a curiously sickly sensation when informed that Miss Southerland was no longer employed in the bureau of statistics, having been promoted to an outside position of great responsibility. His third visit proved anything but satisfactory. He sidled and side-stepped for ten minutes before he dared ask Mr. Keen *where* Miss Southerland had gone. And when the Tracer replied that, considering the business he had undertaken for Mr. Gatewood, he really could not see why Mr. Gatewood should interest himself concerning the whereabouts of Miss Southerland, the young man had nothing to say, and escaped as soon as possible, enraged at himself, at Mr. Keen, and vaguely holding the entire world guilty of conspiracy.

He had no definite idea of what he wanted, except that his desire to see Miss Southerland again seemed out of all proportion to any reasonable motive for seeing her. Occasional fits of disgust with himself for what he had done were varied with moody hours of speculation. Suppose Mr. Keen did find his ideal? What of it?

He no longer wanted to see her. He had no use for her. The savor of the enterprise had gone stale in his mouth; he was by turns worried, restless, melancholy, sulky, uneasy. A vast emptiness pervaded his life. He smoked more and more and ate less and less. He even disliked to see others eat, particularly Kerns.

And one exquisite May morning he came down to breakfast and found the unspeakable Kerns immersed in grapefruit, calm, well balanced, and bland.

"How-de-dee, dear friend?" said that gentleman affably. "Any news from Cupid this beautiful May morning?"

"No; and I don't want any," returned Gatewood, sorting his mail with a scowl and waving away his fruit.

"Tut, tut! Lovers must be patient. Dearie will be found some day—"

"Some day," snarled Gatewood, "I shall destroy you, Tommy."

"Naughty! Naughty!" reflected Kerns, pensively assaulting the breakfast food. "Lovey must *not* worry; Dovey shall be found, and all will be joy and gingerbread. . . . If you throw that orange I'll run screaming to the governors. Aren't you ashamed—just because you're in a love tantrum!"

"One more word and you get it!"

"May I sing as I trifle with this frugal fare, dear friend? My heart is *so* happy that I should love to warble a few wild notes—"

He paused to watch his badgered victim dispose of a Martini.

"I wonder," he mused, "if you'd like me to tell you what a cocktail before breakfast does to the lining of your stomach? Would you?"

"No. I suppose it's what the laundress does to my linen. What do I care?"

"*Don't* be a short sport, Jack."

"Well, I don't care for the game you put me up against. Do you know what has happened?"

"I really don't, dear friend. The Tracer of Lost Persons has not found her—*has* he?"

"He says he has," retorted Gatewood sullenly, pulling a crumpled telegram from his pocket and casting it upon the table.

"I don't want to see her; I'm not interested. I never saw but one girl in my life who interested me in the slightest; and she's employed to help in this ridiculous search."

Kerns, meanwhile, had smoothed out the telegram and was intently perusing it:

"*John Gatewood, Lenox Club, Fifth Avenue:*
"Person probably discovered. Call here as soon as possible.

W. Keen."

"*What* do you make of that?" demanded Gatewood hoarsely.

"Make of it? Why, it's true enough, I fancy. Go and see, and if it's she, be hers!"

"I won't! I don't want to see any ideal! I don't want to marry. Why do you try to make me marry somebody?"

"Because it's good for you, dear friend. Otherwise you'll go to the doggy-dogs. You don't realize how much worry you are to me."

"Confound it! Why don't *you* marry? Why didn't I ask you that when you put me up to all this foolishness? What right have you to—"

"Tut, friend! *I* know there's no woman alive fit to wed me and spend her life in stealing kisses from me. *I* have no ideal. *You* have an ideal."

"I haven't!"

"Oh, yes, dear friend, there's a stub in your check book to prove it. You simply bet $5,000 that your ideal existed. You've won. Go and be her joy and sunshine."

"I'll put an end to this whole business," said Gatewood wrathfully, "and I'll do it now!"

"Bet you that you're engaged within the week!" said Kerns with a placid smile.

The other swung around savagely: "What will you bet, Tommy? You may have what odds you please. I'll make you sit up for this."

"I'll bet you," answered Kerns, deliberately, "an entire silver dinner service against a saddle horse for the bride."

"That's a fool bet!" snapped Gatewood. "What do you mean?"

"Oh, if you don't care to—"

"What do I want of a silver service? But, all right; I'll bet you anything."

"*She'll* want it," replied Kerns significantly, booking the bet. "I may as well canter out to Tiffany's this morning, I fancy. . . . Where are you going, Jack?"

"To see Keen and confess what an ass I've been!" returned Gatewood sullenly, striding across the breakfast room to take his hat and gloves from the rack. And out he went, mad all over.

On his way up the avenue he attempted to formulate the humiliating confession which already he shrank from. But it had to be done. He simply could not stand the prospect of being notified month after month that a lady would be on view somewhere. It was like going for a fitting; it was horrible. Besides, what use was it? Within a week or two an enormous and utterly inexplicable emptiness had yawned before him, revealing life as a hollow delusion. He no longer cared.

Immersed in bitter reflection, he climbed the familiar stairway and sent his card to Mr. Keen, and in due time he was ushered into the presence of the Tracer of Lost Persons.

"Mr. Keen," he began, with a headlong desire to get it over and be done with it, "I may as well tell you how impossible it is for you, or anybody, to find that person I described—"

Mr. Keen raised an expostulatory hand, smiling indulgence.

"It is more than possible, Mr. Gatewood, more than probable; it is almost an accomplished fact. In other words, I think I may venture to congratulate you and say that she *is* found."

"Now, *how* can she be found, when there isn't—"

"Mr. Gatewood, the magician will always wave his magic wand for you and show you his miracles for the price of admission. But for that price he does not show you how he works his miracles," said Keen, laughing.

"But I ought to tell you," persisted Gatewood, "that it is utterly impossible you should find the person I wished to discover, because she—"

"I can only prove that you are wrong," smiled Keen, rising from his easy chair.

"Mr. Keen," said the young man earnestly, "I have been more or less of a chump at times. One of those times was when I came here on this errand. All I desire, now, is to let the matter rest as it is. I am satisfied, and you have lost nothing. Nor have you found anything or anybody. You think you have, but you haven't. I do not wish you to continue the search, or to send me any further reports. I want to forget the whole miserable matter—to be free—to feel myself freed from any obligations to that irritating person I asked you to find."

The Tracer regarded him very gravely.

"Is that your wish, Mr. Gatewood? I can scarcely credit it."

"It is. I've been a fool; I simply want to stop being one if anybody will permit it."

"And you decline to attempt to identify the very beautiful person we have discovered to be the individual for whom you asked us to search?"

"I do. She may be beautiful; but I know well enough she can't compare with—some one."

"I am sorry," said Keen thoughtfully. "We take so much pride in these matters. When one of my agents discovered where this person was, I was rather—happy; for I have taken a peculiar personal interest in your case. However—"

"Mr. Keen," said Gatewood, "if you could understand how ashamed and mortified I am at my own conduct—"

Keen gazed pensively out of the window. "I also am sorry; Miss Southerland was to have received a handsome bonus for her discovery—"

"Miss S-S-S-S-outherland!"

"*Ex*actly; without quite so many *S*'s," said Keen, smiling.

"Did *she* discover that—that person?" exclaimed the young man, startled.

"She thinks she has. I am not sure she is correct; but I am absolutely certain that Miss Southerland could eventually discover

the person you were in search of. It seems a little hard on her—
just on the eve of success—to lose. But that can't be helped now."

Gatewood, more excited and uncomfortable than he had ever
been in all his life, watched Keen intently.

"Too bad, too bad," muttered the Tracer to himself. "The child
needs the encouragement. It meant a thousand dollars to her—"
He shrugged his shoulders, looked up, and, as though rather surprised to see Gatewood still there, smiled an impersonal smile and
offered his hand in adieu. Gatewood winced.

"Could I—I see Miss Southerland?" he asked.

"I am afraid not. She is at this moment following my instructions to—but that cannot interest you now—"

"Yes, it does!—if you don't mind. Where is she? I—I'll take a
look at the person she discovered; I will, really."

"Why, it's only this: I suspected that you might identify a person whom I had reason to believe was to be found every morning
riding in the Park. So Miss Southerland has been riding there
every day. Yesterday she came here, greatly excited—"

"Yes—yes—go on!"

Keen gazed dreamily at the sunny window. "She thought she
had found your—er—the person. So I said you would meet her on
the bridle path, near—but that's of no interest now—"

"Near where?" demanded Gatewood, suppressing inexplicable
excitement. And as Keen said nothing: "I'll go; I want to go, I really do! Can't—can't a fellow change his mind? Oh, I know you think
I'm a lunatic, and there's plenty of reason, too!"

Keen studied him calmly. "Yes, plenty of reason, plenty of reason, Mr. Gatewood. But do you suppose you are the only one? I
know another who was perfectly sane two weeks ago."

The young man waited impatiently; the Tracer paced the room,
gray head bent, delicate, wrinkled hands clasped loosely behind
his bent back.

"You have horses at the Whip and Spur Club," he said abruptly.
"Suppose you ride out and see how close Miss Southerland has
come to solving our problem."

Gatewood seized the offered hand and wrung it with a fervor out of all reason; and it is curious that the Tracer of Lost Persons did not appear to be astonished.

"You're rather impetuous—like your father," he said slowly. "I knew him; so I've ventured to trust his son—even when I heard how aimlessly he was living his life. Mr. Gatewood! May I ask you something—as an old friend of your father?"

The young man nodded, subdued, perplexed, scarcely understanding.

"It's only this: If you *do* find the woman you could love—in the Park—to-day—come back to me some day and let me tell you all those foolish, trite, tiresome things that I should have told a son of mine. I am so old that you will not take offense—you will not mind listening to me, or forgetting the dull, prosy things I say about the curse of idleness, and the habits of cynical thinking, and the perils of vacant-minded indulgence. You will forgive me—and you will forget me. That will be as it should be. Good-by."

Gatewood, sobered, surprised, descended the stairs and hailed a hansom.

SIX

All the way to the Whip and Spur Club he sat buried in a reverie from which, at intervals, he started, aroused by the heavy, expectant beating of his own pulses. But what did he expect, in Heaven's name? Not the discovery of a woman who had never existed. Yet his excitement and impatience grew as he watched the saddling of his horse; and when at length he rode out into the sunshine and cantered through the Park entrance, his sense of impending events and his expectancy amounted to a fever which colored his face attractively.

He saw her almost immediately. Her horse was walking slowly in the dappled shadows of the new foliage; she, listless in her saddle, sometimes watching the throngs of riders passing, at moments turning to gaze into the woodland vistas where, over the thickets of flowering shrubbery, orioles and robins sped flashing on tinted wings from shadow to sun, from sun to shadow. But she looked up as he drew bridle and wheeled his mount beside her; and, "Oh!" she said, flushing in recognition.

"I have missed you terribly," he said quietly.

It was dreamy weather, even for late spring: the scent of lilacs and mock-orange hung heavy as incense along the woods. Their voices unconsciously found the key to harmonize with it all.

She said: "Well, I think I have succeeded. In a few moments she will be passing. I do not know her name; she rides a big roan. She is very beautiful, Mr. Gatewood."

He said: "I am perfectly certain we shall find her. I doubted it until now. But now I know."

"Oh-h, but I *may* be wrong," she protested.

"No; you cannot be."

She looked up at him.

"You can have no idea how happy you make me," he said unsteadily.

"But—I—but I may be all wrong—dreadfully wrong!"

"Y-es; you may be, but I shall not be. For do you know that I have already seen her in the Park?"

"When?" she demanded incredulously, then turned in the saddle, repeating: "Where? Did she pass? How perfectly stupid of me! And *was* she the—the right one?"

"She *is* the right one. . . . Don't turn: I have seen her. Ride on: I want to say something—if I can."

"No, no," she insisted. "I must know whether I was right—"

"You *are* right—but you don't know it yet. . . . Oh, very well, then; we'll turn if you insist." And he wheeled his mount as she did, riding at her bridle again.

"How can you take it so coolly—so indifferently?" she said. "Where has that woman—where has she gone? . . . Never mind; she must turn and pass us sooner or later, for she lives uptown. *What* are you laughing at, Mr. Gatewood?"—in annoyed surprise.

"I am laughing at myself. Oh, I'm so many kinds of a fool—you can't think how many, and it's no use!"

She stared, astonished; he shook his head.

"No, you don't understand yet. But you will. Listen to me: this very beautiful lady you have discovered is nothing to me!"

"Nothing—to you!" she faltered. Two pink spots of indignation burned in her cheeks. "How—how dare you say that!—after all that has been done—all that you have said. You said you loved her; you *did* say so—to *me*!"

"I don't love her now."

"But you did!" Tears of pure vexation started; she faced him, eye to eye, thoroughly incensed.

"What sort of man are you?" she said under her breath. "Your friend Mr. Kerns is wrong. You are not worth saving from yourself."

"Kerns!" he repeated, angry and amazed. "What the deuce has Kerns to do with this affair?"

She stared, then, realizing her indiscretion, bit her lip, and spurred forward. But he put his horse to a gallop, and they pounded along in silence. In a little while she drew bridle and looked around coldly, grave with displeasure.

"Mr. Kerns came to us before you did. He said you would probably come, and he begged us to strain every effort in your behalf, because, he said, your happiness absolutely depended upon our finding for you the woman you were seeking. . . . And I tried—very hard—and now she's found. You admit that—and *now* you say—"

"I say that one of these balmy summer days I'll assassinate Tommy Kerns!" broke in Gatewood. "What on earth possessed that prince of butters-in to go to Mr. Keen?"

"To save you from yourself!" retorted the girl in a low, exasperated voice. "He did not say what threatened you; he is a good friend for a man to have. But we soon found out what you were—a man well born, well bred, full of brilliant possibility, who was slowly becoming an idle, cynical, self-centered egoist—a man who, lacking the lash of need or the spur of ambition, was degenerating through the sheer uselessness and inanity of his life. And, oh, the pity of it! For Mr. Keen and I have taken a—a curiously personal interest in you—in your case. I say, the pity of it!"

Astounded, dumb under her stinging words, he rode beside her through the brilliant sunshine, wheeled mechanically as she turned her horse, and rode north again.

"And now—*now!*" she said passionately, "you turn on the woman you loved! Oh, you are not worth it!"

"You are quite right," he said, turning very white under her scorn. "Almost all you have said is true enough, I fancy. I amount to nothing; I am idle, cynical, selfish. The emptiness of such a life requires a stimulant; even a fool abhors a vacuum. So I drink—not so very much yet—but more than I realize. And it is close enough to a habit to worry me. . . . Yes, almost all you say is true; Kerns knows it; I know it—now that you have told me. You see, he couldn't tell me, because I should not have believed him. But I believe you— all you say, except one thing. And that is only a glimmer of decency left in me—not that I make any merit of it. No, it is merely instinctive. For I have *not* turned on the woman I loved."

Her face was pale as her level eyes met him:

"You said she was nothing to you. . . . Look there! Do you see her? Do you see?"

Her voice broke nervously as he swung around to stare at a rider bearing down at a gallop—a woman on a big roan, tearing along through the spring sunshine, passing them with wind-flushed cheeks and dark, incurious eyes, while her powerful horse carried her on, away through the quivering light and shadow of the woodland vista.

"Is *that* the person?"

"Y-es," she faltered. "Was I wrong?"

"Quite wrong, Miss Southerland."

"But—but you said you had seen her here this morning!"

"Yes, I have."

"Did you speak to her before you met me?"

"No—not before I met you."

"Then you have not spoken to her. Is she still here in the Park?"

"Yes, she is still here."

The girl turned on him excitedly: "Do you mean to say that you will not speak to her?"

"I had rather not—"

"And your happiness depends on your speaking?"

"Yes."

"Then it is cowardly not to speak."

"Oh, yes, it is cowardly. . . . If you wish me to speak to her I will. Shall I?"

"Yes . . . Show her to me."

"And you think that such a man as I am has a right to speak of love to her?"

"I—we believe it will be your salvation. Mr. Kerns says you must marry her to be happy. Mr. Keen told me yesterday that it only needed a word from the right woman to put you on your mettle. . . . And—and that is my opinion."

"Then in charity say that word!" he breathed, bending toward her. "Can't you see? Can't you understand? Don't you know that from the moment I looked into your eyes I loved you?"

"How—how dare you!" she stammered, crimsoning.

"God knows," he said wistfully. "I am a coward. I don't know how I dared. Good-by. . . ."

He walked his horse a little way, then launched him into a gallop, tearing on and on, sun, wind, trees swimming, whirling like a vision, hearing nothing, feeling nothing, save the leaden pounding of his pulse and the breathless, terrible tightening in his throat.

When he cleared his eyes and looked around he was quite alone, his horse walking under the trees and breathing heavily.

At first he laughed, and the laugh was not pleasant. Then he said aloud: "It is worth having lived for, after all!"—and was silent. And again: "I could expect nothing; she was perfectly right to side-step a fool. . . . And *such* a fool!"

The distant gallop of a horse, dulled on the soft soil, but coming nearer, could not arouse him from the bitter depths he had sunk in; not even when the sound ceased beside him, and horse snorted recognition to horse. It was only when a light touch rested on his arm that he looked up heavily, caught his breath.

"Where is the other—woman?" she gasped.

"There never was any other."

"You said—"

"I said I loved my ideal. I did not know she existed—until I saw you."

"Then—then we were searching for—"

"A vision. But it was your face that haunted me. . . . And I am not worth it, as you say. And I know it, . . . for you have opened my eyes."

He drew bridle, forcing a laugh. "I cut a sorry figure in your life; be patient; I am going out of it now." And he swung his horse.

At the same moment she did the same, making a demi-tour and meeting him halfway, confronting him.

"Do you—you mean to ride out of my life without a word?" she asked unsteadily.

"Good-by." He offered his hand, stirring his horse forward; she leaned lightly over and laid both hands in his. Then, her face surging in color, she lifted her beautiful dark eyes to his as the horses approached, nearer, nearer, until, as they passed, flank brushing flank, her eyes fell, then closed as she swayed toward him, and clung, her young lips crushed to his.

There was nobody to witness it except the birds and squirrels—nobody but a distant mounted policeman, who almost fainted away in his saddle.

Oh, it was awful, awful! Apparently she had been kissed speechless, for she said nothing. The man fool did all the talking, incoherently enough, but evidently satisfactory to her, judging from the way she looked at him, and blushed and blushed, and touched her eyes with a bit of cambric at intervals.

All the policeman heard as they passed him was; "I'm going to give you this horse, and Kerns is to give us our silver; and what do you think, my darling?"

"W-what?"

But they had already passed out of earshot; and in a few moments the shady, sun-flecked bridle path was deserted again save for the birds and squirrels, and a single mounted policeman, rigid, wild eyed, twisting his mustache and breathing hard.

SEVEN

The news of Gatewood's fate filled Kerns with a pleasure bordering upon melancholy. It was his work; he had done it; it was good for Gatewood too—time for him to stop his irresponsible cruise through life, lower sail, heave to, set his signals, and turn over matters to this charming pilot.

And now they would come into port together and anchor somewhere east of Fifth Avenue—which, Kerns reflected, was far more proper a place for Gatewood than somewhere east of Suez, where young men so often sail.

And yet, and yet there was something melancholy in the pleasure he experienced. Gatewood was practically lost to him. He knew what might be expected from engaged men and newly married men. Gatewood's club life was ended—for a while; and there was no other man with whom he cared to embark for those brightly lighted harbors twinkling east of Suez across the metropolitan wastes.

"It's very generous of me to get him married," he said frequently to himself, rather sadly. "I did it pretty well, too. It only shows that women have no particular monopoly in the realms of diplomacy and finesse; in fact, if a man really chooses to put his mind to such matters, he can make it no trumps and win out behind a bum ace and a guarded knave."

He was pleased with himself. He followed Gatewood about explaining how good he had been to him. An enthusiasm for marrying off his friends began to germinate within him; he tried it on Darrell, on Barnes, on Yates, but was turned down and severely stung.

Then one day Harren of the Philippine Scouts turned up at the club, and they held a determined reunion until daylight, and they told each other all about it all and what upper-cuts life had handed out to them since the troopship sailed.

And after the rosy glow had deepened to a more gorgeous hue in the room, and the electric lights had turned into silver pin-wheels; and after they had told each other the story of their lives, and the last siphon fizzed impotently when urged beyond its capacity, Kerns arose and extended his hand, and Harren took it. And they executed a song resembling "Auld Lang Syne."

"Ole man," said Kerns reproachfully, "there's one thing you have been deuced careful *not* to mention, and that is about what happened to you three years ago—"

"Steady!" said Harren; "there is nothing to tell, Tommy."

"Nothing?"

"Nothing. I never saw her again. I never shall."

Kerns looked long and unsteadily upon his friend; then very gravely fumbled in his pocket and drew forth the business card of Westrel Keen, Tracer of Lost Persons.

"That," he said, "will be about all." And he bestowed the card upon Harren with magnificent condescension.

And about five o'clock the following afternoon Harren found the card among various effects of his, scattered over his dresser.

It took him several days to make up his mind to pay any attention to the card or the suggestion it contained. He scarcely considered it seriously even when, passing along Fifth Avenue one sunny afternoon, he chanced to glance up and see the sign

KEEN & CO.
TRACERS OF LOST PERSONS

staring him in the face.

He continued his stroll, but that evening, upon mere impulse, he sat down and wrote a letter to Mr. Keen.

The next morning's mail brought a reply and an appointment for an interview on Wednesday week. Harren tossed the letter aside, satisfied to let the matter go, because his leave expired on Tuesday, and the appointment was impossible.

On Sunday, however, the melancholy of the deserted club affected his spirits. A curious desire to see this Tracer of Lost Persons seized him with a persistence unaccountable. He slept poorly, haunted with visions.

On Monday he went to see Mr. Keen. It could do no harm; it was too late to do either harm or good, for his leave expired the next day at noon.

The business of Keen & Co., Tracers of Lost Persons, had grown to enormous proportions; appointments for a personal interview with Mr. Keen were now made a week in advance, so when young Harren sent in his card, the gayly liveried negro servant came back presently, threading his way through the waiting throng with pomp and circumstance, and returned the card to Harren with the date of appointment rewritten in ink across the top. The day named was Wednesday. On Tuesday Harren's leave expired.

"That won't do," said the young man brusquely; "I must see Mr. Keen to-day. I wrote last week for an appointment."

The liveried darky was polite but obdurate.

"Dis here am de 'pintment, suh," he explained persuasively.

"But I want to see Mr. Keen at once," insisted Harren.

"Hit ain't no use, suh," said the darky respectfully; "dey's mi'ions an' mi'ions ob gemmen jess a-settin' roun' an' waitin' foh Mistuh Keen. In dis here perfeshion, suh, de fustest gemman dat has a 'pintment is de fustest gemman dat kin see Mistuh Keen. You is a military gemman yohse'f, Cap'm Harren, an' you is aware dat precedence am de rigger."

The bronzed young man smiled, glanced at the date of appointment written on his card, which also bore his own name followed by the letters U.S.A., then his amused gray eyes darkened and he glanced leisurely around the room, where a dozen or more assorted people sat waiting their turns to interview Mr. Keen: all sorts and conditions of people—smartly gowned women, an anxious-browed business man or two, a fat German truck driver, his greasy cap on his knees, a surly policeman, and an old Irishwoman, wearing a

shawl and an ancient straw bonnet. Harren's eyes reverted to the
darky.

"You will explain to Mr. Keen," he said, "that I am an army officer on leave, and that I am obliged to start for Manila to-morrow.
This is my excuse for asking an immediate interview; and if it's
not a good enough excuse I must cancel this appointment, that is
all."

The darky stood, irresolute, inclined to argue, but something
in the steel-gray eyes of the man set him in involuntary motion,
and he went away once more with the young man's message. Harren
turned and walked back to his seat. The old woman with the faded
shawl was explaining volubly to a handsomely gowned woman beside her that she was looking for her boy, Danny; that her name
was Mrs. Regan, and that she washed for the aristocracy of Hunter's
Point at a liberal price per dozen, using no deleterious substances
in the suds as Heaven was her witness.

The German truck driver, moved by this confidence, was stirred
to begin an endless account of his domestic misfortunes, and old
Mrs. Regan, becoming impatient, had already begun to interrupt
with an account of Regan's recent hoisting on the wings of a pre-
mature petard, when the dark servant reappeared.

"Mistuh Keen will receive you, suh," he whispered, leading the
way into a large room where dozens of attractive young girls sat
very busily engaged at typewriting machines. Door after door they
passed, all numbered on the ground-glass panes, then swung to
the right, where the darky bowed him into a big, handsomely furnished room flooded with the morning sun. A tall, gray man, fault-
lessly dressed in a gray frock suit and wearing white spats, turned
from the breezy, open window to inspect him; the lean, well
groomed, rather lank type of gentleman suggesting a retired colonel of cavalry; unmistakably well bred from the ends of his drooping gray mustache to the last button on his immaculate spats.

"Captain Harren?" he said pleasantly.

"Mr. Keen?"

They bowed. Young Harren drew from his pocket a card. It was
the business card of Keen & Co., and, glancing up at Mr. Keen, he
read it aloud, carefully:

KEEN & CO.
TRACERS OF LOST PERSONS
Keen & Co. are prepared to locate the where-
abouts of anybody on earth. No charges will be
made unless the person searched for is found.
Blanks on Application.
WESTREL KEEN, *Manager.*

Harren raised his clear, gray eyes. "I assume this statement to be correct, Mr. Keen?"

"You may safely assume so," said Mr. Keen, smiling.

"Does this statement include *all* that you are prepared to under-take?"

The Tracer of Lost Persons inspected him coolly. "What more is there, Captain Harren? I undertake to find lost people. I even undertake to find the undiscovered ideals of young people who have failed to meet them. What further field would you suggest?" Harren glanced at the card which he held in his gloved hand; then, very slowly, he re-read, "the whereabouts of anybody *on earth*," accent-ing the last two words deliberately as he encountered Keen's pierc-ing gaze again.

"Well?" asked Mr. Keen laughingly, "is not that sufficient? Our clients could scarcely expect us to invade heaven in our search for the vanished."

"There are other regions," said Harren.

"*Exactly.* Sit down, sir. There is a row of bookcases for your amusement. Please help yourself while I clear decks for action."

Harren stood fingering the card, his gray eyes lost in retrospec-tion; then he sauntered over to the bookcases, scanning the titles. The Searcher for Lost Persons studied him for a moment or two, turned, and began to pace the room. After a moment or two he touched a bell. A sweet-faced young girl entered; she was gowned in black and wore a white collar, and cuffs turned back over her hands.

"Take this memorandum," he said. The girl picked up a pencil and pad, and Mr. Keen, still pacing the room, dictated in a quiet voice as he walked to and fro:

"Mrs. Regan's Danny is doing six months in Butte, Montana. Break it to her as mercifully as possible. He is a bad one. We make no charge. The truck driver, Becker, can find his wife at her mother's house, Leonia, New Jersey. Tell him to be less pig-headed or she'll go for good some day. Ten dollars. Mrs. M., No. 36001, can find her missing butler in service at 79 Vine Street, Hartford, Connecticut. She may notify the police whenever she wishes. His portrait is No. 170529, Rogues' Gallery. Five hundred dollars. Miss K. (No. 3679) may send her letter, care of Cisneros & Co., Rio, where the person she is seeking has gone into the coffee business. If she decides that she really does love him, he'll come back fast enough. Two hundred and fifty dollars. Mr. W. (No. 3620) must go to the morgue for further information. His repentance is too late; but he can see that there is a decent burial. The charge: one thousand dollars to the Florence Mission. You may add that we possess his full record."

The Tracer paused and waited for the stenographer to finish. When she looked up: "Who else is waiting?" he asked.

The girl read over the initials and numbers.

"Tell that policeman that Kid Conroy sails on the *Carania* to-morrow. Fifty dollars. There is nothing definite in the other cases. Report progress and send out a general alarm for the cashier inquired for by No. 3608. You will find details in vol. xxxix under B."

"Is that all, Mr. Keen?"

"Yes. I'm going to be very busy with"—turning slowly toward Harren— "with Captain Harren, of the Philippine Scouts, until to-morrow—a very complicated case, Miss Borrow, involving cipher codes and photography—"

EIGHT

Harren started, then walked slowly to the center of the room as the pretty stenographer passed out with a curious level glance at him.

"Why do you say that photography plays a part in my case?" he asked.

"Doesn't it?"

"Yes. But how—"

"Oh, I only guessed it," said Keen with a smile. "I made another guess that your case involved a cipher code. Does it?"

"Y-es," said the young man, astonished, "but I don't see—"

"It also involves the occult," observed Keen calmly. "We may need Miss Borrow to help us."

Almost staggered, Harren stared at the Tracer out of his astonished gray eyes until that gentleman laughed outright and seated himself, motioning Harren to do likewise.

"Don't be surprised, Captain Harren," he said. "I suppose you have no conception of our business, no realization of its scope—its network of information bureaus all over the civilized world, its myriad sources of information, the immensity of its delicate machinery, the endless data and the infinitesimal details we have at our command. You, of course, have no idea of the number of people of every sort and condition who are in our employ, of the ceaseless yet inoffensive surveillance we maintain. For example, when your letter came last week I called up the person who has charge of the army list. There you were, Kenneth Harren, Captain Philippine

285

Scouts, with the date of your graduation from West Point. Then I called up a certain department devoted to personal detail, and in five minutes I knew your entire history. I then touched another electric button, and in a minute I had before me the date of your arrival in New York, your present address, and"—he looked up quizzically at Harren— "and several items of general information, such as your peculiar use of your camera, and the list of books on Psychical Phenomena and Cryptograms which you have been buying—"

Harren flushed up. "Do you mean to say that I have been spied upon, Mr. Keen?"

"No more than anybody else who comes to us as a client. There was nothing offensive in the surveillance." He shrugged his shoulders and made a deprecating gesture. "Ours is a business, my dear sir, like any other. We, of course, are obliged to know about people who call on us. Last week you wrote me, and I immediately set every wheel in motion; in other words, I had you under observation from the day I received your letter to this very moment."

"You learned much concerning me?" asked Harren quietly.

"*Ex*actly, my dear sir."

"But," continued Harren with a touch of malice, "you didn't learn that my leave is up to-morrow, did you?"

"Yes, I learned that, too."

"Then why did you give me an appointment for the day after to-morrow?" demanded the young man bluntly.

The Tracer looked him squarely in the eye. "Your leave is to be extended," he said.

"What?"

"*Ex*actly. It has been extended one week."

"How do you know that?"

"You applied for extension, did you not?"

"Yes," said Harren, turning red, "but I don't see how you knew that I—"

"By cable?"

"Y-yes."

"There's a cablegram in your rooms at this very moment," said the Tracer carelessly. "You have the extension you desired. And now, Captain Harren," with a singularly pleasant smile, "what can I do to help you to a pursuit of that true happiness which is guaranteed for all good citizens under our Constitution?"

Captain Harren crossed his long legs, dropping one knee over the other, and deliberately surveyed his interrogator.

"I really have no right to come to you," he said slowly. "Your prospectus distinctly states that Keen & Co. undertake to find *live* people, and I don't know whether the person I am seeking is alive or—or—"

His steady voice faltered; the Tracer watched him curiously.

"Of course, that is important," he said. "If she *is* dead—"

"*She!*"

"Didn't you say 'she,' Captain?"

"No, I did not."

"I beg your pardon, then, for anticipating you," said the Tracer carelessly.

"Anticipating? *How* do you know it is not a man I am in search of?" demanded Harren.

"Captain Harren, you are unmarried and have no son; you have no father, no brother, no sister. Therefore I infer—several things—for example, that you are in love."

"I? In love?"

"Desperately, Captain."

"Your inferences seem to satisfy you, at least," said Harren almost sullenly, "but they don't satisfy me—clever as they appear to be."

"*Ex*actly. Then you are *not* in love?"

"I don't know whether I am or not."

"I do," said the Tracer of Lost Persons.

"Then you know more than I," retorted Harren sharply.

"But that is my business—to know more than you do," returned Mr. Keen patiently. "Else why are you here to consult me?" And as Harren made no reply: "I have seen thousands and thousands of people in love. I have reduced the superficial muscular phenomena and facial symptomatic aspect of such people to an exact science founded upon a schedule approximating the Bertillon system of records. And," he added, smiling, "out of the twenty-seven known vocal variations your voice betrays twenty-five unmistakable symptoms; and out of the sixteen reflex muscular symptoms your face has furnished six, your hands three, your limbs and feet six. Then there are other superficial symptoms—"

"Good heavens!" broke in Harren; "how can you prove a man to be in love when he himself doesn't know whether he is or not? If a man isn't in love no Bertillon system can make him so; and if a man doesn't know whether or not he is in love, who can tell him the truth?"

"I can," said the Tracer calmly.

"What! When I tell you I myself don't know?"

"*That*," said the Tracer, smiling, "is the final and convincing symptom. *You* don't know. *I* know because you *don't* know. That is the easiest way to be sure that you are in love, Captain Harren, because you always are when you are not sure. You'd know if you were *not* in love. Now, my dear sir, you may lay your case confidently before me."

Harren, unconvinced, sat frowning and biting his lip and twisting his short, crisp mustache which the tropical sun had turned straw color and curly.

"I feel like a fool to tell you," he said. "I'm not an imaginative man, Mr. Keen; I'm not fanciful, not sentimental. I'm perfectly healthy, perfectly normal—a very busy man in my profession, with no time and no inclination to fall in love."

"Just the sort of man who does it," commented Keen. "Continue."

Harren fidgeted about in his chair, looked out of the window, squinted at the ceiling, then straightened up, folding his arms with sudden determination.

"I'd rather be boloed than tell you," he said. "Perhaps, after all, I *am* a lunatic; perhaps I've had a touch of the Luzon sun and don't know it."

"I'll be the judge," said the Tracer, smiling.

"Very well, sir. Then I'll begin by telling you that I've seen a ghost."

"There are such things," observed Keen quietly.

"Oh, I don't mean one of those fabled sheeted creatures that float about at night; I mean a phantom—a real phantom—in the sunlight—standing before my very eyes in broad day! . . . Now do you feel inclined to go on with my case, Mr. Keen?"

"Certainly," replied the Tracer gravely. "Please continue, Captain Harren."

"All right, then. Here's the beginning of it: Three years ago, here in New York, drifting along Fifth Avenue with the crowd, I looked up to encounter the most wonderful pair of eyes that I ever beheld—that any living man ever beheld! The most—wonderfully—beautiful—"

He sat so long immersed in retrospection that the Tracer said: "I am listening, Captain," and the Captain woke up with a start.

"What was I saying? How far had I proceeded?"

"Only to the eyes."

"Oh, I see! The eyes were dark, sir, dark and lovely beyond any power of description. The hair was also dark—very soft and thick and—er—wavy and dark. The face was extremely youthful, and ornamental to the uttermost verges of a beauty so exquisite that, were I to attempt to formulate for you its individual attractions, I should, I fear, transgress the strictly rigid bounds of that reticence which becomes a gentleman in complete possession of his senses."

"*Exactly*," mused the Tracer.

"Also," continued Captain Harren, with growing animation, "to attempt to describe her figure would be utterly useless, because I am a practical man and not a poet, nor do I read poetry or indulge in futile novels or romances of any description. Therefore I can only add that it was a figure, a poise, absolutely faultless, youthful, beautiful, erect, wholesome, gracious, graceful, charmingly buoyant and—well, I cannot describe her figure, and I shall not try."

"*Exactly*; don't try."

"No," said Harren mournfully, "it is useless"; and he relapsed into enchanted retrospection.

"Who was she?" asked Mr. Keen softly.

"I don't know."

"You never again saw her?"

"Mr. Keen, I—I am not ill-bred, but I simply could not help following her. She was so b-b-beautiful that it hurt; and I only wanted to look at her; I didn't mind being hurt. So I walked on and on, and sometimes I'd pass her and sometimes I'd let her pass me, and when she wasn't looking I'd look—not offensively, but just because I *couldn't* help it. And all the time my senses were humming like a top and my heart kept jumping to get into my throat, and I hadn't a notion where I was going or what time it was or what day of the week. She didn't see me; she didn't dream that I was looking at her; she didn't know me from any of the thousand silk-hatted, frock-coated men who passed and repassed her on Fifth Avenue. And when she went into St. Berold's Church, I went, too, and I stood where I could see her and where she couldn't see me. It was like a touch of the Luzon sun, Mr. Keen. And then she came out and got into a Fifth Avenue stage, and I got in, too. And whenever she looked away I looked at her—without the slightest offense, Mr. Keen, until, once, she caught my eye—"

He passed an unsteady hand over his forehead.

"For a moment we looked full at one another," he continued. "I got red, sir; I felt it, and I couldn't look away. And when I turned color like a blooming beet, she began to turn pink like a rosebud, and she looked full into my eyes with such a wonderful purity, such exquisite innocence, that I—I never felt so near—er—heaven in my life! No, sir, not even when they ambushed us at Manoa Wells— but that's another thing—only it is part of this business."

He tightened his clasped hands over his knee until the knuckles whitened.

"*That's* my story, Mr. Keen," he said crisply.

"All of it?"

Harren looked at the floor, then at Keen: "No, not all. You'll think me a lunatic if I tell you all."

"Oh, you saw her again?"

"N-never! That is—"

"Never?"

"Not in—in the flesh."

"Oh, in dreams?"

Harren stirred uneasily. "I don't know what you call them. I have seen her since—in the sunlight, in the open, in my quarters in Manila, standing there perfectly distinct, looking at me with such strange, beautiful eyes—"

"Go on," said the Tracer, nodding.

"What else is there to say?" muttered Harren.

"You saw her—or a phantom which resembled her. Did she speak?"

"No."

"Did you speak to her?"

"N-no. Once I held out my—my arms."

"What happened?"

"She wasn't there," said Harren simply.

"She vanished?"

"No—I don't know. I—I didn't see her any more."

"Didn't she fade?"

"No. I can't explain. She—there was only myself in the room."

"How many times has she appeared to you?"

"A great many times."

"In your room?"

"Yes. And in the road under a vertical sun; in the forest, in the paddy fields. I have seen her passing through the hallway of a friend's house—turning on the stair to look back at me! I saw her standing just back of the firing-line at Manoa Wells when we were preparing to rush the forts, and it scared me so that I jumped forward to draw her back. But—she wasn't there, Mr. Keen. . . .

"On the transport she stood facing me on deck one moonlit evening for five minutes. I saw her in 'Frisco; she sat in the Pullman twice between Denver and this city. Twice in my room at the Vice-Regent she has sat opposite me at midday, so clear, so beautiful, so real that—that I could scarcely believe she was only a—a—" He hesitated.

"The apparition of her own subconscious self," said the Tracer quietly. "Science has been forced to admit such things, and, as you know, we are on the verge of understanding the alphabet of some of the unknown forces which we must some day reckon with."

Harren, tense, a trifle pale, gazed at him earnestly.

"Do *you* believe in such things?"

"How can I avoid believing?" said the Tracer. "Every day, in my profession, we have proof of the existence of forces for which we have as yet no explanation—or, at best, a very crude one. I have had case after case of premonition; case after case of dual and even multiple personality; case after case where apparitions played a vital part in the plot which was brought to me to investigate. I'll tell you this, Captain: I, personally, never saw an apparition, never was obsessed by premonitions, never received any communications from the outer void. But I have had to do with those who undoubtedly did. Therefore I listen with all seriousness and respect to what you tell me."

"Suppose," said Harren, growing suddenly red, "that I should tell you I have succeeded in photographing this phantom."

The Tracer sat silent. He was astounded, but, he did not betray it.

"You have that photograph, Captain Harren?"

"Yes."

"Where is it?"

"In my rooms."

"You wish me to see it?"

Harren hesitated. "I—there is—seems to be—something almost sacred to me in that photograph. . . . You understand me, do you not? Yet, if it will help you in finding her—"

"Oh," said the Tracer in guileless astonishment, "you desire to find this young lady. Why?"

Harren stared. "Why? Why do I want to find her? Man, I—I can't live without her!"

"I thought you were not certain whether you really could be in love."

The hot color in the Captain's bronzed cheeks mounted to his hair.

"*Exactly*," purred the Tracer, looking out of the window. "Suppose we walk around to your rooms after luncheon. Shall we?"

Harren picked up his hat and gloves, hesitating, lingering on the threshold. "You *don't* think she is—a—dead?" he asked unsteadily.

"No," said Mr. Keen, "I don't."

"Because," said Harren wistfully, "her apparition is so superbly healthy and—and glowing with youth and life—"

"That is probably what sent it half the world over to confront you," said the Tracer gravely; "youth and life aglow with spiritual health. I think, Captain, that she has been seeing you, too, during these three years, but probably only in her dreams—memories of your encounters with her subconscious self floating over continents and oceans in a quest of which her waking intelligence is innocently unaware."

The Captain colored like a schoolboy, lingering at the door, hat in hand. Then he straightened up to the full height of his slim but powerful figure.

"At three?" he inquired bluntly.

"At three o'clock in your room, Hotel Vice-Regent. Good morning, Captain."

"Good morning," said Harren dreamily, and walked away, head bent, gray eyes lost in retrospection, and on his lean, bronzed, attractive face an afterglow of color wholly becoming.

NINE

When the Tracer of Lost Persons entered Captain Harren's room at the Hotel Vice-Regent that afternoon he found the young man standing at a center table, pencil in hand, studying a sheet of paper which was covered with letters and figures.

The two men eyed one another in silence for a moment, then Harren pointed grimly to the confusion of letters and figures covering dozens of scattered sheets lying on the table.

"That's part of my madness," he said with a short laugh. "Can you make anything of such lunatic work?"

The Tracer picked up a sheet of paper covered with letters of the alphabet and Roman and Arabic numerals. He dropped it presently and picked up another comparatively blank sheet, on which were the following figures:

He studied it for a while, then glanced interrogatively at Harren.

"It's nothing," said Harren. "I've been groping for three years—but it's no use. That's lunatics' work." He wheeled squarely on his heels, looking straight at the Tracer. "*Do* you think I've had a touch of the sun?"

"No," said Mr. Keen, drawing a chair to the table. "Saner men than you or I have spent a lifetime over this so-called Seal of Solomon." He laid his finger on the two symbols—

Then, looking across the table at Harren: "What," he asked, "has the Seal of Solomon to do with your case?"

"*She—*" muttered Harren, and fell silent.

The Tracer waited; Harren said nothing.

"Where is the photograph?"

Harren unlocked a drawer in the table, hesitated, looked strangely at the Tracer.

"Mr. Keen," he said, "there is nothing on earth I hold more sacred than this. There is only one thing in the world that could justify me in showing it to a living soul—my—my desire to find—her—"

"No," said Keen coolly, "that is not enough to justify you—the mere desire to find the living original of this apparition. Nothing could justify your showing it unless you love her."

Harren held the picture tightly, staring full at the Tracer. A dull flush mounted to his forehead, and very slowly he laid the picture before the Tracer of Lost Persons.

Minute after minute sped while the Tracer bent above the photograph, his finely modeled features absolutely devoid of expression. Harren had drawn his chair beside him, and now sat leaning forward, bronzed cheek resting in his hand, staring fixedly at the picture.

"When was this—this photograph taken?" asked the Tracer quietly.

"The day after I arrived in New York. I was here, alone, smoking my pipe and glancing over the evening paper just before dressing for dinner. It was growing rather dark in the room; I had not turned on the electric light. My camera lay on the table—there it is!—that kodak. I had taken a few snapshots on shipboard; there was one film left."

He leaned more heavily on his elbow, eyes fixed upon the picture.

"It was almost dark," he repeated. "I laid aside the evening paper and stood up, thinking about dressing for dinner, when my eyes happened to fall on the camera. It occurred to me that I might as well unload it, let the unused film go, and send the roll to be developed and printed; and I picked up the camera—"

"Yes," said the Tracer softly.

"I picked it up and was starting toward the window where there remained enough daylight to see by—"

The Tracer nodded gently.

"Then I saw *her*!" said Harren under his breath.

"Where?"

"There—standing by that window. You can see the window and curtain in the photograph."

The Tracer gazed intently at the picture.

"She looked at me," said Harren, steadying his voice. "She was as real as you are, and she stood there, smiling faintly, her dark, lovely eyes meeting mine."

"Did you speak?"

"No."

"How long did she remain there?"

"I don't know—time seemed to stop—the world—everything grew still. . . . Then, little by little, something began to stir under my stunned senses—that germ of misgiving, that dreadful doubt of my own sanity. . . . I scarcely knew what I was doing when I took the photograph; besides, it had grown quite dark, and I could scarcely see her." He drew himself erect with a nervous movement. "How on earth could I have obtained that photograph of her in the darkness?" he demanded.

"N-rays," said the Tracer coolly. "It has been done in France."

"Yes, from living people, but—"

"What the N-ray is in living organisms, we must call, for lack of a better term, the subaura in the phantom."

They bent over the photograph together. Presently the Tracer said: "She is very, very beautiful?"

Harren's dry lips unclosed, but he uttered no sound.

"She is beautiful, is she not?" repeated the Tracer, turning to look at the young man.

"Can you not see she is?" he asked impatiently.

"No," said the Tracer.

Harren stared at him.

"Captain Harren," continued the Tracer, "I can see nothing upon this bit of paper that resembles in the remotest degree a human face or figure."

Harren turned white.

"Not that I doubt that *you* can see it," pursued the Tracer calmly. "I simply repeat that I see absolutely nothing on this paper except a part of a curtain, a window pane, and—and—"

"What! for God's sake!" cried Harren hoarsely,

"I don't know yet. Wait; let me study it."

"Can you not see her face, her eyes? *Don't* you see that exquisite slim figure standing there by the curtain?" demanded Harren, laying his shaking finger on the photograph. "Why, man, it is as clear, as clean cut, as distinct as though the picture had been taken in sunlight! Do you mean to say that there is nothing there—that I am crazy?"

"No. Wait."

"Wait! How can I wait when you sit staring at her picture and telling me that you can't see it, but that it is doubtless there? Are you deceiving me, Mr. Keen? Are you trying to humor me, trying to be kind to me, knowing all the while that I'm crazy—"

"Wait, man! You are no more crazy than I am. I tell you that I can see something on the window pane—"

He suddenly sprang up and walked to the window, leaning close and examining the glass. Harren followed and laid his hand lightly over the pane.

"Do you see any marks on the glass?" demanded Keen.

Harren shook his head.

"Have you a magnifying glass?" asked the Tracer.

Harren pointed back to the table, and they returned to the photograph, the Tracer bending over it and examining it through the glass.

"All I see," he said, still studying the photograph, "is a corner of a curtain and a window on which certain figures seem to have been cut. . . . Look, Captain Harren, can you see them?"

"I see some marks—some squares."

"You can't see anything written on that pane—as though cut by a diamond?"

"Nothing distinct."

"But you see *her*?"

"Perfectly."

"In minute detail?"

"Yes."

The Tracer thought a moment: "Does she wear a ring?"

"Yes; can't you see?"

"Draw it for me."

They seated themselves side by side, and Harren drew a rough sketch of the ring which he insisted was so plainly visible on her hand:

"Oh," observed the Tracer, "she wears the Seal of Solomon on her ring."

Harren looked up at him. "That symbol has haunted me persistently for three years," he said. "I have found it everywhere—on articles that I buy, on house furniture, on the belts of dead ladrones, on the hilts of creeses, on the funnels of steamers, on the headstalls of horses. If they put a laundry mark on my linen it's certain to be this!

If I buy a box of matches the sign is on it. Why, I've even seen it on the brilliant wings of tropical insects. It's got on my nerves. I dream about it."

"And you buy books about it and try to work out its mystical meaning?" suggested the Tracer, smiling.

But Harren's gray eyes were serious. He said: "*She* never comes to me without that symbol somewhere about her. . . . I told you she never spoke to me. That is true; yet once, in a vivid dream of her, she did speak. I—I was almost ashamed to tell you of that."

"Tell me."

"A—a dream? Do you wish to know what I dreamed?"

"Yes—if it was a dream."

"It was. I was asleep on the deck of the *Mindinao*, dead tired after a fruitless hike. I dreamed she came toward me through a young woodland all lighted by the sun, and in her hands she held masses of that wild flower we call Solomon's Seal. And she said— in the voice I know must be like hers: 'If you could only read! If you would only understand the message I send you! It is everywhere on earth for you to read, if you only would!'

"I said: 'Is the message in the seal? Is that the key to it?'

"She nodded, laughing, burying her face in the flowers, and said:

"'Perhaps I can write it more plainly for you some day; I will try very, very hard.'

"And after that she went away—not swiftly—for I saw her at moments far away in the woods; but I must have confused her with the glimmering shafts of sunlight, and in a little while the woodland grew dark and I woke with the racket of a Colt's automatic in my ears."

He passed his sun-bronzed hand over his face, hesitated, then leaned over the photograph once more, which the Tracer was studying intently through the magnifying glass.

"There is something on that window in the photograph which I'm going to copy," he said. "Please shove a pad and pencil toward me."

Still examining the photograph through the glass which he held in his right hand, Mr. Keen picked up the pencil and, feeling for the pad, began very slowly to form the following series of symbols:

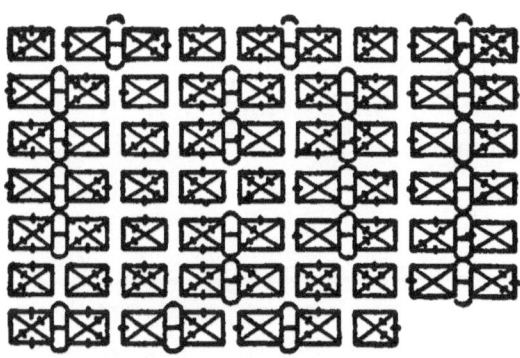

"What on earth are you doing?" muttered Captain Harren, twisting his short mustache in perplexity.

"I am copying what I see through this magnifying glass written on the window pane in the photograph," said the Tracer calmly. "Can't you see those marks?"

"I—I do now; I never noticed them before particularly—only that there were scratches there."

When at length the Tracer had finished his work he sat, chin on hand, examining it in silence. Presently he turned toward Harren, smiling.

"Well?" inquired the younger man impatiently; "do those scratches representing Solomon's Seal mean anything?"

"It's the strangest cipher I ever encountered," said Mr. Keen— "the strangest I ever heard of. I have seen hundreds of ciphers— hundreds—secret codes of the State Department, secret military codes, elaborate Oriental ciphers, symbols used in commercial transactions, symbols used by criminals and every species of male- factor. And every one of them can be solved with time and patience and a little knowledge of the subject. But this"—he sat looking at it with eyes half closed— "this is *too* simple."

"Simple!"

"Very. It's so simple that it's baffling."

"Do you mean to say you are going to be able to find a meaning in squares and crosses?"

"I—I don't believe it is going to be so very difficult to translate them."

"Great guns!" said the Captain. "Do you mean to say that you can ultimately translate that cipher?"

The Tracer smiled. "Let's examine it for repetitions first. Here we have this symbol

repeated five times. It's likely to be the letter E. I think—" His voice ceased; for a quarter of an hour he pored over the symbols, pencil in hand, checking off some, substituting a letter here and there.

"No," he said; "the usual doesn't work in this case. It's an absurdly simple cipher. I have a notion that numbers play a part in it—you see where these crossed squares are bracketed—those must be numbers requiring two figures—"

He fell silent again, and for another quarter of an hour he remained motionless, immersed in the problem before him, Harren frowning at the paper over his shoulder.

TEN

"Come!" said the Tracer suddenly; "this won't do. There are too few symbols to give us a key; too few repetitions to furnish us with any key basis. Come, Captain, let us use our intellects; let us talk it over with that paper lying there between us. It's a simple cipher—a childishly simple one if we use our wits. Now, sir, what I see repeated before us on this sheet of paper is merely one of the forms of a symbol known as Solomon's Seal. The symbol is, as we see, repeated a great many times. Every seal ⊠ has been dotted or crossed on some one of the lines composing it; some seals are coupled with brackets and armatures."

"What of it?" inquired Harren vacantly.

"Well, sir, in the first place, that symbol ⊠ is supposed to represent the spiritual and material, as you know. What else do you know about it?"

"Nothing. I bought a book about it, but made nothing of it."

"Isn't it supposed," asked Mr. Keen, "to contain within itself the nine numerals, 1, 2, 3, 4, 5, 6, 7, 8, 9, and even the zero symbol?"

"I believe so."

"*Ex*actly. Here's the seal ⊠ Now I'll mark the one, two, and three by crossing the lines, like this:

one, ⊠   two, ⊠   three, ⊠

Now, eliminating all lines not crossed there remains

the one, **1**   the two, **Z**   the three, **ろ**

And here is the entire series:

and the zero— ◗ ”

A sudden excitement stirred Harren; he leaned over the paper, gazing earnestly at the cipher; the Tracer rose and glanced around the room as though in search of something.

"Is there a telephone here?" he asked.

"For Heaven's sake, don't give this up just yet," exclaimed Harren. "These things mean numbers; don't you see? Look at that!" pointing to a linked pair of seals,

"That means the number nineteen! You can form it by using only the crossed lines of the seal.

$$\dagger\ \mathbb{Y}$$

Don't you see, Mr. Keen?"

"Yes, Captain Harren, the cipher is, as you say, very plain; quite as easy to read as so much handwriting. That is why I wish to use your telephone—at once, if you please."

"It's in my bedroom; you don't mind if I go on working out this cipher while you're telephoning?"

"Not in the least," said the Tracer blandly. He walked into the Captain's bedroom, closing the door behind him; then he stepped over to the telephone, unhooked the receiver, and called up his own headquarters.

"Hello. This is Mr. Keen. I want to speak to Miss Borrow."

In a few moments Miss Borrow answered: "I am here, Mr. Keen."

"Good. Look up the name Inwood. Try New York first—Edith Inwood is the name. Look sharp, please; I am holding the wire."

He held it for ten full minutes; then Miss Borrow's low voice called him over the wire.

"Go ahead," said the Tracer quietly.

"There is only one Edith Inwood in New York, Mr. Keen—Miss Edith Inwood, graduate of Barnard, 1902—left an orphan 1903 and obliged to support herself—became an assistant to Professor Boggs of the Museum of Inscriptions. Is considered an authority upon Arabian cryptograms. Has written a monograph on the Herati symbol—a short treatise on the Swastika. She is twenty-four years of age. Do you require further details?"

"No," said the Tracer; "please ring off."

Then he called up General Information. "I want the Museum of Inscriptions. Get me their number, please." After a moment: "Is this the Museum of Inscriptions?"

·   ·   ·   ·   ·

"Is Professor Boggs there?"

·   ·   ·   ·   ·

"Is this Professor Boggs?"

·   ·   ·   ·   ·

"Could you find time to decipher an inscription for me at once?"

·   ·   ·   ·   ·

"Of course I know you are extremely busy, but have you no assistant who could do it?"

·   ·   ·   ·   ·

"What did you say her name is? Miss Inwood?"

·   ·   ·   ·   ·

"Oh! And will the young lady translate the inscription at once if I send a copy of it to her by messenger?"

·   ·   ·   ·   ·

"Thank you very much, Professor. I will send a messenger to Miss Inwood with a copy of the inscription. Good-by."

He hung up the receiver, turned thoughtfully, opened the door again, and walked into the sunlit living room.

"Look here!" cried the Captain in a high state of excitement. "I've got a lot of numbers out of it already."

"Wonderful!" murmured the Tracer, looking over the young man's broad shoulders at a sheet of paper bearing these numbers:

$$9-14-5-22-5-18-19-1-23-25-15-21-$$
$$2-21-20-15-14-3-5-9-12-15-22-5-25-$$
$$15-21-5-4-9-20-8-9-14-23-15-15-4.$$

"Marvelous!" repeated the Tracer, smiling. "Now what *do* you suppose those numbers can stand for?"

"Letters!" announced the Captain triumphantly. "Take the number nine, for example. The ninth letter in the alphabet is I! Mr. Keen, suppose we try writing down the letters according to that system!"

"Suppose we do," agreed the Tracer gravely.

So, counting under his breath, the young man set down the letters in the following order, not attempting to group them into words:

INEVERSAWYOUBUTONCEILOVEYOUEDITHINWOOD.

Then he leaned back, excited, triumphant.

"There you are!" he said; "only, of course, it makes no sense." He examined it in silence, and gradually a hopeless expression effaced the animation. "How the deuce am I going to separate that mass of letters into words?" he muttered.

"This way," said the Tracer, smilingly taking the pencil from his fingers, and he wrote: I—NEVER—SAW—YOU—BUT—ONCE. I—LOVE—YOU. EDITH INWOOD.

Then he laid the pencil on the table and walked to the window.

Once or twice he fancied that he heard incoherent sounds behind him. And after a while he turned, retracing his steps leisurely. Captain Harren, extremely pink, stood tugging at his short mustache and studying the papers on the desk.

"Well?" inquired the Tracer, amused.

The young man pointed to the translation with unsteady finger. "W-what on earth does that mean?" he demanded shakily. "Who is Edith Inwood? W-what on earth does that cryptogram mean on the window pane in the photograph? How did it come there? It isn't on my window pane, you see!"

The Tracer said quietly: "That is not a photograph of your window."

"What!"

"No, Captain. Here! Look at it closely through this glass. There are sixteen small panes in that sash; now count the panes in your window—eight! Besides, look at that curtain. It is made of some figured stuff like chintz. Now, look at your own curtain yonder! It is of plain velour."

"But—but I took that photograph! She stood there—there by that very window!"

The Tracer leaned over the photograph, examining it through the glass. And, studying it, he said: "Do you still see *her* in this photograph, Captain Harren?"

"Certainly. Can you not see her?"

"No," murmured the Tracer, "but I see the window which she really stood by when her phantom came here seeking you. And that is sufficient. Come, Captain Harren, we are going out together."

The Captain looked at him earnestly; something in Mr. Keen's eyes seemed to fascinate him.

"You think that—that it's likely we are g-going to see—*her*!" he faltered.

"If I were you," mused the Tracer of Lost Persons, joining the tips of his lean fingers meditatively— "If I were you I should wear a silk hat and a frock coat. It's—it's afternoon, anyhow," he added deprecatingly, "and we are liable to make a call."

Captain Harren turned like a man in a dream and entered his bedroom. And when he emerged he was dressed and groomed with pathetic precision.

"Mr. Keen," he said, "I—I don't know why I am d-daring to hope for all s-sorts of things. Nothing you have said really warrants it. But somehow I'm venturing to cherish an absurd notion that I may s-see her."

"Perhaps," said the Tracer, smiling.

"Mr. Keen! You wouldn't say that if—if there was no chance, would you? You wouldn't dash a fellow's hopes—"

"No, I wouldn't," said Mr. Keen. "I tell you frankly that I ex-pect to find her."

"To-day?"

"We'll see," said Mr. Keen guardedly. "Come, Captain, don't look that way! Courage, sir! We are about to execute a turning movement; but you look like a Russian general on his way to the south front."

Harren managed to laugh; they went out, side by side, descended the elevator, and found a cab at the *porte-cochère*. Mr. Keen gave the directions and followed the Captain into the cab.

"Now," he said, as they wheeled south, "we are first going to visit the Museum of Inscriptions and have this cipher translation verified. Here is the cipher as I copied it. Hold it tightly, Captain; we've only a few blocks to drive."

Indeed they were already nearly there. The hansom drew up in front of a plain granite building wedged in between some rather elaborate private dwelling-houses. Over the door were letters of dull bronze:

AMERICAN MUSEUM OF INSCRIPTIONS

and the two men descended and entered a wide marble hall lined with glass-covered cabinets containing plaster casts of various ancient inscriptions and a few bronze and marble originals. Several female frumps were nosing the exhibits.

An attendant in livery stood in the middle distance. The Tracer walked over to him. "I have an appointment to consult Miss Inwood," he whispered.

"This way, sir," nodded the attendant, and the Tracer signaled the Captain to follow.

They climbed several marble stairways, crossed a rotunda, and entered a room—a sort of library. Beyond was a door which bore the inscription:

ASSISTANT CURATOR

"Now," said the Tracer of Lost Persons in a low voice to Captain Harren, "I am going to ask you to sit here for a few minutes while I interview the assistant curator. You don't mind, do you?"

"No, I don't mind," said Harren wearily, "only, when are we going to begin to search for—*her*?"

"Very soon—I may say extremely soon," said Mr. Keen gravely. "By the way, I think I'll take that sheet of paper on which I copied the cipher. Thank you. I won't be long."

The attendant had vanished. Captain Harren sat down by a window and gazed out into the late afternoon sunshine. The Tracer of Lost Persons, treading softly across the carpeted floor, approached the sanctuary, turned the handle, and walked in, carefully closing the door behind him.

There was a young girl seated at a desk by an open window; she looked up quietly as he entered, then rose leisurely.

"Miss Inwood?"

"Yes."

She was slender, dark-eyed, dark-haired—a lovely, wholesome young creature; gracious and graceful. And that was all—for the Tracer of Lost Persons could not see through the eyes of Captain Harren, and perhaps that is why he was not able to discern a miracle of beauty in the pretty girl who confronted him—no magic and matchless marvel of transcendent loveliness—only a quiet, sweet-faced, dark-eyed young girl whose features and figure were attractive in the manner that youth is always attractive. But then it is a gift of the gods to see through eyes anointed by the gods.

The Tracer touched his gray mustache and bowed; the girl bowed very sweetly.

"You are Mr. Keen," she said; "you have an inscription for me to translate."

"A mystery for young eyes to interpret," he said, smiling. "May I sit here—and tell my story before I show you my inscription?"

"Please do," she said, seating herself at her desk and facing him, one slender white hand supporting the oval of her face.

The Tracer drew his chair a little forward. "It is a curious matter," he said. "May I give you a brief outline of the details?"

"By all means, Mr. Keen."

"Then let me begin by saying that the inscription of which I have a copy was probably scratched upon a window pane by means of a diamond."

"Oh! Then—then it is not an ancient inscription, Mr. Keen."

"The theme is ancient—the oldest theme in the world—love! The cipher is old—as old as King Solomon." She looked up quickly. The Tracer, apparently engrossed in his own story, went on with it.

"Three years ago the young girl who wrote this inscription upon the window pane of her—her bedroom, I think it was—fell in love. Do you follow me, Miss Inwood?"

Miss Inwood sat very still—wide, dark eyes fixed on him.

"Fell in love," repeated the Tracer musingly, "not in the ordinary way. That is the point, you see. No, she fell in love at first sight; fell in love with a young man whom she never before had seen, never again beheld—and never forgot. Do you still follow me, Miss Inwood?"

She made the slightest motion with her lips.

"No," mused the Tracer of Lost Persons, "she never forgot him. I am not sure, but I think she sometimes dreamed of him. She dreamed of him awake, too. Once she inscribed a message to him, cutting it with the diamond in her ring on the window pane—"

A slight sound escaped from Miss Inwood's lips. "I beg your pardon," said the Tracer, "did you say something?"

The girl had risen, pale, astounded, incredulous.

"Who are you?" she faltered. "What has this—this story to do with me?"

"Child," said the Tracer of Lost Persons, "the Seal of Solomon is a splendid mystery. All of heaven and earth are included within its symbol. And more, more than you dream of, more than I dare fathom; and I am an old man, my child—old, alone, with nobody to fear for, nothing to dread, not even the end of all—because I am ready for that, too. Yet I, having nothing on earth to dread, dare not fathom what that symbol may mean, nor what vast powers it may exert on life. God knows. It may be the very signet of Fate itself; the sign manual of Destiny."

He drew the paper from his pocket, unrolled it, and spread it out under her frightened eyes.

"*That!*" she whispered, steadying herself blindly against the arm he offered. She stood a moment so, then, shuddering, covered her eyes with both hands. The Tracer of Lost Persons looked at her, turned and opened the door.

"Captain Harren!" he called quietly. Harren, pacing the anteroom, turned and came forward. As he entered the door he caught sight of the girl crouching by the window, her face hidden in her hands, and at the same moment she dropped her hands and looked straight at him.

"*You!*" she gasped.

The Tracer of Lost Persons stepped out, closing the door. For a moment he stood there, tall, gaunt, gray, staring vacantly into space.

"She *was* beautiful—when she looked at him," he muttered.

For another minute he stood there, hesitating, glancing backward at the closed door. Then he went away, stooping slightly, his top hat held close against the breast of his tightly buttoned frock coat.

ELEVEN

During his first year of wedded bliss, Gatewood cut the club. When Kerns wanted to see him he had to call like other people or, like other people, accept young Mrs. Gatewood's invitations.

"Why," said Gatewood scornfully, "should I, thirty-four years of age and safely married, go to a club? Why should I, at my age, idle with a lot of idlers and listen to stuffy stories from stuffier individuals? Do you think that stale tobacco smoke, and the idiotically reiterated click of billiard balls, and the vacant stare of the fashionably brainless, and the meaningless exchange of banalities with the intellectually aimless have any attractions for me?"

Mrs. Gatewood raised her pretty eyes in silence; Kerns returned her amused gaze rather blankly.

"Clubs!" sniffed Gatewood. "What are clubs but pretexts for wasting time? What mental, what spiritual stimulus can a man expect to find in a club? Why, Kerns, when I look back a year and think what I was, and when I look at you and think what you still arc "

"John," said Mrs. Gatewood softly.

"Oh, he knows it!" insisted her husband, "don't you, Tommy? You know the sort of life you're leading, don't you? You know what a miserable, aimless, selfish, unambitious, pitiable existence an unmarried man leads who lives at his club; don't you?"

"Certainly," said Kerns, blinking into the smiling gaze of Mrs. Gatewood.

"Then why don't you marry?"

But Kerns had risen and was making his adieus with cheerful decision; and Mrs. Gatewood was laughing as she gave him her slender hand.

"Now I know a girl—" began Gatewood; but his wife was still speaking to Kerns, so he circled around them, politely suppressing the excitement of a sudden idea struggling for utterance.

Mrs. Gatewood was saying: "I do wish John would go to his clubs occasionally. Because a man is married is no reason for his losing touch with his clubs—"

"I know a girl," broke in Gatewood excitedly, laying his arm on Kerns's to detain him; but Kerns slid sideways through the door with a smile so noncommittal that Mrs. Gatewood laughed again and, linking her arm in her husband's, faced partly toward him. This maneuver, and the slightest pressure of her shoulder, obliged her husband to begin a turning movement, so that Kerns might reasonably make his escape in the middle of Gatewood's sentence; which he did with nimble and circumspect agility.

"I—I know a—" began Gatewood desperately, twisting his head over his shoulder, only to hear the deadened patter of his friend's feet over the velvet stair carpet and the subdued clang of the front door.

"Isn't it extraordinary?" he said to his wife. "I've been trying to tell Tommy, every time he comes here, about a girl I know—just the very girl he ought to marry; and something prevents him from listening every time."

The attractive young matron beside him turned her face so that her eyes were directly in line with his.

"Did you ever know any people named Manners?" she asked.

"No. Why?"

"You never knew a girl named Marjorie Manners, did you, John?"

"No. What about her?"

"You never heard Mr. Kerns speak of her, did you, dear?"

"No, never. Tommy doesn't talk about girls."

"You never heard him speak of a Mrs. Stanley?"

"Never. Who are these two women?"

"One and the same, dear. Marjorie Manners married an Englishman named Stanley six years ago. Do you happen to recollect that Mr. Kerns took his vacation in England six years ago?"

"Yes. What of it?"

"He crossed to Southampton with Marjorie and her mother. He didn't know she was going over to be married, and she didn't tell him. She wrote to me about it, though. I was in school at Farmington; she left school to marry—a mere child of eighteen, undeveloped for her age, thin, almost scrawny, with pipe-stem arms and neck, red hair, a very sweet, full-lipped mouth, and gray eyes that were too big for her face."

"Well," said Gatewood with a short laugh, "what about it? You don't think Kerns fell in love with an insect of that genus, do you?"

"Yes, I do," smiled Mrs. Gatewood.

"Nonsense. Besides, what of it? She's married, you say."

"Her husband died of enteric at Ladysmith. She wrote me. She has never remarried. Think of it, John—in all these years she has never remarried!"

"Oh!" said Gatewood pityingly; "do you really suppose that Tommy Kerns has been nursing a blighted affection all these years without ever giving *me* an inkling? Besides, men don't do that; men don't curl up and blight. Besides, men don't take any stock in big-eyed, flat-chested, red-headed pipe stems. Why do you think that Kerns ever cared for her?"

"I know he did."

"How do you know it?"

"From Marjorie's letters."

"The conceited kid! Well, of all insufferable nerve! A man like Kerns—a man—one of the finest, noblest characters—spiritually, intellectually, physically—a practically faultless specimen of manhood! And a red-headed, spindle-legged—Oh, my! Oh, fizz! Dearest, men don't worship a cage of bones with an eighteen-year-old soul in it—like a nervous canary pecking out at the world!"

"She created a furor in England," observed his wife, smiling.

"Oh, I dare say she might over there. Besides, she's doubtless fattened up since then. But if you suppose for one moment that Tommy could even remember a girl like that—"

Mrs. Gatewood smiled again—the wise, sweet smile of a young matron in whom her husband's closest friend had confided. And after a moment or two the wise smile became more thoughtful and less assured; for that very day the Tracer of Lost Persons had called on her to inquire about a Mrs. Stanley—a new client of his who had recently bought a town house in East Eighty-third Street and a country house on Long Island; and who had applied to him to find her fugitive butler and a pint or two of family jewels. And, after her talk with the Tracer of Lost Persons, Mrs. Gatewood knew that her favorite among all her husband's friends, Mr. Kerns, would never of his own volition go near that same Marjorie Manners who had flirted with him to the very perilous verge before she told him why she was going to England—and who, now a widow, had returned with her five-year-old daughter to dwell once more in the city of her ancestors.

Kerns had said very simply: "She has spoiled women for me— all except you, Mrs. Gatewood. And if Jack hadn't married you—"

"I understand, Mr. Kerns. I'm awfully sorry."

"Don't feel sorry; only, if you can, call Jack off. He's been perfectly possessed to marry me to somebody ever since he married you. And if I told him why I don't care to consider the matter he wouldn't believe me—he'd spend his life in trying to bring me around. Besides, I couldn't ever tell him about—Marjorie Manners. Anyhow, nothing on earth could ever induce me to look at her again. . . . You say she is now a widow?"

"Yes, Mr. Kerns, and very beautiful."

"Never again," muttered Kerns. "Never! She was homely enough when I asked her to marry me. I don't want to see her; I don't want to know what she looks like. I'm glad she has changed so I wouldn't recognize her, for that means the end of it all—the final elimination of the girl I remember on the ship. . . . It was probably a sort of diseased infatuation, wasn't it, Mrs. Gatewood? Think of it! A few days on shipboard and—and I asked her to marry me! . . . I don't blame her, after all, for letting me dangle. It was an excellent opportunity for her to study a rare species of idiot. She was justified and I am satisfied. Only, do call Jack off with a hint or two."

"I shall try," said young Mrs. Gatewood thoughtfully—very thoughtfully, for already every atom and fiber of her femininity was aroused in behalf of these two estranged young people whom Providence certainly had not meant to put asunder.

TWELVE

"Nothing," said Gatewood firmly, "can make me believe that Kerns ought not to marry somebody; and I'm never going to let up on him until he does. I'll bet I could fix him for life if I called in the Tracer to help me. Isn't it extraordinary how Kerns has kept out of it all these years?"

The attractive girl beside him turned her face once more so that her clear, sweet eyes were directly in line with his.

"It *is* extraordinary," she said seriously. "I think you ought to drop in at the club some day when you can corner him and bully him."

"I don't want to go to the club," said the infatuated man.

"Why, dear?"

He looked straight at her and she flushed prettily, while a tint of color touched his own face. Which was very nice of him. So she didn't say what she was going to say—that it would be perhaps better for them both if he practiced on her an artistic absence now and then. Younger in years, she was more mature than he. She knew. But she was too much in love with him to salt their ambrosia with common sense or suggest economy in their use of the nectar bottle.

However, the gods attend to that, and she knew they would, and she let them. So one balmy evening late in May, when the new moon's ghost floated through the upper haze, and the golden Diana above Manhattan turned flame color, and the electric lights began to glimmer along Fifth Avenue, and the first faint scent of the young summer freshened the foliage in square and park, Kerns, stopping at the club for a moment, found Gatewood seated at the same window they both were wont to haunt in earlier and more flippant days.

"Are you dining here?" inquired Kerns, pushing the electric button with enthusiasm. "Well, that's the first glimmer of common sense you've betrayed since you've been married!"

"Dining *here*!" repeated Gatewood. "I should hope not! I am just going home—"

"He's thoroughly cowed," commented Kerns; "every married man you meet at the club is just going home." But he continued to push the button, nevertheless.

Gatewood leaned back in his chair and gazed about him, nose in the air. "What a life!" he observed virtuously. "It's all I can do to stand it for ten minutes. You're here for the evening, I suppose?" he added pityingly.

"No," said Kerns; "I'm going uptown to Billy Lee's house to get my suit case. His family are out of town, and he is at Seabright, so he let me camp there until the workmen finish papering my rooms upstairs. I'm to lock up the house and send the key to the Burglar Alarm Company to-night. Then I go to Boston on the 12.10. Want to come? There'll be a few doing."

"To Boston! What for?"

"Contracts! We can go out to Cambridge when I've finished my business. There'll be *etwas* doing."

"*Can't* you ever recover from being an undergraduate?" asked Gatewood, disgusted.

"Well—is there anything the matter with a man getting next to a little amusement in life?" asked Kerns. "Do you object to my being happy?"

"Amusement? You don't know how to amuse yourself. You don't know how to be happy. Here you sit, day after day, swallowing Martinis—" He paused to finish his own, then resumed: "Here you sit, day after day, intellectually stultified, unemotionally ignorant of the higher and better life—"

"No, I don't. I've a book upstairs that tells all about that. I read it when I have holdovers—"

"Kerns, I wish to speak seriously. I've had it on my mind ever since I married. May I speak frankly?"

"Well, when I come back from Boston—"

"Because I know a girl," interrupted Gatewood— "wait a moment, Tommy!"—as Kerns rose and sauntered toward the door— "you've plenty of time to catch your train and be civil, too! I mean to tell you about that girl, if you'll listen."

Kerns halted and turned upon his friend a pair of eyes, unwinking in their placid intelligence.

"I was going to say that I know a girl," continued Gatewood, "who is just the sort of a girl you—"

"No, she isn't!" said Kerns, wheeling to resume his progress toward the cloakroom.

"Tom!"

Kerns halted.

"*You're* a fine specimen!" commented Gatewood scornfully. "You spent the best years of your life in persuading me to get married, and the first time I try to do the same for you, you make for the tall timber!"

"I know it," admitted Kerns, unashamed; "I'm bashful. I'm a chipmunk for shyness, so I'll say good night—"

"Come back," said Gatewood coldly.

"But my suit case—"

"You left it at the Lee's, didn't you? Well, you've time enough to go there, get it, make your train, and listen to me, too. Look here, Kerns, have you any of the elements of decency about you?"

"No," said Kerns, "not a single element." He seated himself defiantly in the club window facing Gatewood and began to button his gloves. When he had finished he settled his new straw hat more comfortably on his head, and, leaning forward and balancing his malacca walking stick across his knees, gazed at Gatewood with composure.

"Crank up!" he said pleasantly; "I'm going in less than three minutes." He pushed the electric knob as an afterthought, and when the gilt buttons of the club servant glimmered through the dusk, "Two more," he explained briskly. After a few moments' silence,

broken by the tinkle of ice in thin glassware, Gatewood leaned forward, menacing his friend with an impressive forefinger:

"Did you or didn't you once tell me that a decent citizen ought
to marry?"

"I did, dear friend."

"Did I or didn't I do it?"

"In the words of the classic, you *done* it," admitted Kerns.

"Was I or wasn't I going to the devil before I had the sense to
marry?" persisted Gatewood.

"You was! You *was*, dear friend!" said Kerns with enthusiasm.
"You had almost went there ere I appeared and saved you."

"Then why shouldn't you marry and let me save you?"

"But I'm not going to the bowwows. *I'm* all right. I'm a decent
citizen. I awake in the rosy dawn with a song on my lips; I softly
whistle rag time as I button my collar; I warble a few delicious
vagrant notes as I part my sparse hair; I'm not murderous before
breakfast; I go down town, singing, to my daily toil; I fish for fat
contracts in Georgia marble; I return uptown immersed in a holy
calm and the evening paper. I offer myself a cocktail; I bow and
accept; I dress for dinner with the aid of a rascally valet, but—*do* I
swear at him? No, dear friend; I say, 'Henry, I have known far, far
worse scoundrels than you. Thank you for filling up my bay rum
with water. Bless you for wearing my imported hosiery! I deeply
regret that my new shirts do not fit you, Henry!' And my smile is a
benediction upon that wayward scullion. Then, dear friend, why,
why do you desire to offer me up upon the altar of unrest? What is
a little wifey to me or I to any wifey?"

"Because," said Gatewood irritated, "you offered me up. I'm
happy and I want you to be—you great, hulking, self-satisfied symbol of supreme self-centered selfishness—"

"Oh, splash!" said Kerns feebly.

"Yes, you are. What do you do all day? Grub for money and
study how to make life agreeable to yourself! Every minute of the
day you are occupied in having a good time! You've admitted it!
You wake up singing like a fool canary; you wear imported hosiery;
you've made a soft, warm wallow for yourself at this club, and here

you bask your life away, waddling downtown to nail contracts and cut coupons, and uptown to dinners and theaters, only to return and sprawl here in luxury without one single thought for posterity. *Your* crime is race suicide!"

"I—my—*what*!"

"Certainly. Some shirk taxes, some jury duty. *You* shirk fatherhood, and all its happy and sacred obligations! You deny posterity! You strike a blow at it! You flout it! You menace the future of this Republic! Your inertia is a crime against the people! Instead of *pro bono publico* your motto is *pro bono tempo*—for a good time! And, dog Latin or not, it's the truth, and our great President—"

"Splash!" said Kerns, rising.

"I've a good mind," said Gatewood indignantly, "to put the Tracer of Lost Persons on your trail. He'd rope you and tie you in record time!"

Kerns's smile was a provocation.

"I'll do it, too!" added Gatewood, losing his temper, "if you dare give me the chance."

"Seriously," inquired Kerns, delighted, "*do* you think your friend, Mr. Keen, could encompass my matrimony against my better sense and the full enjoyment of my unimpaired mental faculties?"

"Didn't he—fortunately for me—force me into matrimony when I had never seen a woman I would look at twice? Didn't you put him up to it? Very well, why can't I put him on your trail then? Why can't *he* do the same for you?"

"Try it, dear friend," retorted Kerns courteously.

"Do you mean that you are not afraid? Do you mean you give me full liberty to set him on you? And do you realize what that means? No, you don't; for you haven't a notion of what that man, Westrel Keen, can accomplish. You haven't the slightest idea of the machinery which he controls with a delicacy absolutely faultless; with a perfectly terrifying precision. Why, man, the Pinkerton system itself has become merely a detail in the immense complexity of the system of control which the Tracer of Lost Persons exercises over this entire continent. The urban police, the State constabulary of Pennsylvania, the rural systems of surveillance, the Secret Service, all municipal, provincial, State, and national organizations form but a few strands in the universal web he has woven. Custom officials, revenue officers, the militia of the States, the army, the navy, the personnel of every city, State, and national legislative bodies form interdependent threads in the mesh he is master of; and, like a big beneficent spider, he sits in the center of his web, able to tell by the slightest tremor of any thread exactly where to begin investigations!"

Flushed, earnest, a trifle out of breath with his own eloquence, Gatewood waved his hand to indicate a Ciceronian period, adding, as Kerns's incredulous smile broadened: "Say splash again, and I'll put you at his mercy!"

"Ker-splash! dear friend," observed Kerns pleasantly. "If a man doesn't want to marry, the army, the navy, the Senate, the white wings, and the great White Father at Washington can't make him."

"I tell you I want to see you happy!" said Gatewood angrily.

"Then gaze upon me. I'm it!"

"You're not! You don't know what happiness is."

"Don't I? Well, I don't miss it, dear friend—"

"But if you've never had it, and therefore don't miss it, it's time somebody found some real happiness for you. Kerns, I simply can't bear to see you missing so much happiness—"

"Why grieve?"

"Yes, I will! I do grieve—in spite of your grinning skepticism and your bantering attitude. See here, Tom; I've started about a thousand times to say that I knew a girl—"

"Do you want to hear that splash again?"

Gatewood grew madder. He said: "I could easily lay your case before Mr. Keen and have you in love and married and happy whether you like it or not!"

"If I were not going to Boston, my son, I should enjoy your misguided efforts," returned Kerns blandly.

"Your going to Boston makes no difference. The Tracer of Lost Persons doesn't care where you go or what you do. If he starts in on your case, Tommy, you can't escape."

"You mean he can catch me now? Here? At my own club? Or on the public highway? Or on the classic Boston train?"

"He *could*. Yes, I firmly believe he could land you before you ever saw the Boston State House. I tell you he can work like lightning, Kerns. I know it; I am so absolutely convinced of it that I—I almost hesitate—"

"Don't feel delicate about it," laughed Kerns; "you may call him on the telephone while I go uptown and get my suit case. Perhaps I'll come back a blushing bridegroom; who knows?"

"If you'll wait here I'll call him up now," said Gatewood grimly.

"Oh, very well. Only I left my suit case in Billy's room, and it's full of samples of Georgia marble, and I've got to get it to the train."

"You've plenty of time. If you'll wait until I talk to Mr. Keen I'll dine with you here. Will you?"

"What? Dine in this abandoned joint with an outcast like me? Dear friend, are you dippy this lovely May evening?"

"I'll do it if you'll wait. Will you? And I'll bet you now that I'll have you in love and sprinting toward the altar before we meet again at this club. Do you dare bet?"

"The terms of the wager, kind friend?" drawled Kerns, delighted; and he fished out a notebook kept for such transactions.

"Let me see," reflected Gatewood; "you'll need a silver service when you're married. . . . Well, say, forks and spoons and things against an imported trap gun—twelve-gauge, you know."

"Done. Go and telephone to your friend, Mr. Keen." And Kerns pushed the electric button with a jeering laugh, and asked the servant for a dinner card.

THIRTEEN

Gatewood, in the telephone booth, waited impatiently for Mr. Keen; and after a few moments the Tracer of Lost Persons' agreeable voice sounded in the receiver.

"It's about Mr. Kerns," began Gatewood; "I want to see him happy, and the idiot won't be. Now, Mr. Keen, you know what happiness you and he brought to me! You know what sort of an idle, selfish, aimless, meaningless life you saved me from? I want you to do the same for Mr. Kerns. I want to ask you to take up his case at once. Besides, I've a bet on it. Could you attend to it at once?"

"To-night?" asked the Tracer, laughing.

"Why—ah—well, of course, that would be impossible. I suppose—"

"My profession is to overcome the impossible, Mr. Gatewood. Where is Mr. Kerns?"

"Here, in this club, defying me and drinking cocktails. He won't get married, and I want you to make him do it."

"Where is he spending the evening?" asked the Tracer, laughing again.

"Why, he's been stopping at the Danforth Lees' in Eighty-third Street until the workmen at the club here finish putting new paper on his walls. The Lees are out of town. He left his suit case at their house and he's going up to get it and catch the 12.10 train for Boston."

"He goes from the Lenox Club to the residence of Mr. W. Danforth Lee, East Eighty-third Street, to get a suit case," repeated the Tracer. "Is that correct?"

"Yes."

"What is in the suit case?"

"Samples of that new marble he's quarrying in Georgia."

"Is it an old suit case? Has it Mr. Kerns's initials on it?"

"Hold the wire; I'll find out."

And Gatewood left the telephone and walked into the great lounging room, where Kerns sat twirling his stick and smiling to himself.

"All over, dear friend?" inquired Kerns, starting to rise. "I've ordered a corking dinner."

"Wait!" returned Gatewood ominously. "What sort of a suit case is that one you're going after?"

"What sort? Oh, just an ordinary—"

"Is it old or new?"

"Brand new. Why?"

"Is your name on it?"

"No; why? Would that thicken the plot, dear friend? Or is the Tracer foiled, ha! ha!"

Gatewood turned on his heel, went back to the telephone, and, carefully shutting the door of the booth, took up the receiver.

"It's a new suit case, Mr. Keen," he said; "no initials on it—just an ordinary case."

"Mr. Lee's residence is 38 East Eighty-third Street, between Madison and Fifth, I believe."

"Yes," replied Gatewood.

"And the family are out of town?"

"Yes."

"Is there a caretaker there?"

"No; Mr. Kerns camped there. When he leaves to-night he will send the key to the Burglar Alarm Company."

"Very well. Please hold the wire for a while."

For ten full minutes Gatewood sat gleefully cuddling the receiver against his ear. His faith in Mr. Keen was naturally boundless; he believed that whatever the Tracer attempted could not result in failure. He desired nothing in the world so ardently as to see Kerns safely married. His own happiness may have been the

motive power which had set him in action in behalf of his friend—
that and a certain indefinable desire to practice a species of heavenly revenge, of grateful retaliation upon the prime mover and
collaborateur, if not the sole author, of his own wedded bliss. Kerns
had made him happy.

"And I'm hanged if I don't pay him off and make him happy,
too!" muttered Gatewood. "Does he think I'm going to sit still and
see him go tearing and gyrating about town with no responsibility,
no moral check to his evolutions, no wholesome home duties to
limit his acrobatics, no wife to clip his wings? It's time he had somebody to report to; time he assumed moral burdens and spiritual
responsibilities. A man is just as happy when he is certain where
he is going to sleep. A man can find just as much enjoyment in life
when he feels it his duty to account for his movements. I don't care
whether Kerns is comparatively happy or not—there's nothing
either sacred or holy in that kind of happiness, and I'm not going
to endure the sort of life he likes any longer!"

Immersed in moral reflections, inspired by affectionate obligations to violently inflict happiness upon Kerns, the minutes
passed very agreeably until the amused voice of the Tracer of Lost
Persons sounded again in the receiver.

"Mr. Gatewood?"

"Yes, I am here, Mr. Keen."

"Do you really think it best for Mr. Kerns to fall in love?"

"I do, certainly!" replied Gatewood with emphasis.

"Because," continued the Tracer of Lost Persons, "I see little
chance for him to do otherwise if I take up this case. Fate itself, in the
shape of a young lady, is already on the way here in a railroad train."

"Good! Good!" exclaimed Gatewood. "Don't let him escape, Mr.
Keen! I beg of you to take up his case! I urge you most seriously to
do so. Mr. Kerns is now exactly what I was a year ago—an utterly
useless member of the community—a typical bachelor who lives at
his clubs, shirking the duties of a decent citizen."

"*Exactly*," said the Tracer. "Do you insist that I take this case?
That I attempt to trace and find for Mr. Kerns a sort of happiness
he himself has never found?"

ROBERT W. CHAMBERS

"I implore you to do so, Mr. Keen."

"*Ex*actly. If I do—if I carry it out as it has been arranged—or rather as the case seems to have already arranged itself, for it is rather a simple matter, I fancy—I do not exactly see how Mr. Kerns can avoid experiencing a—ahem—a tender sentiment for the very charming young lady whom I—and chance—have designed for him as a partner through life."

"Excellent! Splendid!" shouted Gatewood through the telephone. "Can I do anything to aid you in this?"

"Yes," replied the Tracer, laughing. "If you can keep him amused for an hour or two before he goes after his suit case it might make it easier for me. This young lady is due to arrive in New York at eight o'clock—a client of mine—coming to consult me. Her presence plays an important part in Mr. Kerns's future. I wish you to detain Mr. Kerns until she is ready to receive him. But of this he must know nothing. Good-by, Mr. Gatewood, and would you be kind enough to present my compliments to Mrs. Gatewood?"

"Indeed I will! We never can forget what you have done for us. Good-by."

"Good-by, Mr. Gatewood. Try to keep Mr. Kerns amused for two or three hours. Of course, if you can't do this, there are other methods I may employ—a dozen other plans already partly outlined in my mind; but the present plan, which accident and coincidence make so easy, is likely to work itself out to your entire satisfaction within a few hours. We are already weaving a web around Mr. Kerns; we already have taken exclusive charge of his future movements after he leaves the Lenox Club. I do not believe he can escape us, or his charming destiny. Good night!"

Gatewood, enchanted, hung up the receiver. Song broke softly from his lips as he started in search of Kerns; his step was springy, buoyant—sort of subdued and modest prance.

"Now," he said to himself, "Tommy must take out his papers. The time is ended when he can issue letters of marque to himself, hoist sail, square away, and go cruising all over this metropolis at his own sweet will."

FOURTEEN

In the meanwhile, at the other end of the wire, Mr. Keen, the Tracer of Lost Persons, was preparing to trace for Mr. Kerns, against that gentleman's will, the true happiness which Mr. Kerns had never been able to find for himself.

He sat in his easy chair within the four walls of his own office, inspecting a line of people who stood before him on the carpet forming a single and attentive rank. In this rank were five men: a policeman, a cab driver, an agent of the telephone company, an agent of the electric company, and a reformed burglar carrying a kit of his trade tools.

The Tracer of Lost Persons gazed at them, meditatively joining the tips of his thin fingers.

"I want the number on 36 East Eighty-third Street changed to No. 38, and the number 38 replaced by No. 36," he said to the policeman. "I want it done at once. Get a glazier and go up there and have it finished in an hour. Mrs. Kenna, caretaker at No. 36, is in my pay; she will not interfere. There is nobody in No. 38: Mr. Kerns leaves there to-night and the Burglar Alarm Company takes charge to-morrow."

And, turning to the others: "You," nodding at the reformed burglar, "know your duty. Mike!" to the cab driver, "don't miss Mr. Kerns at the Lenox Club. If he calls you before eleven, drive into the park and have an accident. And you," to the agent of the telephone company, "will sever all telephone connection in Mrs. Stanley's house; and you," to the official of the electric company, "will see that the circuit in Mrs. Stanley's house is cut so that no electric light may be lighted and no electric bell sound."

The Tracer of Lost Persons stroked his gray mustache thoughtfully. "And that," he ended, "will do, I think. Good night."

He rose and stood by the door as the policeman headed the solemn file which marched out to their duty; then he looked at his watch, and, as it was already a few minutes after eight, he called up No. 36 East Eighty-third Street, and in a moment more had Mrs. Stanley on the wire.

"Good evening," he said pleasantly. "I suppose you have just arrived from Rosylyn. I may be a little late—I may be very late, in fact, so I called you up to say so. And I wished to say another thing; to ask you whether your servants could recollect ever having seen a young man about the place, a rather attractive young man with excellent address and manners, five feet eleven inches, slim but well built, dark hair, dark eyes, and dark mustache, offering samples of Georgia marble for sale."

"Really, Mr. Keen," replied a silvery voice, "I have heard them say nothing about such an individual. If you will hold the wire I will ask my maid." And, after a pause: "No, Mr. Keen, my maid cannot remember any such person. Do you think he was a confederate of that wretched butler of mine?"

"I am scarcely prepared to say that; in fact," added Mr. Keen, "I haven't the slightest idea that this young man could have been concerned in anything of that sort. Only, if you should ever by any chance see such a man, detain him if possible until you can communicate with me; detain him by any pretext, by ruse, by force if you can, only detain him until I can get there. Will you do this?"

"Certainly, Mr. Keen, if I can. Please describe him again?"

Mr. Keen did so minutely.

"You say he sells Georgia marble by samples, which he carries in a suit case?"

"He *says* that he has samples of Georgia marble in his suit case," replied the Tracer cautiously. "It might be well, if possible, to see what he has in his suit case."

"I will warn the servants as soon as I return to Rosylyn. When may I expect you this evening, Mr. Keen?"

"It is impossible to say, Mrs. Stanley. If I am not there by midnight I shall try to call next morning."

So they exchanged civil adieus; the Tracer hung up his receiver and leaned back in his chair, smiling to himself.

"Curious," he said, "that chance should have sent that pretty woman to me at such a time. . . . Kerns *is* a fine fellow, every inch of him. It hit him hard when he crossed with her to Southampton six years ago; it hit him harder when she married that Englishman. I don't wonder he never cared to marry after that brief week of her society; for she is just about the most charming woman I have ever met—red hair and all. . . . And if quick action is what is required, it's well to break the ice between them at once with a dreadful misunderstanding."

FIFTEEN

The dinner that Kerns had planned for himself and Gatewood was an ingenious one, cunningly contrived to discontent Gatewood with home fare and lure him by its seductive quality into frequent revisits to the club which was responsible for such delectable wines and viands.

A genial glow already enveloped Gatewood and pleasantly suffused Kerns. From time to time they held some rare vintage aloft, squinting through the crystal-imprisoned crimson with deep content.

"Not that *my* word is necessarily the *last* word concerning Burgundy," said Gatewood modestly; "but I venture to doubt that any club in America can match this bottle, Kerns."

"Now, Jack," wheedled Kerns, "isn't it pleasant to dine here once in a while? Be frank, man! Look about at the other tables—at all the pleasant, familiar faces—the same fine fellows, bless 'em—the same smoky old ceiling, the same bum portraits of dead governors, the same old stag heads on the wall. Now, Jack, isn't it mighty pleasant, after all? Be a gentleman and admit it!"

"Y-yes," confessed Gatewood, "it's all right for me once in a while, because I know that I am presently going back to my own home—a jolly lamplit room and the prettiest girl in Manhattan curled up in an armchair—"

"You're fortunate," said Kerns shortly. And for the first time there remained no lurking mockery in his voice; for the first time his retort was tinged with bitterness. But the next instant his eyes glimmered with the same gay malice, and the unbelieving smile twitched at his clean-cut lips, and he raised his hand, touching the short ends of his mustache with that careless, amused cynicism which rather became him.

"All that you picture so entrancingly is forbidden the true believer," he said; and began to repeat:

> "'O weaver! weave the flowers of Feraghan
> Into the fabric that thy birth began;
> Iris, narcissus, tulips cloud-band tied,
> These thou shalt picture for the eye of Man;
> Henna, Herati, and the Jhelums tide
> In Sarraband and Saruk be thy guide,
> And the red dye of Ispahan beside
> The checkered Chinese fret of ancient gold;
> —So heed the ban, old as the law is old,
> Nor weave into thy warp the laughing face,
> Nor limb, nor body, nor one line of grace,
> Nor hint, nor tint, nor any veiled device
> Of Woman who is barred from Paradise!'"

"A nice sentiment!" said Gatewood hotly.

"Can't help it; you see I'm forbidden to monkey with the eternal looms or weave the forbidden into the pattern of my life."

Gatewood sat silent for a moment, then looked up at Kerns with something so closely akin to a grin that his friend became interested in its scarcely veiled significance, and grinned in reply.

"So you really expect that your friend, Mr. Keen, is going to marry me to somebody, *nolens volens*?" asked Kerns.

"I do. That's what I dream of, Tommy."

"My poor friend, dream on!"

"I am. Tommy, you're lost! I mean you're as good as married now!"

"You think so?"

"I *know* it! There you sit, savoring your Burgundy, idling over a cigar, happy, care free, fancy free, at liberty, as you believe, to roam off anywhere at any time and continue the eternal hunt for pleasure! That's what you *think*! Ha! Tommy, I know better! That's not the sort of man *I* see sitting on the same chair where you are now sprawling in such content! I see a doomed man, already in the shadow of the altar, wasting his time unsuspiciously while Chance comes whirling into the city behind a Long Island locomotive, and Fate, the footman, sits outside ready to follow him, and Destiny awaits him no matter what he does, what he desires, where he goes, wherever he turns to-night! Destiny awaits him at his journey's end!"

"Very fine," said Kerns admiringly. "Too bad it's due to the Burgundy."

"Never mind what my eloquence is due to," retorted Gatewood, "the fact remains that this is probably your last bachelor dinner. Kerns, old fellow! Here's to her! Bless her! I—I wish sincerely that we knew who she is and where to send those roses. Anyway, here's to the bride!"

He stood up very gravely and drank the toast, then, reseating himself, tapped the empty glass gently against the table's edge until it broke.

"You are certainly doing your part well," said Kerns admiringly. Then he swallowed the remainder of his Burgundy and looked up at the club clock.

"Eleven," he said with regret. "I've about time to go to Eighty-third Street, get my suit case, and catch my train at 125th Street." To a servant he said, "Call a hansom," then rose and sauntered downstairs to the cloakroom, where presently both men stood, hatted and gloved, swinging their sticks.

"That was a fool bet you made," began Kerns; "I'll release you, Jack."

"Sorry, but I must insist on holding you," replied Gatewood, laughing. "You're going to your doom. Come on! I'll see you as far as the cab door."

They walked out, and Kerns gave the cabby the street and number and entered the hansom.

"Now," said Gatewood, "you're in for it! You're done for! You can't help yourself! I've won my twelve-gauge trap gun already, and I'll have to set you up in table silver, anyway, so it's an even break. You're all in, Tommy! The Tracer is on your trail!"

In the beginning of a flippant retort Kerns experienced a curious sensation of hesitation. Something in Gatewood's earnestness, in his jeering assurance and delighted certainty, made him, for one moment, feel doubtful, even uncomfortable.

"What nonsense you talk," he said, recovering his equanimity. "Nothing on earth can prevent me driving to 38 East Eighty-third Street, getting my luggage, and taking the Boston express. Your Tracer doesn't intend to stop my hansom and drag me into a cave, does he? You haven't put knock-outs into that Burgundy, have you? Then what in the dickens are you laughing at?"

But Gatewood, on the sidewalk under the lamplight, was still laughing as Kerns drove away, for he had recognized in the cab driver a man he had seen in Mr. Kern's office, and he knew that the Tracer of Lost Persons had Kerns already well in hand.

The hansom drove on through the summer darkness between rows of electric globes drooping like huge white moon flowers from their foliated bronze stalks, on up the splendid avenue, past the great brilliantly illuminated hotels, past the white cathedral, past clubs and churches and the palaces of the wealthy; on, on along the park wall edged by its double rows of elms under which shadowy forms moved—lovers strolling in couples.

"Pooh," sniffed Kerns, "the whole world has gone love mad, and I'm the only sane man left."

But he leaned back in his cab and fell a-thinking of a thin girl with red hair and great gray eyes—a thin, frail creature, scarcely more than a child, who had held him for a week in a strange sorcery only to release him with a frightened smile, leaving her indelible impression upon his life forever.

And, thinking, he looked up, realizing that the cab had stopped in East Eighty-third Street before one of a line of brownstone houses, all externally alike.

Then he leaned out and saw that the house number was thirty-eight. That was the number of the Lees' house; he descended, bade the cabman await him, and, producing his latch key, started up the steps, whistling gayly.

But he didn't require his key, for, as he reached the front door, he found, to his surprise and concern, that it swung partly open—just a mere crack.

"The mischief!" he muttered; "could I have failed to close it? Could anybody have seen it and crept in?"

He entered the hallway hastily and pressed the electric knob. No light appeared in the sconces.

"What the deuce!" he murmured; "something wrong with the switch!" And he hurriedly lighted a match and peered into the darkness. By the vague glimmer of the burning match he could distinguish nothing. He listened intently, tried the electric switch again without success. The match burned his fingers and he dropped it, watching the last red spark die out in the darkness.

Something about the shadowy hallway seemed unfamiliar; he went to the door, stepped out on the stoop, and looked up at the number on the transom. It was thirty-eight; no doubt about the house. Hesitating, he glanced around to see that his hansom was still there. It had disappeared.

"What an idiot that cabman is!" he exclaimed, intensely annoyed at the prospect of lugging his heavy suit case to a Madison Avenue car and traveling with it to Harlem.

He looked up and down the dimly lighted street; east, an electric car glided down Madison Avenue; west, the lights of Fifth Avenue glimmered against the dark foliage of the Park. He stood a moment, angry at the desertion of his cabman, then turned and reëntered the dark hall, closing the door behind him.

Up the staircase he felt his way to the first landing, and, lighting a match, looked for the electric button.

"Am I crazy, or was there no electric button in this hall?" he thought. The match burned low; he had to drop it. Perplexed, he struck another match and opened the door leading into the front room, and stood on the threshold a moment, looking about him at the linen-shrouded furniture and pictures. This front room, closed for the summer, he had not before entered, but he stepped in now, poking about for any possible intruder, lighting match after match.

"I suppose I ought to go over this confounded house inch by inch," he murmured. "What could have possessed me to leave the front door ajar this morning?"

For an instant he thought that perhaps Mrs. Nolan, the woman who came in the morning to make his bed, might have left the door open, but he knew that couldn't be so, because he always waited for her to finish her work and leave before he went out. So either he must have left the door open, or some marauder had visited the house—was perhaps at that moment in the house! And it was his duty to find out.

"I'd better be about it, too," he thought savagely, "or I'll never make my train."

He struck his last match, looked around, and, seeing gas jets among the clustered electric bulbs of the sconces, tried to light one and succeeded.

He had left his suit case in the passageway between the front and rear rooms, and now, cautiously, stick in hand, he turned toward the dim corridor leading to the bedroom. There was his suit case, anyway! He picked it up and started to push open the door of the rear room; but at the same time, and before he could lay his hand on the knob, the door before him opened suddenly in a flood of light, and a woman stood there, dark against the gas-lit glare, a pistol waveringly extended in the general direction of his head.

SIXTEEN

"Good heavens!" he said, appalled, and dropped his suit case with a crash.

"W-what are you d-doing—" She controlled her voice and the wavering weapon with an effort. "What are you doing in this house?"

"Doing? In *this* house?" he repeated, his eyes protruding in the direction of the unsteady pistol muzzle. "What are *you* doing in this house—if you don't mind saying!"

"I—I m-must ask you to put up your hands," she said. "If you move I shall certainly s-shoot off this pistol."

"It will go off, anyway, if you handle it like that!" he said, exasperated. "What do you mean by pointing it at me?"

"I mean to fire it off in a few moments if you don't raise your hands above your head!"

He looked at the pistol; it was new and shiny; he looked at the athletic young figure silhouetted against the brilliant light.

"Well, if you make a point of it, of course." He slowly held up both hands, higher, then higher still. "Upon my word!" he breathed. "Held up by a woman!" And he said aloud, bitterly: "No doubt you have assistance close at hand."

"No doubt," she said coolly. "What have you been packing into that valise?"

"P-packing into *what*? Oh, into that suit case? That is my suit case."

"Of course it is," she said quietly, "but what have you inside it?"

"Nothing *you* or your friends would care for," he said meaningly.

"I must be the judge of that," she retorted. "Please open that suit case."

"How can I if my hands are in the air?" he expostulated, now intensely interested in the novelty of being held up by this graceful and vaguely pretty silhouette.

"You may lower your arms to unpack the suit case," she said.

"I—I had rather not if you are going to keep me covered with your pistol."

"Of course I shall keep you covered. Unpack your booty at once!"

"My—*what*?"

"Booty."

"Madam, do you take *me* for a thief? Have you, by chance, entered the wrong house? I—I cannot reconcile your voice with what I am forced to consider you—a housebreaker—"

"We will discuss that later. Unpack that bag!" she insisted.

"But—but there is nothing in it except samples of marble—"

"What!" she exclaimed nervously. "*What* did you say? Samples of *marble*?"

"Marble, madam! Georgia marble!"

"Oh! So *you* are the young man who goes about pretending to peddle Georgia marble from samples! Are you? The famous marble man I have heard of."

"I? Madam, I don't know what you mean!"

"Come!" she said scornfully; "let me see the contents of that suit case. I—I am not afraid of you; I am not a bit afraid of you. And I shall catch your accomplice, too."

"Madam, you speak like an honest woman! You *must* have managed to enter the wrong house. This is number thirty-eight, where I live."

"It is number thirty-six; my house!"

"But I *know* it is number thirty-eight; Mr. Lee's house," he protested hopefully. "This is some dreadful mistake."

"Mr. Lee's house is next door," she said. "Do you not suppose I know my own house? Besides, I have been warned against a plausible young man who pretends he has Georgia marble to sell—"

"There is a dreadful mistake somewhere," he insisted. "Please p-p-put up your p-pistol and aid me to solve it. I am no robber, madam. I thought at first that you were. I'm living in Mr. Lee's house, No. 38 East Eighty-third Street, and I've looked carefully at the number over the door of this house and the number is thirty-eight, and the street is East Eighty-third. So I naturally conclude that I am in Mr. Lee's house."

"Your arguments and your conclusions are very plausible," she said, "but, fortunately for me, I have been expressly warned against a young man of your description. *You* are the marble man!"

"It's a mistake! A very dreadful one."

"Then how did you enter this house?"

"I have a key—I mean I found the front door unlatched. Please don't misunderstand me; I know it sounds unconvincing, but I really have a key to number thirty-eight."

He attempted to reach for his pocket and the pistol glittered in his face.

"Won't you let me prove my innocence?" he asked.

"You can't prove it by showing me a key. Besides, it's probably a weapon. Anyhow, if, as you pretend, you have managed to get into the wrong house, why did you bring that suit case up here?"

"It was here. It's mine. I left it here in this passageway."

"In *my* house?" she asked incredulously.

"In number thirty-eight; that is all I know. I'll open the suit case if you will let me. I have already described its contents. If it has samples of marble in it you *must* be convinced!"

"It will convince me that it is your valise. But what of that? I know it is yours already," she said defiantly. "I know, at least, that you are the marble man—if nothing worse!"

"But malefactors don't go about carrying samples of Georgia marble," he protested, dropping on one knee under the muzzle of her revolver and tugging at the straps and buckles. In a second or two he threw open the case—and the sight of the contents staggered him. For there, thrown in pellmell among small square blocks of polished marble was a complete kit of burglar's tools, including also a mask, a dark lantern, and a blackjack.

"What—w—w—what on earth is this?" he stammered. "These things don't belong to me. I won't have them! I don't want them. Who put them into my suit case? How the deuce—"

"You *are* the marble man!" she said with a shudder. "Your crimes are known! Your wretched accomplice will be caught! You are the marble man—or something worse!"

Kneeling there, aghast, bewildered, he passed his hand across his eyes as though to clear them from some terrible vision. But the suit case was still there with its incriminating contents when he looked again.

"I am sorry for you," she said tremulously. "I—if it were not for the marble—I would let you go. But you are the marble man!"

"Yes, and I'm probably a madman, too. I don't know what I am! I don't know what is happening to me. I ought to be going, that is all I know—"

"I cannot let you go."

"But I must! I've got to catch a train."

The feebleness of his excuse chilled her pity.

"I shall not let you go," she said, resting the hand which held the pistol on her hip, but keeping him covered. "I know you came to rob my house; I know you are a thoroughly bad and depraved young man, but for all that I could find it in my heart to let you go if you were not also the *marble man!*"

"What on earth is the marble man?" he asked, exasperated.

"I don't know. I have been earnestly warned against him. Probably he is a relative of my butler—"

"I'm not a relative of anybody's butler!"

"You *say* you are not. How do I know? I—I will make you an offer. I will give you one last chance. If you will return to me the jewels that my butler took—"

"Good heavens, madam! Do you really take me for a professional burglar?"

"How can I help it?" she said indignantly. "Look at your suit case full of lanterns and masks—full of *marble*, too!"

Speechless, he stared at the burglar's kit.

"I am sorry—" Her voice had altered again to a tremulous sweetness. "I can't help feeling sorry for you. You do not seem to be hardened; your voice and manner are not characteristically criminal. I—I can't see your face very clearly, but it does not seem to be a brutally inhuman face—"

An awful desire to laugh seized Kerns; he struggled against it; hysteria lay that way; and he covered his face with both hands and pinched himself.

She probably mistook the action for the emotion of shame and despair born of bitter grief; perhaps of terror of the law. It frightened her a little, but pity dominated. She could scarcely endure to do what she must do.

"This is dreadful, dreadful!" she faltered. "If you only would give me back my jewels—"

Sounds, hastily smothered, escaped him. She believed them to be groans, and it made her slightly faint.

"I—I've simply got to telephone for the police," she said pityingly. "I must ask you to sit down there and wait—there is a chair. Sit there—and please don't move, for I—this has unnerved me—I am not accustomed to doing cruel things; and if you should move too quickly or attempt to run away I feel certain that this pistol would explode."

"Are you going to telephone?" he asked.

"Yes, I am."

She backed away, cautiously, pistol menacing him, reached for the receiver, and waited for Central. She waited a long time before she realized that the telephone as well as the electric light was out of commission.

"Did *you* cut all these wires?" she demanded angrily.

"I? What wires?"

She reached out and pressed the electric button which should have rung a bell in her maid's bedroom on the top floor. She kept her finger on the button for ten minutes. It was useless.

"You laid deliberate plans to rob this house," she said, her cheeks pink with indignation. "I am not a bit sorry for you. I shall *not* let you go! I shall sit here until somebody comes to my assistance, if I have to sit here for weeks and weeks!"

"If you'd let me telephone to my club—" he began.

"Your club! You are very plausible. You didn't offer to call up any club until you found that the telephone was not working!"

He thought a moment. "I don't suppose you would trust me to go out and get a policeman?"

"Certainly not."

"Or go into the front room and open a window and summon some passer-by?"

"How do I know you haven't confederates waiting outside?"

"That's true," he said seriously.

There was a silence. Her nerves seemed to trouble her, for she began to pace to and fro in front of the passageway where he sat comfortably on his chair, arms folded, one knee dropped over the other.

The light being behind her he could not as yet distinguish her features very clearly. Her figure was youthful, slender, yet beautifully rounded; her head charming in contour. He watched her restlessly walking on the floor, small hand clutching the pistol resting on her hip.

The ruddy burnished glimmer on the edges of her hair he supposed, at first, was caused by the strong light behind her.

"This is atrocious!" she murmured, halting to confront him. "How dared you sever every electric connection in my house?"

As she spoke she stepped backward a pace or two, resting herself for a moment against the footboard of the bed—full in the gaslight. And he saw her face.

For a moment he studied her; an immense wave of incredulity swept over him—of wild unbelief, slowly changing to the astonishment of dawning conviction. Astounded, silent, he stared at her from his shadowy corner; and after a while his pulses began to throb and throb and hammer, and the clamoring confusion of his senses seemed to deafen him.

She rested a moment or two against the footboard of the bed, her big gray eyes fixed on his vague and shadowy form.

"This won't do," she said.

"No," he said, "it won't do."

He spoke very quietly, very gently. She detected the alteration in his voice and started slightly, as though the distant echo of a familiar voice had sounded.

"What did you say?" she asked, coming nearer, pistol glittering in advance.

"I said 'It won't do.' I don't know what I meant by it. If I meant anything I was wrong. It *will* do. The situation is perfectly agreeable to me."

"Insolence will not help you," she said sharply. And under the sharpness he detected the slightest quaver of a new alarm.

"I am going to free myself," he said coolly.

"If you move I shall certainly shoot!" she retorted.

"I am going to move—but only my lips. I have only to move my lips to free myself."

"I should scarcely advise you to trust to your eloquence. I have been duly warned, you see."

"Who warned you?" he asked curiously. And, as she disdained to reply: "Never mind. We can clear that up later. Now let me ask you something."

"You are scarcely in a position to ask questions," she said.

"May I not speak to you?"

"Is it necessary?"

He thought a moment. "No, not necessary. Nothing is in this life, you know. I thought differently once. Once—when I was younger—six years younger—I thought happiness was necessary. I found that a man might live without it."

She stood gazing at him through the shadows, pistol on hip.

"What do you mean?" she asked.

"I mean that happiness is not necessary to life. Life goes on all the same. My life has continued for six years without that happiness which some believe to be essential."

After a silence she said: "I can tell by the way you speak that you are well born. I—I dread to do what I simply must do."

He, too, sat silent a long time—long enough for an utterly perverse and whimsical humor to take complete possession of him.

"*Won't* you let me go—*this* time?" he pleaded.

"I cannot."

"You had better let me go while you can," he said, "because, perhaps, you may find it difficult to get rid of me later."

Affronted, she shrank back from the doorway and stood in the center of her room, angry, disdainful, beautiful, under the ruddy glory of her lustrous hair.

His perverse mood changed, too; he leaned forward, studying her minutely—the splendid gray eyes, the delicate mouth and nose, the full, sweet lips, the witchery of wrist and hand, and the flowing, rounded outline of limb and body under the pretty gown. Could this be *she*? This lovely, mature woman, wearing scarcely a trace of the young girl he had never forgotten—scarcely a trace save in the beauty of her eyes and hair—save in the full, red mouth, sweet and sensitive even in its sudden sullenness?

"Once," he said, and his voice sounded to him like voices heard in dreams— "once, years and years ago, there was a steamer, and a man and a young girl on board. Do you mind my telling you about it?"

She stood leaning against the footboard of the bed, not even deigning to raise her eyes in reply. So he made the slightest stir in his chair; and then she looked up quickly enough, pistol poised.

"The steamer," said Kerns slowly, "was coming into Southampton—six years ago. On deck these two people stood—a man of twenty-eight, a girl of eighteen—six years ago. The name of the steamer was the *Carnatic*. Did you ever hear of that ship?"

She was looking at him attentively. He waited for her reply; she made none; and he went on.

"The man had asked the girl something—I don't know what—I don't know why her gray eyes filled with tears. Perhaps it was because she could not do what the man asked her to do. It may have been to love him; it may have been that he was asking her to marry him and that she couldn't. Perhaps that is why there were tears in her eyes—because she may have been sorry to cause him the pain of refusal—sorry, perhaps, perhaps a little guilty. Because she must have seen that he was falling in love with her, and she—she let him—knowing all the time that she was to marry another man. Did you ever hear of that man before?"

She had straightened up, quivering, wide eyed, lips parted. He rose and walked slowly into her room, confronting her under the full glare of light.

Her pistol fell clattering to the floor. It did not explode because it was not loaded.

"Now," he said unsteadily, "will you give me my freedom? I have waited for it—not minutes—but years—six years. I ask it now—the freedom I enjoyed before I ever saw you. Can you give it back to me? Can you restore to me a capacity for happiness? Can you give me a heart to love with—love some woman, as other men love? Is it very much I ask of you—to give me a chance in life—the chance I had before I ever saw you?"

Her big gray eyes seemed fascinated; he looked deep into them, smiling; and she turned white.

"Will you give me what I ask?" he said, still smiling.

She strove to speak; she could not, but her eyes never faltered. Suddenly the color flooded her neck and cheeks to the hair, and the quick tears glimmered.

"I—I did not understand; I was too young to be cruel," she faltered. "How could I know what I was doing? Or what—what you did?"

"I? To *you*?"

"Y-yes. Did you think that I escaped heart free? Do you realize what *my* punishment was—to—to marry—and *remember*! If I was too young, too inexperienced to know what I was doing, I was not too young to suffer for it!"

"You mean—" He strove to control his voice, but the sweet, fearless gray eyes met his; the old flame leaped in his veins. He reached out to steady himself and his hand touched hers—that soft, white hand that had held him all these years in the hollow of its palm.

"Did you *ever* love me?" he demanded.

Her eyes, wet with tears, met his straight as the starry gaze of a child.

"Yes," she said.

His hand tightened over hers; she swayed a moment, quivering from head to foot; then drawing a quick, sobbing breath, closed her eyes, imprisoned in his arms; and, after a long while, aroused, she looked up at him, her divine eyes unclosing dreamily.

"Somebody is hammering at the front door," he breathed. "Listen!"

"I hear. I believe it must be the Tracer of Lost Persons."

"What?"

"Only a Mr. Keen."

"O Lord!" said Kerns faintly, and covered his face with her fragrant hands.

Very tenderly, very gravely, she drew her hands away, and, laying them on his shoulders, looked up at him.

"You—you know what there is in your suit case," she faltered; "*are* you a burglar, dear?"

"Ask the Tracer of Lost Persons," said Kerns gently, "what sort of a criminal I am!"

They stood together for one blissful moment listening to the loud knocking below, then, hand in hand, they descended the dark stairway to admit the Tracer of Lost Persons.

SEVENTEEN

On the thirteenth day of March, 1906, Kerns received the following cable from an old friend:

"Is there anybody in New York who can find two criminals for me? I don't want to call in the police.
"J.T. Burke."

To which Kerns replied promptly:

"Wire Keen, Tracer of Lost Persons, N.Y."

And a day or two later, being on his honeymoon, he forgot all about his old friend Jack Burke.

On the fifteenth day of March, 1906, Mr. Keen, Tracer of Lost Persons, received the following cablegram from Alexandria, Egypt:

"*Keen, Tracer, New York:*—Locate Joram Smiles, forty, stout, lame, red hair, ragged red mustache, cast in left eye, pallid skin; carries one crutch; supposed to have arrived in America per S. S. *Scythian Queen*, with man known as Emanuel Gandon, swarthy, short, fat, light bluish eyes, Eurasian type.

"I will call on you at your office as soon as my steamer, *Empress of Babylon*, arrives. If you discover my men, keep them under surveillance, but on

346

no account call in police. Spare no expense. Dundas,
Gray & Co. are my bankers and reference.

"John Templeton Burke."

On Monday, April 2d, a few minutes after eight o'clock in the morning, the card of Mr. John Templeton Burke was brought to Mr. Keen, Tracer of Lost Persons, and a moment later a well-built, wiry, sun-scorched young man was ushered into Mr. Keen's private office by a stenographer prepared to take minutes of the interview.

The first thing that the Tracer of Lost Persons noted in his visitor was his mouth; the next his eyes. Both were unmistakably good—the eyes which his Creator had given him looked people squarely in the face at every word; the mouth, which a man's own character fashions agreeably or mars, was pleasant, but firm when the trace of the smile lurking in the corners died out.

There were dozens of other external characteristics which Mr. Keen always looked for in his clients; and now the rapid exchange of preliminary glances appeared to satisfy both men, for they advanced toward each other and exchanged a formal hand clasp.

"Have you any news for me?" asked Burke.

"I have," said the Tracer. "There are cigars on the table beside you—matches in that silver case. No, I never smoke; but I like the aroma—and I like to watch men smoke. Do you know, Mr. Burke, that no two men smoke in the same fashion? There is as much character in the manner of holding a cigar as there is difference in the technic of artists."

Burke nodded, amused, but, catching sight of the busy stenographer, his bronzed features became serious, and he looked at Mr. Keen inquiringly.

"It is my custom," said the Tracer. "Do you object to my stenographer?"

Burke looked at the slim young girl in her black gown and white collar and cuffs. Then, very simply, he asked her pardon for objecting to her presence, but said that he could not discuss his case if she remained. So she rose, with a humorous glance at Mr. Keen;

and the two men stood up until she had vanished, then reseated themselves *vis-à-vis*. Mr. Keen calmly dropped his elbow on the concealed button which prepared a hidden phonograph for the reception of every word that passed between them.

"What news have you for me, Mr. Keen?" asked the younger man with that same directness which the Tracer had already been prepared for, and which only corroborated the frankness of eyes and voice.

"My news is brief," he said. "I have both your men under observation."

"Already?" exclaimed Burke, plainly unprepared. "Do you actually mean that I can see these men whenever I desire to do so? Are these scoundrels in this town—within pistol shot?"

His youthful face hardened as he snapped out his last word, like the crack of a whip.

"I don't know how far your pistol carries," said Mr. Keen. "Do you wish to swear out a warrant?"

"No, I do not. I merely wish their addresses. You have not used the police in this matter, have you, Mr. Keen?"

"No. Your cable was explicit," said the Tracer. "Had you permitted me to use the police it would have been much less expensive for you."

"I can't help that," said the young man. "Besides, in a matter of this sort, a man cannot decently consider expense."

"A matter of what sort?" asked the Tracer blandly.

"Of *this* sort."

"Oh! Yet even now I do not understand. You must remember, Mr. Burke, that you have not told me anything concerning the reasons for your quest of these two men, Joram Smiles and Emanuel Gandon. Besides, this is the first time you have mentioned pistol range."

Burke, smoking steadily, looked at the Tracer through the blue fog of his cigar.

"No," he said, "I have not told you anything about them."

Mr. Keen waited a moment; then, smiling quietly to himself, he wrote down the present addresses of Joram Smiles and Emanuel

Gandon, and, tearing off the leaf, handed it to the younger man, saying: "I omit the pistol range, Mr. Burke."

"I am very grateful to you," said Burke. "The efficiency of your system is too famous for me to venture to praise it. All I can say is 'Thank you'; all I can do in gratitude is to write my check—if you will be kind enough to suggest the figures."

"Are you sure that my services are ended?"

"Thank you, quite sure."

So the Tracer of Lost Persons named the figures, and his client produced a check book and filled in a check for the amount. This was presented and received with pleasant formality. Burke rose, prepared to take his leave, but the Tracer was apparently busy with the combination lock of a safe, and the young man lingered a moment to make his adieus.

As he stood waiting for the Tracer to turn around he studied the writing on the sheet of paper which he held toward the light:

> Joram Smiles, no profession, 613 West 24th Street. Emanuel Gandon, no profession, same address. Very dangerous men.

It occurred to him that these three lines of pencil-writing had cost him a thousand dollars—and at the same instant he flushed with shame at the idea of measuring the money value of anything in such a quest as this.

And yet—and yet he had already spent a great deal of money in his brief quest, and—*was* he any nearer the goal—even with the penciled addresses of these two men in his possession? Even with these men almost within pistol shot!

Pondering there, immersed in frowning retrospection, the room, the Tracer, the city seemed to fade from his view. He saw the red sand blowing in the desert; he heard the sickly squealing of camels at the El Teb Wells; he saw the sun strike fire from the rippling waters of Saïs; he saw the plain, and the ruins high above it; and the odor of the Long Bazaar smote him like a blow, and he heard the far call to prayer from the minarets of Sa-el-Hagar, once

Saïs, the mysterious—Saïs of the million lanterns, Saïs of that splendid festival where the Great Triad's worship swayed dynasty after dynasty, and where, through the hot centuries, Isis, veiled, impassive, looked out upon the hundredth king of kings, Meris, the Builder of Gardens, dragged dead at the chariot of Upper and Lower Egypt.

Slowly the visions faded; into his remote eyes crept the consciousness of the twentieth century again; he heard the river whistles blowing, and the far dissonance of the streets—that iron undertone vibrating through the metropolis of the West from river to river and from the Palisades to the sea.

His gaze wandered about the room, from telephone desk to bookcase, from the table to the huge steel safe, door ajar, swung outward like the polished breech of a twelve-inch gun.

Then his vacant eyes met the eyes of the Tracer of Lost Persons, almost helplessly. And for the first time the full significance of this quest he had undertaken came over him like despair—this strange, hopeless, fantastic quest, blindly, savagely pursued from the sand wastes of Saïs to the wastes of this vast arid city of iron and masonry, ringing to the sky with the menacing clamor of its five monstrous boroughs.

Curiously weary of a sudden, he sat down, resting his head on one hand. The Tracer watched him, bent partly over his desk. From moment to moment he tore minute pieces from the blotter, or drew imaginary circles and arabesques on his pad with an inkless pen.

"Perhaps I could help you, after all—if you'd let me try," he said quietly.

"Do you mean—*me*?" asked Burke, without raising his head.

"If you like—yes, you—or any man in trouble—in perplexity—in the uncertain deductions which arise from an attempt at self-analysis."

"It is true; I am trying to analyze myself. I believe that I don't know how. All has been mere impulse—so far. No, I don't know how to analyze it all."

"I do," said the Tracer.

Burke raised his level, unbelieving eyes.

"You are in love," said the Tracer.

After a long time Burke looked up again. "Do you think so?"

"Yes. Can I help you?" asked the Tracer pleasantly.

The young man sat silent, frowning into space; then:

"I tell you plainly enough that I have come here to argue with two men at the end of a pistol; and—you tell me I'm in love. By what logic—"

"It is written in your face, Mr. Burke—in your eyes, in every feature, every muscle's contraction, every modulation of your voice. My tables, containing six hundred classified superficial phenomena peculiar to all human emotions, have been compiled and scientifically arranged according to Bertillon's system. It is an absolutely accurate key to every phase of human emotion, from hate, through all its amazingly paradoxical phenomena, to love, with all its genera under the suborder—all its species, subspecies, and varieties."

He leaned back, surveying the young man with kindly amusement.

"You talk of pistol range, but you are thinking of something more fatal than bullets, Mr. Burke. You are thinking of love—of the first, great, absorbing, unreasoning passion that has ever shaken you, blinded you, seized you and dragged you out of the ordered path of life, to push you violently into the strange and unexplored! That is what stares out on the world through those haunted eyes of yours, when the smile dies out and you are off your guard; that is what is hardening those flat, clean bands of muscle in jaw and cheek; that is what those hints of shadow mean beneath the eye, that new and delicate pinch to the nostril, that refining, almost to sharpness, of the nose, that sensitive edging to the lips, and the lean delicacy of the chin."

He bent slightly forward in his chair.

"There is all that there, Mr. Burke, and something else—the glimmering dawn of desperation."

"Yes," said the other, "that is there. I am desperate."

"*Exactly*. Also you wear two revolvers in a light, leather harness strapped up under your armpits," said the Tracer, laughing. "Take them off, Mr. Burke. There is nothing to be gained in shooting up Mr. Smiles or converting Mr. Gandon into nitrates."

"If it is a matter where one man can help another," the Tracer added simply, "it would give me pleasure to place my resources at your command—without recompense—"

"Mr. Keen!" said Burke, astonished.

"Yes?"

"You are very amiable; I had not wished—had not expected anything except professional interest from you."

"Why not? I like you, Mr. Burke."

The utter disarming candor of this quiet, elderly gentleman silenced the younger man with a suddenness born of emotions long crushed, long relentlessly mastered, and which now, in revolt, shook him fiercely in every fiber. All at once he felt very young, very helpless in the world—that same world through which, until within a few weeks, he had roved so confidently, so arrogantly, challenging man and the gods themselves in the pride of his strength and youth.

But now, halting, bewildered, lost amid the strange maze of byways whither impulse had lured and abandoned him, he looked out into a world of wilderness and unfamiliar stars and shadow shapes undreamed of, and he knew not which way to turn—not even how to return along the ways his impetuous feet had trodden in this strange and hopeless quest of his.

"How can you help me?" he said bluntly, while the quivering undertone rang in spite of him. "Yes, I am in love; but how can any living man help me?"

"Are you in love with the dead?" asked the Tracer gravely. "For that only is hopeless. Are you in love with one who is not living?"

"Yes."

"You love one whom you know to be dead?"

"Yes; dead."

"How do you know that she is dead?"

"That is not the question. I knew that when I fell in love with her. It is not that which appalls me; I ask nothing more than to live my life out loving the dead. I—I ask very little."

He passed his unsteady hand across his dry lips, across his eyes and forehead, then laid his clinched fist on the table.

"Some men remain constant to a memory; some to a picture—sane, wholesome, normal men. Some men, with a fixed ideal, never encounter its facsimile, and so never love. There is nothing strange, after all, in this; nothing abnormal, nothing unwholesome. Grünwald loved the marble head and shoulders of the lovely Amazon in the Munich Museum; he died unmarried, leaving the charities and good deeds of a blameless life to justify him. Sir Henry Guest, the great surgeon who worked among the poor without recompense, loved Gainsborough's 'Lady Wilton.' The portrait hangs above his tomb in St. Clement's Hundreds. D'Epernay loved Mlle. Jeanne Vacaresco, who died before he was born. And I—I love in my own fashion."

His low voice rang with the repressed undertone of excitement; he opened and closed his clinched hand as though controlling the lever of his emotions.

"What can you do for a man who loves the shadow of Life?" he asked.

"If you love the shadow because the substance has passed away—if you love the soul because the dust has returned to the earth as it was—"

"It has *not*!" said the younger man.

The Tracer said very gravely: "It is written that whenever 'the Silver Cord' is loosed, 'then shall the dust return unto the earth as it was, and the spirit shall return unto Him who gave it.'"

"The spirit—yes; *that* has taken its splendid flight—"

His voice choked up, died out; he strove to speak again, but could not. The Tracer let him alone, and bent again over his desk, drawing imaginary circles on the stained blotter, while moment after moment passed under the tension of that fiercest of all struggles, when a man sits throttling his own soul into silence.

And, after a long time, Burke lifted a haggard face from the cradle of his crossed arms and shook his shoulders, drawing a deep, steady breath.

"Listen to *me*!" he said in an altered voice.

And the Tracer of Lost Persons nodded.

EIGHTEEN

"When I left the Point I was assigned to the colored cavalry. They are good men; we went up Kettle Hill together. Then came the Philippine troubles, then that Chinese affair. Then I did staff duty, and could not stand the inactivity and resigned. They had no use for me in Manchuria; I tired of waiting, and went to Venezuela. The prospects for service there were absurd; I heard of the Moorish troubles and went to Morocco. Others of my sort swarmed there; matters dragged and dragged, and the Kaiser never meant business, anyway.

"Being independent, and my means permitting me, I got some shooting in the back country. This all degenerated into the merest nomadic wandering—nothing but sand, camels, ruins, tents, white walls, and blue skies. And at last I came to the town of Sa-el-Hagar."

His voice died out; his restless, haunted eyes became fixed.

"Sa-el-Hagar, once ancient Saïs," repeated the Tracer quietly; and the young man looked at him.

"You know *that*?"

"Yes," said the Tracer.

For a while Burke remained silent, preoccupied, then, resting his chin on his hand and speaking in a curiously monotonous voice, as though repeating to himself by rote, he went on:

"The town is on the heights—have you a pencil? Thank you. Here is the town of Sa-el-Hagar, here are the ruins, here is the wall, and somewhere hereabouts should be the buried temple of

Neith, which nobody has found." He shifted his pencil. "Here is the lake of Saïs; here, standing all alone on the plain, are those great monolithic pillars stretching away into perspective—four hundred of them in all—a hundred and nine still upright. There were one hundred and ten when I arrived at El Teb Wells."

He looked across at the Tracer, repeating: "One hundred and ten—when I arrived. One fell the first night—a distant pillar far away on the horizon. Four thousand years had it stood there. And it fell—the first night of my arrival. I heard it; the nights are cold at El Teb Wells, and I was lying awake, all a-shiver, counting the stars to make me sleep. And very, very far away in the desert I heard and felt the shock of its fall—the fall of forty centuries under the Egyptian stars."

His eyes grew dreamy; a slight glow had stained his face.

"Did you ever halt suddenly in the Northern forests, listening, as though a distant voice had hailed you? Then you understand why that far, dull sound from the dark horizon brought me to my feet, bewildered, listening, as though my own name had been spoken.

"I heard the wind in the tents and the stir of camels; I heard the reeds whispering on Saïs Lake and the yap-yap of a shivering jackal; and always, always, the hushed echo in my ears of my own name called across the star-lit waste.

"At dawn I had forgotten. An Arab told me that a pillar had fallen; it was all the same to me, to him, to the others, too. The sun came out hot. I like heat. My men sprawled in the tents; some watered, some went up to the town to gossip in the bazaar. I mounted and cast bridle on neck—you see how much I cared where I went! In two hours we had completed a circle—like a ruddy hawk above El Teb. And my horse halted beside the fallen pillar."

As he spoke his language had become very simple, very direct, almost without accent, and he spoke slowly, picking his way with that lack of inflection, of emotion characteristic of a child reading a new reader.

"The column had fallen from its base, eastward, and with its base it had upheaved another buried base, laying bare a sort of cellar and a flight of stone steps descending into darkness.

"Into this excavation the sand was still running in tiny rivulets. Listening, I could hear it pattering far, far down into the shadows.

"Sitting there in the saddle, the thing explained itself as I looked. The fallen pillar had been built upon older ruins; all Egypt is that way, ruin founded on the ruin of ruins—like human hopes.

"The stone steps, descending into the shadow of remote ages, invited me. I dismounted, walked to the edge of the excavation, and, kneeling, peered downward. And I saw a wall and the lotus-carved rim of a vast stone-framed pool; and as I looked I heard the tinkle of water. For the pillar, falling, had unbottled the ancient spring, and now the stone-framed lagoon was slowly filling after its drought of centuries.

"There was light enough to see by, but, not knowing how far I might penetrate, I returned to my horse, pocketed matches and candles from the saddlebags, and, returning, started straight down the steps of stone.

"Fountain, wall, lagoon, steps, terraces half buried—all showed what the place had been: a water garden of ancient Egypt—probably royal—because, although I am not able to decipher hieroglyphics, I have heard somewhere that these picture inscriptions, when inclosed in a cartouch like this"—he drew rapidly—

"or this

indicate that the subject of the inscription was once a king.

"And on every wall, every column, I saw the insignia of ancient royalty, and I saw strange hawk-headed figures bearing symbols engraved on stone—beasts, birds, fishes, unknown signs and symbols; and everywhere the lotus carved in stone—the bud, the blossom half-inclosed, the perfect flower."

His dreamy eyes met the gaze of the Tracer, unseeing; he rested his sunburned face between both palms, speaking in the same vague monotone:

"Everywhere dust, ashes, decay, the death of life, the utter annihilation of the living—save only the sparkle of reborn waters slowly covering the baked bed of the stone-edged pool—strange, luminous water, lacking the vital sky tint, enameled with a film of dust, yet, for all that, quickening with imprisoned brilliancy like an opal.

"The slow filling of the pool fascinated me; I stood I know not how long watching the thin film of water spreading away into the dimness beyond. At last I turned and passed curiously along the wall where, at its base, mounds of dust marked what may have been trees. Into these I probed with my riding crop, but discovered nothing except the depths of the dust.

"When I had penetrated the ghost of this ancient garden for a thousand yards the light from the opening was no longer of any service. I lighted a candle; and its yellow rays fell upon a square portal into which led another flight of steps. And I went down.

"There were eighteen steps descending into a square stone room. Strange gleams and glimmers from wall and ceiling flashed dimly in my eyes under the wavering flame of the candle. Then the flame grew still—still as death—and Death lay at my feet—there on the stone floor—a man, square shouldered, hairless, the cobwebs of his tunic mantling him, lying face downward, arms outflung.

"After a moment I stooped and touched him, and the entire prostrate figure dissolved into dust where it lay, leaving at my feet a shadow shape in thin silhouette against the pavement—merely a gray layer of finest dust shaped like a man, a tracery of impalpable powder on the stones.

"Upward and around me I passed the burning candle; vast figures in blue and red and gold grew out of the darkness; the painted walls sparkled; the shadows that had slept through all those centuries trembled and shrank away into distant corners.

"And then—and then I saw the gold edges of her sandals sparkle in the darkness, and the clasped girdle of virgin gold around her slender waist glimmered like purest flame!"

Burke, leaning far across the table, interlocked hands tightening, stared and stared into space. A smile edged his mouth; his voice grew wonderfully gentle:

"Why, she was scarcely eighteen—this child—there so motionless, so lifelike, with the sandals edging her little upturned feet, and the small hands of her folded between the breasts. It was as though she had just stretched herself out there—scarcely sound asleep as yet, and her thick, silky hair—cut as they cut children's hair in these days, you know—cradled her head and cheeks.

"So marvelous the mimicry of life, so absolute the deception of breathing sleep, that I scarce dared move, fearing to awaken her.

"When I did move I forgot the dusty shape of the dead at my feet, and left, full across his neck, the imprint of a spurred riding boot. It gave me my first shudder; I turned, feeling beneath my foot the soft, yielding powder, and stood aghast. Then—it is absurd!—but I felt as a man feels who has trodden inadvertently upon another's foot—and in an impulse of reparation I stooped hastily and attempted to smooth out the mortal dust which bore the imprint of my heel. But the fine powder flaked my glove, and, looking about for something to compose the ashes with, I picked up a papyrus scroll. Perhaps he himself had written on it; nobody can ever know, and I used it as a sort of hoe to scrape him together and smooth him out on the stones."

The young man drew a yellowish roll of paper-like substance from his pocket and laid it on the table.

"This is the same papyrus," he said. "I had forgotten that I carried it away with me until I found it in my shooting coat while packing to sail for New York."

The Tracer of Lost Persons reached over and picked up the scroll. It was flexible still, but brittle; he opened it with great care, considered the strange figures upon it for a while, then turned almost sharply on his visitor.

"Go on," he said.

And Burke went on:

"The candle was burning low; I lighted two more, placing them at her head and feet on the edges of the stone couch. Then, lighting a third candle, I stood beside the couch and looked down at the dead girl under her veil-like robe, set with golden stars."

He passed his hand wearily over his hair and forehead.

"I do not know what the accepted meaning of beauty may be if it was not there under my eyes. Flawless as palest amber ivory and rose, the smooth-flowing contours melted into exquisite symmetry; lashes like darkest velvet rested on the pure curve of the cheeks; the closed lids, the mouth still faintly stained with color, the delicate nose, the full, childish lips, sensitive, sweet, resting softly upon each other—if these were not all parts of but one lovely miracle, then there is no beauty save in a dream of Paradise. . . .

"A gold band of linked scarabs bound her short, thick hair straight across the forehead; thin scales of gold fell from a necklace, clothing her breasts in brilliant discolored metal, through which ivory-tinted skin showed. A belt of pure, soft gold clasped her body at the waist; gold-edged sandals clung to her little feet.

"At first, when the stunned surprise had subsided, I thought that I was looking upon some miracle of ancient embalming, hitherto unknown. Yet, in the smooth skin there was no slit to prove it, no opening in any vein or artery, no mutilation of this sculptured masterpiece of the Most High, no cerements, no bandages, no gilded carven case with painted face to stare open eyed through the wailing cycles.

"This was the image of sleep—of life unconscious—not of death. Yet it was death—death that had come upon her centuries and centuries ago; for the gold had turned iridescent and magnificently discolored; the sandal straps fell into dust as I bent above them, leaving the sandals clinging to her feet only by the wired silver core of the thongs. And, as I touched it fearfully, the veil-like garment covering her, vanished into thin air, its metal stars twinkling in a shower around her on the stone floor."

The Tracer, motionless, intent, scarcely breathed; the younger man moved restlessly in his chair, the dazed light in his eyes clearing to sullen consciousness.

"What more is there to tell?" he said. "And to what purpose? All this is time wasted. I have my work cut out for me. What more is there to tell?"

"What you have left untold," said the Tracer, with the slightest ring of authority in his quiet voice.

And, as though he had added "Obey!" the younger man sank back in his chair, his hands contracting nervously.

"I went back to El Teb," he said; "I walked like a dreaming man. My sleep was haunted by her beauty; night after night, when at last I fell asleep, instantly I saw her face, and her dark eyes opening into mine in childish bewilderment; day after day I rode out to the fallen pillar and descended to that dark chamber where she lay alone. Then there came a time when I could not endure the thought of her lying there alone. I had never dared to touch her. Horror of what might happen had held me aloof lest she crumble at my touch to that awful powder which I had trodden on.

"I did not know what to do; my Arabs had begun to whisper among themselves, suspicious of my absences, impatient to break camp, perhaps, and roam on once more. Perhaps they believed I had discovered treasure somewhere; I am not sure. At any rate, dread of their following me, determination to take my dead away with me, drove me into action; and that day when I reached her silent chamber I lighted my candle, and, leaning above her for one last look, I touched her shoulder with my finger tip.

"It was a strange sensation. Prepared for a dreadful dissolution, utterly unprepared for cool, yielding flesh, I almost dropped where I stood. For her body was neither cold nor warm, neither dust-dry nor moist; neither the skin of the living nor the dead. It was firm, almost stiff, yet not absolutely without a certain hint of flexibility.

"The appalling wonder of it consumed me; fear, incredulity, terror, apathy succeeded each other; then slowly a fierce shrinking happiness swept me in every fiber.

"This marvelous death, this triumph of beauty over death, was mine. Never again should she lie here alone through the solitudes of night and day; never again should the dignity of Death lack the tribute demanded of Life. Here was the appointed watcher—I, who had found her alone in the wastes of the world—all alone on the outermost edges of the world—a child, dead and unguarded. And standing there beside her I knew that I should never love again."

He straightened up, stretching out his arm: "I did not intend to carry her away to what is known as Christian burial. How could

I consign her to darkness again, with all its dreadful mockery of marble, all its awful emblems?

"This lovely stranger was to be my guest forever. The living should be near her while she slept so sweetly her slumber through the centuries; she should have warmth, and soft hangings and sunlight and flowers; and her unconscious ears should be filled with the pleasant stir of living things. . . . I have a house in the country, a very old house among meadows and young woodlands. And I—I had dreamed of giving this child a home—"

His voice broke; he buried his head in his hands a moment; but when he lifted it again his features were hard as steel.

"There was already talk in the bazaar about me. I was probably followed, but I did not know it. Then one of my men disappeared. For a week I hesitated to trust my Arabs; but there was no other way. I told them there was a mummy which I desired to carry to some port and smuggle out of the country without consulting the Government. I knew perfectly well that the Government would never forego its claim to such a relic of Egyptian antiquity. I offered my men too much, perhaps. I don't know. They hesitated for a week, trying by every artifice to see the treasure, but I never let them out of my sight.

"Then one day two white men came into camp; and with them came a government escort to arrest me for looting an Egyptian tomb. The white men were Joram Smiles and that Eurasian, Emanuel Gandon, who was partly white, I suppose. I didn't comprehend what they were up to at first. They escorted me forty miles to confront the official at Shen-Bak. When, after a stormy week, I was permitted to return to Saïs, my Arabs and the white men were gone. And the stone chamber under the water garden wall was empty as the hand I hold out to you!"

He opened his palm and rose, his narrowing eyes clear and dangerous.

"At the bazaar I learned enough to know what had been done. I traced the white men to the coast. They sailed on the *Scythian Queen*, taking with them all that I care for on earth or in heaven! And you ask me why I measure their distance from me by a bullet's flight!"

The Tracer also rose, pale and grave.

"Wait!" he said. "There are other things to be done before you prepare to face a jury for double murder."

"It is for them to choose," said Burke. "They shall have the choice of returning to me my dead, or of going to hell full of lead."

"*Ex*actly, my dear sir. That part is not difficult," said the Tracer quietly. "There will be no occasion for violence, I assure you. Kindly leave such details to me. I know what is to be done. You are outwardly very calm, Mr. Burke—even dangerously placid; but though you maintain an admirable command over yourself superficially, you are laboring under terrible excitement. Therefore it is my duty to say to you at once that there is no cause for your excitement, no cause for your apprehension as to results. I feel exceedingly confident that you will, in due time, regain possession of all that you care for most—quietly, quietly, my dear sir! You are not yet ready to meet these men, nor am I ready to go with you. I beg you to continue your habit of self-command for a little while. There is no haste—that is to say, there is every reason to make haste slowly. And the quickest method is to seat yourself. Thank you. And I shall sit here beside you and spread out this papyrus scroll for your inspection."

Burke stared at the Tracer, then at the scroll.

"What has that inscription to do with the matter in hand?" he demanded impatiently.

"I leave you to judge," said the Tracer. A dull tint of excitement flushed his lean cheeks; he twisted his gray mustache and bent over the unrolled scroll which was now held flat by weights at the four corners.

"Can you understand any of these symbols, Mr. Burke?" he asked.

"No."

"Curious," mused the Tracer. "Do you know it was fortunate that you put this bit of papyrus in the pocket of your shooting coat— so fortunate that, in a way, it approaches the miraculous?"

"What do you mean? Is there anything in that scroll bearing on this matter?"

"Yes."

"And you can read it? Are you versed in such learning, Mr. Keen?"

"I am an Egyptologist—among other details," said the Tracer calmly.

The young man gazed at him, astonished. The Tracer of Lost Persons picked up a pencil, laid a sheet of paper on the table beside the papyrus, and slowly began to copy the first symbol:

NINETEEN

"The ancient Egyptian word for the personal pronoun 'I' was
anuk," said the Tracer placidly. "The phonetic for *a* was the
hieroglyph

q

a reed; for *n* the water symbol

〰〰〰

for *u* the symbols

𓄿,𓂝

for *k*

𓎡

Therefore this hieroglyphic inscription begins with the personal
pronoun

q〰〰𓄿,𓂝𓎡

or *I*. That is very easy, of course.

"Now, the most ancient of Egyptian inscriptions read vertically
in columns; there are only two columns in this papyrus, so we'll
try it vertically and pass downward to the next symbol, which is
inclosed in a sort of frame or cartouche. That immediately signifies that royalty is mentioned; therefore, we have already translated as much as 'I, the king (or queen).' Do you see?"

"Yes," said Burke, staring.

"Very well. Now this symbol, number two,

spells out the word '*Meris*,' in this way: M (pronounced *me*) is phonetically symbolized by the characters

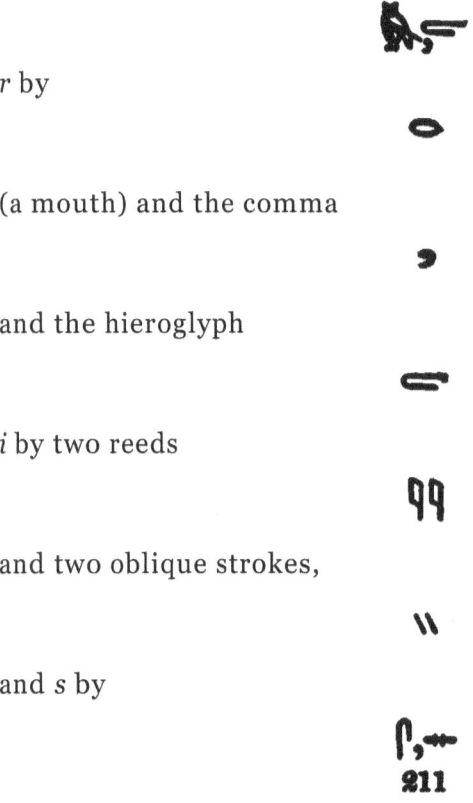

r by

(a mouth) and the comma

and the hieroglyph

i by two reeds

and two oblique strokes,

and *s* by

211

This gives us Meris, the name of that deposed and fugitive king of Egypt who, after a last raid on the summer palace of Mer-Shen, usurping ruler of Egypt, was followed and tracked to Saïs, where, with an arrow through his back, he crawled to El Teb and finally died there of his wound. All this Egyptologists are perfectly familiar with in the translations of the boastful tablets and inscriptions erected near Saïs by Mer-Shen, the three hundred and twelfth sovereign after Queen Nitocris."

He looked up at Burke, smiling. "Therefore," he said, "this papyrus scroll was written by Meris, ex-king, a speculative thousands of years before Christ. And it begins: 'I, Meris the King.'"

"How does all this bear upon what concerns me?" demanded Burke.

"Wait!"

Something in the quiet significance of the Tracer's brief command sent a curious thrill through the younger man. He leaned stiffly forward, studying the scroll, every faculty concentrated on the symbol which the Tracer had now touched with the carefully sharpened point of his pencil:

"That," said Mr. Keen, "is the ancient Egyptian word for 'little,' '*Ket*.' The next, below, written in two lines, is 'Samaris,' a proper name—the name of a woman. Under that, again, is the symbol for the number 18; the decimal sign,

and eight vertical strokes,

Under that, again, is a hieroglyph of another sort, an ideograph representing a girl with a harp; and, beneath that, the symbol which always represented a dancing girl

and also the royal symbol inclosed in a cartouch,

which means literally 'the Ruler of Upper and Lower Egypt.' Under that is the significant symbol

representing an arm and a hand holding a stick. This always means *force*—to take forcibly or to use violence. Therefore, so far, we have the following literal translation: 'I, Meris the King, little Samaris, eighteen, a harpist, dancing girl, the Ruler of Upper and Lower Egypt, to take by violence—'"

"What does that make?" broke in Burke impatiently.

"*Wait!* Wait until we have translated everything literally. And, Mr. Burke, it might make it easier for us both if you would remember that I have had the pleasure of deciphering many hundreds of papyri before you had ever heard that there were such things."

"I beg your pardon," said the young man in a low voice.

"I beg yours for my impatience," said the Tracer pleasantly. "This deciphering always did affect my nerves and shorten my temper. And, no doubt, it is quite as hard on you. Shall we go on, Mr. Burke?"

"If you please, Mr. Keen."

So the Tracer laid his pencil point on the next symbol

"That is the symbol for night," he said; "and that

is the water symbol again, as you know; and that

is the ideograph, meaning a ship. The five reversed crescents

record the number of days voyage; the sign

means a house, and is also the letter H in the Egyptian alphabet.

"Under it, again, we have a repetition of the first symbol meaning *I*, and a repetition of the second symbol, meaning 'Meris, the King.' Then, below that cartouche, comes a new symbol,

which is the feminine personal pronoun, *sentus*, meaning '*she*'; and the first column is completed with the symbol for the ancient Egyptian verb, *nehes*, 'to awake,'

"And now we take the second column, which begins with the jackal ideograph expressing slyness or cleverness. Under it is the hieroglyph meaning 'to run away,' 'to escape.' And under that, Mr. Burke, is one of the rarest of all Egyptian symbols; a symbol seldom seen on stone or papyrus,

except in rare references to the mysteries of Isis. The meaning of it, so long in dispute, has finally been practically determined through a new discovery in the cuneiform inscriptions. It is the symbol of two hands holding two *closed* eyes; and it signifies power."

"You mean that those ancients understood hypnotism?" asked Burke, astonished.

"Evidently their priests did; evidently hypnotism was understood and employed in certain mysteries. And there is the symbol of it; and under it the hieroglyphs

O ❥

meaning 'a day and a night,' with the symbol

⌊⌋

as usual present to signify force or strength employed. Under that, again, is a human figure stretched upon a typical Egyptian couch. And now, Mr. Burke, *note carefully* three modifying signs: first, that it is a *couch* or *bed* on which the figure is stretched, not the funeral couch, not the embalming slab; second, there is no mummy mask covering the face, and no mummy case covering the body; third, that under the recumbent figure is pictured an *open* mouth, not a *closed* one.

"All these modify the ideograph, apparently representing death. But the sleep symbol is not present. Therefore it is a sound inference that all this simply confirms the symbol of hypnotism."

Burke, intensely absorbed, stared steadily at the scroll.

"Now," continued Mr. Keen, "we note the symbol of force again, always present; and, continuing horizontally, a cartouche quite empty except for the midday sun. That is simply translated; the midday sun illuminates nothing. Meris, deposed, is king only in name; and the sun no longer shines on him as 'Ruler of Upper and Lower Egypt.' Under that despairing symbol, 'King of Nothing,' we have

the phonetics which spell *sha*, the word for garden. And, just beyond this, horizontally, the modifying ideograph meaning 'a *water* garden';

a design of lotus and tree alternating on a terrace. Under that is the symbol for the word '*aneb*,'

a 'wall.' Beyond that, horizontally, is the symbol for 'house.' It should be placed under the wall symbol, but the Egyptians were very apt to fill up spaces instead of continuing their vertical columns. Now, beneath, we find the imperative command

'arise!' And the Egyptian personal pronoun '*entuten*,'

which means 'you' or 'thou.'

"Under that is the symbol

which means 'priest,' or, literally, 'priest man.' Then comes the imperative 'awake to life!'

After that, our first symbol again, meaning '*I*,' followed horizontally by the symbol

Λ

signifying 'to go.'

"Then comes a very important drawing—you see?—the picture of a man with a jackal's head, not a dog's head. It is not accompanied by the phonetic in a cartouche, as it should be. Probably the writer was in desperate haste at the end. But, nevertheless, it is easy to translate that symbol of the man with a jackal's head. It is a picture of the Egyptian god, Anubis, who was supposed to linger at the side of the dying to conduct their souls. Anubis, the jackal-headed, is the courier, the personal escort of departing souls. And this is he.

"And now the screed ends with the cry 'Pray for me!'

the last symbol on this strange scroll—this missive written by a deposed, wounded, and dying king to an unnamed priest. Here is the literal translation in columns:

I	cunning
Meris the King	escape
little	hypnotize
Samaris	King of Nothing ⎱
eighteen	place forcibly ⎰
a harpist	garden ⎱
a dancing girl—Ruler of	water garden ⎰
Upper and Lower	wall
Egypt	house
took forcibly—night	Arise. Do
by water	Thou
five days	Priest Man
ship	Awake ⎱
house	To life ⎰
I	I go
Meris the King	Anubis
she	Pray
awake	

"And this is what that letter, thousands of years old, means in this language of ours, hundreds of years young: 'I, Meris the King, seized little Samaris, a harpist and a dancing girl, eighteen years of age, belonging to the King of Upper and Lower Egypt, and carried her away at night on shipboard—a voyage of five days—to my house. I, Meris the King, lest she lie awake watching cunningly for a chance to escape, hypnotized her (or had her hypnotized) so that she lay like one dead or asleep, but breathing, and I, King no longer of Upper and Lower Egypt, took her and placed her in my house under the wall of the water garden. Arise! therefore, O thou priest; (go) and awaken her to life. I am dying (I go with Anubis!). Pray for me!'"

TWENTY

For a full minute the two men sat there without moving or speaking. Then the Tracer laid aside his pencil.

"To sum up," he said, opening the palm of his left hand and placing the forefinger of his right across it, "the excavation made by the falling pillar raised in triumph above the water garden of the deposed king, Meris, by his rival, was the subterranean house of Meris. The prostrate figure which crumbled to powder at your touch may have been the very priest to whom this letter or papyrus was written. Perhaps the bearer of the scroll was a traitor and stabbed the priest as he was reading the missive. Who can tell how that priest died? He either died or betrayed his trust, for he never aroused the little Samaris from her suspended animation. And the water garden fell into ruins and she slept; and the Ruler of Upper and Lower Egypt raised his columns, lotus crowned, above the ruins; and she slept on. Then—*you* came."

Burke stared like one stupefied.

"I do not know," said the Tracer gravely, "what balm there may be in a suspension of sensation, perhaps of vitality, to protect the human body from corruption after death. I do not know how soon suspended animation or the state of hypnotic coma, undisturbed, changes into death—whether it comes gradually, imperceptibly freeing the soul; whether the soul hides there, asleep, until suddenly the flame of vitality is extinguished. I do not know how long she lay there with life in her."

He leaned back and touched an electric bell, then, turning to Burke:

"Speaking of pistol range," he said, "unstrap those weapons and pass them over, if you please."

And the young man obeyed as in a trance.

"Thank you. There are four men coming into this room. You will keep your seat, if you please, Mr. Burke."

After a moment the door opened noiselessly. Two men hand-cuffed together entered the room; two men, hands in their pockets, sauntered carelessly behind the prisoners and leaned back against the closed door.

"That short, red-haired, lame man with the cast in his eye—do you recognize him?" asked the Tracer quietly.

Burke, grasping the arms of his chair, had started to rise, fury fairly blazing from his eyes; but, at the sound of the Tracer's calm, even voice, he sank back into his chair.

"That is Joram Smiles? You recognize him?" continued Mr. Keen.

Burke nodded.

"*Exactly*—alias Limpy, alias Red Jo, alias Big Stick Joram, alias Pinky; swindler, international confidence man, fence, burglar, gambler; convicted in 1887, and sent to Sing Sing for forgery; convicted in 1898, and sent to Auburn for swindling; arrested by my men on board the S. S. *Scythian Queen*, at the cabled request of John T. Burke, Esquire, and held to explain the nature of his luggage, which consisted of the contents of an Egyptian vault or underground ruin, declared at the customhouse as a mummy, and passed as such."

The quiet, monotonous voice of the Tracer halted, then, as he glanced at the second prisoner, grew harder:

"Emanuel Gandon, general international criminal, with over half a hundred aliases, arrested in company with Smiles and held until Mr. Burke's arrival."

Turning to Burke, the Tracer continued: "Fortunately, the *Scythian Queen* broke down off Brindisi. It gave us time to act on your cable; we found these men aboard when she was signaled off the Hook. I went out with the pilot myself, Mr. Burke."

Smiles shot a wicked look at Burke; Gandon scowled at the floor.

"Now," said the Tracer pleasantly, meeting the venomous glare of Smiles, "I'll get you that warrant you have been demanding to have exhibited to you. Here it is—charging you and your amiable friend Gandon with breaking into and robbing the Metropolitan Museum of ancient Egyptian gold ornaments, in March, 1903, and taking them to France, where they were sold to collectors. It seems that you found the business good enough to go prowling about Egypt on a hunt for something to sell here. A great mistake, my friends—a very great mistake, because, after the Museum has finished with you, the Egyptian Government desires to extradite you. And I rather suspect you'll have to go."

He nodded to the two quiet men leaning against the door.

"Come, Joram," said one of them pleasantly.

But Smiles turned furiously on the Tracer. "You lie, you old gray rat!" he cried. "That ain't no mummy; that's a plain dead girl! And there ain't no extrydition for body snatchin', so I guess them niggers at Cairo won't get us, after all!"

"Perhaps," said the Tracer, looking at Burke, who had risen, pale and astounded. "Sit down, Mr. Burke! There is no need to question these men; no need to demand what they robbed you of. For," he added slowly, "what they took from the garden grotto of Saïs, and from you, I have under my own protection."

The Tracer rose, locked the door through which the prisoners and their escorts had departed; then, turning gravely on Burke, he continued:

"That panel, there, is a door. There is a room beyond—a room facing to the south, bright with sunshine, flowers, soft rugs, and draperies of the East. *She* is there—like a child asleep!"

Burke reeled, steadying himself against the wall; the Tracer stared at space, speaking very slowly:

"Such death I have never before heard of. From the moment she came under my protection I have dared to doubt—many things. And an hour ago you brought me a papyrus scroll confirming my doubts. I doubt still—Heaven knows what! Who can say how long

the flame of life may flicker within suspended animation? A week?
A month? A year? Longer than that? Yes; the Hindoos have proved
it. How long? The span of a normal life? Or longer? Can the life
flame burn indefinitely when the functions are absolutely suspended—generation after generation, century after century?"

Burke, ghastly white, straightened up, quivering in every limb;
the Tracer, as pale as he, laid his hand on the secret panel.

"If—if you dare say it—the phrase is this: '*O Ket Samaris,
Nehes!*'— 'O Little Samaris, awake!'"

"I—dare. In Heaven's name, open that door!"

Then, averting his head, the Tracer of Lost Persons swung open
the panel.

A flood of sunshine flashed on Burke's face; he entered; and
the paneled door closed behind him without a sound.

Minute after minute passed; the Tracer stood as though turned
to stone, gray head bent.

Then he heard Burke's voice ring out unsteadily:

"O Ket Samaris—Samaris! O Ket Samaris—*Nehes!*"

And again: "Samaris! Samaris! O beloved, awake!"

And once more: "*Nehes!* O Samaris!"

Silence, broken by a strange, sweet, drowsy plaint—like a child
awakened at midnight by a dazzling light.

"Samaris!"

Then, through the stillness, a little laugh, and a softly tremulous voice:

"*Ari un aha, O Entuk sen!*"

TWENTY-ONE

"What we want to do," said Gatewood over the telephone, "is to give you a corking little dinner at the Santa Regina. There'll be Mr. and Mrs. Tommy Kerns, Captain and Mrs. Harren, Mr. and Mrs. Jack Burke, Mrs. Gatewood, and myself. We want you to set the date for it, Mr. Keen, and we also wish you to suggest one more deliriously happy couple whom you have dragged out of misery and flung head-first into terrestrial paradise."

"Do you young people really care to do this for me?" asked the Tracer, laughing.

"Of course we do. We're crazy about it. We want one more couple, and you to set the date."

There was the slightest pause; then the Tracer's voice, with the same undertone of amusement ringing through it:

"How would your cousin, Victor Carden, do?"

"He's all right, only he isn't married. We want two people whom you have joined together after hazard has put them asunder and done stunts with them."

"Very well; Victor Carden and his very lovely wife will be just the people."

"Is Victor married?" demanded Gatewood, astonished.

"No," said the Tracer demurely, "but he will be in time for that dinner." And he set the date for the end of the week in an amused voice, and rang off.

Then he glanced at the clock, touched an electric bell, and again unhooking the receiver of the telephone, called up the Sherwood Studios and asked for Mr. Carden.

"Is *this* Mr. Carden? Oh, good morning, Mr. Carden! This is Mr. Keen, Tracer of Lost Persons. Could you make it convenient to call—say in course of half an hour? Thank you. . . . What? . . . Well, speaking with that caution and reserve which we are obliged to employ in making any preliminary statements to our clients, I think I may safely say that you have every reason to feel moderately encouraged."

"You mean," said Carden's voice, "that you have actually solved the proposition?"

"It has been a difficult proposition, Mr. Carden; I will not deny that it has taxed our resources to the uttermost. Over a thousand people, first and last, have been employed on this case. It has been a slow and tedious affair, Mr. Carden—tedious for us all. We seldom have a case continue as long as this has; it is a year ago to-day since you placed the matter in our hands. . . . What? Well, without committing myself, I think that I may venture to express a carefully qualified opinion that the solution of the case is probably practically in the way of being almost accomplished! . . . Yes, I shall expect you in half an hour. Good-by!"

The Tracer of Lost Persons' eyes were twinkling as he hung up the receiver and turned in his revolving chair to meet the pretty young woman who had entered in response to his ring.

"The Carden case, if you please, Miss Smith," he said, smiling to himself.

The young woman also smiled; the Carden case had become a classic in the office. Nobody except Mr. Keen had believed that the case could ever be solved.

"Safe-deposit box 108923!" said Miss Smith softly, pressing a speaking tube to her red lips. In a few moments there came a hissing thud from the pneumatic tube; Miss Smith unlocked it and extracted a smooth, steel cylinder.

"The combination for that cylinder is A-4-44-11-X," observed the Tracer, consulting a cipher code, "which, translated," he added, "gives us the setting combination, One, D, R-R,-J-'24."

Miss Smith turned the movable disks at the end of the cylinder until the required combination appeared. Then she unscrewed the cylinder head and dumped out the documents in the famous Carden case.

"As Mr. Carden will be here in half an hour or so I think we had better run over the case briefly," nodded the Tracer, leaning back in his chair and composing himself to listen. "Begin with my preliminary memorandum, Miss Smith."

"Case 108923," began the girl. Then she read the date, Carden's full name, Victor Carden, a terse biography of the same gentleman, and added: "Case accepted. Contingent fee, $5,000."

"Quite so," said Mr. Keen; "now, run through the minutes of the first interview."

And Miss Smith unrolled a typewritten scroll and read:

"Victor Carden, Esquire, the well-known artist, called this evening at 6.30. Tall, well-bred, good appearance, very handsome; very much embarrassed. Questioned by Mr. Keen he turned pink, and looked timidly at the stenographer (Miss Colt). Asked if he might not see Mr. Keen alone, Miss Colt retired. Mr. Keen set the recording phonograph in motion by dropping his elbow on his desk."

A brief *résumé* of the cylinder records followed:

"Mr. Carden asked Mr. Keen if he (Mr. Keen) knew who he (Mr. Carden) was. Mr. Keen replied that everybody knew Mr. Carden, the celebrated painter and illustrator who had created the popular type of beauty known as the 'Carden Girl.' Mr. Carden blushed and fidgeted. (*Notes from. Mr. Keen's Observation Book, pp. 291-297.*) Admitted that he was the creator of the 'Carden Girl.' Admitted he had drawn and painted that particular type of feminine beauty many times. Fidgeted some more. (*Keen's O.B., pp. 298-299.*) Volunteered the statement that this type of beauty, known as the 'Carden Girl,' was the cause of great unhappiness to himself. Questioned, turned pinker and fidgeted. (*K.O.B., page 300.*) Denied that his present trouble was caused by the model who had posed for the 'Carden Girl.' Explained that a number of assorted models had posed for that type of beauty. Further explained that none of them resembled the type; that the type was his own creation; that he used models merely for the anatomy, and that he always idealized form and features.

"Questioned again, admitted that the features of the 'Carden Girl' were his ideal of the highest and loveliest type of feminine beauty. Did not deny that he had fallen in love with his own creation. Turned red and tried to smoke. (*K.O.B., page 303.*) Admitted he had been fascinated himself with his own rendering of a type of beauty which he had never seen anywhere except as rendered by his own pencil on paper or on canvas. Fidgeted. (*K.O.B., page 304.*) Admitted that he could easily fall in love with a woman who resembled the 'Carden Girl.' Didn't believe she ever really existed. Confessed he had hoped for years to encounter her, but had begun to despair. Admitted that he had ventured to think that Mr. Keen might trace such a girl for him. Doubted Mr. Keen's success. Fidgeted (*K.O.B., page 306*), and asked Mr. Keen to take the case. Promised to send to Mr. Keen a painting in oil which embodied his loftiest ideal of the type known as the 'Carden Girl.' (*Portrait received; lithographs made and distributed to our agents according to routine, from Canada to Mexico and from the Atlantic to the Pacific.*)

"Mr. Keen terminated the interview with characteristic tact, accepting the case on the contingent fee of $5,000."

"Very well," said the Tracer, as Miss Smith rolled up the scroll and looked at him for further instructions. "Now, perhaps you had better run over the short summary of proceedings to date. I mean the digest which you will find attached to the completed records."

Miss Smith found the paper, unrolled it, and read:

"During the twelve months' investigation and search (*in re Carden*) seven hundred and nine young women were discovered who resembled very closely the type sought for. By process of elimination, owing to defects in figure, features, speech, breeding, etc., etc., this list was cut down to three. One of these occasionally chewed gum, but otherwise resembled the type. The second married before the investigation of her habits could be completed. The third is apparently a flawless replica of Mr. Carden's original in face, figure, breeding, education, moral and mental habits. (*See Document 23, A.*)"

"Read Document 23, A," nodded Mr. Keen.

And Miss Smith read:

ROSALIND HOLLIS, M.D.

Age 24
Height . . . . 5 feet 9 inches
Weight . . . . 160 pounds
Hair . . . . Thick, bright, ruddy golden,
                              and inclined to curl.
Teeth . . . . Perfect
Eyes . . . . Dark violet-blue
Mouth . . . . Perfect
Color . . . . Fair. An ivory-tinted blonde.
Figure . . . . Perfect
Health . . . . Perfect
Temper . . . . Feminine
Habits . . . . Austere, with a resolutely
                         suppressed capacity for romance.
Business . . . . None
Profession . . . . Physician
Mania . . . . A Mission

"Note.—Dr. Rosalind Hollis was presented to society in her eighteenth year. At the end of her second season she withdrew from society with the determination to devote her entire life to charity. Settlement work and the study of medicine have occupied her constantly. Recently admitted to practice, she spends her mornings in visiting the poor, whom she treats free of all charge; her afternoons and evenings are devoted to what she expects is to be her specialty: the study of the rare malady known as Lamour's Disease. (*See note on second page.*)

"It is understood that Dr. Hollis has abjured the society of all men other than her patients and such of her professional *confrères* as she is obliged to

consult or work with. Her theory is that of the bee-
hive: drones for mates, workers for work. She adds,
very decidedly, that she belongs to the latter divi-
sion, and means to remain there permanently.

"Note (*Mr. Keen's O.B., pp. 916-18*).—Her eccen-
tricity is probably the result of a fine, wholesome,
highly strung young girl taking life and herself too
seriously. The remedy will be the *Right Man*."

"*Ex*actly," nodded Mr. Keen, joining the tips of his thin fingers
and partly closing his eyes. "Now, Miss Smith, the disease which
Dr. Hollis intends to make her specialty—have you any notes on
that?"

"Here they are," said Miss Smith; and she read: "Lamour's Disease; the rarest of all known diseases; first discovered and described by Ero S. Lamour, M.D., M.S., F.B.A., M.F.H., in 1861. Only
a single case has ever been observed. This case is fully described
in Dr. Lamour's superb and monumental work in sixteen volumes.
Briefly, the disease appears without any known cause, and is ultimately supposed to result fatally. The first symptom is the appearance of a faintly bluish circle under the eyes, as though the patient
was accustomed to using the eyes too steadily at times. Sometimes
a slight degree of fever accompanies this manifestation; pulse and
temperature vary. The patient is apparently in excellent health,
but liable to loss of appetite, restlessness, and a sudden flushing
of the face. These symptoms are followed by others unmistakable:
the patient becomes silent at times; at times evinces a weakness
for sentimental expressions; flushes easily; is easily depressed;
will sit for hours looking at one person; and, if not checked, will
exhibit impulsive symptoms of affection for the opposite sex.
The strangest symptom of all, however, is the physical change in
the patient, whose features and figure, under the trained eye of
the observer, gradually from day to day assume the symmetry
and charm of a beauty almost unearthly, sometimes accompanied
by a spiritual pallor which is unmistakable in confirming the

diagnosis, and which, Dr. Lamour believes, presages the inexorable approach of immortality.

"There is no known remedy for Lamour's Disease. The only case on record is the case of the young lady described by Dr. Lamour, who watched her for years with unexampled patience and enthusiasm; finally, in the interest of science, marrying his patient in order to devote his life to a study of her symptoms. Unfortunately, some of these disappeared early—within a week—but the curious manifestation of physical beauty remained, and continued to increase daily to a dazzling radiance, with no apparent injury to the patient. Dr. Lamour, unfortunately, died before his investigations, covering over forty years, could be completed; his widow survived him for a day or two only, leaving sixteen children.

"Here is a wide and unknown field for medical men to investigate. It is safe to say that the physician who first discovers the bacillus of Lamour's Disease and the proper remedy to combat it will reap as his reward a glory and renown imperishable. Lamour's Disease is a disease not yet understood—a disease whose termination is believed to be fatal—a strange disease which seems to render radiant and beautiful the features of the patient, brightening them with the forewarning of impending death and the splendid resurrection of immortality."

The Tracer of Lost Persons caressed his chin reflectively. "*Exactly*, Miss Smith. So this is the disease which Dr. Hollis has chosen for her specialty. And only one case on record. *Exactly*. Thank you."

Miss Smith replaced the papers in the steel cylinder, slipped it into the pneumatic tube, sent it whizzing below to the safe-deposit vaults, and, saluting Mr. Keen with a pleasant inclination of her head, went out of the room.

The Tracer turned in his chair, picked up the daily detective report, and scanned it until he came to the name Hollis. It appeared that the daily routine of Rosalind Hollis had not varied during the past three weeks. In the mornings she was good to the poor with bottles and pills; in the afternoons she tucked one of Lamour's famous sixteen volumes under her arm and walked to Central Park, where, with democratic simplicity, she sat on a secluded bench and pored over the symptoms of Lamour's Disease. About five she retired to her severely simple apartments in the big brownstone office building devoted to physicians, corner of Fifty-eighth Street and Madison Avenue. Here she took tea, read a little, dined all alone, and retired about nine. This was the guileless but determined existence of Rosalind Hollis, M.D., according to McConnell, the detective assigned to observe her.

The Tracer refolded the report of his chief of detectives and pigeonholed it just as the door opened and a tall, well-built, attractive young man entered.

Shyness was written all over him; he offered his hand to Mr. Keen with an embarrassed air and seated himself at that gentleman's invitation.

"I'm almost sorry I ever began this sort of thing," he blurted out, like a big schoolboy appalled at his own misdemeanors. "The truth is, Mr. Keen, that the prospect of actually seeing a 'Carden Girl' alive has scared me through and through. I've a notion that my business with that sort of a girl ends when I've drawn her picture."

"But surely," said the Tracer mildly, "you have some natural curiosity to see the living copy of your charming but inanimate originals, haven't you, Mr. Carden?"

"Yes—oh, certainly. I'd like to see one of them alive—say out of a window, or from a cab. I should not care to be too close to her."

"But merely seeing her does not commit you," interposed Mr. Keen, smiling. "She is far too busy, too much absorbed in her own affairs to take any notice of you. I understand that she has something of an aversion for men."

"Aversion!"

"Well, she excludes them as unnecessary to her existence."

"Why?" asked Carden.

"Because she has a mission in life," said Mr. Keen gravely.

Carden looked out of the window. It was pleasant weather— June in all its early loveliness—the fifth day of June. The sixth was his birthday.

"I've simply got to marry somebody before the day after to-morrow," he said aloud— "that is, if I want my legacy."

"What!" demanded the Tracer sharply.

Carden turned, pink and guilty. "I didn't tell you all the circumstances of my case," he said. "I suppose I ought to have done so."

"*Exactly*," said the Tracer severely. "Why is it necessary that you marry somebody before the day after to-morrow?"

"Well, it's my twenty-fifth birthday—"

"Somebody has left you money on condition that you marry before your twenty-fifth birthday? Is that it, Mr. Carden? An uncle? An imbecile grandfather? A sentimental aunt?"

"My Aunt Tabby Van Beekman."

"Where is she?"

"In Trinity churchyard. It's too late to expostulate with her, you see. Besides, it wouldn't have done any good when she was alive."

The Tracer knitted his brows, musing, the points of his slim fingers joined.

"She was very proud, very autocratic," said Carden. "I am the last of my race and my aunt was determined that the race should not die out with me. I don't want to marry and increase, but she's trying to make me. At all events, I am not going to marry any woman inferior to the type I have created with my pencil—what the public calls the 'Carden Girl.' And now you see that your discovery of this living type comes rather late. In two days I must be legally married if I want my Aunt Tabby's legacy; and to-day for the first time I hear of a girl who, you assure me, compares favorably to my copyrighted type, but who has a mission and an aversion to men. So you see, Mr. Keen, that the matter is perfectly hopeless."

"I don't see anything of the kind," said Mr. Keen firmly.

"What?—do you believe there is any chance—"

"Of your falling in love within the next hour or so? Yes, I do. I think there is every chance of it. I am sure of it. But that is not the difficulty. The problem is far more complicated."

"You mean—"

"*Ex*actly; how to marry that girl before day after to-morrow. That's the problem, Mr. Carden!—not whether you are capable of falling in love with her. I have seen her; I *know* you can't avoid falling in love with her. Nobody could. I myself am on the verge of it; and I am fifty: you can't avoid loving her."

"If that were so," said Carden gravely; "if I were really going to fall in love with her—I would not care a rap about my Aunt Tabby and her money—"

"You ought to care about it for this young girl's sake. That legacy is virtually hers, not yours. She has a right to it. No man can ever give enough to the woman he loves; no man has ever done so. What *she* gives and what *he* gives are never a fair exchange. If you can balance the account in any measure, it is your duty to do it. Mr. Carden, if she comes to love you she may think it very fine that you bring to her your love, yourself, your fame, your talents, your success, your position, your gratifying income. But I tell you it's not enough to balance the account. It is never enough—no, not all your devotion to her included! You can never balance the account on earth—all you can do is to try to balance it materially and spiritually. Therefore I say, endow her with *all* your earthly goods. Give all you can in every way to lighten as much as possible man's hopeless debt to all women who have ever loved."

"You talk about it as though I were already committed," said Carden, astonished.

"You are, morally. For a month I have, without her knowledge, it is true, invaded the privacy of a very lovely young girl—studied her minutely, possessed myself of her history, informed myself of her habits. What excuse had I for this unless I desired her happiness and yours? Nobody could offer me any inducement to engage in such a practice unless I believed that the means might justify a moral conclusion. And the moral conclusion of this investigation is your marriage to her."

"Certainly," said Carden uneasily, "but how are we going to accomplish it by to-morrow? How is it going to be accomplished at all?"

The Tracer of Lost Persons rose and began to pace the long rug, clasping his hands behind his back. Minute after minute sped; Carden stared alternately at Mr. Keen and at the blue sky through the open window.

"It is seldom," said Mr. Keen with evident annoyance, "that I personally take any spectacular part in the actual and concrete demonstrations necessary to a successful conclusion of a client's case. But I've got to do it this time."

He went to a cupboard, picked out a gray wig and gray side whiskers and deliberately waved them at Carden.

"You see what these look like?" he demanded.

"Y-yes."

"Very well. It is now noon. Do you know the Park? Do you happen to recollect a shady turn in the path after you cross the bridge over the swan lake? Here; I'll draw it for you. Now, here is the lake; here's the esplanade and fountain, you see. Here's the path. You follow it—so!—around the lake, across the bridge, then following the lake to the right—so!—then up the wooded slope to the left—so! Now, here is a bench. I mark it Number One. *She* sits there with her book—there she is!"

"If she looks like *that*—" began Carden. And they both laughed with the slightest trace of excitement.

"Here is Bench Number Two!" resumed the Tracer. "Here you sit—and there you are!"

"Thanks," said Carden, laughing again.

"Now," continued the Tracer, "you must be there at one o'clock. She will be there at one-thirty, or earlier perhaps. A little later I will become benignly visible. Your part is merely a thinking part; you are to do nothing, say nothing, unless spoken to. And when you are spoken to you are to acquiesce in whatever anybody says to you, and you are to do whatever anybody requests you to do. And, above all, don't be surprised at *anything* that may happen. You'll be nervous enough; I expect that. You'll probably color up and flush and fidget; I expect that; I count on that. But don't lose your nerve entirely; and don't think of attempting to escape."

388 ROBERT W. CHAMBERS

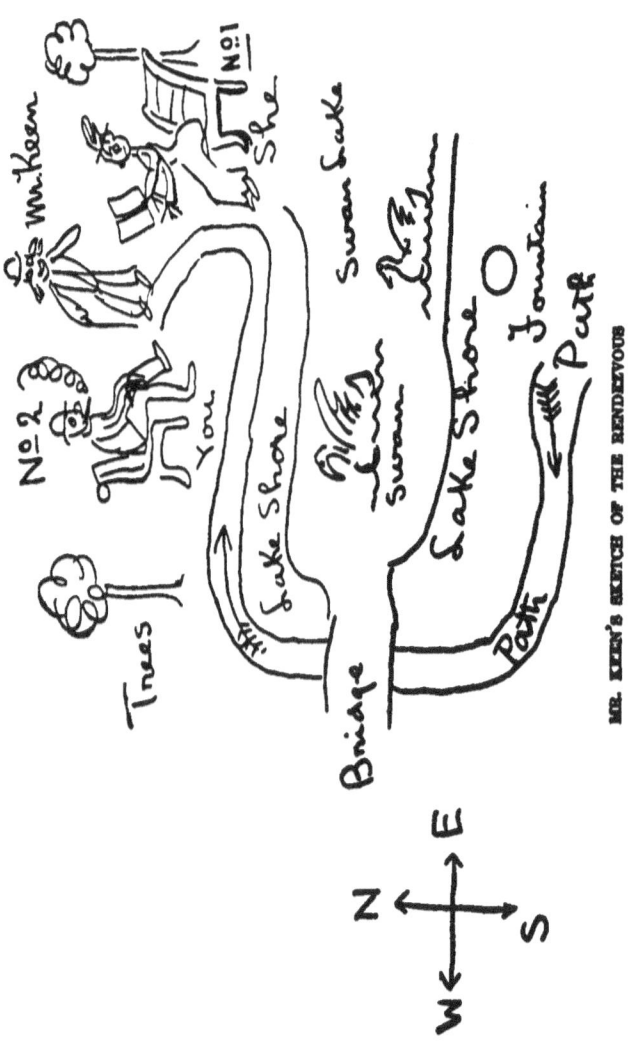

MR. KERR'S SKETCH OF THE RENDEZVOUS

"Escape! From what? From whom?"

"From her."

"*Her?*"

"Are you going to follow my instructions?" demanded the Tracer of Lost Persons.

"I—y-yes, of course."

"Very well, then, I am going to rub some of this under your eyes." And Mr. Keen produced a make-up box and, walking over to Carden, calmly darkened the skin under his eyes.

"I look as though I had been on a bat!" exclaimed Carden, surveying himself in a mirror. "Do you think any girl could find any attraction in such a countenance?"

"*She* will," observed the Tracer meaningly. "Now, Mr. Carden, one last word: The moment you find yourself in love with her, and the first moment you have the chance to do so decently, make love to her. She won't dismiss you; she will repulse you, of course, but she won't let you go. I know what I am saying; all I ask of you is to promise on your honor to carry out these instructions. Do you promise?"

"I do."

"Then here is the map of the rendezvous which I have drawn. Be there promptly. Good morning."

TWENTY-TWO

At one o'clock that afternoon a young man earnestly consulting a map might have been seen pursuing his solitary way through Central Park. Fresh green foliage arched above him, flecking the path with fretted shadow and sunlight; the sweet odor of flowering shrubs saturated the air; the waters of the lake sparkled where swans swept to and fro, snowy wings spread like sails to the fitful June wind.

"This," he murmured, pausing at a shaded bend in the path, "must be Bench Number One. I am not to sit on that. This must be Bench Number Two. I *am* to sit on that. So here I am," he added nervously, seating himself and looking about him with the caution of a cat in a strange back yard.

There was nobody in sight. Reassured, he ventured to drop one knee over the other and lean upon his walking stick. For a few minutes he remained in this noncommittal attitude, alert at every sound, anxious, uncomfortable, dreading he knew not what. A big, fat, gray squirrel racing noisily across the fallen leaves gave him a shock. A number of birds came to look at him—or so it appeared to him, for in the inquisitive scrutiny of a robin he fancied he divined sardonic meaning, and in the blank yellow stare of a purple grackle, a sinister significance out of all proportion to the size of the bird.

"What an absurd position to be in!" he thought. And suddenly he was seized with a desire to flee.

He didn't because he had promised not to, but the desire persisted to the point of mania. Oh, how he could run if he only hadn't promised not to! His entire being tingled with the latent possibilities of a burst of terrific speed. He wanted to scuttle away like a scared rabbit. The pace of the kangaroo would be slow in comparison. What a record he could make if he hadn't promised not to.

He crossed his knees the other way and brooded. The gray squirrel climbed the bench and nosed his pockets for possible peanuts, then hopped off hopefully toward a distant nursemaid and two children.

Growing more alarmed every time he consulted his watch Carden attempted to stem his rising panic with logic and philosophy, repeating: "Steady! my son! Don't act like this! You're not obliged to marry her if you don't fall in love with her; and if you do, you won't mind marrying her. That is philosophy. That is logic. Oh, I wonder what will have happened to me by this time to-morrow! I wish it *were* this time to-morrow! I wish it were this time next month! Then it would be all over. Then it would be—"

His muttering speech froze on his lips. Rooted to his bench he sat staring at a distant figure approaching—the figure of a young girl in a summer gown.

Nearer, nearer she came, walking with a free-limbed, graceful step, head high, one arm clasping a book.

That was the way the girls he drew would have walked had they ever lived. Even in the midst of his fright his artist's eyes noted that: noted the perfect figure, too, and the witchery of its grace and contour, and the fascinating poise of her head, and the splendid color of her hair; noted mechanically the flowing lines of her gown, and the dainty modeling of arm and wrist and throat and ear.

Then, as she reached her bench and seated herself, she raised her eyes and looked at him. And for the first time in his life he realized that ideal beauty was but the pale phantom of the real and founded on something more than imagination and thought; on something of vaster import than fancy and taste and technical skill; that it was founded on Life itself—on breathing, living, palpitating, tremulous Life!—from which all true inspiration must come.

Over and over to himself he was repeating: "Of course, it is perfectly impossible that I can be in love already. Love doesn't happen between two ticks of a watch. I am merely amazed at that girl's beauty; that is all. I am merely astounded in the presence of perfection; that is all. There is nothing more serious the matter with me. It isn't necessary for me to continue to look at her; it isn't vital to my happiness if I never saw her again. . . . That is—of course, I should like to see her, because I never did see living beauty such as hers in any woman. Not even in my pictures. What superb eyes! What a fascinately delicate nose! *What* a nose! By Heaven, that nose *is* a nose! I'll draw noses *that* way in future. My pictures are all out of drawing; I must fit arms into their sockets the way hers fit! I must remember the modeling of her eyelids, too—and that chin! and those enchanting hands—"

She looked up leisurely from her book, surveyed him calmly, absent-eyed, then bent her head again to the reading.

"There *is* something the matter with me," he thought with a suppressed gulp. "I—if she looks at me again—with those iris-hued eyes of a young goddess—I—I think I'm done for. I believe I'm done for anyway. It seems rather mad to think it. But there *is* something the matter—"

She deliberately looked at him again.

"It's all wrong for them to let loose a girl like that on people," he thought to himself, "all wrong. Everybody is bound to go mad over her. I'm going now. I'm mad already. I know I am, which proves I'm no lunatic. It isn't her beauty; it's the way she wears it—every motion, every breath of her. I know exactly what her voice is like. Anybody who looks into her eyes can see what her soul is like. She isn't out of drawing anywhere—physically or spiritually. And when a man sees a girl like that, why—why there's only one thing that can happen to him as far as I can see. And it doesn't take a year either. Heavens! How awfully remote from me she seems to be."

She looked up again, calmly, but not at him. A kindly, gray-whiskered old gentleman came tottering and rocking into view, his rosy, wrinkled face beaming benediction on the world as he passed through it—on the sunshine dappling the undergrowth, on the furry squirrels sitting up on their hind legs to watch him pass, on the stray dickybird that hopped fearlessly in his path, at the young man sitting very rigid there on his bench, at the fair, sweet-faced girl who met his aged eyes with the gentlest of involuntary smiles. And Carden did not recognize him!

Who could help smiling confidently into that benign face, with its gray hair and gray whiskers? Goodness radiated from every wrinkle.

"Dr. Atwood!" exclaimed the girl softly as she rose to meet this marvelous imitation of Dr. Austin Atwood, the great specialist on children's diseases.

The old man beamed weakly at her, halted, still beaming, fumbled for his eyeglasses, adjusted them, and peered closely into her face.

"Bless my soul," he smiled, "our pretty Dr. Hollis!"

"I—I did not suppose you would remember me," she said, rosy with pleasure.

"Remember you? Surely, surely." He made her a quaint, old-fashioned bow, turned, and peeped across the walk at Carden. And Carden, looking straight into his face, did not know the old man, who turned to Dr. Hollis again with many mysterious nods of his doddering head.

"You're watching him, too, are you?" he chuckled, leaning toward her.

"Watching whom, Dr. Atwood?" she asked surprised.

"Hush, child! I thought you had noticed that unfortunate and afflicted young man opposite."

Dr. Hollis looked curiously at Carden, then at the old gentleman with gray whiskers.

"Please sit down, Dr. Atwood, and tell me," she murmured. "I have noticed nothing in particular about the young man on the bench there." And she moved to give him room; and the young man opposite stared at them both as though bereft of reason.

"A heavy book for small hands, my child," said the old gentleman in his quaintly garrulous fashion, peering with dimmed eyes at the volume in her lap.

She smiled, looking around at him.

"My, my!" he said, tremblingly raising his eyeglasses to scan the title on the page; "Dr. Lamour's famous works! Are *you* studying Lamour, child?"

"Yes," she said with that charming inflection youth reserves for age.

"Astonishing!" he murmured. "The coincidence is more than remarkable. A physician! And studying Lamour's Disease! Incredible!"

"Is there anything strange in that, Dr. Atwood?" she smiled.

"Strange!" He lowered his voice, peering across at Carden. "Strange, did you say? Look across the path at that poor young man sitting there!"

"Yes," she said, perplexed, "I see him."

"*What* do you see?" whispered the old gentleman in a shakily portentous voice. "Here you sit reading about what others have seen; now what do *you* see?"

"Why, only a man—rather young—"

"No *symptoms*?"

"Symptoms? Of what?"

The old gentleman folded his withered hands over his cane. "My child," he said, "for a year I have had that unfortunate young man under secret observation. He was not aware of it; it never entered his mind that I could be observing *him* with minutest attention. He may have supposed there was nothing the matter with him. He was in error. I have studied him carefully. Look closer! *Are* there dark circles under his eyes—or are there not?" he ended in senile triumph.

"There are," she began, puzzled, "but I—but of what interest to me—"

"Compare his symptoms with the symptoms in that book you are studying," said the old gentleman hoarsely.

"Do you mean—do you suppose—" she stammered, turning her eyes on Carden, who promptly blushed to his ears and began to fidget.

"*Every symptom*," muttered the old gentleman. "Poor, poor young man!"

She had seen Carden turn a vivid pink; she now saw him fidget with his walking stick; she discovered the blue circles under his eyes. Three symptoms at once!

"Do you believe it *possible*?" she whispered excitedly under her breath to the old gentleman beside her. "It seems incredible! Such a rare disease! Only one single case ever described and studied! It seems impossible that I could be so fortunate as actually to see a case! Tell me, Dr. Atwood, do you believe that young man is really afflicted with Lamour's Disease?"

"There is but one way to be absolutely certain," said the old gentleman in a solemn voice, "and that is to study him; corroborate your suspicions by observing his pulse and temperature, as did Dr. Lamour."

"But—how can I?" she faltered. "I—he would probably object to becoming a patient of mine—"

"Ask him, child! Ask him."

"I have not courage—"

"Courage should be the badge of your profession," said the old gentleman gravely. "When did a good physician ever show the white feather in the cause of humanity?"

"I—I know, but this requires a different sort of courage."

"How," persisted the old gentleman, "can you confirm your very natural suspicions concerning this unfortunate young man unless you corroborate your observations by studying him at close range? Besides, already it seems to me that certain unmistakable signs are visible; I mean that strange physical phase which Dr. Lamour dwells on: the symmetry of feature and limb, the curiously spiritual beauty. Do you not notice these? Or is my sight so dim that I only imagine it?"

"He is certainly symmetrical—and—in a certain way—almost handsome in regard to features," she admitted, looking at Carden.

"Poor, poor boy!" muttered the old gentleman, wagging his gray whiskers. "I am too old to help him—too old to dream of finding a remedy for the awful malady which I am now convinced has seized him. I shall study him no more. It is useless. All I can do now is to

mention his case to some young, vigorous, ambitious physician—
some specialist—"

"Don't!" she whispered almost fiercely, "don't do that, Dr.
Atwood! I want him, please! I—you helped me to discover him, you
see. And his malady is to be my specialty. Please, do you mind if I
keep him all to myself and study him?"

"But you refused, child."

"I didn't mean to. I—I didn't exactly see how I was to study
him. But I must study him! Oh, I *must*! There will surely be some
way. Please let me. You discovered him, I admit, but I will promise
you faithfully to devote my entire life to studying him, as the great
Lamour devoted his life for forty years to his single patient."

"But Dr. Lamour married his patient," said the Tracer mildly.

"He—I—that need not be necessary—"

"But if it should prove necessary?"

"I—you—"

"Answer me, child."

She stared across at Carden, biting her red lips. He turned pink
promptly and fidgeted.

"He *has* got it!" she whispered excitedly. "Oh, *do* you mind if I
take him for mine? I am perfectly wild to begin on him!"

"You have not yet answered my question," said the old gentleman gravely. "Do you lack the courage to marry him if it becomes
necessary to do so in order to devote your entire life to studying
him?"

"Oh—it *cannot* be necessary—"

"You lack the courage."

She was silent.

"Braver things have been done by those of your profession who
have gone among lepers," said the old gentleman sadly.

She flushed up instantly; her eyes sparkled; her head proudly
high, delicate nostrils dilated.

"I am not afraid!" she said. "If it ever becomes necessary, I *can*
show courage and devotion, as well as those of my profession who
minister to the lepers of Molokai! Yes; I do promise you to marry
him if I cannot otherwise study him. And I promise you solemnly

to devote my entire life to observing his symptoms and searching for proper means to combat them. My one ambition in life is personally to observe and study a case of Lamour's Disease, and to give my entire life to investigating its origin, its course, and its cure."

The old gentleman rose, bowing with that quaintly obsolete courtesy which was in vogue in his youth.

"I am contented to leave him exclusively to you, Dr. Hollis. And I wish you happiness in your life's work—and success in your cure of this unhappy young man."

Hat in hand, he bowed again as he tottered past her, muttering and smiling to himself and shaking his trembling head as he went rocking on unsteady legs out into the sunshine, where the nursemaids and children flocked along the lake shore throwing peanuts to the waterfowl and satiated goldfish.

Dr. Hollis looked after him, her small hand buried among the pages of her open book. Carden viewed his disappearing figure with guileless emotions. He was vaguely aware that something important was about to happen to him. And it did before he was prepared.

TWENTY-THREE

When Rosalind Hollis found herself on her feet again a slight sensation of fright checked her for a moment. Then, resolutely suppressing such unworthy weakness, the lofty inspiration of her mission in life dominated her, and she stepped forward undaunted. And Carden, seeing her advance toward him, arose in astonishment to meet her.

For a second they stood facing each other, he astounded, she a trifle pale but firm. Then in a low voice she asked his pardon for disturbing him.

"I am Rosalind Hollis, a physician," she said quietly, "and physicians are sometimes obliged to do difficult things in the interest of their profession. It is dreadfully difficult for me to speak to you in this way. But"—she looked fearlessly at him— "I am confident you will not misinterpret what I have done."

He managed to assure her that he did not misinterpret it.

She regarded him steadily; she examined the dark circles under his eyes; she coolly observed his rising color under her calm inspection; she saw him fidgeting with his walking stick. She *must* try his pulse!

"Would you mind if I asked you a few questions in the interest of science?" she said earnestly.

"As a m-m-matter of fact," he stammered, "I don't know much about science. Awfully glad to do anything I can, you know."

"Oh, I don't mean it that way," she reassured him. A hint of a smile tinted her eyes with brilliant amethyst. "Would you mind if I sat here for a few moments? *Could* you overlook this horrid un-conventionality long enough for me to explain why I have spoken to you?"

"I could indeed!" he said, so anxiously cordial that her lovely face grew serious and she hesitated. But he was standing aside, hat off, placing the bench at her disposal, and she seated herself, placing her book on the bench beside her.

"Would you mind sitting here for a few moments?" she asked him gravely.

Dazed, scarcely crediting the evidence of his senses, he took possession of the end of the bench with the silent obedience of a schoolboy. His attitude was irreproachable. She was grateful for this, and her satisfaction with herself for not having misjudged him renewed her confidence in him, in herself, and in the difficult situation.

She began, quietly, by again telling him her name and profession; where she lived, and that she was studying to be a specialist, though she did not intimate what that specialty was to be.

Outwardly composed and attentively deferential, his astonishment at times dominated a stronger sentiment that seemed to grow and expand with her every word, seizing him in a fierce possession absolutely and hopelessly complete.

The bewildering fascination of her mastered him. No cool analysis of what his senses were confirming could be necessary to convince him of his condition. Every word of hers, every gesture, every inflection of her sweet, clear voice, every lifting of her head, her eyes, her perfectly gloved hands, only repeated to him what he knew was a certainty. Never had he looked upon such physical loveliness; never had he dreamed of such a voice.

She had asked him a question, and, absorbed in the pure delight of looking at her, he had not comprehended or answered. She flushed sensitively, accepting his silence as refusal, and he came out of his trance hastily.

"I beg your pardon; I did not quite understand your question, Miss Hollis—I mean, Dr. Hollis."

"I asked you if you minded my noting your pulse," she said.

He stretched out his right hand; she stripped off her glove, laid the tip of her middle finger on his wrist, and glanced down at the gold watch which she held.

"I am wondering," he said, laughing uncertainly, "whether you believe me to be ill. Of course it is easy to see that you have found something unusual about me—something of particular interest to a physician. Is there anything very dreadful going to happen to me, Dr. Hollis? I feel perfectly well."

"Are you sure you feel well?" she asked, so earnestly that the smile on his lips faded out.

"Absolutely. Is my pulse queer?"

"It is not normal."

He could easily account for that, but he said nothing.

She questioned him for a few minutes, noted his pulse again, looked closely at the bluish circles under his eyes. Naturally he flushed up and grew restless under the calm, grave, beautiful eyes.

"I—I have an absolutely new and carefully sterilized thermom-eter—" She drew it from a tiny gold-initialed pocket case, and looked wistfully at him.

"You want to put that into my mouth?" he asked, astonished.

"If you don't mind."

She held it up, shook it once or twice, and deliberately inserted it between his lips. And there he sat, round-eyed, silent, the end of the thermometer protruding at a rakish angle from the corner of his mouth. And he grew redder and redder.

"I *don't* wish to alarm you," she was saying, "but all this is so deeply significant, so full of vital interest to me—to the world, to science—"

"*What* have I got, in Heaven's name?" he said thickly, the ther-mometer wiggling in his mouth.

"Ah!" she exclaimed with soft enthusiasm, clasping her pretty ungloved hands, "I cannot be sure yet—I dare not be too sanguine—"

"Do you mean that you *want* me to have something queer?" he blurted out, while the thermometer wiggled with every word he uttered.

"N-no, of course, I don't *want* you to be ill," she said hastily. "Only, if you *are* ill it will be a wonderful thing for me. I mean—a—that I am intensely interested in certain symptoms which—"

She gently withdrew the glass tube from his lips and examined it carefully.

"*Is* there anything the matter?" he insisted, looking at the instrument over her shoulder.

She did not reply; pure excitement rendered her speechless.

"I seem to *feel* all right," he added uneasily. "If you really believe that there's anything wrong with me, I'll stop in to see my doctor."

"Your doctor!" she repeated, appalled.

"Yes, certainly. Why not?"

"Don't do that! Please don't do that! I—why *I* discovered this case. I beg you most earnestly to let me observe it. You don't understand the importance of it! You don't begin to dream of the rarity of this case! How much it means to me!"

He flushed up. "Do you intend to intimate that I am afflicted with some sort of rare and s-s-trange d-d-disease?" he stammered.

"I dare not pronounce upon it too confidently," she said with enthusiasm; "I have not yet absolutely determined the nature of the disease. But, oh, I am beginning to hope—"

"Then I *am* diseased!" he faltered. "I've got *something* anyhow; is that it? Only you are not yet perfectly sure what it is called! Is that the truth, Miss Hollis?"

"How can I answer positively until I have had time to observe these symptoms? It requires time to be certain. I do not wish to alarm you, but it is my duty to say to you that you should immediately place yourself under medical observation."

"You think that?"

"I do; I am convinced of it. Please understand me; I do not pronounce upon these visible symptoms; I do not express an unqualified opinion; but I could be in a position to do so if you consent to place yourself under my observations and care. For these suspicious symptoms are not only very plainly apparent to me, but were even noted by that old gentleman whom you may perhaps have observed conversing with me."

"Yes, I saw him. Who is he?"

"Dr. Austin Atwood," said the girl solemnly.

"Oh! And you say he also observed something queer about me? What did he see? Are there spots on me? Am I turning any remarkable color? Am I—" And in the very midst of his genuine alarm he suddenly remembered the make-up box and what the Tracer of Lost Persons had done to his eyes. Was *that* it? Where was the Tracer, anyway? He had promised to appear. And then Carden recollected the gray wig and whiskers that the Tracer had waved at him from the cupboard, bidding him note them well. *Could* that beaming, benignant, tottering old gentleman have been the Tracer of Lost Persons himself? And the same instant Carden was sure of it, spite of the miraculous change in the man.

Then logic came to his aid; and, deducing with care and patience, an earnest conviction grew within him that the dark circles under his eyes and the tottering old gentleman resembling Dr. Austin Atwood had a great deal to do with this dreadful disease which Dr. Hollis desired to study.

He looked at the charming girl beside him, and she looked back at him very sweetly, very earnestly, awaiting his decision.

For a moment he realized that she had really scared him, and in the reaction of relief an overwhelming desire to laugh seized him. He managed to suppress it, to compose himself. Then he remembered the Tracer's admonition to acquiesce in everything, do what he was told to do, not to run away, and to pay his court at the first decent opportunity.

He had no longer any desire to escape; he was quite willing to do anything she desired.

"Do you really want to study me, Dr. Hollis?" he asked, feeling like a hypocrite.

"Indeed I do," she replied fervently.

"You believe me worth studying?"

"Oh, truly, truly, you are! You don't suspect—you cannot conceive how important you have suddenly become to me."

"Then I think you had better take my case, Dr. Hollis," he said seriously. "I begin now to realize that you believe me to be a sort of freak—an afflicted curiosity, and that, in the interest of medicine, I ought to go to an asylum or submit myself to the ceaseless observation of a competent private physician."

"I—I think it best for you to place yourself in my care," she said. "Will you?"

"Yes," he said, "I will. I'll do anything in the world you ask."

"That is very—very generous, very noble of you!" she exclaimed, flushing with excitement and delight. "It means a great deal to me—it means, perhaps, a fame that I scarcely dared dream of even in my most enthusiastic years. I am too grateful to express my gratitude coherently; I am trying to say to you that I thank you; that I recognize in you those broad, liberal, generous qualities which, from your appearance and bearing, I—I thought perhaps you must possess."

She colored again very prettily; he bowed, and ventured to remind her that she had not yet given him the privilege of naming himself.

"That is true!" she said, surprised. "I had quite forgotten it." But when he named himself she raised her head, startled.

"Victor Carden!" she repeated. "You are the *artist*, Victor Carden!"

"Yes," he said, watching her dilated eyes like two violet-tinted jewels.

For a minute she sat looking at him; and imperceptibly a change came into her face, and its bewildering beauty softened as the vivid tints died out, leaving her cheeks almost pale.

"It is—a pity," she said under her breath. All the excitement, all the latent triumph, all the scarcely veiled eager enthusiasm had gone from her now.

"A pity?" he repeated, smiling.

"Yes. I wish it had been only an ordinary man. I—why should this happen to you? You have done so much for us all—made us forget ourselves in the beauty of what you offer us. Why should this happen to *you*!"

"But you have not told me yet what has happened to me, Miss Hollis."

She looked up, almost frightened.

"*Are* you our Victor Carden? I do not wish to believe it! You have done so much for the world—you have taught us to understand and desire all that is noble and upright and clean and beautiful!—to desire it, to aspire toward it, to venture to live the good, true, wholesome lives that your penciled creations must lead—*must* lead to wear such beautiful bodies and such divine eyes!"

"Do *you* care for my work?" he asked, astonished and moved.

"I? Yes, of course I do. Who does not?"

"Many," he replied simply.

"I am sorry for them," she said.

They sat silent for a long while.

At first his overwhelming desire was to tell her of the deception practiced upon her; but he could not do that, because in exposing himself he must fail in loyalty to the Tracer of Lost Persons. Besides, she would not believe him. She would think him mad if he told her that the old gentleman she had taken for Dr. Atwood was probably Mr. Keen, the Tracer of Lost Persons. Also, he himself was not absolutely certain about it. He had merely deduced as much.

"Tell me," he said very gently, "what is the malady from which you believe I am suffering?"

For a moment she remained silent, then, face averted, laid her finger on the book beside her.

"That," she said unsteadily.

He read aloud: "Lamour's Disease. A Treatise in sixteen volumes by Ero S. Lamour, M.D., M.S., F.B.A., M.F.H."

"All that?" he asked guiltily.

"I don't know, Mr. Carden. Are you laughing at me? Do you not believe me?" She had turned suddenly to confront him, surprising a humorous glimmer in his eyes.

"I really do not believe I am seriously ill," he said, laughing in spite of her grave eyes.

"Then perhaps you had better read a little about what Lamour describes as the symptoms of this malady," she said sadly.

"Is it fatal?" he inquired.

"Ultimately. That is why I desire to spend my life in studying means to combat it. That is why I desire you so earnestly to place yourself under my observation and let me try."

"Tell me one thing," he said; "is it contagious? Is it infectious? No? Then I don't mind your studying me all you wish, Dr. Hollis. You may take my temperature every ten minutes if you care to. You may observe my pulse every five minutes if you desire. Only please tell me how this is to be accomplished; because, you see, I live in the Sherwood Studio Building, and you live on Madison Avenue."

"I—I have a ward—a room—fitted up with every modern surgical device—every improvement," she said. "It adjoins my office. *Would* you mind living there for a while—say for a week at first—until I can be perfectly certain in my diagnosis?"

"Do you intend to put me to bed?" he asked, appalled.

"Oh, no! Only I wish to watch you carefully and note your symptoms from moment to moment. I also desire to try the effects of certain medicines on you—"

"What kind of medicines?" he asked uneasily.

"I cannot tell yet. Perhaps antitoxin; I don't know; perhaps formalin later. Truly, Mr. Carden, this case has taken on a graver, a more intimate significance since I have learned who you are. I would have worked hard to save any life; I shall put my very heart and soul into my work to save you, who have done so much for us all."

The trace of innocent emotion in her voice moved him.

"I am really not ill," he said unsteadily. "I cannot let you think I am—"

"Don't speak that way, Mr. Carden. I—I am perfectly miserable over it; I don't feel any happiness in my discovery now—not the least bit. I had rather live my entire life without seeing one case of Lamour's Disease than to believe you are afflicted with it."

"But I'm not, Miss Hollis!—really, I am not—"

She looked at him compassionately for a moment, then rose.

"It is best that you should be informed as to your probable condition," she said. "In Lamour's works, volume nine, you had better read exactly what Lamour says. Do you mind coming to the office with me, Mr. Carden?"

"Now?"

"Yes. The book is there. Do you mind coming?"

"No—no, of course not." And, as they turned away together under the trees: "You don't intend to begin observing me this afternoon, do you?" he ventured.

"I think it best if you can arrange your affairs. Can you, Mr. Carden?"

"Why, yes, I suppose I can. Did you mean for me to begin to occupy that surgical bedroom at once?"

"Do you mind?"

"N-no. I'll telephone my servants to pack a steamer trunk and send it around to your apartment this evening. And—where am I to board?"

"I have a dining room," she said simply. "My apartment consists of the usual number of servants and rooms, including my office, and my observation ward which you will occupy."

He walked on, troubled.

"I only w-want to ask one or two things, Dr. Hollis. Am I to be placed on a diet? I hate diets!"

"Not at once."

"May I smoke?"

"Certainly," she said, smiling.

"And you won't p-put me—send me to bed too early?"

"Oh, no! The later you sit up the better, because I shall wish to take your temperature every ten minutes and I shall feel very sorry to arouse you."

"You mean you are coming in to wake me up every ten minutes and put that tube in my mouth?" he asked, aghast.

"Only every half-hour, Mr. Carden. Can't you stand it for a week?"

"Well," he said, "I—I suppose I can if *you* can. Only, upon my honor, there is really nothing the matter with me, and I'll prove it to you out of your own book."

"I wish you could, Mr. Carden. I should be only too happy to give you back to the world with a clear bill of health if you can convince me I am wrong. Do you not believe me? Indeed, indeed I am not selfish and wicked enough to wish you this illness, no matter how rare it is!"

"The rarer a disease is the madder it makes people who contract it," he said. "I should be the maddest man in Manhattan if I really did have Lamour's malady. But I haven't. There is only one malady afflicting me, and I am waiting for a suitable opportunity to tell you all about it, but—"

"Tell me now," she said, raising her eyes to his.

"Not now."

"To-night?"

"I hope so. I will if I can, Miss Hollis."

"But you must not fear to tell a physician about anything which troubles you, Mr. Carden."

"I'll remember that," he said thoughtfully, as they emerged from the Park and crossed to Madison Avenue.

A moment later he hailed a car and they both entered.

TWENTY-FOUR

No, there could be no longer any doubt in her mind as she went into her bedroom, closed the door, and, unhooking the telephone receiver, called up the great specialist in rare diseases, Dr. Austin Atwood, M.S., F.B.A., M.F.H.

"Dr. Atwood," she said with scarcely concealed emotion, "this is Dr. Rosalind Hollis."

"How-de-do?" squeaked the aged specialist amiably.

"Oh, I am well enough, thank you, doctor—except in spirits. Dr. Atwood, you were right! He *has* got it, and I am perfectly wretched!"

"*Who* has got *what*?" retorted the voice of Atwood.

"The unfortunate young gentleman we saw to-day in the Park."

"What park?"

"Why, Central Park, doctor."

"Central Park! *I* haven't been in Central Park for ten years, my child."

"Why, Dr. Atwood!—A—*is* this Dr. Austin Atwood with whom I am talking?"

"Not the least doubt! And you are that pretty Dr. Hollis—Rosalind Hollis, who consulted me in those charity cases, are you not?"

"I certainly am. And I wanted to say to you that I have the unfortunate patient now under closest observation here in my own apartment. I have given him the room next to the office. And, doctor, you were perfectly right. He shows every symptom of the disease—he is even inclined to sentimentalism; he begins to blush and fidget and look at me—a—in that unmistakable manner—not that he isn't well-bred and charming—indeed he is most attractive, and it grieves me dreadfully to see that he already is beginning to believe himself in love with the first person of the opposite sex he encounters—I mean that he—that I cannot mistake his attitude toward me—which is perfectly correct, only one cannot avoid seeing the curious infatuation—"

"*What* the dickens is all this?" roared the great specialist, and Dr. Hollis jumped.

"I was only confirming your diagnosis, doctor," she explained meekly.

"What diagnosis?"

"Yours, doctor. I have confirmed it, I fear. And the certainty has made me perfectly miserable, because his is such a valuable life to the world, and he himself is such a splendid, wholesome, noble specimen of youth and courage, that I cannot bear to believe him incurably afflicted."

"Good Heavens!" shouted the doctor, "*what* has he got and *who* is he?"

"He is Victor Carden, the celebrated artist, and he has Lamour's Disease!" she gasped.

There was a dead silence; then: "Keep him there until I come! Chloroform him if he attempts to escape!"

And the great specialist rang off excitedly.

So Rosalind Hollis went back to the lamp-lit office where, in a luxurious armchair, Carden was sitting, contentedly poring over the ninth volume of Lamour's great treatise and smoking his second cigar.

"Dr. Atwood is coming here," she said in a discouraged voice, as he rose with alacrity to place her chair.

"Oh! What for?"

"T-to see you, Mr. Carden."

"Who? Me? Great Scott! I don't want to be slapped and pinched and polled by a man! I didn't expect that, you know. I'm willing enough to have you observe me in the interest of humanity—"

"But, Mr. Carden, he is only called in for consultation. I—I have a dreadful sort of desperate hope that perhaps I may have made a mistake; that possibly I am in error."

"No doubt you are," he said cheerfully. "Let me read a few more pages, Dr. Hollis, and then I think I shall be all ready to dispute my symptoms, one by one, and convince you what really is the trouble with me. And, by the way, did Dr. Atwood seem a trifle astonished when you told him about me?"

"A trifle—yes," she said uncertainly. "He is a very, very old man; he forgets. But he is coming."

"Oh! And didn't he appear to recollect seeing me in the Park?"

"N-not clearly. He is very old, you know. But he is coming here."

"*Ex*actly—as a friend of mine puts it," smiled Carden. "May I be permitted to use your telephone a moment?"

"By all means, Mr. Carden. You will find it there in my bedroom."

So he entered her pretty bedroom and, closing the door tightly, called up the Tracer of Lost Persons.

"Is that you, Mr. Keen? This is Mr. Carden. I'm head over heels in love. I simply must win her, and I'm going to try. If I don't—if she will not listen to me—I'll certainly go to smash. And what I want you to do is to prevent Atwood from butting in. Do you understand? . . . Yes, Dr. Austin Atwood. Keep him away somehow. . . . Yes, I'm here, at Dr. Hollis's apartments, under anxious observation. . . . She is the *only* woman in the world! I'm mad about her—and getting madder every moment! She is the most perfectly splendid specimen of womanhood—*what*? Oh, yes; I rang you up to ask you whether it was *you* in the Park to-day?—that old gentleman—*What!* Yes, in Central Park. Yes, this afternoon! No, he didn't resemble you; and Dr. Hollis took him for Dr. Atwood. . . . What are you laughing about? . . . I can *hear* you laughing. . . . *Was* it you? . . . What do I think? Why, I don't know exactly what to think, but I suppose it must have been you. Was it? . . . Oh, I see. You don't wish me to know. Certainly, you are quite right. Your clients have no business behind the scenes. I only asked out of curiosity. . . . All right. Good-by."

He came back to the lamp-lit office, which was more of a big, handsome, comfortable living room than a physician's quarters, and for a moment or two he stood on the threshold, looking around.

In the pleasant, subdued light of the lamp Rosalind Hollis looked up and around, smiling involuntarily to see him standing there; then, serious, silent, she dropped her eyes to the pages of the volume he had discarded—volume nine of Lamour's great works.

Even with the evidence before her, corroborated in these inexorably scientific pages which she sat so sadly turning, she found it almost impossible to believe that this big, broad-shouldered, attractive young man could be fatally stricken.

Twice her violet eyes stole toward him; twice the thick lashes veiled them, and the printed pages on her knee sprang into view, and the cold precision of the type confirmed her fears remorselessly:

"The trained scrutiny of the observer will detect in the victim of this disease a peculiar and indefinable charm—a strange symmetry which, on closer examination, reveals traces of physical beauty almost superhuman—"

Again her eyes were lifted to Carden; again she dropped her white lids. Her worst fears were confirmed.

Meanwhile he stood on the threshold looking at her, his pulses racing, his very soul staring through his eyes; and, within him, every sense clamoring out revolt at the deception, demanding confession and its penalty.

"I can't stand this!" he blurted out; and she looked up quickly, her face blanched with foreboding.

"Are you in pain?" she asked.

"No—not that sort of pain! I—*won't* you please believe that I am not ill? I'm imposing on you. I'm an impostor! There's nothing whatever the trouble with me except—something that I want to tell you—if you'll let me—"

"Why should you hesitate to confide in a physician, Mr. Carden?"

He came forward slowly. She laid her small hand on the empty chair which faced hers and he sank into it, clasping his restless hands under his chin.

"You are feeling depressed," she said gently. Depression was a significant symptom. Three chapters were devoted to it.

"I'm depressed, of course. I'm horribly depressed and ashamed of myself, because there is nothing on earth the matter with me, and I've let you think there is."

She smiled mournfully; this was another symptom of a morbid state. She turned, unconsciously, to page 379 to verify her observation.

"See here, Miss Hollis," he broke out, "haven't I any chance to convince you that I am not ill? I want to be honest without involving a—a friend of mine. I can't endure this deception. Won't you let me prove to you that these symptoms are—are only significant of something else?"

She looked straight at him, considering him in silence.

"Let us begin with those dark circles under my eyes," he said desperately. "I found some cold-cream in my room and—look! They are practically gone! At any rate, if there is a sort of shadow left it's because I use my eyes in my profession."

"Dr. Lamour says that the dark circles disappear, anyway," said the girl, unconvinced. "Cold-cream had nothing to do with it."

"But it *did*! Really it did. And as for the other symptoms, I— well, I can't help my pulses when y-you t-t-touch me."

"Please, Mr. Carden."

"I don't mean to be impertinent. I am trying my hardest to tell the truth. And my pulses *do* gallop when you test them; they're galloping now! This very moment!"

"Let me try them," she said coolly, laying her hand on his wrist.

"Didn't I say so!" he insisted grimly. "And I'm turning red, too. But those symptoms mean something else; they mean *you*!"

"Mr. Carden!"

"I can't help saying so—"

"I know it," she said soothingly; "these sentimental outbursts are part of the disease—"

"Good Heavens! *Won't* you try to believe me! There's nothing in the world the matter with me except that I am—am—p-p-perfectly f-f-fascinated—"

"You must struggle against it, Mr. Carden. That is only part of the—"

"It isn't! It isn't! It's you! It's your mere presence, your personality, your charm, your beauty, your loveliness, your—"

"Mr. Carden, I beg of you! I—it is part of my duty to observe symptoms, but—but you are making it very hard for me very difficult—"

"I am only proving to you that it isn't Lamour's Disease which does stunts with my pulses, my temperature, my color. I'm not morbid except when I realize my deception. I'm not depressed except when I think how far you are from me—how far above me—how far out of reach of such a man as I am—how desperately I—I—"

"D-don't you think I had better administer a s-s-sedative, Mr. Carden?" she said, distressed.

"I don't care. I'll take anything you give me—as long as *you* give it to me. I'll swallow pint after pint of pills! I'll fletcherize 'em! I'll luxuriate in poison—anything—"

She was hastily running through the pages of the ninth volume to see whether the symptoms of sentimental excitement ever turned into frenzy.

"What can you learn from that book?" he insisted, leaning forward to see what she was reading. "Anyway, Dr. Lamour married his patient so early in the game that all the symptoms disappeared. And I believe the trouble with his patient was my trouble. She had every symptom of it until he married her! She was in love with him, that is absolutely all!"

Rosalind Hollis raised her beautiful, incredulous eyes.

"What do you mean, Mr. Carden?"

"I mean that, in my opinion, there's no such disease as Lamour's Disease. That young girl was in love with him. Then he married her at last, and—presto!—all the symptoms vanished—the pulse, the temperature, the fidgets, the blushes, the moods, the whole business!"

"W-what about the strangely curious manifestations of physical beauty—superhuman symmetry, Mr. Carden?"

"Do you notice them in *me*?" he gasped.

"A—yes—in a m-modified measure—"

"In *me*?"

"Certainly!" she said firmly; but the slow glow suffusing her cheeks was disconcerting her. Then his own face began to reflect the splendid color in hers; their eyes met, dismayed.

"There are sixteen volumes about this disease," she said. "There *must* be such a disease!"

"There is," he said. "I have it badly. But I never had it before I first saw you in the Park!"

"Mr. Carden—this is the wildest absurdity—"

"I know it. Wildness is a symptom. I'm mad as a hatter. I've got every separate symptom, and I wish it was infectious and contagious and catching and fatal!"

She made an effort to turn the pages to the chapter entitled "Manias and Illusions," but he laid his hand across the book and his clear eyes defied her.

"Mr. Carden—"

Her smooth hand trembled under his, then, suddenly nerveless, relaxed. With an effort she lifted her head; their eyes met, spellbound.

"*You* have *every* symptom," he said unsteadily— "every one! What have you to say?"

Her fascinated eyes held his.

"What have you to say?" he repeated under his breath— "you, with every symptom, and your heavenly radiant beauty to confirm them—that splendid youthful loveliness which blinds and stuns me as I look—as I speak—as I tell you that I love you. That is my malady; that is the beginning and the end of it; love!"

She sat speechless, immovable, as one under enchantment.

"All my life," he said, "I have spent in painting shadows. But the shadows were those dim celestial shapes cast by your presence in the world. You tell me that the world is better for my work; that I have offered my people beauty and a sort of truth, which they had never dreamed of until I revealed it? Yet what inspired me was the shadow only, for I had never seen the substance; I had never believed I should ever see the living source of the shadows which inspired me. And now I see; now I have seen with my own eyes. Now the confession of faith is no longer a blind creed, born of instinct. You live! You are you! What I believed from necessity I find proved in fact. The occult no longer can sway one who has seen. And you, who, without your knowledge or mine, have always been the one and only source of any good in me or in my work—why is it strange that I loved you at first sight?—that I worshiped you at first breath?—I, who, like him who raises his altar to 'the unknown god,' raised my altar to truth and beauty? And a miracle has answered me."

She rose, the beautiful dazed eyes meeting his, both hands clasping the ninth volume of Lamour's great monograph to her breast as though to protect it from him—from him who was threatening her, enthralling her, thrilling her with his magic voice, his enchanted youth, the masterful mystery of his eyes. What was he saying to her? What was this mounting intoxication sweeping her senses—this delicious menace threatening her very will? What did he want with her? What was he asking? What was he doing now—with both her hands in his, and her gaze deeply lost in his—and the ninth volume of Lamour on the floor between them, sprawling there, abandoned, waving its helpless, discredited leaves in air—discredited, abandoned, obsolete as her own specialty—her life's work! He had taken that, too—taken her life's work from her. And in return she was holding nothing!—nothing except a young man's hands—strong, muscular hands which, after all, were holding her own imprisoned. So she had nothing in exchange for the ninth volume of Lamour; and her life's work had been annihilated by a smile; and she was very much alone in the world—very isolated and very youthful.

After a while she emerged from the chaos of attempted reflection and listened to what he was saying. He spoke very quietly, very distinctly, not sparing himself, laying bare every deception without involving anybody except himself.

He told her the entire history of his case, excluding Mr. Keen in person; he told her about his aunt, about his birthday, about his determination to let the legacy go. Then in a very manly way he told her that he had never before loved a woman; and fell silent, her hands a dead weight in his.

She was surprised that she could experience no resentment. A curious inertia crept over her. She was tired of expectancy, tired of effort, weary of the burden of decision. Life and its problems overweighted her. Her eyes wandered to his broad young shoulders, then were raised to his face.

"What shall we do?" she asked innocently.

Unresisting, she suffered him to explain. His explanation was not elaborate; he only touched his lips to her hands and straightened up, a trifle pale.

After a moment they walked together to the door and he took his hat and gloves from the rack.

"Will you come to-morrow morning?" she asked.

"Yes."

"Come early. I am quite certain of how matters are with me. Everything has gone out of my life—everything I once cared for—all the familiar things. So come early, for I am quite alone without you."

"And I without you, Rosalind."

"That is only right," she said simply. "I shall cast no more shadows for you. . . . Are you going? . . . Oh, I know it is best that you should go, but—"

He halted. She laid both hands in his.

"We both have it," she faltered— "every symptom. And—you will come early, won't you?"

Coachwhip Publications

CoachwhipBooks.com

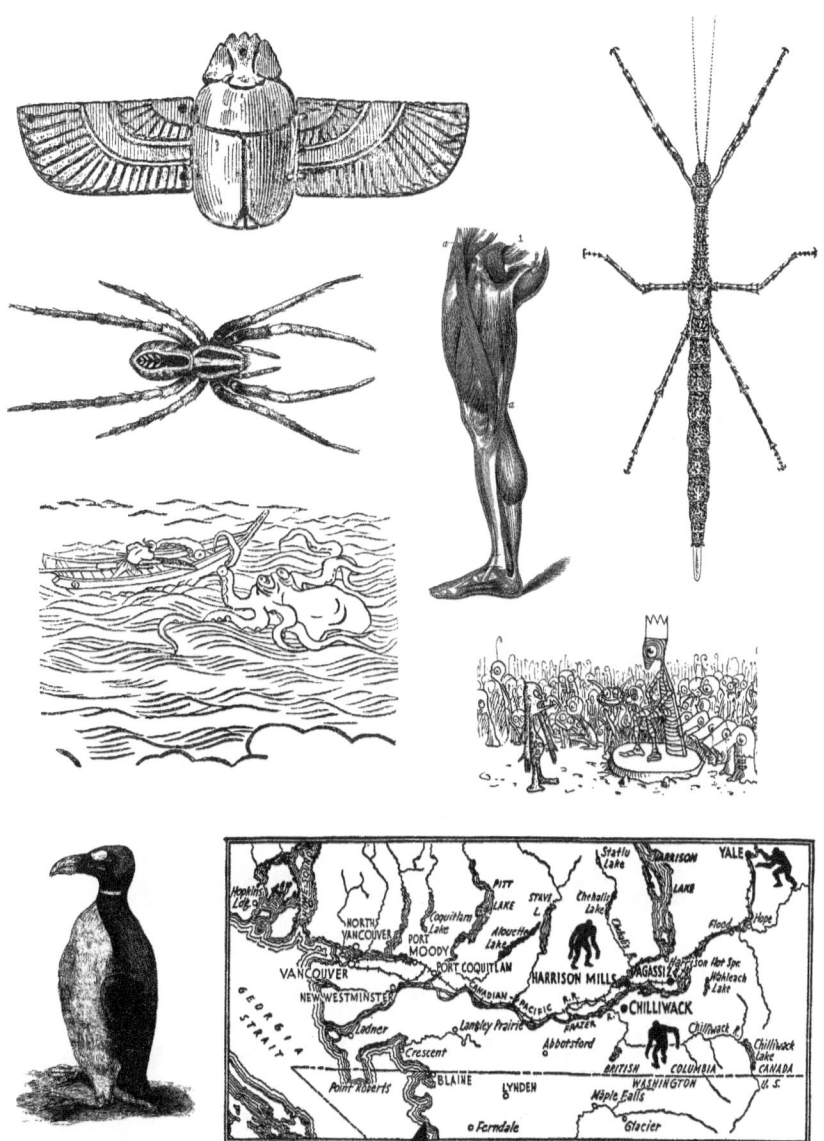

AVERAGE JONES/
DR. FURNIVALL, PHYSICIAN-DETECTIVE

ISBN 1-61646-098-9

THE CHRONICLES OF ADDINGTON PEACE /
LUTHER TRANT, PSYCHOLOGICAL DETECTIVE

ISBN 1-61646-097-0

THE COMPLETE ADVENTURES OF

ROMNEY PRINGLE

R. AUSTIN FREEMAN &
JOHN J. PITCAIRN

(AS BY CLIFFORD ASHDOWN)

THE COMPLETE ADVENTURES OF
ROMNEY PRINGLE

ISBN 1-61646-090-3

12 CASES FOR MAX CARRADOS

ISBN 1-61646-018-0

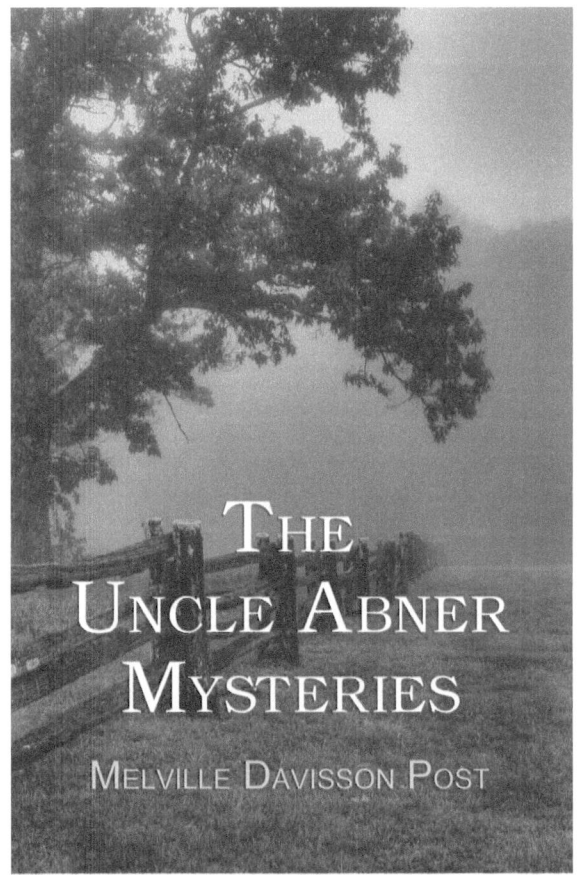

THE UNCLE ABNER MYSTERIES

ISBN 1-61646-016-4

SHERLOCK HOLMES, VOL. 1

ISBN 1-61646-006-7

www.ingramcontent.com/pod-product-compliance
Lightning Source LLC
Chambersburg PA
CBHW021844010726
47493CB00005B/1551